I0685165

FLIGHT

Kate Christie

SECOND GROWTH

Copyright © 2013 by Kate Christie

Second Growth Books
Seattle, WA

All rights reserved. No part of this book may be reproduced
or transmitted in any form or by any means, electronic or
mechanical, including photocopying, without permission in
writing from the author.

Printed in the United States of America on acid-free paper
First published 2013

Cover Design: Kate Christie

ISBN: 0985367725
ISBN-13: 978-0-9853677-2-5

DEDICATION

To the latest additions to the family, Sydney and Ellie: May you and big sister Alex run fast, play hard, and always look out for each other. And when you fall, because you will on occasion, remember what Mama likes to say: *Fall down seven times, get up eight.*

PROLOGUE

Lately I've been thinking a lot about family. Maybe that's not so surprising given that in a few weeks, I'll be traveling to Chicago with my wife and children to observe the thirty-fifth anniversary of the plane crash that killed my parents. Our daughter and son are young still, so they won't be present for the official ceremony of remembrance. Instead, my wife will take them downtown to the Chicago Children's Museum to draw and play while I return to the airport for only the fourth time in thirty-five years. At O'Hare, the families of those lost will once again mingle with airline representatives, rescue workers, and other airport personnel who were there on the sunlit October afternoon when Flight 108 from Orlando crashed on landing, killing everyone on board except a three-year-old girl—me.

Outwardly, I suffered only a broken leg, second-degree burns, cuts, and bruises. But after the paramedics pulled me out of the wreckage, I didn't talk for ten whole days. I didn't cry, either, my aunt told me later. I just stared straight ahead, unmoving and unresponsive in my hospital bed as doctors and psychiatrists and social workers tried to break through the protective walls my immature brain had raised. At last, exhausted and lonely, I woke to life again, missing my parents with a pain I still associate with the flames that consumed much of the crash site.

I don't remember the crash itself, or my week of silence. Intellectually, I know what happened, but I can't remember the instant the plane struck the runway, rose up again, and cartwheeled across the air field. Which is just as well, everyone has always assured me. There's a reason I can't remember, but even without the memory, I am marked by the accident in a way that I know I'll never fully escape. Up to that point, it had never occurred to me that I could lose my family. But in the few seconds it took the landing gear on an aging jet to fail, my parents were gone, leaving me in a world that no longer felt safe. Like anyone who experiences tragedy, I am a different person because of the crash. I will never know the person I might have become, nor the people my parents might have already been.

"And I alone survived…"

The melodramatic statement, also the title of an actually quite good book about, of all things, the sole survivor of a plane crash, occurs to me semi-frequently, though less and less as I get older. Three and a half decades have changed me so much that I no longer feel like the same person who, as a young child, survived a tragedy too immense for her brain to grasp. I don't feel like the rebellious teenager I grew into, either, or the motivated college student or, later, the young adult with a wedding album and mortgage.

Technically, in fact, I am no longer any of these people. According to my college biology professor, the human body is made up mostly of water that is replaced on a monthly basis, while many other human cells have a life cycle measured only in days or months. Our bodies are constantly changing, evolving, shedding bits and pieces of who we once were. We couldn't remain the same person from year to year, decade to decade, even if we wanted to.

This transitory nature of the body makes sense to me. Most days I simply feel like the current me—half of an old married couple, full-time parent to two lovely kids under the age of five, and part-time writing instructor at the local community college, with never, seemingly, enough time to get much of anything done.

We haven't told Madison, the oldest at four going on forty, or Jack, our plucky yet wobbly toddler, the reason for our upcoming trip to Chicago. They know they have only one set of doting grandparents to Skype with and to visit at the holidays. But they don't know details. Those will come later—perhaps at the next Flight 108 reunion, or the one after that. We meet in Chicago, survivors of our common tragedy, every five years to share stories and photos of the dead, and to celebrate our own lives, too, for most of us have managed to move forward in spite of the loss we all keenly still feel.

Lost loved ones never go away completely, of course, particularly those ripped away in violence. Your heart never fully heals. But you do go on, if you're lucky, to become someone almost recognizable—a person with different loves and losses, new families and friends, hoping all the while that the swift injustice of tragedy won't target you again; that untimely death will leave you in peace forever after.

I wasn't that fortunate, myself. But when loss decided to set up shop on my front stoop again, I didn't stop talking this time. I kept moving away from who and what I had been, hoping my new life would find me sooner rather than later.

CHAPTER ONE
~SUMMER 1993~

A year and a day after he left home for good, Austin Taylor knocked on my front door and strolled right in. It was June 1993, and I'd owed him a letter for months now. Apparently he'd gotten tired of waiting.

"Hey there, Ash," he said, dropping his sea bag and smiling at me across the living room as if it had been no time at all since we had last seen each other.

"Austin! What are you doing here?" I lowered the dust rag clenched in my right hand and stared at him.

"What does it look like? What—no hug?"

He crossed to where I knelt beside the once-busted rocking chair my aunt, Selma, had restored and refinished years before in her garage workshop. Half an hour earlier, I had discovered a thick coat of dust on the lower support rails, which had led to a concerted attack with a can of Pledge and an old T-shirt that had long since been repurposed.

I stood up and let him embrace me, my arms loose about his waist as a lump rose in my throat. I swallowed hard, trying without success to force it away. In general, I was not a fan of crying. Lately, I'd done more than my share. Not that Austin would know.

We'd been best friends ever since his family moved in next door when he was ten and I was nine. Nearly a decade later, life was not as simple as it had been when we first met. For one thing, Austin had graduated from high school a year ahead of me and joined the Navy, leaving behind Signal Mountain, Tennessee, and me in one fell swoop. The day he left, he promised to come back some day and steal me away from our hometown. I told him he was dreaming—I would never need rescuing.

"I swear, girl, you are even skinnier than last time I saw you," Austin said, pulling away to give me the once-over.

"That's slender to you."

I returned the perusal. He had filled out in his year at sea, shoulders broader than I remembered, biceps straining the short sleeves of his white T-shirt, features more chiseled than delicate now.

"What are you doing here?" I asked again. "Aren't you supposed to be out on a boat somewhere in the middle of the ocean?"

"They call 'em ships, you know." His gaze slid away and settled on my half-full glass on the coffee table. "Hey, is that lemonade?"

For a moment, I pictured Selma standing at the kitchen counter running lemons through her beloved juicer, her shock of prematurely white hair disheveled from the habit she'd had of lifting her bangs away from her face when the Tennessee swelter got to be too much for her Northern blood.

"It's Minute Maid," I said.

Austin ducked his head in the way girls at our high school had always found endearing. Boys, on the other hand, had usually wanted to kick the crap out of him.

"I'm sorry I couldn't be here for the funeral," he said. "Did you get my letters?"

I nodded. Throughout the spring, he had written long letters full of bittersweet remembrances that only he and I, now, shared.

"I can't believe she's gone," he added, "just like that? Feels like she should come walking in any minute in that bandanna and those ratty old gloves of hers."

I smiled at the image he'd conjured of Selma in her gardening uniform, half-expecting to look out the back window myself and see her wiping the sweat from her eyes with her faded blue bandanna as she toiled over the raised beds she'd built back before I could remember. As far as I was concerned, the garden had always been there, just like Selma herself. Now it was wasting away, no matter how hard I worked to keep the neat plots watered and weed-free—as if the plants, sensing Selma's absence, had given up on life; as if photosynthesis and cell division were impossible without the plant food she brewed from scratch, the songs she crooned as she worked in the garden, her whispered words not intended for human ears.

Those songs had led some of the less progressive people in town to whisper the word "witch" behind her back. Or maybe it was the informative display on the history of paganism she'd created a few years back, smack dab in the middle of Lent. Being director of the local library had its perks, she'd told me, her serene smile never faltering as even the liberal Christians on the library board of trustees privately expressed their concerns with this rather "creative" exhibition.

"Want some lemonade anyway?" I asked Austin. "Even if it is from a can?"

"Totally. I forget how hot it gets here."

In the kitchen, I poured Austin's lemonade and leaned against the stove, watching him. When he'd left the summer before, Selma had been alive and supposedly well, the cancer cells attacking her body as yet undetected. A year later, she was gone and the house, a cozy Craftsman cottage on half an acre at the edge of the town's historic district, was now mine to do with as I chose, along with the shockingly large sum of money Selma had left me. As of yet, I had put off choosing.

He fingered a pot holder hanging from a hook on the side of the fridge, then peered down at the counter. "Jesus, Ash, it's cleaner in here than the flight deck on my ship."

"I've had a little time on my hands," I said, and folded my arms across my chest.

His eyes scrunched at the corners. "I really wanted to be at the funeral. I practically begged my CO, but he claimed it was out of his control."

"It's okay. I knew you couldn't help it."

"Then why didn't you write back?"

I shrugged. "I didn't know what to say."

To tell the truth, I still didn't. The last few months were a blur. For my high school graduation two weeks earlier, Claire, Austin's mother and Selma's best friend, had bought me a dress to wear to graduation. Even though I was more of a sweats and T-shirt kind of girl, I'd worn the dress to the ceremony down at U-T

Chattanooga, and then again to the party Claire had thrown for me. I'd put my hair up the way Selma had always liked, and I'd smiled at the people I'd known my whole life, classmates and teachers and the parents of schoolmates and former teammates, most of whom regarded me now with even more pity than they had before Selma got sick, their kind eyes and offers of assistance making me grit my teeth and long to be someplace—any place—else.

In the days since, I'd tackled house and yard chores that seemed to multiply like kudzu vines, while at night I lay awake for hours trying to piece back together a future I had once regarded as immutable. I had been accepted into three universities for the fall—two here in Tennessee and one in Chicago—but I couldn't seem to choose between them. It didn't help that not one of the track coaches at these fine institutions had expressed anything more than tepid interest in my athletic abilities. So much for my dream of becoming another Wilma Rudolph, triumphing over early tragedy to flourish on the college and international track scene.

Orphan—I had always hated the word the would-be bullies and mean girls whispered loudly in my hearing, taunting me on the playground before they learned better. When I was little, Selma had been there to kiss away my tears of rage, to bandage my skinned knuckles as she explained to me why violence was never an acceptable response.

Now she was gone, too. Ever since the day in April that Claire and I had sprinkled Selma's ashes from the overlook at Signal Point, I'd been sleepwalking through the scenery of my old life, waiting for something to come along and wake me up.

"What are you really doing here?" I asked Austin. "If they wouldn't let you come home for Christmas or the funeral, how are you here now?"

He held his glass in both hands. "It's a long story."

"I have time." A thought occurred to me. "Your parents don't know you're here, do they?"

They would have told me if they had, would have joyfully announced his impending arrival as if he were able to dispel storm clouds with a single smile. To them, that was what he had always been—their golden-haired child, their sunny son. During his final year of high school, Austin's parents had appeared to overlook signs of the increasingly troubled boy I'd recognized beneath his compulsively cheerful surface. No wonder they'd been stunned

7

when he announced he was putting off college to join the Navy.

He shook his head now and glanced guiltily out the window, as if his family would somehow be able to detect his presence despite the mature stand of trees and the eight-foot wooden fence—*deer obstacle*, Selma had liked to call it—that lay between his house and ours.

"You're my first stop," he admitted. "I actually have to tell you something."

But instead of continuing, he set his empty glass on the counter and spun on his heel all military precise-like, angling for the living room.

Selma had used that same portentous phrase the day after Halloween when she sat me down at the kitchen table to tell me that she had metastatic pancreatic cancer. Stage IV. The oncologist down in Chattanooga was very sorry, but he didn't think she had much time left. She was welcome, of course, to seek another opinion.

"I'm going to fight it," she'd insisted, holding both of my hands, her blue-gray eyes darker than I'd ever seen them. Normally she reminded me of Santa Claus with her white hair, rosy cheeks, and easy belly laugh. That fall, though, she'd moved more and more slowly about the roomy bungalow she'd bought just before I came to live with her. The cancer diagnosis made everything click into place—that was why she seemed tired all the time, why she sometimes moaned in her sleep as she dozed on the couch after a dinner she'd only picked at. Cancer was the reason my aunt, the only mother I could remember, wouldn't live long enough to see me finish high school.

As a distance runner, I thought I understood pain. But in the months that followed that talk, I learned what a body was capable of withstanding. And, simply, what it couldn't.

In the living room, Austin and I sat on the antique wicker couch, and I folded my feet under me while he rested his on the cherry wood coffee table I had helped Selma refinish the summer I turned twelve. Half a dozen magazines lay strewn across the surface, subscriptions I hadn't yet been able to bring myself to cancel. *National Geographic, Journal of the Smithsonian, National Gardener,* and *American Heritage* occupied the place usually reserved in Southern homes for colorful books on plantation architecture and the War Between the States. Selma, raised with my mother in

Wisconsin, had steadfastly refused to give up her Yankee roots. Maybe that was why I didn't feel like a true Southerner, either.

Austin, on the other hand, could trace his ancestors back to the Civil War—mostly gray-jacketed Rebs, though not all, as Eastern Tennessee had seen its fair share of divided loyalties—and beyond. So what was his excuse? Except I thought I knew why he had always held himself slightly apart from the other kids.

"Dude," I said, regarding him evenly, "what's up?"

He slouched down on the couch. "It's not that big of a deal, really. Not after everything you've been through."

"You're not dying, are you?"

"No." He looked at me quickly. "It's nothing like that."

"Just checking." I plucked at a loose thread on one of the cushions.

"Honestly, this whole thing is idiotic. I don't even know why the stupid government has half the rules it does."

"Spill it, Austin."

"Same old Ash." He cleared his throat. "Okay. So, um, I kind of got kicked out of the Navy."

"You did?" I pretended to be surprised.

"Yeah." He paused, squinted, seemed to hold his breath. "For being gay."

I shook my head. "Stupid-ass military. Why do they even care?"

He stared at me, blinking. "That's it? That's all you have to say?"

"Austin, I've known you half your life. I even used to think we'd get married someday. It's cool if you're gay."

His shoulders visibly relaxed. "I used to think we'd get married, too. I like women, I really do. I'm just not, you know, attracted to them."

"Fine with me. It's not like kissing me turned you off girls permanently."

In middle school, during an ill-advised game of "Spin the Bottle" in Mitch Allen's basement, Austin and I had landed in the designated make-out closet for six whole minutes. Curious what the fuss was about, as soon as the door swung shut I'd leaned forward and kissed him. After an awkward moment, we'd both pulled back. Clearly there was nothing to be found between us other than a warm, fuzzy sort of affection.

"If you recall, you kissed me. And I'm pretty sure that's exactly what made me gay."

"Liar!" I slugged him, my fist connecting with solid muscle.

Austin recoiled. "Ow! Jackass."

"*I'm* the jackass, Mr. I-Have-A-Huge-Confession-To-Make? Like I wouldn't know."

Just before her diagnosis, Selma and I had rented *Torch Song Trilogy*. Afterward, I'd asked her if she thought Austin might be gay. She'd turned the question back on me, only allowing that it was possible after I admitted I believed he was queerer than a two-dollar bill. Looking back, she'd probably brought the movie home as a conversation-starter. A transplanted Midwesterner, Selma wasn't exactly the direct type.

Although maybe her preference for subtlety was innate rather than a product of geography—I'd been raised nearly entirely in the South, the land of good manners, and my mouth had gotten me into trouble too many times to count. *Just like your mother*, Selma used to say.

"You really knew?" Austin asked. "Seriously?"

"I suspected. So did Selma." I hesitated.

His eyes narrowed. "What?"

"We weren't the only ones. Selma said Claire—your mom thought you probably joined the Navy because of it. You know, to escape the Bible Belt bangers."

"Jesus H. Christ. Here I've been trying for the past month to work out a way to tell you guys, and you already knew?"

"Not everyone. Your mom wasn't sure about your dad."

He exhaled noisily and rubbed his head, palm grazing the short blond hairs standing up seemingly at attention. "He's the one I'm most worried about."

I looked a little closer, noticing that while his hair was short, it wasn't military issue. "Wait. You've been out of the Navy for a month?"

He winced. "I know, I'm a jerk. I just didn't know how to tell you guys."

"You could have been here for graduation," I said, folding my arms across the front of my T-shirt again.

"I know," Austin repeated. "I'm sorry, Ash. I was going through a rough time, mooching off the friend of a friend. I finally found a place to live this weekend, so I caught a Greyhound and here I am. I don't have long, though. I have to be back in a couple of days to start my new job. Nothing fancy, just waiting tables. Work is hard to come by in the city without a college degree."

"And which city would that be?"

"*The* city." He grinned. "New York, of course."

Just like Austin to hope his dimple would smooth things over.

"New York City?" I shook my head, most definitely not smiling.

His grin slipped. "Come on, now. What's wrong?"

I stared at him, recalling the sleepless nights when I lay in bed listening to Selma moan in pain on the other side of the wall; the trips down the mountain to the oncology clinic at Chattanooga General, the news inevitably worse each time; the abysmal day we drove into the city to check her into the hospital for the last time; the final hour of Selma's life when her breathing slowed to thirteen breaths a minute and twice her heart stopped only to restart itself as Claire and I sat on opposite sides of the hospital bed each holding onto a hand that was already deathly cold, waiting; all while my supposed best friend was thousands of miles away trying to decipher a part of himself I'd long since figured out.

"Gee, I don't know, Austin," I said. "You take off because you can't deal, and all this shit comes down and you're not here and now you come back and just expect—I don't know. What do you expect?"

He looked at me levelly. "I don't expect anything. I was hoping—my mom wrote me after the funeral and said you might not go to college right away. I'm subletting this apartment in the West Village for a year, and it's amazing but seriously expensive. I could use some help with the rent. What do you say?"

I frowned. "About what?"

"About moving to New York. That's why I'm here, Ash. Come back with me."

At the earnest look in his eyes, the urgency in his voice, my anger ebbed. I looked around the living room, a familiar emptiness coiling in my stomach. I still expected to see Selma tending to her many indoor plants or relaxing on the patio out back. I still listened for her voice belting out one of the Janises—Ian or Joplin—in the kitchen as she cooked, for her footsteps creaking on the wood floors at night, even as I reminded myself these sounds would never—could never—come again. I had freed all that remained of her physical body myself, jettisoning her dusty, gritty ashes out into the air high above the Tennessee River. Yet somehow I still felt her all around me in this home we had shared for so long.

Could I leave her now? Someday I would have to, but someday could still be a long way off. Or it could be tomorrow.

"Up north, huh?" I said. "You livin' with a bunch of Yankees?"

"Shoot, they put their pants on same's me 'n you," Austin said in his best redneck accent.

"I still can't believe you."

"Why not? I told you I'd come back and rescue you from this old mountain."

"It's a ridge, not a mountain, fool. Besides, I told you I wouldn't need rescuing."

"How's that working out for you?" He waved an arm presumably in reference to the house, Signal Mountain, my current state of being.

My eyes narrowed. "You can't just waltz back in and expect me to jump at the idea of moving up north with you."

"Why not? You're more of a Yankee than I'll ever be."

"It's not that easy, Austin, and you know it."

He nodded. "I get it, Ash. Really. But will you at least think about it? I only have a couple of days before I have to head back."

I hesitated, glancing again around the bright living room. This house, with its exposed beams and well-crafted built-ins, had been my home ever since I could remember, its light and smell and feel the most familiar things to me in the world. But without Selma there to complete the picture, even home didn't feel right anymore.

"I'll consider it," I said at last.

"You will?" He leaned forward and held up his hand for a high-five. "Dude, that's awesome!"

I ignored the gesture. "In the meantime, have you thought about how you're going to tell your dad?"

His hand sank. "Only for the last month, and I still have no idea."

Austin's father was a good person, but Tennessee born and bred. And Southern men, even more so than other American men, are rarely pleased to discover they have a homosexual in the family, particularly when the gay is their only son.

"More lemonade?" I offered.

He leaned back against the couch. "Yes, please."

CHAPTER TWO

After Austin left, I was too restless to stay in watching yet another Braves game, so I made myself a sandwich and went for a drive. I backed the station wagon down the long driveway, pulled out onto our tree-lined road, and headed east across the mountain, which isn't, as I'd reminded Austin, a mountain at all. Walden's Ridge occupies the southern edge of the Cumberland Plateau. Signal Mountain, our town, was named for Signal Point, the promontory that overlooks Chattanooga and the Tennessee River Gorge, the so-called Grand Canyon of Tennessee. Our ridge has been used by various factions—Creeks, Cherokees, Confederate soldiers, Federal troops—throughout the centuries to signal important messages and to observe enemy movements along the Tennessee River.

Herself a Yankee descendant of Midwestern abolitionists and Union soldiers, Selma had first traveled to Walden's Ridge in the mid-'70s when an old professor from library school had recommended her to his cousin, a prominent physician who was then President of the Signal Mountain Library Board of Trustees. Selma had worked for ten years already as a librarian in Milwaukee, and only accepted the invitation to interview for the library directorship out of respect for her one-time mentor. She'd fully intended to say no if they offered her the job, she told me later. But then she spent a lovely autumn weekend at the Signal Mountain Bed and Breakfast in the historic district, with its attractive cottages and stately summer homes. Almost against her will, my aunt found herself charmed by Signal Mountain's leisurely pace, its Southern hospitality, and the unexpectedly progressive area residents who were ardently committed to community arts and, most importantly, to their library.

As her old professor had promised, directing the Signal Mountain Library was a dream job, and Selma knew she would probably never again be offered such an opportunity. By the time she returned home to busy, working class Milwaukee, she was ruined both for city life and urban library work. A small town girl at heart, she accepted the job even though it would take her far away from her baby sister in Chicago—and her sister's young daughter, barely walking and already a handful. Natalie, my mother, encouraged her to go, even though Selma, who was ten years older, had practically raised her after their mother died of breast cancer and their grieving father buried himself in his work. For someone who had never conceived, I'd always thought that Selma had managed to pack more than her share of mothering into her short lifetime.

Was dying young something you could inherit, like freckles or a receding hairline? This question had shadowed me in the aftermath of Selma's diagnosis. My mother, father, and maternal grandmother had all died before their thirty-fifth birthdays, while my maternal grandfather had managed to drink himself to death in the decades after the loss of his wife. We went to Wisconsin for his funeral when I was ten, the summer after Austin and his family moved to Signal Mountain. In Oshkosh, on the shores of Lake Winnebago, Selma and I attended the memorial service with scores of people who seemed to know all about me. My father's parents, Judy and Sherman Lake, stayed close throughout the services, stealing glances at me with their customary looks that even as a child I could tell featured a mixture of joy and pain.

Selma had told me that I looked just like my dad, lean and tall for a girl and brown-skinned from the sun just like he always was, swimming in Lake Winnebago and camping out under the Wisconsin stars with his older brother and their buddies. My dad, Ben, an avid outdoorsman, had loved growing up in Wisconsin, as had my mom, according to everyone who loved them. High school sweethearts, they planned to move back to their hometown someday, Selma told me. My father's law career was just taking off when we took that vacation to Disney World. Sometimes I think I can remember the amusement rides and the giant stuffed characters featured on the camera that, along with my mother's purse, managed to survive the crash the same way I did—tucked between my parents' sheltering bodies, their arms about each other and me as the plane disintegrated around us. A rescue worker found me among the debris immediately after the crash, still clinging to my mother's body.

Thank God I can't remember anything about that. Denial ain't just a river in Egypt, as one of my therapists used to say. Turns out it's also a sophisticated coping mechanism.

Blessed be denial, Selma repeated often, offering me a hug when I was little, an affectionate pat or squeeze as I got older and started ducking her embrace. It hurt now to remember the petty slights I'd slung at her. Typical teenager, I'd assumed she would be around forever. But I of all people should have known better.

My arm hanging out the open car window, I turned up the stereo—Whitney Houston alternately crooning and belting out lyrics to her beloved bodyguard—and drove alongside the golf course at the northern edge of town. The Old Town district had originally been built by Chattanoogans fleeing urban outbreaks of yellow fever and cholera in the late nineteenth century. Fortunately, the ghosts that lurked along the ridges and trails of my adopted hometown didn't feel personal to me. They were part of a world that had existed without me or anyone else whose DNA I shared. Growing up, I'd never had to wonder about intimate connections to the stories that made up Chattanooga and Signal Mountain's rich anecdotal history. In Southeast Tennessee, I could just be me— Ashley Lake, Selma Bishop's Yankee kid. We were a family; perhaps not a traditional one, but a happy one nonetheless.

And then we weren't. Like Austin had said, *just like that.*

Whitney Houston still doing her thing, I cruised past the local country club, where I'd worked a couple of summers waiting tables; past the stately homes that graced the land around the country club; and finally on to the unassuming public library where Selma had worked for seventeen years. Well, not this building, exactly—six years earlier, work had been completed on what I still thought of as the "new" library, a structure funded entirely by local donors. I slowed as I passed the familiar building, memories of Storytime and leisurely strolls among the stacks competing with those of Selma holding court at the central counter or bent over the cluttered desk of her glass-walled office. Accompanying all these images was the familiar smell of books—the musty, dusty scent of thousands upon thousands of books bound with thread, glue, wood, crowding the library shelves from floor to ceiling.

The nostalgic sights and scents still dancing in my head, I drove on about my hometown, passing my old elementary school where I had often reigned supreme during games of kickball or King of the Mountain; the pizza place where my cross country teammates and I would hold court as we proceeded to demolish pie after pie in the wake of an autumn meet; and, of course, churches of all persuasions: Latter-Day Saints, Methodist, Church of Christ, Baptist—American and Southern, Episcopal, and the grand Presbyterian Church in the old part of town, just to name a few. They don't call it the Bible Belt for nothing.

My agnostic aunt's daughter, I bypassed all of these traditional spiritual havens and guided Selma's car instead toward what had always been our mutual favorite place of worship: Signal Point. The sun was sinking in the pale summer sky, tingeing the clouds pink and gray while darkness crept in from the east. I parked the station wagon and followed the paved path to the low stone wall that edged the cliff hundreds of feet above the Tennessee River. I came here when I wanted to be alone. Of course, with Austin and Selma both gone, recently I'd been alone most of the time whether I liked it or not.

Stepping over the wall, I sat down, my back against the mortared stones, my feet pointing toward empty space as the clouds overhead changed colors. The sky darkened, while in Chattanooga and over on Raccoon and Lookout Mountains, the opposite walls of the gorge, yellow lights blinked on a handful at a time like lightning bugs in a field at dusk.

When I was little, I used to catch lightning bugs in a jar and put them on my dresser, using their faint glow as a nightlight as I drifted off to sleep. A few months before she died, I mentioned this memory to Selma, telling her I had always been a little shocked that she had allowed me to kill creatures as amazing as lightning bugs. She'd thrown back her head and laughed, as in days of old, and assured me that she had freed any and all creatures I'd ever caught, waiting until I fell asleep to sneak into my room and replace the natural nightlight with my trusty electric one.

Did you ever even once wake up in the morning to find a jar of lightning bugs on your dresser? she'd asked. And I'd had to shake my head, wondering as I did what other important clues I'd failed to notice during our too-short time together.

Now I gazed out across the gorge, thinking of my mother-aunt and her love of the birds and bats and trees of Signal Mountain. Almost daily, as long as it wasn't too hot, she and I would walk one of the many trails Walden's Ridge offered. Weekdays, with work and school constraining our time, we stuck to after-dinner walks on the golf course if the sun had already set, or opted for the one and a half mile loop around Rainbow Lake if the light still held. That was how I started trail-running—at ten, I could run two full loops of the lake in the time it took Selma to walk one. Later, as I grew taller and faster, my two loops became three. Afterward, we would walk home together, sharing the water bottles she carried in her fanny pack and remarking on the natural beauty of our home.

This wasn't to say that her passion for "the mountain" had been entirely unswerving. Not far below my current perch, leaf-clad trees hid an old rock quarry from view. Long since abandoned, the quarry was filled with water, making it a natural draw for kids and the worst fear of some Signal Mountain parents, including Selma. In high school, Austin and I had often smuggled a boom box and a six-pack of beer down to the quarry on summer nights. We would sit on the edge of the cliff, thirty feet up over the water, listening to Top Forty and jawing about anything and everything while the sun set and the air cooled. In the distance, a thousand feet below, we could see the river snaking toward downtown Chattanooga, once distinguished as the EPA's Most Polluted City. The 1980s had seen a rash of renewal projects sweep the region, though, and tourism was beginning to pick up again. Now, in the early '90s, people were coming from all over again to see Rock City, hike to Ruby Falls, and ride the Incline Railway up Lookout Mountain where, on a clear day, you could see seven states from the bluff at Lover's Leap.

On those summer nights way up above the world, Austin and I would talk about high school, our families, The Future. We complained about how little our parents understood us as we predicted endlessly wonderful destinies for ourselves far from Signal Mountain. I was going to be a great runner, with NCAA titles and Olympic medals aplenty. Austin wasn't sure yet what he wanted to do with his life, but he knew that whatever he achieved, it wouldn't be anywhere near Chattanooga. All we wanted then, both of us, was to get as far away from Signal Mountain, from Tennessee, from the South, as we could.

Funny thing, though—now all I wanted was to return to those lost days of drinking illicit beers in the quarry, knowing that our parents would be waiting for us when we got home. Knowing that Selma would have fallen asleep on the couch, a blanket around her legs, newsletter of the National Audubon Society or the World Wildlife Fund open on her lap. Waiting for me.

Except she hadn't waited. She had gone on without me, just like my parents. The only person waiting for me now was Austin, the boy I had loved most of my life. My brother, my friend. He had left without me, too, but unlike the others, he had come back. He'd come back for me, and he was waiting for me even now, assuming his father hadn't kicked him out.

When dusk fell in earnest, the early summer darkness carrying with it the usual mosquito blitzkrieg, I left Signal Point and headed home. But as I approached my dark, silent house, I didn't stop. Instead, I pulled over on the gravel shoulder at the foot of a different driveway. There, I got out and headed up the long drive, brushing away buzzing insects and sticking to the silent grass at the edge of the gravel-strewn pavement. Around the back of the house, a two-story Colonial with an attached garage and vinyl siding, I saw a light on in a familiar window. I held a few pieces of gravel in my left hand and, with the other, tossed a pebble upward in a nearly forgotten motion. It took a couple of tries, but soon Austin's head appeared behind the screen, backlit by the overhead lamp. Still here, at least for now.

"Ash," he said. "Where were you? I tried to call."

"Did you mean it?" I asked, ignoring his question. "Are you serious about me going back with you?"

He seemed to perk up a little. "Totally."

"Okay then," I said, "I'm in."

And then I spun on my heel, all military-precise-like myself, and strode away into the darkness. I had to blink back tears as I guided Selma's car up our driveway. I couldn't stay here indefinitely with only her ghost to keep me company, but it was difficult to think about abandoning the only home I had ever known for the city of all cities a thousand miles away. Still, I had a year to figure out how to jump-start my stalled college plans. New York City was as good a place as any to do the figuring. Better, even, because it contained

Austin, my once and future—I hoped—best friend.

I parked Selma's car in the carport and went inside, accidentally banging the kitchen screen behind me. I froze, half-expecting to hear a familiar, mildly admonishing voice: *Ashley, dear girl, please don't slam the door.*

But the only sounds that reached me were the steady hum of the refrigerator and the velvety call of an owl echoing through the summer-thick trees.

The next morning, Austin called early to make sure I hadn't changed my mind and to see if I could be ready to leave in twenty-four hours. I swallowed a bite of toast, said I hadn't and I could.

"Good," he said, and then again, "good."

"How did things go with your dad?"

"You know," he said evasively.

"Um, no, I don't."

"It was okay. But you'd better get packing. Do you need help?"

"Not yet. Maybe later?"

"Okay." He sounded disappointed, and I knew then that things at the Taylor house were not good.

I didn't press him, though. I had a lot to do, and there would be plenty of time to hear the details once we hit the road. *Hit the road*—holy crap. I was moving to the North. To New York City, even. Hadn't seen that one coming.

When the screen door banged a half hour later, I looked up from the silverware drawer, expecting to see Austin. Instead, it was his mother.

"Good morning," Claire said. "Okay if I join you?"

"Of course."

I turned back to the drawer, resuming the search for pieces of flatware that had belonged to my parents. They were easy to pick out, wide and rounded and engraved with loopy, cheerful daisies. The sublet was fully furnished, Austin had told me, but I wanted to have some of my own things there to make it feel more like home.

"You're packing, then?" she asked, clutching her elbows with her hands.

"Yes." The thought of everything I had to do in the next twenty-four hours made my heart pound like I'd just run a mile for time, so I changed the subject. "Did Austin tell you what happened with the Navy?"

"He did," she confirmed, pulling up a chair at the kitchen table. "How did it go?"

"Not well."

Briefly I pictured Austin's response if he knew his mother and I were discussing their private family affairs, but he had left town and not looked back until now. Meanwhile, Claire and I had shared the intimate moments of Selma's illness and death. At this point, I almost felt closer to her.

"I wasn't surprised," Claire said, "but Bruce was stunned. He refused to accept it. In fact, he went off to work this morning operating as if it was all just one big mistake that needed sorting out."

I faced her, silverware in hand. "You're kidding."

"Didn't Austin tell you?"

"Not exactly. I figured I'd get the details of who said what tomorrow."

Claire leaned her elbows on the table. "There wasn't much discussion, really. Austin informed us that another boy on the ship turned him in during a 'witch hunt,' as he called it. Bruce insisted that it had to be a mistake, that his son couldn't possibly be one of *those people*. Austin tried to speak up, but Bruce wouldn't listen. He kept blustering on about the Navy and its byzantine bureaucracy, about what a long, distinguished record of service to their country the Taylors have. He swore he would go to Washington himself to petition the government to withdraw its claim, if he had to. And do you know what? I didn't stop him. I just sat at the dining room table and watched him rant and rave. I didn't say a word."

She passed a hand over her eyes. A marriage and family therapist by profession, she was accustomed to capably managing the upheaval in other people's lives. Why, then, hadn't she broached the subject of Austin's sexual orientation with her husband before now? But just as Austin couldn't have predicted Selma's death, Claire couldn't have known that the US Navy, in all its wisdom, would suddenly decide that their son was no longer welcome to risk his life for his country solely because he found other men attractive.

"Just give it some time," I offered, recycling one of the many platitudes I'd heard in recent months.

"I don't think we have any choice. You know what I keep thinking? Austin must have suspected his father would react this way, or he would have confided in us sooner. Maybe he knows his father better than I do after all." She shook her head. "They didn't even speak this morning, just passed politely in the hall. I don't know if I can fix this one. I don't know if they'll ever forgive each other."

"Of course they will," I said. "They've always been so close. Besides, nothing's forever."

She blinked and seemed to focus right on me for the first time. "I'm sorry, honey. I don't mean to dump this on you. I'm just so used to heading over here when I need to talk."

"You miss her, too, don't you?"

"I sure do."

The woods beyond the window were lit by morning sunshine. This would be my last afternoon on the mountain for an indeterminate time, I reminded myself. On cue, my pulse quickened again.

"Well, anyway," Claire said, "Austin told me that you're planning to go up north with him, so I came over to see if you need any help packing."

I hesitated, wishing I could accept her offer, but this was Austin's last afternoon on the mountain, too. "No, thanks. I'll be fine."

I was still holding my parents' silverware. Turning away, I dropped it into an open Ziploc bag. Next on my list was cleaning out the refrigerator, a task I was not looking forward to. Fortunately, it wasn't exactly full these days, given my predilection for sandwiches and pizza.

"What do you want to do about the house?" Claire asked.

"I don't know. I was thinking I could rent it out, maybe."

"You could. It would have to be packed up, but I suppose that wouldn't be too difficult, given…"

She paused, but I knew what she meant. Together, she and I had gone through Selma's things a few weeks after the funeral. The boxes were still in the attic, waiting for me to decide what to do with them. The night we lugged the last box up the rickety old drop-down ladder, Claire had asked me to move in with her and Bruce and Julie, Austin's younger sister who was a year behind me in school. I'd refused, mostly because I couldn't bear to leave Selma's house.

Now here I was six short—or abysmally long, depending on

your perspective—weeks later, ready to leave at the drop of a sailor's hat.

"I could probably pay someone to move everything into storage," I suggested.

In fact, Selma and I had discussed this exact course of action when it became clear that her efforts to fight the cancer were failing. She hadn't wanted me to sell the house right away, but at the same time, she knew I would be leaving for college soon. I ignored the flicker of guilt this memory elicited. I could go to school anytime; it wasn't like there was an expiration date on undergraduate education. Eighty-year-olds earned degrees all the time, didn't they?

"A realtor would know what to do," Claire said. "I could call Janet Gothard, if you'd like. She should be able to recommend next steps, along with a good property manager."

"Is that too much to ask? I mean, I don't have to leave tomorrow. I could always wait a little while if all of this is too fast."

"It is quick," she agreed. "But you know Bruce and I worry about you alone over here. It's not healthy. I don't know that New York City necessarily is, either, but you need to get on with your life, Ashley. And to be honest, I'm relieved to think of you and Austin together, even if it is so far away."

"Thanks, Claire," I said, aware of the pale yellow light filtering into the kitchen, illuminating the normally invisible dust motes floating in the air between us.

"You're welcome, hon. I just want you both to be happy. You know that, don't you? And Austin? He knows that too, doesn't he?"

I nodded.

After a moment, her voice grew brisk again. "All right, then. I'll let you know what Janet says about the house. Right now, however, I'd better get back." She set her hands palms-down on the old pedestal table and pushed herself up out of the wood-backed chair, one of a mismatched set Selma had rescued over the years and lovingly restored, one chair at a time. "Come over for dinner tonight, will you?"

"Are you sure? I don't want to intrude."

"Don't be silly," she said, her smile purposely cheerful. "It's your last night on the mountain. We'd love to have you. Say, six-thirty?"

"Okay."

She nodded once, business-like almost, and strode from the house, waving briefly through the kitchen screen before disappearing around the side of the station wagon. I went back to packing, crossing off "Kitchen" from the list I had hastily scrawled after Austin's breakfast phone call. By the end of the day, I would be ready to leave Selma's house.

Despite the heat of the summer day, I shivered.

CHAPTER THREE

That night, after a tense, awkward dinner at the Taylors, I tossed in my comfortable, familiar bed and wondered what the hell I had been thinking. I may have been born and lived my first few years in a skyscraper-bedecked city of millions, but I had spent the past decade and a half in a forested suburb where seventy percent of the residents were college-educated, as Selma liked to point out whenever I complained about the backwoods quality of our town, and where deer, coyotes, and the occasional bear and mountain lion still roamed. The residents of New York City promised to be of a very different, far more intimidating nature, if *Law and Order* were even a smidgeon accurate.

It was scarcely light out when I rose and pulled on my running gear. Carrying my shoes outside, I sat on the front stoop to tie my laces, listening to the cheerful trills of the resident summer songbirds. Then I rose and did a few push-ups and jumping jacks to get my blood pumping before heading down the long gravel drive to the road. It would be too dark yet for the tree roots on the trail around Rainbow Lake, so I started out across the golf course, sticking to the paved walkways and keeping an eye out for any early risers. The sun slowly rose over Chattanooga as I ran, but it wouldn't top the trees here on the ridge until well after Austin and I had hit the road, assuming everything went as planned. Even so, there was enough light to see where I was going and to pick out the khaki pants of the occasional country club member.

As I ran, my heart rate increased and my anxiety slowly ebbed, unable to compete with the endorphins flooding my addled brain. I chanted my mantra as I ran: "Pain is weakness leaving the body," timing the words to my foot strikes, my breath to the words. For a while, when Selma was going through chemo and radiation, my mantra shifted to "If she can do it, I can do it." In the wake of her death, I had gone back to the old tried and true, a phrase I'd learned under the tutelage of Butch Halvorson, former Marine, current P.E. teacher, and longtime coach of the Redbank High School track team.

I'd known since I was ten that I wanted to be a runner. Sophomore and junior years of high school, my times in the 1500, 3000, and 5000 meters had helped get my team into the All-State meet at Tennessee State University, storied alma mater of Wilma Rudolph and her Olympic teammates. Sophomore year I surprised everyone by winning the 3000 and taking second place in the 5000, attracting the interest of regional scouts. But the following spring, I ignored Butch's advice, over trained, and had to withdraw from the 1500 prelims with a groin pull. Senior year, I missed most of the cross country season with a hamstring injury. Then Selma got sick and I quit the track team outright, offering only a vague excuse about "personal obligations." Running could wait. Cancer couldn't.

Butch didn't say much when I told him I was leaving the team. Even before that, we'd barely gotten along. Privately he let me know he thought I was a selfish runner who didn't give a whit about anyone but myself. Privately I let him know that I ran in spite of his role as coach, not because of it. Looking back, I may not have had the best attitude when it came to high school team sports. Hadn't helped that Butch was a small-town—and small-minded, in my opinion—good ole Southern boy, while I was the smartass tomboy daughter of a Yankee librarian. It may have been wiser to cultivate his support rather than his enmity, but with me, what you see is usually what you get. Unfortunately, as a direct result of my inability to coexist with Butch, I now had as much likelihood of achieving my long-term running goals as a crow did of flying a mile upside down.

There was a lesson here, no doubt. But I wasn't in the mood to learn from past mistakes. I didn't want to think about Butch or what might have been; I didn't even want to think about what might still yet be. As the sky slowly lightened and my vision sharpened, I murmured my mantra wordlessly and focused on the dew sparkling on bright green blades of grass; on the slap of my rubber soles against the paved path; on the sound of my own breathing steady in my ears. I felt good again, finally, running. Throughout the spring I had backed off my usual punishing training routine, cruising around the mountain on my bike instead, a lightweight ten-speed I had bought in eighth grade with babysitting money. The cross-training—another of Butch's ideas—had worked. My hamstrings were strong again, my quads more powerful than ever, my groin back to normal.

"Pain is weakness leaving the body," I reminded myself, repeating the phrase over and over again until the past and future faded and the only sights and sounds accosting me were of my hometown on a summer's morning, coming to life around me.

By the time Austin and I got the car packed and our goodbyes proffered to those we were leaving behind, the sun was threatening to break through trees on the eastern horizon. With a final wave at the Taylors, who stood on the front walkway of Selma's house watching us, we backed down the long driveway and onto the main road in a sputter of gravel.

"You ready?" I asked Austin.

Busy pretending not to watch his family out of the corner of his eye, he missed the question.

"Guess so," I said to myself, and then paused the car for a long moment, gazing back at the house I'd shared with my aunt. I couldn't remember another home, or another parent, for that matter. But Selma had joined my mother and father in some other place, and now all I had left of any of them were a few photos destined to fade and crack.

Although that wasn't true, not really. Selma had told me again and again that I was part of my parents, physical evidence of their existence. My presence made them both come alive again for her—my father's physique, my mother's temperament, my grandfather's eyes, even. While she was alive, I could feel that connection because she saw them in me. Now I was left without even that tenuous hold on a family I couldn't remember.

Tears filled my eyes, and I felt Austin's hand on my arm.

"You okay, Ash?"

"Fine," I said quickly. I sniffed back my tears, waved at Claire and Bruce and Julie, and hit the gas.

One hand on the steering wheel and the other on the gear shift, I guided Selma's car down from Signal Mountain to the edge of the city, where we followed the Olgiati Bridge over the brown-green Tennessee River. Soon we were crossing Chattanooga, Signal Mountain receding behind us, to I-75 at the far eastern edge of the city. The last time I'd been on this interstate with Austin had been almost exactly a year before, coming back from Hilton Head the day before he went into the service. We'd raced the sun from Atlanta to Chattanooga, driving all night so that he would make his bus to land-locked New Mexico where he was scheduled to be inducted into the United States Navy. Now we were headed north again, but toward Knoxville this time along the edge of the Cumberland Plateau, the Appalachian Mountains an imposing yet unseen barrier between East Tennessee and the Atlantic Coast.

"You okay?" Austin asked again, looking over at me as Chattanooga, the Tennessee River Gorge, and our hometown slipped from sight in the rearview mirror.

It wasn't forever, I told myself. It *wasn't.*

"Totally," I said. "But what about you? You still haven't told me what went down with your parents."

"Not much to tell."

"Really? Didn't seem like it at dinner."

The night before, Bruce Taylor had stared morbidly around the table at everyone except his son throughout the meal, brandishing the blank school administrator's expression that I had only ever observed on him in public. Almost even before the meal was over, he had excused himself and vanished into his study, where I heard the murmur of the television set to low, the unmistakable rhythms of a baseball broadcast audible in the momentarily quiet dining room. Julie, a smart, popular girl who I liked well enough, had offered me a raised-brow look while Austin glowered at the tablecloth and Claire sighed quietly, her eyes on the closed study door.

As dinner wound down, I'd found myself thinking that there were perhaps some very minor advantages, after all, to losing one's parents at a young age—such as never having to watch your father shun you for becoming the very person his genes and upbringing had made you. The person you couldn't help but be.

Austin drummed his fingers on the car door frame. "Huh. I didn't notice."

"Come on, I'm not blind, and neither are you. Anyway, your mom told me that you and your dad weren't exactly thrilled with each other over this whole thing."

"Dude," Austin said, leaning against the passenger door, "that is so not cool. You've been my best friend since we were ten, and now you're talking to my *mom* about our family stuff?"

"A lot happened after you left," I pointed out.

He didn't know about the hospital visits when his mom and I had talked or read while Selma slept the day away. He didn't know that when Selma checked into the hospital in April for the last time, I'd stayed at his house, sleeping in his bed and eating at his dining room table, the same table I'd helped Claire and Julie clear the night before while Austin retired to his room to pack. That was the South for you—even in supposedly "liberated" households, men didn't often do housework.

Which reminded me: If Austin thought I was moving north to be his glorified maid, he had a whole other thing coming.

"I know a lot happened," he said. "It's just hard to picture you guys as, like, *friends*. I wish I could've—well, anyway. If you talked to my mom, you probably know more about what happened the other night than I do."

"I doubt that," I said, speeding up to pass a semi. The station wagon was filled to the hilt, my bike lying flat across the pile like a steel-framed king of the mountain, which meant I had to rely on my mirrors.

"Did she tell you he pretty much refused to believe anything I said?"

I shook my head and turned on my blinker.

"Well, he did. At first he didn't even want to accept that I'd been kicked out of the Navy. Then he kept asking me what I was going to do, how I would ever be able to get into a good school or get a job with this on my record. I told him the discharge was honorable, but he didn't care. He said I was ruining my life."

"That doesn't sound like your dad."

I knew Bruce as my former middle school principal, a man who seemed to genuinely care about the teachers and kids at his school. He was soft-spoken and always looked a little ruffled in dress shirts with the sleeves rolled up. I couldn't imagine him getting worked up about much of anything.

"Honestly, he was better than a lot of dads," Austin said.

"Fathers aren't exactly known for their tolerance. That's why most guys come out to people they barely know long before they come out to their families."

"That sucks. But he'll come around eventually, won't he? It just takes time, right?"

The mind-numbing cliché I had heard so many times since Selma's death that sometimes I thought I ought to have it tattooed to my forehead, and here I was repeating it for the second time in twenty-four hours.

"Sure." But he didn't look at me as he rifled through my padded cassette carrier. "Damn, girl, even your tapes are organized. What did you do, alphabetize them?"

I had, but that didn't stop me from smacking him.

Rubbing his arm and grumbling good-naturedly, he put in the Eagles and we sang along to "Take it Easy" as we drove along the tree-lined interstate, leaving the Tennessee River Valley behind. We'd looked at Selma's beat-up road atlas before starting out, and I knew that a little ways up the road was Knoxville where we would switch over to I-40 and then to I-81, the road that would take us all the way to Pennsylvania. From there, we would make our way to New Jersey, and then Austin would take the wheel. He was planning to drive us into Manhattan—which I hadn't actually realized was an island until he pointed this out on the map—via the Holland Tunnel. A tunnel under a river into New York City struck me as an almost too-perfect terrorist target. After all, it had only been a few years since the Pan-Am bombing over Lockerbie, and less than a handful of months since the "unsuccessful" World Trade Center attack. But I didn't share my fears with Austin. I was old enough to understand that most people didn't anticipate disaster quite the way I did.

The morning grew hotter as we continued on toward the land of Yankees. Technically, as Austin had reminded me, I was one. In grade school, I used to take out the road atlas and stare at the map of Illinois with its half-page spread on Chicago: Sears Tower, Shedd Aquarium, Navy Pier, University of Chicago, Midway, and O'Hare. O'Hare, where our jet had crashed on the way back from Orlando. I didn't remember Chicago as a city where I had once lived, but rather as the place where my parents had died. In all of our educational wanderings, Selma had never planned a trip that included the Windy City. Washington, DC, yes, and Jefferson's

Charlottesville, including Monticello and the Blue Ridge Parkway, and even once a tour of New England where we ate lobster and walked the Cape Cod beach where the *Mayflower* had landed in 1620. As a result, the route Austin and I traveled now was not entirely unfamiliar to me, only our ultimate destination. Selma had not liked cities, and worried that New York, with its skyscrapers and hordes of pedestrians, might trigger long-buried memories of the Second City. So we'd avoided the Big Apple on our journeys, along with Boston and Philadelphia and any other urban center that could possibly remind me—and her, though she never said as much—of Chicago.

Would the streets of New York suddenly set my memories to flowing, as Selma had feared? Somehow I doubted it. Nothing else ever had. But still, as we headed north, I wondered.

Captive audience members that we were, Austin and I caught each other up on the goings-on since he'd left for the Navy. I filled him in on Signal Mountain gossip: who had married whom, who'd gone to college or otherwise left the mountain, and who had died, while he told me about the places he'd gone and the guys he'd dated in the ten months since he'd come to terms with being gay. He told me about military witch hunts, when they cracked down on specific units and tried to get gay soldiers to rat each other out. One of his friends, threatened with a dishonorable discharge and possible jail time, had turned Austin in.

"It's ridiculous," he said, looking out the window at the land rushing by. "Some of the best sailors on our ship were gay."

"The whole thing doesn't make any sense. It'll change eventually, won't it?"

"Maybe. But I wouldn't hold my breath." He paused, fiddled with the tape case handle while he chose his next words. "The thing is, Ash, I know about Selma from my mom. I know she tried to fight it, and that you and my mom were with her at the end. But I don't know how it was for you. I can imagine, but I can't really know. I guess what I'm trying to say is that if you want to talk about it, I'm here, okay?"

I blinked, surprised that such a roundabout inquiry could nonetheless leave me with watering eyes and a tightness in my throat yet again. Would I always be dealing with Selma's cancer, the way I seemed unable to escape the aftereffects of Flight 108?

"Okay," I said, my eyes on the gray road before us. "Thanks."

"You're welcome."

A little while later he fell asleep, leaving me alone with my thoughts and a Sting tape. In sleep Austin looked more like the kid I used to know, less like the grown man he'd morphed into over the past year. Even at the age of ten, when his parents abandoned low-lying Chattanooga for the friendly community of Signal Mountain, Austin had seemed different from other boys. *They* were miniature versions of their fathers, future Vanderbilt frat boys who'd known how to throw a baseball and swing a golf club almost before they could walk. But Austin wasn't a clone of his father or any other man, for that matter. He seemed sweeter than the other boys, with slender hips, long eyelashes, and a mouth made to smile. The first time we met, when Selma and I walked next door bearing welcome tidings and a homemade cherry pie, I knew that Austin wouldn't last long in the crowd of boys at school. Jimmy Walters and Tad Berghorst would knock the laughter right out of him. I decided then and there not to let that happen.

"Want to ride bikes tomorrow?" I'd asked him after we finished our pie that first night. His sister Julie had already earned my disgust by asking if I wanted to play Barbies. I hated Barbie dolls with a passion that pleased Selma. After promising Julie that I would *never* want to play Barbies, I'd turned back to Austin, who was trying to balance a spoon on his nose the way I'd shown him.

At my invitation, Austin glanced at his mother, who was laughing with Selma about something beyond our grasp.

"Yeah," he said, looking back at me. "Sure."

And that was the start of Austin and me. The month before school we played in the woods and on our bikes and in my tree house. By the time school started, I'd taught Austin secretly how to box. Tad Berghorst's father, a Golden Gloves champ who had given up fighting for a lucrative surgeon's career, had taught Tad and me the summer before, back when we were still best friends.

At the end of third grade, Tad and I had gotten into a fight. Trying to do the right thing after he punched me for beating him on the monkey bars, I punched him back, magnanimously pronounced us even, and turned to walk away. He kicked me in the back, knocking me to the ground so hard I was sure I would never walk again and causing my immortal humiliation—I actually cried in front of all of the kids on the playground, a first and only, as it turned out, for me. A couple of days later, again on the playground,

I hit Tad in the face so hard he fell down and his nose bled and he cried like a little kid. We hadn't spoken a friendly word to each other since. To a kid one month feels more like a year, so to my mind, it had been ages since Tad and I had been buddies. Austin was my new best friend. Anyone who messed with him would be messing with me, too.

Fortunately, half the boys at school were afraid of me. For one thing, everyone in Signal Mountain knew that I had survived a fiery plane crash with barely a scratch, which, it was said, must indicate that I possessed mystical powers of some sort—just like my Yankee witch aunt. For another, I wasn't like most other girls in Signal Mountain. I didn't play hopscotch or jump rope or wear pink. I rode my bike all over, if I wasn't running, and I wrestled and played tackle football during recess with the boys. In gym class, I played a mean game of kick ball.

Then Austin came along, his head full of poetry and his body unskilled in the territorial battles of the playground. We were good for each other, Austin and me. With my help he learned to tolerate math and how to hold his own with the boys. Under his influence, I learned to like the game of Pretend and most musicals, especially anything with Garland or Streisand. We helped balance each other out, so that we weren't such misfits in a part of the world that didn't approve of sensitivity in its boys or stubbornness in its girls.

"You okay driving, Ash?" Austin was awake and watching me. "I can take a turn if you want."

"I'm fine," I said. "Don't you worry your pretty little head, darlin.'"

He snorted. "You'll fit in fine in the Village. They have a saying there—'Greenwich Village, where the men are pretty and the women are strong.'"

"Why doesn't that surprise me? Dude, this tape's putting me to sleep. How about some Abba?"

"Now you're talking."

As we sang along to the music, it occurred to me that our roles had reversed since the day Austin had moved to Signal Mountain. When we got to New York, it would be his turn to teach me the games everyone else already knew.

Late that night, we emerged from the neat New Jersey farm fields into the industrial wasteland of Newark and its sprawling suburbs. Despite the industrialization of Tennessee, I'd never seen such a mass of twisted metal structures, smoke stack after smoke stack billowing clouds of white gases into the air, the smell of rotten eggs and burning rubber wafting across the highway.

"Night's the best time to see the city," Austin told me as we headed up I-95 along the Hudson. It was almost midnight, and we still hadn't reached the New York state line. But we were close. Over a small hill, beyond the complicated steel structure of some type of factory, I got my first look at New York City, a mass of lights across the river. The twin towers of the World Trade Center presided over the rest of the buildings at the southern tip of Manhattan. I had seen photos, of course, but in person the towers' sheer dominance of a skyline filled already with buildings taller than any I'd previously encountered was stunning.

As planned, Austin was at the wheel for the final leg of the trip. But at the last minute, he bypassed the Holland Tunnel exit.

"We're going to take the GW instead," he announced, keeping his eyes on the traffic flitting restlessly around us.

"What's the GW?" I asked, hoping it wouldn't be another tunnel.

"It's a bridge. This way you'll see more of the city instead of just the Village."

A bridge sounded much safer than a tunnel. I say *sounded*, because once I saw the George Washington Bridge, I sort of wished we'd taken the tunnel. The bridge, like the city itself, was immense. As we crossed high above the Hudson amidst a sea of roaring, honking cars, I decided that what I really wished was that Manhattan wasn't an island. Building the free market capital of the world on a slip of land that could only be reached by tunnel, bridge, or ferry struck me as perhaps not the best example of urban planning.

I stared out the window, looking out upon the city that stretched southward below us. Hundreds, maybe thousands of buildings poked up like an irregular forest from the thin slab of land. From my vantage point on the bridge, it seemed as if the island should surely sink beneath all of that weight, tipping like the Titanic into the water that lapped at its southern edge.

"What do you think?" Austin asked as we exited onto Henry Hudson Parkway. "Isn't it amazing?"

I nodded, staring across the river at the yellow lights of New

Jersey. "Amazing is a good word. It's gigantic."

"I know. Isn't it fantastic?"

I didn't answer as I watched black Cadillacs, yellow cabs, and old, wide Chevys fly past us on a narrow-laned parkway that had seen better days. Once again, I was only too happy to have Austin at the wheel.

To the left of the highway, up a hill, were lights, buildings, concrete roads, and walkways. A train rumbled past on a track built above the city streets, graffitied sides revealed in sporadic streetlights. I couldn't get over how light it was at midnight. On cloudy nights Signal Mountain was as dark as a windowless room. Sometimes the moon might light the way through the wooded paths near my house, but usually you needed a flashlight to see where you were going.

"The apartment's on the west side," Austin said as we careened down the highway with buildings and billboards to our left, the river and New Jersey to our right.

I just nodded. All at once I couldn't wait to go to sleep in a bed, any bed, anywhere.

"Don't worry," Austin said, looking away from the road to flash me a quick smile. "We're almost there."

I'd assumed we would be living in the midst of fifty-floor buildings, but the highway turned into a regular road and we soon turned left at a stop light. Then we drove through a series of twisting, winding one-way streets. People were out in shorts and tank tops and sandals walking the streets on this, a Tuesday night. Grocery stores seemed to occupy every other corner. Most were still open. Back in Signal Mountain everything closed by ten o'clock, even in the summer.

Eventually Austin turned the car down a quiet residential block with trees and the occasional tiny grass yard. The buildings were all the same size and built one next to the other, but the stairs and exteriors varied. New York brownstones, I realized—just like on *The Cosby Show*.

We double parked in front of a four-story building with flower pots in the front windows and a wide brick stairway with a wrought iron handrail.

"This is it," Austin said as he turned on the hazards and turned off the car engine.

"It looks nice," I said. "A little loud, though."

"For Manhattan, this is about as quiet as it gets unless you're forty stories up." He slipped out of the car and stretched. "Let's go. Time to unpack."

I felt like a zombie, exhausted from the trip and already overwhelmed by the noise of the city. I needed darkness and quiet, and was afraid I would find neither.

"It's almost one," I said. "Can't we unpack in the morning?"

"Only if you don't mind seeing your stuff for sale on a blanket at St. Marks." As I stared at him blankly, he clarified: "We can't leave your car on the street as it is, not even in a good neighborhood, or someone else will unpack it for you."

"Are you serious?"

"Come on, Toto," he said, unlocking the hatchback as I climbed out of the car and wrinkled my nose at the sour stench I would come to recognize as the mingled odor of trash and urine. "We're not in Tennessee anymore."

It took forever to move my stuff into the apartment on the first floor of the brownstone, given that Austin insisted on staying with the car while I lugged everything up the steps and inside. I piled my bags, boxes, and bike in the spacious, high-ceilinged living room, careful not to soil the tan linen couch or the Persian rug that covered most of the wood floor.

I was almost unconscious on my feet when Austin said, "That's it. I'll move the car if you want to head to bed."

"Okay. Thanks." I turned away, yawning, and climbed the steps for the last time that night.

"Lock the door!" Austin called after me.

I waved over my shoulder and went into the apartment, turning one of the many bolts behind me. Then I trudged past my boxes and bags to the small bedroom off the living room. I had an impression of peach walls and cool air and what I thought at first was a bunk bed. Then I remembered that New Yorkers called it a "loft." I climbed the ladder to the bed, lay down fully clothed, and sighed at the unquestionably lovely feeling of being prone.

We definitely weren't in Tennessee anymore.

CHAPTER FOUR

I awoke to the sound of birds singing beyond my window—not exactly what I'd expected of New York City. I sat up in bed, careful not to hit my head on the ceiling above the loft, and glanced out the window. My small room overlooked a courtyard, which explained the relative quiet. The people who lived in the daylight basement apartment below us had planted a flower garden along the edge of their deck. Across the way, a willow tree hung over a Japanese garden, complete with bonsai trees and a friendly statue of Buddha. Just outside my window grew a tall elm tree, home to the half dozen birds whose singing had greeted me.

Not at all what I'd expected, especially after my introduction to city life the night before.

I climbed down, eager to explore my new home. There was no sign of Austin yet, so I wandered our shared living space, opening drawers and cupboards in the kitchen and reading the spines of books neatly arrayed in the entertainment center in the living room. In the heart of the West Village on Perry Street between Bleecker and West Fourth, the apartment was indeed awesome, as Austin had promised during the drive north—fully furnished, high-ceilinged, and, best of all, rent-controlled. We had it for a full year while its usual inhabitant, an NYU professor of European history who had lived here for close to twenty years, was on sabbatical in France. Ours was the largest unit in the building, with polished wooden floors, two bedrooms with queen-sized beds built into lofts, and air conditioning units in every room. The front bedroom, which Austin had claimed for himself, was bigger and closer to the tiny bathroom. My bedroom in the back was smaller and less furnished; the guest room, Austin had explained. But my windows were wider and afforded a quieter view of urban life, which suited me fine.

Austin got up a little later and joined me for orange juice and toasted English muffins with butter and the blackberry jam his mom and Selma had canned the previous fall, before the cancer diagnosis. But we didn't discuss the jam's creation story as we sat at the table in the dining alcove overlooking the back yard.

"What do you want to do today?" he asked.

"I don't know. When do you have to be at work?"

Austin's new job was waiting tables at a gay-owned restaurant not far from the apartment. He was expected to work every night except Mondays, a busy schedule that nonetheless sounded to him like coasting after the Navy, he'd told me.

"At five. We close at midnight, so it's kind of a long night. But the tips should be good."

"I'll bet."

I eyed Austin across the table, taking in the still new (to me) muscles in his chest and arms, the sheen of his short hair tamed by pomade, the slight lift of his lips, as if he might break into a smile at any moment. No doubt about it, my best friend had grown into a far more fabulous version of his high school self.

"Seriously, what do you want to do?" he asked. "We could always go to the Empire State Building. Or maybe the World Trade Center."

"I thought you were afraid of heights."

"I got over it."

I tilted my head, considering the odds of a terrorist attack at either site. "How about the Empire State Building?"

"Cool. I haven't gone to any of the touristy places yet. Too embarrassing to do alone."

It was ten by the time we left the apartment. As we walked through the West Village, I gazed around at the buildings and people, at the streets just as narrow and twisty as I remembered from our drive in the night before. Just as crowded, too—at home, I was used to running miles without encountering another person, but here you couldn't walk even half a block without having to dodge oncoming pedestrian traffic.

"Where do you go to be alone?" I asked Austin as we waited underground for the subway train that would carry us to Midtown and the Empire State Building.

"Alone?" he echoed, glancing over at me.

He was wearing cut-off jeans shorts and another tight T-shirt that showcased his tanned arms nicely. During our short walk to the subway station, we'd passed several other men of varying ages and races similarly clad—gay men, Austin had informed me, as if I couldn't pick up on the interested, half-lidded looks they smoldered at him.

"Yeah, you know, by yourself?"

Austin shrugged and looked back at the empty train tracks. "I don't like being alone much anymore."

"*You* don't like being by yourself?"

Was there really no trace left of the moody teenager who had sometimes blown off even me to sit in his room alone for hours listening to U2 and the Eurythmics?

"When you're at sea for months at a time, you get over needing space of any kind pretty quickly."

Maybe that explained why he didn't appear to mind the stifling nature of the subway station. The air underground was heavy, hot, and reeked of urine. I caught a glimpse of a rat skittering along the tracks and looked up as a train neared. I'd ridden the subway on trips to DC. How different could it be?

The train slowed to a stop, brakes shrieking as metal scraped against metal. We stepped aboard and found seats, relaxing in the air-conditioned car.

"You've changed a lot, haven't you?" I commented as the train pulled away from the station and entered a dimly lit tunnel.

"Not really," he said. "Or maybe so. I feel the same, but different, too. I know now why I was so unhappy in high school. I just couldn't be myself there. I had to get away from everyone who thought they knew me. You know?"

"Yeah, I know."

I looked out the train window, trying to see into the dark tunnel. Red lights glowed sporadically, illuminating the graffiti-covered walls of passageways that snaked away to unknown destinations. We moved too quickly for me to make sense of what I saw, but I kept staring anyway, trying to read the spray-painted slogans.

Then the tunnel walls narrowed again, and we slowed and entered another station, car lights flickering as the conductor applied the brakes. After a moment, the doors opened and hot air gusted along with people into the car.

"Four more stops," Austin said, looking at the subway map on the far wall.

Good thing he knew where we were going.

When the train doors closed again, we crept away from the station, steadily picking up speed. We'd been going for less than a minute when a thirty-something black man in scruffy clothes stepped to the center of the car and said, "Excuse me please, ladies and gentlemen. I do not want to disturb you, but my name is David, and I would like to ask for your attention. My family lost our home in a fire, and as a result of this fire I lost my job and now we live in a cardboard box and I ask you, is that any way for my little boy and little girl to grow up?"

I glanced at Austin, but he was staring straight ahead, apparently ignoring the speaker. Around me, the blank faces of other train passengers reflected a corresponding lack of interest.

The man continued: "If you could find it in your heart to offer up any of your spare change, my wife and I would greatly appreciate the chance to buy a hot meal for our little ones. Thank you very much."

He began to move around the car, holding out a frayed paper cup that jingled slightly as he paused in front of one unmoving, unmoved passenger after the next. I shifted uncomfortably in my seat and started to reach into my shorts pocket, where I knew for a fact there were a couple of quarters and maybe a dime or two that I didn't need. But Austin touched my hand and shook his head almost imperceptibly.

The homeless man paused in front of me longer than he did anyone else, but Austin kept his hand on mine, and soon the stranger moved on.

"You'll get used to the act," Austin said once the man was out of earshot. "Usually the stories are much more creative and involve something more catastrophic than a fire."

"The act? You mean you don't believe him?"

Austin shrugged. "Most of the time, they're lying."

"What about when they aren't?"

"There's no way to tell the difference. But the majority are just

39

out for drug money."

I looked again through the window at the darkness pressing in on the train. First Austin had said it wasn't safe to leave a locked car filled with my possessions unattended for even a few minutes, and now he was counseling me not to give away my pocket change to someone who could clearly use it.

Apparently there was a reason the Huxtables had spent so much time inside their brownstone. Real city life didn't work quite as well with a laugh track.

Leaning my head against the train window, I watched red lights and painted words whip past out of focus, and wondered what I had gotten myself into.

Selma had always said that all I needed was a routine and I could get used to almost anything. Normally, I would have agreed. But New York, in all of its concrete, people-jammed immensity, was a beast of an altogether different sort. I was accustomed to trees and grass and Craftsman bungalows, not paved expanses and steel high-rises. I wasn't sure the comfort of routine would help me settle in here.

I had to admit, though, the sheer variety of possibilities in New York was exhilarating. The weekend after we arrived was Pride. If you've never been to Pride in the city that single-handedly started the gay civil rights crusade, then I highly recommend you add it to your bucket list. A mile-long throng filled the streets, with fine boys in fishnets and gorgeous girls in pasties. This was The City, after all, filled with Beautiful People. Austin and I stayed out late with his friends three nights in a row, putting our fake IDs to good use with more dancing and drinking than I'd accomplished in the previous five years. The whole weekend was one big party, and though the lights and drinks and crowds were semi-addictive, I was relieved when Monday came and the city settled down from Gay Party Town to its usual merely flamboyant self.

My first full week in the city, I awoke each morning and lay in bed staring for a few minutes at the sun-dappled backyard and the green branches beyond my window. Then I would climb down from my loft and pad barefoot into the kitchen for a breakfast of bagels and cream cheese over the previous day's *New York Times*. After breakfast came a shower. Then I would leave Austin a note and head out on daily wanderings. At first I went on foot, guide book and map in hand, venturing into some part of the city I had yet to explore. But after a week of watching bicycle messengers and delivery boys running red lights and blasting past pedestrians on their two wheels, I got my nerve up to take my bike out for its first NYC spin.

I left the apartment mid-morning on my second Saturday in the city, carrying my bike down the brick steps in front of our building and setting off in the wrong direction along our one-way street. I'd plotted my route the night before on a bike map I'd picked up at the public library on Tenth Street, drawing out a wide loop that started in the Village, wound down to SoHo, and cut across Delancey to First Avenue, which I planned to follow north to Midtown before taking a spin through Central Park. A weekend day would be better, I figured, because the roads would be less clogged with cars and bicycles.

Turned out I was half-right—there were definitely fewer cars on the road as I headed down Bleecker Street to Seventh Avenue on my old school Schwinn, but there were also more cyclists and roller bladers than I'd ever seen in my life. Narrow New York streets were always getting backed up with delivery trucks, double-parked cars, and city buses. Given that the island of Manhattan is only a little over two miles wide and thirteen miles long, bikes and blades are often the fastest above-ground travel option, especially if your route takes you both crosstown and up or downtown. Most public transit options only cover a single axis.

But I didn't know any of this yet. I only knew that tree-lined Perry Street, with its four-story brownstones and townhouses built shoulder to shoulder with next to no gap between neighboring structures, was atypical in its relative livability.

Bleecker Street grew grittier the further south I rode, with six-story tenements harboring neon-signed businesses at street level, while Seventh Avenue offered four lanes and timed stoplights that allowed the traffic to shoot past frighteningly close. While Austin's street—I couldn't think of it as mine yet—had plentiful trees offering up oxygen to combat the exhaust generated by minimal traffic, the streets I traveled that morning had only a few spindly hardwoods that were no match for the bounty of diesel fumes spewed by trucks and buses or the gray gases coughed out by old El Dorados and yellow cabs in need of a tune-up.

To say that riding a lightweight piece of metal with thin rubber wheels along the main streets of New York City was a little intimidating would be like saying skydiving could a tad nerve-wracking. As cabs turned corners with little concern for my presence and pedestrian after pedestrian jay-walked into my direct path, I quickly rethought my plan for the day. Twenty minutes after leaving the apartment, I coasted into Union Square and literally heaved a sigh of relief as I jumped off my still-moving bike.

I was alive. A bit surprising, really.

On the steps that faced Fourteenth Street, I gulped water and chomped one of the two bagels I'd packed, trying to justify to myself my change in plans. It was only natural that New York would take some getting used to. After all, I'd grown up in suburbia, and was better schooled in watching out for mountain lions with razor-sharp claws than dodging cabbies with a death-to-cyclists wish. Probably, I should allow myself another couple of weeks to learn my way around the city before tackling it again on two wheels, given how hard it was to concentrate on riding when I had no idea what kind of terrain the next turn would bring, or even where, exactly, the next turn might be.

That was it, I told myself, hunching my shoulders and trying not to feel ill as I remembered how many times I could have been killed in a mere twenty minutes. That was totally it. I just needed to get used to the city, and then I would kick its ass.

Right.

It wasn't like I wasn't used to fear. I just wasn't used to being its bitch. Back in Signal Mountain, I'd earned the nickname Crazy Eights Lake, and not only because I'd been something of a card shark in grade school. Before I had a potential future as a track star to keep me on the straight and narrow, I'd earned a rep as a bit of a daredevil, climbing trees higher than any of the other kids, jumping my bike off ramps in the parking lot of the Methodist Church, even for one particularly ill-advised, white-knuckled moment swinging out over the Signal Point precipice on a rope looped over a sturdy white oak branch at the edge of the thousand-foot drop. As I hung in mid-air, I imagined letting go. The urge scared me more than the actual stunt, though I blustered and boasted to the crowd of classmates who had gathered to witness my brief flight.

Officially Selma had remained unaware of these exploits. Looking back now, I had a feeling there wasn't much she hadn't known about my summer days of running wild across Signal

Mountain while she worked at the library to support us.

Now I hung my hands between my legs and examined my feet. Maybe coming to New York with Austin had been a mistake. Maybe I was a small fish who belonged back in her small pond, where she could tend a dying garden and wander through empty halls pondering the ghosts of her dead family for all eternity. Assuming ponds had gardens. And halls.

Beside me, a guy with well-defined muscles visible beneath his olive green tank top dropped onto the steps, lowering his bike at his feet.

"Hey," he said, nodding at me. "Nice wheels."

I eyed him doubtfully. Was he making fun of the bike I'd bought seven years earlier with money saved up from babysitting a mouthy seven-year-old two summers in a row?

"I'm serious," he said. "It's a classic."

"Right," I said neutrally, just in case he was making fun.

I glanced down at his bike, but it was nondescript and bare bones, with only one chain ring and no brakes that I could see. I didn't know they made bikes without brakes or gears. Had someone stolen his? How did he ride anywhere, let alone around the city?

"Man, she thinks I'm yanking her chain," he said to the air, his smile revealing a slight gap between his front teeth. "Listen up, I'm about to give you some free advice. You need to get yourself to a hardware store and buy yourself a chain. I'm talking a real chain, with hardened links and a solid padlock, none of that lightweight bullshit."

"But I have a lock," I said, gesturing at the U-lock resting in its holder on the frame.

"I'm telling you, that thing is not going to keep your ride safe."

"Who would want my bike? I mean, look at it."

He laughed and rubbed a hand over the crown of his head from back to front. "You must be new here. Where are you from? Wait, let me guess." And he leaned away, eying me critically. "The heartland, right? You're from Ohio, or Kentucky, some place like that."

I frowned. I didn't know this guy from a can of paint, and yet he'd pegged me right off.

"Tennessee," I admitted.

"That explains the accent. I love a girl with Southern charm."

"I'm not a real Southerner. What about you? Where are you from?"

"Brooklyn, baby, born and bred. Jeremiah, at your service."

He held out his hand. I hesitated, and then shook it, pulling my own hand away as he tried to hold on longer.

"All right, all right," he said. "I feel you. How long you been in the city?"

"A couple of weeks."

"First time out on two wheels?"

"How did you know?"

"Don't worry. It gets better. Oh, wait, I see my boys," he added, nodding at a couple of guys who were riding their bikes up the steps on the other side of the park. "What was your name, again?"

I hesitated. What could it hurt for him to know my name? "Ash."

"Ash? Like a fire?"

"Short for Ashley, but no one calls me that."

He nodded in apparent approval. "Cool. Welcome to New York, Fire Girl. Now, I'm serious, you go get yourself a fat chain if you want to keep that classic of yours. Peace out."

And with that, he hopped onto his bike and did a wheelie across the pavement as his friends hooted and whistled.

Bikes are like dogs in New York. If you go out in public with one on a nice day, people who would never have looked twice at you otherwise will chat you up about a variety of topics—how old your baby is, how you came to be in possession of her, where to get her fixed.

And as a bonus, a bicycle won't shed or pee on your carpet. It won't love you unconditionally, either, but that doesn't mean you can't love your bike.

After my first illustrious spin through the city, I stuck to my feet for a while, determined to learn my way around New York before venturing out again on two wheels. Still, I stopped by a bike store and bought the chain and padlock the clerk claimed were his best sellers among commuters, delivery boys, and messengers—people who needed their bikes to stay where they left them.

Everywhere I went my first month in the city, I saw bikes—mountain bikes, sleek ten speeds, careworn "classics" like mine, tricked-out track bikes like Jeremiah's without brakes or gears, and granny bikes—upright cruisers with generous padded saddles, low crossbars, and the ever-useful basket suspended from wide-set handlebars. Most of the messengers I saw favored track bikes or old ten-speeds like mine fitted with needle-thin slick tires. Track bikes were so popular because messing, one of Austin's new friends told me, wasn't just a job. It was a way of life.

"Isn't that the Marines?" I asked.

Marcus snorted and shook his head. "Most Marines wish they had the balls to mess. Sorry," he added, with a nod in my direction. "I mean, the guts."

"Dude," I said, "I'm surrounded by balls most of the time, in case you haven't noticed."

He snorted again, but with laughter this time, and glanced at Austin.

"Don't look at me," my best friend said, lifting his arm to shield his eyes. "I ain't the one what brung her."

"Actually, you kind of are," I said, and lay back beside him, pillowing my head on my upraised arms and studying the nearby silver skyline gleaming in mid-day sun.

"Details," Austin muttered, and sighed in what sounded like a cross between exhaustion and satisfaction.

It was a glorious summer day in New York City, not too hot or humid, and Austin, Marcus, and I were lying on a blanket in Central Park's Sheep Meadow, whiling away a Sunday afternoon under the careful watch of the skyscrapers of Midtown. Not far off, a handful of Marcus and Austin's friends were jockeying over a football. We'd played with them for a while, but the excessive displays of testosterone had begun to irritate me, while Austin's late nights out after waiting tables had left him as fussy as a nap-deprived toddler. Meanwhile Marcus, a professional bike messenger putting himself through architecture school, had a strict policy against "the pursuit of athletic endeavors" on the weekends. His days off the bike, he'd told us, were for eating, sleeping, reading, and lazing in the sunshine, weather permitting.

I squinted in the sunlight and watched the half dozen half-naked men trash-talking and tackling each other. Some former military, some college kids, Austin's friends were a diverse bunch— black, white, Asian, Hispanic. But Austin was the only Southerner in the group, and as such, was the target of regular "You might be a redneck if…" jokes. Jeff Foxworthy had recently made a name for himself with his redneck routine, neatly equating those of us who have Southern accents with mobile homes, binge drinking, and taxidermy. I'm not saying the equation is entirely inaccurate, just that gross generalizations are more than a little irritating to those of us who don't fit the bill.

The first time a couple of Austin's friends came over to eat pizza, drink beer, and talk about guys, one of them tried the redneck routine on me. I just shrugged and said, "I was born in Chicago and my parents were from Wisconsin, so technically I'm a Northerner."

"Traitor." Austin stuck his tongue out at me.

"You might be a redneck," I countered, "if you wag your tongue like a frog and think it's sexy."

José and Ben, NYU students who worked at the restaurant, snickered.

"Shut up," Austin said to the room at large, sipping from his beer.

Now I watched Ben, a pale boy with dark hair and a skinny frame, tackle Tommy, a tall black man with baby dreads. Tommy fell awkwardly, and in a flash, Marcus was up off the blanket, sprinting across the green expanse. Austin and I both sat up and watched as Marcus tossed Ben aside like so much chaff. Apparently messing was pretty good for your upper body strength, too.

"Are they together?" I asked Austin.

"I don't think so. They go way back, though. They went to Columbia together."

We watched as Marcus helped Tommy up and brushed the grass and dirt from his thin frame. Tommy said something, his mouth twisted in an indulgent smile. Reluctantly, Marcus turned around and bumped fists with Ben. Drama over, the game resumed. But the play was less boisterous now.

Marcus returned to our blanket and lowered himself onto his elbows, keeping an eye on Tommy's athletic leaps and spins with the football.

"Everything okay?" Austin asked.

"Fine," Marcus said. But his voice was more reserved now too, his dark eyes no longer quite as carefree as he watched the other men cavort in the sun on a fine day.

Another week passed before I decided I was almost ready to

take my bike out on city streets again. Saturday morning, I rose at five and headed out on a long, slow run along the route I had planned for my original ride. As I ran, I made mental notes of particular intersections that seemed busier than others, even at that early hour, and tricky spots where multiple streets came together. When Marcus had heard that I was planning to take my bike out again, he'd offered me all sorts of useful tips—when to run reds and when not to, which cars to give way to (trucks had the right of way, no matter what, because they couldn't stop easily but could squash you like a melon if you got caught under their wheels), how to handle jay-walking pedestrians—*peds*, as he called them—who always seemed surprised to see a cyclist barreling down on them in one of the few bike lanes that existed in New York in the '90s.

"You come as close to them as you can without running them down," Marcus instructed, "unless it's an old person or a kid or someone with a handicap. You have to let them know it's our road, our right of way. Not theirs."

His attitude reminded me of the different factions in Signal Mountain arguing over trail maintenance and use in the local parks. The hunters and dirt bike aficionados were always at odds with the bird-watchers and hikers over some plan or other.

The run, I decided midway through, didn't feel like a real run because even though it was early and the sparse traffic made jay-walking a snap, I still had to pay attention to the stoplights at the end of practically every block, not to mention the bikes and trucks and cabs content to nearly clip me as we all jockeyed for position on the city streets. No wonder NYC runners wax poetic about Central Park—it's the only place in Manhattan where you can run long distance stoplight-free. An alternative only five blocks from Austin's apartment was Washington Square Park, the exterior of which offers a half-mile loop. Repeated loops, I'd discovered, afforded plentiful people-watching, from potheads and acoustic guitarists smoking up brazenly in the open to wealthy shih tzu owners taking advantage of the dog runs at opposite corners of the park. Not to mention the chance to run timed splits.

But while Central Park trumped the Village's running options for sheer number of car-free trails and walkways, it didn't feel like "nature" the same way park systems in other, smaller cities might. Not with litter scattered everywhere and the inescapable smell of the city tarnishing even the unpaved trails—exhaust odor, animal and human waste, the musty scent of steam rising from ever-present manholes. As I ran north along East Park Drive, closed to motorized traffic on weekends, I decided that Central Park felt more like a model of what nature could be, if only you weren't smack dab in the middle of one of the most over-developed urban areas in the world.

The only part of the route that didn't feel like NYC was the reservoir between Eighty-Fifth and Ninety-Sixth Streets. The cinder path around the reservoir reminded me of my middle school track, while the scent of fresh water managed to overcome every other smell competing for olfactory attention. For ten minutes as I ran in early morning light, I could almost convince myself I wasn't really in the middle of a ginormous city.

The next morning, I got up early again. Only instead of strapping on running gear, I pulled on bike shorts that I promptly covered with long Umbros. I added a nondescript bike jersey I'd picked up at the same shop where I'd bought my new, heavy-duty lock. I was ready to ride New York. I hoped.

I carried my bike down to street level and set off along Perry, flexing my shoulder muscles as I slowly coasted the wrong way again on our one-way street. After living in New York for a few weeks, I felt more confident in the saddle, more sure of my ability to navigate the urban center I'd begun to know if not as well as the sprawling lawns and shady trails of my hometown, then at least as well as the grid-like neighborhoods that surrounded the University of Tennessee at Chattanooga, where my high school teammates and I had run all our important meets.

I rode leisurely at first, stopping at every red light and pausing whenever the burn became more than a little intense. But soon I was pumping at the pedals and barely slowing at some reds where the visibility was good and the foot and motor traffic scarce. By the time I had pedaled north up First Avenue past St. Marks to Stuy Town, I was feeling pretty good. Why had I freaked out so badly before? But I knew why—this was New York, the mother of all cities. And while I may have been born in Chicago, I had spent most of my sheltered life in a picturesque town on the Cumberland Plateau within walking distance of the Grand Canyon of the South. Nothing I had experienced so far had prepared me for the reality of living in Manhattan.

Except, maybe, running on the track team at Red Bank High.

Red Bank, like Signal Mountain, is a suburb of Chattanooga. But the city of Chattanooga is a pretty diverse place, racially and economically speaking, and, therefore, so are some of its suburbs. While the student body at my elementary school had been mostly white and middle-upper class, Red Bank High offered a bit more variation. The sports teams offered even more diversity. In Tennessee, it was rare for a white girl to be fast enough to make the track team, and even rarer for someone like me to beat out most of the runners I competed against. My teammates had a nickname for me: White Lightning, which they shortened to WL and then, somehow, to L-Dub.

The first time Selma heard my nickname was at a meet my freshman year, when I made it to the finals of the 1500.

"Go Dub!" the guys and girls on my team exhorted each time I streaked past. "Go on, girl!"

After the meet, as the station wagon chugged up Signal Mountain Boulevard, lined by trees draped in kudzu except in a handful of places where the sky dropped away and you realized you were traveling along at the edge of a precipitous drop, Selma asked, "What was that they were calling you?"

"Dub," I said, and watched her face carefully.

My aunt would have made a terrible poker player, which was why, as a rule, she didn't play cards.

"Dub?"

"Yeah, short for L-Dub, short for WL, short for White Lightning."

Her eyes widened briefly in alarm. "Oh. Well, that's interesting, isn't it?"

"Come on, Selma."

She looked at me quickly, her lips already lifting.

"*White lightning* means moonshine, and you know it," I said.

"I do know it. I just wasn't sure you were aware of the connotations."

"Besides which Dub is a total redneck nickname," I added, hoping she wasn't about to ask me about my drinking habits. I didn't like lying to her.

"Well, now that you mention it… But I think it suits you all the same."

"Hey, now," I said, laughing.

She angled her Santa Claus smile at me, and we laughed the rest of the way home to our spacious bungalow on its wide lot, situated on a quiet street not far from the Rainbow Lake trailhead.

I remembered that drive now as I wove through traffic on the island of Manhattan, and instead of feeling sad like I expected I would, I smiled a little. We had laughed most days, more than we'd argued or cried, perhaps because we knew we couldn't take each other for granted. For each of us, there was no one else in the world. In theory, I had my dad's family, but in reality it had always been too painful to be around them—too painful for them, which made it too much for me. Selma was the one who had set aside her grief to take care of me, while I was the child who had needed her during what she later told me were the darkest days of her life. We had saved each other.

And then she'd gone and died on me, just like everybody else. Was I cursed? Was I a jinx? Did the people around me die because I'd done something wrong in another life, or broken one too many mirrors, or walked under a ladder? Was it somehow my fault that other people died while I stayed undeniably, wholly alive?

Probably, I wasn't that important, I reminded myself, coasting through a red light at the south end of Central Park. But as the sole survivor of Flight 108 and, now, my own family, it was hard not to feel like I'd been singled out for some as yet unknown reason.

As I pedaled through the interior of Central Park, I looked up at the trees arcing overhead and pretended I was back in Signal Mountain, riding along the spine of the plateau on a cool—for Tennessee—summer morning, and Selma was back at home gathering tomatoes and basil leaves to add to a huge omelet I would scarf down within minutes of returning home, my appetite exhorted by exertion, while she looked on smiling half in pride and half in wonder.

CHAPTER FIVE

By the time August settled like a hot, humid blanket over the city, I knew my way around the Village and Midtown pretty well. I still hadn't ventured much into the Financial District at the southern tip of the island, which I continued to view as the riskiest area of the city given the attack on the World Trade Center earlier in the year. Fortunately, I didn't have any reason to visit Wall Street or the WTC.

Most days when there wasn't a heat or air quality warning, I jogged over to Washington Square Park. Eight laps at a good pace around the exterior of the park, and I had my exercise for the day. It wasn't exactly the same as running around Signal Mountain, of course. Instead of the smell of dew-dampened vegetation and summer wildflowers, the trill of songbirds and the rustle of small animals, my senses were assailed by the honking of cab horns and the odor of sizzling franks each time I passed the vendor's carts along University Place. But with my headphones on and music pounding in my ears, stopwatch tracking my splits, I could be anywhere I wanted in my head.

The passage of time meant more than just that I had been in the Big Apple for almost two months. It also signaled the steadily declining balance of the Citibank checking account I'd opened my first week in the city with funds "borrowed" from the money market account back in Tennessee. Unless I wanted to contact the Chattanooga investment firm Selma had put in charge of our finances and request an advance, it was time to find a job. Besides,

I wasn't used to so many unfettered days and nights. In middle school, I had spent two summers babysitting a neighbor boy while his parents worked full-time in Chattanooga. Later, in high school, I'd worked part-time during the school year and nearly full-time during the summers as a library page, repairing and shelving books and helping out occasionally with the Bookmobile. Before now, I had never gone more than a few days without either working, going to school, or both, and to be honest, the lack of productive activity was getting to me. In theory I was rich enough never to have to work again. But my sudden wealth, which I'd only learned about a few weeks before Selma died, didn't feel genuine. What felt real was the fact that I should be doing something other than watching soaps with Austin on summer days when it was too hot to venture out into the city.

One Sunday in mid-August, Austin invited a handful of friends over to our air-conditioned apartment for brunch. Afterward, while the boys sprawled over the furniture sighing and patting their full bellies as they sipped coffee and talked about Bosnia and RuPaul, Sampras's chances at the Open and LA's new ban on smoking in restaurants, I sat on the floor and opened that morning's *New York Times* to the classifieds section. I felt simultaneously grown-up and clichéd—a wealthy, privileged cliché because of course I didn't really have to have a job; I was only marking time until college and trying not to dip too deeply into the inheritance Selma had left me. If I did manage to find my way into one of the positions listed in the paper—"Get Paid to Make a Difference in the World" sounded interesting, although the ad didn't specify how much or doing what—I would likely be taking a job away from someone who needed it.

I trolled through the ads, circling a few here and there—dog-walking sounded like a possibility, or maybe "Community Organizing," though I had no idea what that meant. But then I was a job-search novice. Any work I had done before now had been offered to me by people I'd known most of my life. No application necessary, and no résumé, for that matter, which was good because I wasn't sure what I could put on a résumé, other than the library gig. Did people list babysitting under work experience? If they did, they probably invented creative descriptions like "Professional Child Care in Client's Home." As if the person reading such an entry would fail to grasp its meaning.

"Whatcha doin'?" Marcus asked, dropping to the floor beside me.

"Looking for a job."

He traced a short, blunt finger across my margin scribbles. "*Dialoguer*?" he asked, pausing at one of my circles. "You know that means selling things door-to-door, right?"

In fact, I had not known that. I drew a line through the ad and chewed on the end of the pen, decorated with the inscription, "MTV Video Music Awards." Where exactly had this pen come from? I removed the tip from my mouth and wiped it on my Umbro soccer shorts. Well, technically they were Austin's Umbros. The good thing about living with someone roughly the same size, I had discovered, was that you could share clothes—as long as you didn't mind dressing like a gay dude.

"Have you thought about temping?" Marcus asked.

"What's temping?"

"Jesus, you really are a hick, aren't you?"

I shot him the bird.

"It means signing up with a temporary agency for clerical or light industrial work."

I stared at him blankly. Clerical work I could guess at, but *light industrial work*? As far as I knew, jobs came in a limited assortment of flavors—educational (including library work), professional (doctor, lawyer, accountant), laborer (Parks and Recreation workers, trash collectors, and so on and so forth), and other (everyone else). But I also knew that New York currently had more than seven million residents, the majority of whom needed to work in some capacity. Clearly there were a great number of employment types outside the few I recognized.

Marcus elaborated further: "You sign up with a temp agency, tell them what kind of skills you have, and they send you out to work at jobs that either only last a few weeks or offer a temp-to-permanent situation. That way the company doesn't have to keep you if they decide you're not going to work out. I did it for a little while the summer after I graduated from college, but I couldn't stand office work. Made me want to jump out a window."

"I don't think I'd like it, either," I said, my tone unaccountably certain given that I had never actually tried office work.

Selma had always encouraged, even forced me at times, to try new things. Judging from her many tales of me as a toddler stomping my foot and refusing to do a variety of tasks without the influence of bribery—half an hour of *Sesame Street*, for example, or a serving of berry-flavored yogurt—I'd been born both stubborn and opinionated. *Just like your mother*, Selma used to murmur, shaking her head with a smile that let me knew I was loved in spite of this flaw in temperament.

Marcus snapped his fingers in a non-gay-dude way and pointed at me. "I have an idea."

"What?"

"That's your bike, right?"

My "classic" was leaning against the living room wall in its usual spot, just outside my bedroom door. I nodded.

"Austin said you've been riding it all over. Why don't you come with me to work tomorrow and see if you like it? I could show you the ropes, and then when I go back to school in a few weeks, you could have my spot at Mercury's."

Me, a bike messenger? I thought back to my first, shaky ride through the Village and SoHo, heart pounding and hands sweating as I struggled to make my way amid the fast-flying city traffic.

"I don't know," I hedged.

The conversation on the couch had slid into momentary silence, and Austin said lazily, "Wait, Ashley Lake is admitting she doesn't know something?"

"Piss off." I threw the pen at him.

He caught it easily and flung it back. "Keep your slobber to yourself."

"Dick," I said, but mildly, because I didn't really think he was.

"What are you guys all in cahoots about, anyway?" Austin pressed.

"I was just telling Ash she should tag along on the road with me this week, see if messing could be her thing."

Austin's eyes moved from Marcus to me and back again in rapid succession. "Wait. You're not serious, are you?"

"As a heart attack," Marcus intoned.

"Ash, a bike messenger?"

"Why not?" I asked. "It'd be way more fun than anything else I'm qualified for, like nannying or working at the Gap."

"At least if you worked at the Gap I'd get your discount," Austin said. "Being a bike messenger is dangerous, especially if you don't know your way around the city."

"Ooh, danger. I thought you said the Navy made you tough."

"I could still kick your skinny little butt."

"I'm not skinny."

"You go right ahead and tell yourself that."

The conversation shifted to caloric intake and lifting routines, one of the more popular topics among Austin's group of friends, and I returned to the classifieds. But I couldn't focus on the tiny newsprint. I was too busy picturing myself doing a track stand at a stoplight in Midtown, a messenger bag strapped to my back. I'd been practicing my track stand here in our living room where it didn't hurt as much to fall—and where no one was around to witness said fall, more to the point—and soon I would be able to pull one at will, I was pretty sure.

Maybe I could give messing a whirl. Riding a bike around the city had to be more interesting than any job that leveraged my clerical skills. Somehow, I doubt Selma had my employability by New York City temp agencies in mind when she insisted I take typing in high school. Or, really, temp agencies anywhere. I was supposed to be in college, studying science and literature and mathematics, not trying to figure out how to pay my half of the rent on a sublet in the West Village.

Soon, I told myself, turning the pages of the newspaper.

Later, after everyone except Tommy had left, Austin returned to the subject of my potential career.

"Seriously, Ash, I don't know about the whole bike messenger thing."

"You don't have to worry," I said. "It's me we're talking about."

"That's exactly why I am worried—you and your nothing-can-touch-me dream world."

"I don't think I can't be touched. But why live in fear? Might as well enjoy life."

"Are you sure that's what you're trying to do?"

I stared at him with the look that had made more than a few boys at Red Bank High visibly wilt. "What's that supposed to mean?"

"Just seems like you're trying to prove something."

"Like what?"

He shook his head. "I don't know. What about when you jumped into the quarry? That was a twenty-foot cliff."

"Yeah, well, Tad and Jimmy dared me."

My back had hurt for days after that one, and I'd worried I might have seriously injured myself. But the pain had gone away, never to return, while my reputation for dare-devilry had continued to flourish for years afterward.

"What, you couldn't walk away from a couple of future frat boys? How about when you wrecked Selma's car on the W road? You didn't even know how to drive."

The W road zig-zags down Signal Mountain in such sharp turns that it literally looks like a W. When we were fourteen, Tad and Jimmy, both sons of surgeons and resident troublemakers, had bet me fifty dollars that I didn't have the nerve to take Selma's car down it. I won the bet, but I had to work odd jobs for a full year to pay Selma back for the repairs to the station wagon after I drove into a low stone wall on one of the curves. Only the wall had prevented the car from careening over the edge of the road and down the side of the mountain.

Selma had taken one look at the accident scene and proclaimed that I'd used another of my nine lives. Took me down to six, or was it five? I'd lost count.

"I know, but—"

Austin cut me off. "Tad and Jimmy dared you, right?"

"No, they bet me fifty bucks." Which had seemed like serious cash back then.

He shook his head again. "It's like you're daring God or something. And as your friend, I have to tell you, it's hard to watch."

"I'm not daring God," I said. "Anyway, since when are you such a believer? No, wait, I know. Since the Navy, right? They made you religious, too."

"I only used the word God because I don't know what else to call it."

"How about fate? Or karma, or luck, or providence? Because somehow I doubt there's a God who gives a crap one way or the other if you or I live or die."

It came out more bitterly than I intended, and out of the corner of my eye, I saw Tommy watching me. Did he know about my situation? I had asked Austin to keep my past private, but he and Tommy had been spending a lot of time together lately. More and more at the end of a weekend outing, it somehow ended up the three of us.

"Maybe not," Austin conceded, "but I care what happens to you. And so do my parents, and your grandparents, and somewhere I have to believe Selma is looking down on us, too, hoping you'll have the sense she gave you to take care of yourself, since she…"

He trailed off, but I finished his sentence: "Since she can't anymore?"

He nodded, his brow furrowed, and we stared at each other, sitting on opposite ends of the couch, sunlight leaking in through the open door to Austin's south-facing bedroom. He looked so mournful, and belatedly I remembered I wasn't the only one who had lost my aunt. Austin hadn't even had a chance to say goodbye to her, the woman whose house had been a second home.

Tommy, who was sitting in the armchair with his feet up on the coffee table, said, "If it's any consolation, Austin, she wouldn't be out there alone. Marcus will look out for her."

"Maybe for a while, but he's going back to school soon."

"He wouldn't have asked her if he thought she couldn't do it."

Austin squinted at him, the wheels in his head visible, at least to me. At twenty-four, Tommy was older, well-educated, an adult with a "real job" at a public relations firm in Midtown. A friend of José's, the ex-Navy man turned student who had let Austin crash at his Chelsea loft after the Navy unceremoniously dumped him, Tommy was the one who had hooked Austin up with the sublet.

Austin sighed and glanced at me. "I'm not going to talk you out of this, am I?"

Actually… "No," I said, once again with a resolve I didn't necessarily feel.

"Then how about we start over. You say you want to be a bike messenger? That sounds great, Ash," he said with exaggerated enthusiasm. "Have fun with that."

"I promise I won't get killed, okay?"

"Uh-huh." He didn't sound much like he believed me. That made two of us.

Marcus called after dinner to see what I'd decided. I swallowed hard and told him I was in, and we made a plan. He would meet me at Mercury's headquarters in Midtown the next morning at seven, and we would see how the day's rides went. I hung up feeling the butterflies normally reserved for competition careening about my mid-section, and hoped I wasn't about to throw up my spaghetti dinner. I already had buyer's remorse, but I couldn't back out now without looking chicken. And I wasn't chicken. I wasn't.

That night, lying in my loft bed overlooking the tree-shrouded courtyard, I couldn't fall asleep. I was going to be a bicycle messenger in New York City, one of the coolest, slickest, raddest jobs available, it seemed to me at that moment.

Assuming, of course, Marcus's bosses would hire me.

CHAPTER SIX

Mercury's Messengers was a small company run by Victor and Javi Boneta, brothers from the Lower East Side. The office occupied a storefront sandwiched between a check cashing center and a coffee shop in the east forties, just off Lexington Avenue. Most of their clients were publishing companies and law firms, Marcus explained as he led me inside to "meet the guys." And guys it was, I soon realized—among the riders and dispatchers milling about the wide main room we entered, there only appeared to be one female rider drinking coffee out of a chipped mug with a picture of Shakespeare and the inscription, "I am not bound to please thee with my answers." I say "appeared" because with short hair, an unwavering glare, and camo pants, the rider's gender seemed debatable.

Introductions took place in a tiny inner office with grungy walls and a streaked window that overlooked an alley. Victor, the brother in charge of hiring, chatted me up, asking about my bike experience and my background. When I revealed I was from Tennessee, Victor leaned back in his chair and folded his arms across his chest.

"You should know," he said, "that we are a very diverse company. Our riders and dispatchers come to us from throughout the New York Metro area. We expect all of our employees to treat each other with respect, regardless of difference."

"Great. You know, not everyone in the South is hung up on the Civil War."

Victor cleared his throat. "No, of course not," he said. "Just so

59

we understand each other."

We talked another few minutes about business, bikes, and New York traffic. Victor explained that his riders were independent contractors with no benefits, described all the possible ways I could be injured or killed as a messenger, and stressed how easily my bike could be stolen. I just nodded again and again. Then Marcus said he thought he'd give me a trial run, train me on the go, as it were.

"You sharing commissions?" Victor asked.

"No need," I said. "I can train without pay."

I didn't add that I wasn't sure I would be able to keep Marcus's wheel for a few hours, let alone a few days.

"Works for me if it works for you," Victor announced. "Let's plan to talk again after a week or two, see how things are going."

"Awesome," Marcus said. "Thanks, man."

"No—thank you," Victor said sarcastically, and waved us out of his office.

By now the garage door off the alley was open, and would stay that way throughout the day, Marcus told me. The company's cadre of riders was all present in various stages of wakefulness, waiting for the dispatchers to assign runs. No one appeared to have showered, and the pungent odor of male sweat reminded me of my high school track days. I reminded myself that I could do this, that I was an athlete who knew how to demand the best from her body, but I still felt smaller and weaker than even the smallest rider in the room, Jackson, nick-named JR for his speed.

"Jack Rabbit," the little white guy explained, puffing out his chest under a tight tank top, "not the guy from *Dallas*."

For the most part, the riders treated me with respect and made me feel welcome as Marcus introduced me around. Only one, a Hispanic twenty-something, gave me a look as if to say, *Are you kidding?* He turned away without a word and started talking to another messenger, his back firmly to me.

"Don't mind Fido," Marcus said in a low tone.

"Fido?"

"You know, like the dog? It fits, trust me."

So much for treating each other with respect—apparently all bets were off if you were a girl.

The riders lounged around in apparent relaxation, talking about people I didn't know and bike races I hadn't known existed—informal "alleycat" competitions among messengers after work and on the weekends, marked by checkpoints and tasks, spoke cards and points. I only listened quietly as the smelly, grungy group of boys and men (JR looked barely out of high school, while Brian "The Stone" had to be pushing forty, by my bet) joked and pummeled and harassed each other the way the boys I'd known back in Tennessee had always done. Some things transcended geography.

But as soon as the phones started ringing and the dispatchers began barking out orders, the mood in the room shifted. Riders elbowed each other out of the way to gain their dispatcher's attention, each jockeying for the "best" jobs. Except Marcus. He just leaned against a wall at one side of the room waiting for the initial frenzy to cool.

"I'm not in this to get the chance to see a model," he told me, nodding at Jake the Snake and Fido the Dick (as I had christened him in my head) compete over a garment bag pick-up at Donna Karan's headquarters on Seventh Avenue.

"What are you in it for?"

"To make some money and see the city in the summer. And to stay alive, first and foremost. I don't ride like some of these guys, just so you know."

"Fine with me," I said. Maybe I would be able to keep up with him after all.

Steph, one of the dispatchers, nodded at Marcus, and he stepped forward. Looked like I was about to find out.

Half an hour later we paused at an intersection in SoHo where five streets with multiple lanes each came together in a misshapen star. I rested one foot on the pavement and adjusted the chain hanging from one shoulder. It was heavy, but Marcus had nodded in approval when he saw it.

"Now that's a messenger's chain," he'd said.

As we waited for the light, Marcus pulled a pad from a pocket of his baggy cargo shorts. A pencil materialized out of somewhere, and as I watched, he began to sketch the façade of the building next to us, a large rectangular edifice with cast-iron ornamentation.

"I told you I ride to stay alive," he said, pencil moving quickly over the page. "That means the only lights I like to run are at intersections with two one-way streets. Places like this, where the traffic is unpredictable, I wait."

"Cool," I said, watching over his shoulder as, bit by bit, the building took shape. We'd picked up a satchel from a law firm in Midtown, not far from Mercury's, and were headed downtown to the Manhattan Municipal Building for delivery.

"The other guys will tell you it's because I'm a pansy-ass pussy," Marcus went on, his hand never faltering as cars from another of the intersection's pentagonal points accelerated past us, "but really, it's because I'm smart. I have something to live for."

In those days, my knowledge of art would have fit on the tip of a bicycle spoke, but even I could tell that Marcus had talent. Probably, the other riders were just jealous.

"And another thing, don't go thinking messenger culture is this cool thing. Trust me—you have better things to do with your time than sit around drinking and talking about the job."

I hesitated, then asked the question that had been on my mind ever since I first walked into Mercury's: "Do the other messengers care that you're gay?"

He looked up from his sketch and smiled. "I don't know. I never asked. But messenger culture in general tends to be pretty laissez-faire."

"Except when it comes to female riders?"

"Well, yeah," he admitted. "You do sometimes encounter that shit, like with Fido. But for the most part, riders only care if you can do the work and observe the code."

The light changed and in a flash, Marcus had stowed his sketchpad and I was pedaling hard to catch up to him. Six blocks later we hit another red, and our conversation resumed.

"The code?" I asked.

"Get the package to the client on time, don't ever cut off a fellow rider, and if you can help another guy keep his line, you do it."

Keeping the line, he explained as we cut through a deserted alley, meant finding the most efficient route through city traffic, be it a congested corner or a wide avenue with multiple lanes. It took time and experience, but most riders could see their next three moves, at least. Like a soccer player, only instead of a grassy expanse occupied by teammates and foes, the rider's field of play consisted of city streets, cars, and pedestrians.

The worst pedestrians, according to Marcus, were the dancers—jaywalkers who stepped out, saw you bearing down on them and backed up, then moved forward again, repeating the steps of a dance routine known only to them.

"Have you ever hit anyone?" I asked as we slowed at the end of the alley.

"Of course," he said. "So will you, if you do this long enough." And he pulled onto a cross-street, leaving me to trail after him.

Bike messengering, I'd already known, is not for the faint of heart. But not just because of the daily risk-taking and impressive potential for personal injury. Messengers tend to have a stigma associated with them. People assume that they're uneducated, or that they're former convicts who can't find a real job, particularly the African-American riders. Sometimes the stereotype fits, Marcus told me. A lot of the guys he knew had been in jail, or otherwise had issues that precluded them from seeking office work. But there were many more others like him, guys and a handful of women who messengered to put themselves through school, or who chose messing over a more conventional route because they loved getting paid to ride their bikes. People who couldn't imagine "wasting" their lives, stuck indoors forty or fifty hours every week punching time as a clerical cog in some corporate machine.

When he put it like that, I couldn't imagine being satisfied with an indoor life, either.

Whether it was because he rode smart or because I was in good shape, or possibly both, I managed to keep Marcus's wheel that first day. Mostly. Time passed quickly as I shadowed him around the city, learning to read the flow of traffic, to pick the best spot to lock up my bike, to look through the windows of nearby cars for potential hazards—jaywalking pedestrians and open cab doors, mostly, along with the occasional homicidal sports car or city bus. We spent an inordinate amount of time waiting for and riding slow, smelly freight elevators, since security in most office buildings wouldn't allow us to "pollute" the main elevators. Marcus took advantage of these lengthy pauses in among the brief bursts of activity—or sometimes long, as in the ride that took us across the Brooklyn Bridge and back within twenty minutes—to impart as much of his knowledge as he could, peppered with sometimes overly explicit real-world examples.

I wouldn't remember everything he said over the next few days, of course, but some part of my brain must have absorbed his advice because I would find myself recalling it again and again as the weeks and months passed:

Marcus's Messing Rules

1. Pedestrians are the number one road hazard. Remember that if one steps out in front of you, better them than you— if you can, just hit them and keep going. Otherwise, if you try to dodge the ped, you could end up road kill. ("I once saw a guy swerve around a ped and get his head run over by a garbage truck. Not a good way to go, seriously—his eyes were [unnecessary details of grisly carnage omitted] and his brain was [ditto].")

2. Watch for slowed or stopped vehicles, especially cabs, where idiot passengers might door you. "This one time, on Fifth, a passenger opened his door right into me. I had a nasty deep muscle bruise in my quad, couldn't walk or ride for days. And the guy who couldn't be bothered to look first? He just stepped over me and kept right on his merry way."

3. Never run a red light blind. "Enough said."

4. Always carry food with you, or be prepared to eat on the go. It takes fifteen minutes for what you eat to get into your bloodstream, so learn to recognize the signs of depletion of glycogen stores early. "If you get dizzy when you get off the bike, have a banana or turkey sandwich. To prevent the bonk, carbo load every night—pasta, bread, rice, potatoes. You don't look like you can afford to lose much weight, Lake, which is exactly what's going to happen if you ride forty or fifty miles a day and don't eat right."

5. If a cop tells you to stop, pedal away as fast as you can. "Then change your shirt or your jacket or your bike. Cops have memories like elephants. Or more like a really officious, autocratic elephant, if such a thing exists, which it doesn't."

6. Watch out for open car windows—"The shit that flies out can mess you up. Not that it's shit, per se, but spit, cigarettes, and one time, I punctured my front tire on a diamond engagement ring. Actually, that one was worth it."

7. Don't drink too much in the course of a day, and keep a running list in your head of places where you can pee.

"You're a girl, so if you smile pretty, a client or a guard might let you use the facilities. But you're better off either not needing to go or knowing a messenger-friendly restroom or two in every borough. Or both."

8. Don't ever lock your bike to anything that weighs less than half a ton. "You know, like a United States Post Office mailbox. Don't ask."

9. Know how to change a flat, and keep your tools on you at all times.

10. Carry bungee cords. Lots of them.

11. Finally, and again, watch for doors. "I'm serious. Being doored blows. And not in the good kind of way."

Fortunately, I didn't have to learn everything that first day. With Marcus watching out for me, I managed to avoid being doored or crushed to death by passing trucks or waylaid by rogue pedestrians. By mid-afternoon, I was actually enjoying myself on the bike, something I hadn't been certain would happen in New York City. During our last run, as we cruised along Ninth Avenue headed for an art gallery in Chelsea, I even thought I caught a glimpse of the flow Marcus had been talking about—that sweet sense of foreshadowing, as if I could predict where each car and truck and pedestrian would be before they got there. The sixth sense I would eventually carry with me at all times, Marcus promised, if I stuck with the job.

When it came time to part ways that evening, Marcus gave me the bro hug, one arm plus a chest bump, and grinned at me over his shoulder as he rode off toward the East Village, where he and Tommy lived in neighboring buildings.

"Nice riding, Lake," he called. "For a girl."

Too tired to do anything other than laugh, I turned for home. I *had* done well, I congratulated myself, unsure whether the warm feeling spreading through my chest was the result of excessive pride or extreme exhaustion.

Austin was waiting for me on the front stoop of our building as I coasted my bike to a stop on the sidewalk. After a long day on the streets of New York, I was tired but happy, and had been fantasizing about an enormous dinner even as I tried to remember all of Marcus's advice on the ride home. At one point, as I carefully ran a red a few blocks from Perry Street, I remembered my first foray into New York City traffic, and I had to laugh at my own scared-shitlessness. What a difference a couple of months could make.

"Yo, Ash," Austin said as I slid off my bike in front of him. "You survived."

"Yo, strictly dickly," I said. "Of course I did."

"Nice. I can tell you've been hanging out with a fag."

"Lately, I seem only and always to be hanging out with fags." I saw him wince, and added as I shouldered my bike and started up the steps, "I mean, if I can say that."

"Given you've become a fag hag, albeit a slightly unorthodox one, I guess it's okay."

"Unorthodox how?" I asked as he unlocked the three bolts to the apartment and held the door open for me.

"You're kind of butch for the role. I mean, you don't exactly like to shop or dish on hot guys."

"True."

"And why is that?" he asked, locking the door again behind us.

"I never liked shopping. You know that."

"And guys? Do you like them more than you used to?"

I shrugged. "I don't know. It's not like there was much of a pool to choose from back home."

"Maybe not when we were younger, but high school provided more opportunity. I don't remember you dating much, except for Eric. And you know as well as I do that he doesn't count."

Eric James had been just about the only virgin on the Red Bank High soccer team. Or, at least, one of the few to admit it. The son of a Baptist minister, he broke the preacher's wild child mold, and how. He was saving himself for marriage, which meant that instead of fooling around, we did other things—go out for dinner, rent movies with Selma, visit the tourist traps around Chattanooga, explore the Signal Mountain hiking trails with his parents and little brother. He was Austin's year, and when he left for Florida State, I missed him, but not as much as I missed Austin.

Unlike Austin, Eric managed to make Selma's funeral. I was glad to see him, and more than happy to meet his college girlfriend, another minister's kid who didn't believe in drinking or premarital sex. Somehow in among the heathens of Tallahassee they had managed to find each other. Must be a miracle, I'd imagined telling Selma, who would have appreciated the sacrilegious pun.

"He does too count," I said now, brushing past Austin. "Not everyone in high school obsesses about sex."

I went to park my bike outside my room, my mind back on dinner: pasta with meat sauce, garlic bread, a spinach salad, and a slice of the chocolate cake I'd had the sense to pick up the day before from the gourmet bakery around the corner. My mouth literally began to water.

"Wait. You're still a virgin, aren't you?" Austin asked, his dimples showing.

"Wouldn't you like to know."

"We're not in Chattanooga anymore, Toto. It'd be easy to find a nice het boy for you here."

I rolled my eyes at yet another *Wizard of Oz* reference— seriously, could you get any gayer?—and closed my bedroom door. Growing up sexy had made Austin a little too full of himself. But I would gladly take him this way, I reminded myself as I changed out of my smelly bike clothes and into soft, worn Red Bank High sweats I hadn't bothered to give back at the end of the cross country season. Butch hadn't come looking for them, so either he hadn't noticed or he was sick of butting heads. Then again, maybe he'd simply felt sorry for me.

Like my lone ex-boyfriend, my ex-coach had come to Selma's funeral, too. Despite her pagan Yankee ways, Selma had been much loved by the community of Signal Mountain, and her funeral was a crowded affair. I'd been only too happy to have Claire and Bruce at my side throughout the service. Still, they couldn't help me deliver the eulogy I'd written the night before. I had to stand up and do that all by myself, face down a church full of friends and strangers all waiting to hear what I would say about the woman who had loved me like her own, even though I wasn't.

Standing at the podium looking out over the crowded pews, I froze, unable to find my voice. But then my gaze had come to rest on my former coach's broad impassive features, his tattooed forearms hidden in a sports jacket I recognized from three years of annual end-of-season banquets, his pale blue eyes focused squarely on me. We stared at each other until he nodded at me, and somehow I could hear his calm, encouraging voice inside my head: "You can do this, Lake. It'll be over soon, and then you'll have done it. You can do this."

I took a deep breath, and then another, and I did it. I read the eulogy Claire had helped me write, and then it was done. Afterward, to my surprise, Butch gave me a hug, his eyes bright, and told me gruffly he hoped I would call him if I ever needed anything.

Sometimes I still woke from dreams of standing at the front of the church, Selma's ashes on the podium in front of me, and either I was naked or I'd knocked the urn over, sending what remained of my aunt, my mother, out across the first row where my father's parents sat, the old grief blooming in their eyes. Sometimes my birth mother and father were there in the dream too, their creased photo selves with indistinct features and foreign expressions. Those were the hardest dreams to wake from—horror (the funereal aspect) mingled with joy at seeing my parents again. Then, as I emerged sputtering from dreamland, I would have to acknowledge that only the horror part was real.

One of the good things about exercise is that it makes me sleep so deeply I don't remember my dreams. Bike messengering, I was hoping, would have just such a soporific effect.

"You should see Marcus," I told Austin that night over dinner. "He's so smooth on the bike."

"Not only on the bike."

"Seriously, I learned a ton from him in just one day. All about peds—that's pedestrians to you, civilian—and how to feel the traffic flow and keep from being doored."

"Feel the traffic flow? You guys smoke up out there or something?"

"I'm serious, Austin. Marcus is cool, and so is the job."

"What does it pay?"

"I don't know yet, but I don't really have to…" I trailed off. In the months we'd been living together, Austin hadn't asked about my financial situation, and I hadn't been able to think how to tell him I was suddenly richer than one of Donald Trump's ex-wives.

"You don't have to worry about money, is that it?" Austin asked. "My mom said she thought Selma must have left you in pretty good shape. She was a total planner."

"That she was."

I thought about the airline settlement and my parents' insurance money that had been invested for fifteen years now. Even if Selma hadn't been a planner, it would have been hard to burn through all that cash without the good people of Signal Mountain noticing.

"How much did she leave you?" he asked.

"Um, I'm not sure exactly."

"If you want, I can cover the rent for a little while until you get it sorted out. The tips are better than I expected."

"No, no, you don't have to do that." I put my fork down and wiped spaghetti sauce from the corner of my mouth. "The thing is, I actually just found out a little while ago that there's, um..." I paused. "Turns out there's a few million dollars sitting in a bank account down in Chattanooga with my name on it."

Five million, plus or minus a few thousand, but he didn't have to know that.

The ballpark figure was enough—Austin choked on a bite of bread and coughed copiously before gulping down half a glass of water. No wonder he'd ruled the drama club at Red Bank High.

"You're kidding," he said when he finally caught his breath. "You cannot be serious."

"I didn't think the news would make you choke to death."

"How? There's no way librarians get paid that much."

"Settlement money from the airline plus my parents' insurance policies. I didn't know about it until March. Selma said she wanted to raise me like a normal kid, or at least as normal as possible, given the circumstances."

"Of course there'd be money," Austin said. "I just never thought about it. So you could buy this whole building, then?"

"I doubt I could afford the whole building. Either way, the money's invested. I've been living on Selma's insurance since graduation, which, after paying all the bills for the house, is seriously dwindling. It's still enough that I can work as a messenger and not have to worry, but not indefinitely."

"Jesus, Ash. What are you going to do with all that cash?"

"Go to school, for one thing. I wasn't ready this year, but I want to reapply. When Selma got sick, I pretty much tuned out of the college thing."

"Seems like you tuned out of a lot more than just school." He reached across the table to touch my hand. "Not that I blame you. I was worried about you, though, especially when your letters stopped. Now it seems like you're waking up again, if that makes sense."

"I know." I hesitated, and then turned my palm up to his. "Thanks for coming back for me, Austin."

He squeezed my hand. "That's what gay best friends are for. Speaking of which, want to come out dancing tonight? Ben and Cruz want to try a new club over on Seventh."

"I can't. I have to be up at the crack tomorrow morning."

"Sucks for you. Then again, you're a multi-millionaire, so you could always call in sick."

"Shut it," I said, and threw a crouton at him.

"Just sayin'."

We slipped back into our familiar fake bickering as we finished dinner. Later, as we loaded the dishwasher, working efficiently together like an old, asexual, married couple, I wondered what I would have done if Austin had never come back to Signal Mountain. Grown moldy tending the wilting garden and cleaning the house for the bizillionth time? Pissed away my fortune on fast cars and beer? Married Jimmy Walters and raised a mess of kids?

Yeah, probably not.

Still, it might've taken me longer to snap out of the stupor I'd fallen into. Without Austin, I definitely wouldn't have been a messenger-in-training living in New York's Greenwich Village and beginning to think hopeful thoughts about the future again.

Life in New York in the early 1990s wasn't completely idyllic, though, especially not for gay men. A decade into the AIDS crisis, there was no sign of a cure yet. Among Austin and Tommy's circle of friends, there were several men whose failing health was obvious. Austin never brought it up, so I didn't, either. I figured if he wanted to talk to me about AIDS, he would. During the road trip north when he had shared his coming out story—falling in lust with a beautiful sailor who was only too happy to introduce him to the love that dare not speak its name, particularly not in the US military—I'd alluded to the dangers of HIV. He'd assured me that he was always careful, and I believed him. Austin was no dummy. But even if he had been, he didn't need me to remind him of a fact he couldn't escape living in the Village.

I knew how it was to be in denial. And denial wasn't always a bad thing.

After two weeks of learning the ropes on the job with Marcus, I graduated from messenger-in-training to rookie on the job. Victor doled out a pager and a clipboard (the cost of which would be taken out of my first week's pay), reminded me of all the ways I could die, warned me again of all the creeps in New York just waiting to steal my bike, and then assigned me to Marcus's dispatcher, Steph, a well-dressed white girl who always looked as if she had stopped in for a free makeover at Macy's on her way to work. The week before, when Marcus had introduced me, Steph had given me the sort of critical onceover I recognized from non-jock girls back home, and then, seemingly, dismissed me. To her, I figured, I was invisible—I wasn't anyone she would ever have to compete with, nor was I anyone who might share valuable feminine tips or tricks.

But when Victor assigned me to her, Steph smiled widely at me from her desk at the back of the office.

"Way to go, Lake," she said, nodding appreciatively. "I didn't think you would last an hour, but here you are."

Then she held out her hand for a fist bump. After a bemused moment, I hurried to comply.

"Us ladies gotta stick together," she said. "There aren't all that many of us up in here, in case you didn't notice."

"I noticed," I said, glancing around.

The other riders seemed to be ignoring me, except Marcus who leaned against the wall in his usual spot, smiling in my direction, and Fido the Dick, who had apparently overheard our conversation and was glaring from Steph to me and back again. He would bear watching, I thought, mentally adding his name to the litany of dangers Victor had recited.

As they'd done each morning the previous two weeks, the phones started ringing promptly at seven-thirty as if a switch had been flicked. I leaned against the wall beside Marcus, waiting patiently while most of the other riders jockeyed for position in the melee that marked the start of our work day. Then Steph turned to us. At first, I wasn't sure who her nod was directed at. Then she said, "Rookie, you're up."

I stepped forward, my heart racing. It was official: I was a bike messenger in New York City.

What had I been thinking?

Fortunately, the terror didn't last long. Almost as soon as I had mapped my route to a Midtown law firm for pick-up and slipped my feet into my toe straps, messenger bag containing my lock, snacks, and other gear strapped to my back, my heart rate began to settle. It was just like a race—the worst moment, I'd always found, came when I lined up at the start with my opponents. As soon as the starting signal sounded, my heart slowed and I settled into my breathing, into myself. The frenetic energy—along with the psychosomatic pressure on my bladder—faded, and I ran smoothly, with confidence.

The same was true of biking around New York—once I got started, I didn't have time to worry. Instead, I had to be on at every minute, aware of my surroundings, looking ten moves ahead down the street and trying to anticipate the motion of the traffic the way Marcus had taught me. There were delivery entrances to find, guards to woo, lock-up spots to claim. And, most of all, there was the hunger that shadowed me at every turn.

It would take some time to figure out how to keep my energy balanced, Marcus had told me. And he was right—that first week on my own, without Marcus calling the shots, I had to learn how to pace myself. Bonking wasn't an option. *Get the package there on time*—that was our primary objective. Excuses wouldn't wash if you missed a court deadline to file a legal brief, or failed to deliver a contract before it expired. Fortunately, Steph gave me lower key assignments to start out with.

"She has your back," Marcus told me mid-week as we caught a quick lunch of pizza and dried fruit on the Great Lawn at Bryant Park, located behind the iconic Midtown public library.

A summer performance series brought a variety of musicians to the park each Wednesday over the lunch hour. This week's guest was a mariachi band, minus the stereotypical outfits. Would have been too hot for those suits, Marcus and I agreed as we staked out a spot in the shade at the edge of a walkway.

"Glad someone has my best interests at heart," I said.

"Fido?"

"Yup."

"He been harassing you?"

"Nothing blatant, just stares and whispers. And here I thought I'd left middle school behind for good."

Marcus giggled. Usually he didn't "let his hair down," as he called it, around the other riders. But with me, every once in a while he did something that reminded me he was gay.

"Has he ever given you a hard time?" I asked.

Marcus shrugged and looked away, eyes hidden behind expensive wraparound shades. "Nothing I can't handle. But you let me know if he does anything more than talk, got it?"

"Yes, sir."

He threw a dried apricot at me, which I caught and tossed into my mouth—would have been a crime to waste food on a work day. As I chewed the squishy fruit, I leaned back on my hands and gazed across the lawn, where people in business suits and pantyhose sat on blankets next to teenagers in tank tops and Daisy Dukes, all talking and laughing and eating lunch on a warm day in New York City. Skyscrapers crowded the park, standing shoulder to shoulder and sheltering unseen multitudes, some of whom were looking down upon us from behind glass-walled offices, others exercising in air-conditioned gyms or eating at gourmet restaurants.

Messing offers a glimpse into diverse worlds occupied by profoundly different people. One day you might deliver a bottle of champagne to a Hollywood producer's New York loft; the next drop off samples at an internationally renowned fashion designer's townhouse. Or you could be asked to deliver architectural plans for a new skyscraper that would take the place of an existing postwar walk-up whose residents didn't even know their building was slated for demolition. Every day was different on the bike.

After twenty minutes, Marcus's pager sounded. We stood up and did the bro hug, and then we were strapping on our gear bags and walking our bikes toward the street. Lunchtime was over.

Just before I rode off, I noticed a teenage girl with short hair and obviously bickering parents sitting on a park bench watching me. I smiled at her, and she smiled back. *Tourist*, I thought, setting off at a break in traffic. When I looked back, just before I rounded a corner, the girl was still watching me wistfully, almost as if she wished she could be me.

CHAPTER SEVEN

After a month officially on the job at Mercury's, I could barely remember the terror that had caused me to fail to make it out of the Village on my inaugural bike ride. New York wasn't bad. In fact, I was even starting to like living in the city, I decided one warm Saturday afternoon in late September as I ran around Washington Square Park. I was on my eighth and final lap, listening to Arrested Development on my Walkman and picturing the Cumberland Plateau rolling off into the distance, when WHACK! A Frisbee nailed me in the head, sending my headphones flying.

"Jesus!" I stopped running and grabbed the side of my head, glancing around for the abysmally talented thrower.

"Oh, hey, sorry," a guy about my age said, jogging toward me. He had shoulder-length brown hair and was dressed in a pair of worn khaki shorts, no shirt. His skin was brown, as if he'd spent all summer lounging in Washington Square throwing Frisbees at passersby.

"That's okay," I said grudgingly, stooping to pick up my headphones. I retrieved the Frisbee, too, and handed it back to him.

"Thanks. Again, I'm really sorry. My friends totally can't aim." He waved at a couple of other shirtless guys by the arch, watching us with obvious interest.

"It's really no problem," I said, ready to resume my run. Compared to some of the spills I'd taken on my bike—a taxi mirror had clipped me one of my first mornings out, while a trash can lid had tripped me up a couple of days earlier—this was nothing.

"I'm Drew, by the way." He stuck out his hand.

I hesitated. Selma would never have approved of this meeting. He could be a murderer or a rapist, she would have pointed out. Or worse, a frat boy. But his hazel eyes were warm, his smile engaging. Just like Ted Bundy.

I gave his hand a squeeze and let go. "Ashley."

"What a great name," he said.

And what a pathetic line. Still, something about the way he looked at me, his face open and uncomplicated, stopped me from rolling my eyes. "Um, thanks."

"What are you listening to, anyway?"

"Arrested Development."

His eyebrows shot up. "Seriously?"

"What, did you think it would be Whitney Houston?"

"More like Bobby Brown. You definitely look like the Bobby Brown type."

I bit my lip. Probably best not to smile at a serial killer.

A warm breeze circled us, and Drew shook his hair back from his face. "Guess I should let you get back to your run. What are you training for?"

"I'm not in training."

"You aren't? I thought for sure you must be on the NYU team. We all did." He gestured toward his friends.

Which meant they'd been talking about me before the Frisbee incident.

"I mean," he added quickly, "we've seen you out here before, and we figured you must be on the team, or whatever. Since you're always running."

"I'm not in school," I said. "I'm taking a year off."

"That's cool."

I looked at my watch. I was supposed to meet Tommy and Marcus for dinner in less than an hour, and I still had to shower. "Anyway, it was nice meeting you."

"Even if you did almost suffer a concussion?" he asked.

"Yeah, but in a good way," I replied, noticing his eyes again. They were somewhere on the color spectrum between green and brown, with a golden ring around the pupil.

"Maybe I'll see you around?"

"You never know."

"Actually," he said, his voice endearingly tentative, "what are you doing tonight?"

"Going out with friends."

"Oh, okay. Gotcha." And he smiled as if to say, *No harm, no foul.*

I paused, still channeling Selma. But she was gone and I was here, and frankly Austin's habitual haranguing about finding me a "groovy straight boy" was getting on my last nerve.

"We'll be at the Limelight after midnight," I said. "You know, in case you like to dance."

"Awesome. Maybe I'll see you there."

"Whatever." I flashed him a smile finally and turned away, replacing my headphones as I took off for home.

What was I doing with random man at Washington Square? Selma was right—he could be a psycho killer for all I knew. But it didn't really matter, I thought as I raced home, dodging traffic and pedestrians and wishing I had my bike. Drew might not even show up at the club.

Not that I cared, of course.

After only a few months in Manhattan, it seemed as if Austin was acquainted with half the city. We'd be eating lunch at a sidewalk café or having a drink at a bar in the Village, and inevitably a gorgeous man with a perfect body would lean in and say, "Well, hello, sweetie, I haven't seen you in ages!"

And Austin would smile coyly and reply, "Well, Steve," or *Adam* or *Scott*, "you must not have been looking very hard." Then he would introduce me, they'd chat for a few minutes as I finished my sandwich or beer, and off would go the beautiful boy. Austin would look back at me, shrugging helplessly.

I understood why so many men were drawn to him—Austin was full of love and light again like he used to be before adolescence struck. Instead of locking himself away to brood and listen to depressing music, he was out in the world again enjoying himself, and I was lucky enough to be along for the ride. On weekends after his shift at the restaurant, we'd go clubbing with his group of friends, spinning and laughing beneath the disco lights. They cracked me up whenever Abba's "Dancing Queen" came on—onto the dance floor they would sashay, twirling each other in circles. Another favorite was anything by Madonna, especially

"Deeper and Deeper" and the gay favorite, "Vogue." One of our first weekends out, Tommy and Marcus couldn't believe that Austin and I didn't know that voguing had been popular in gay Harlem for decades before Madonna brought it into the mainstream. They promptly rented *Paris is Burning* and brought it over to "expand" our "Southern horizons."

One of Austin's favorite hangouts was the Limelight, a trendy Chelsea club frequented by drug dealers from Brooklyn and Club Kids from the Upper West Side. In its previous life, the building that housed the Limelight had served for more than a century as an Episcopal Church. Inside, the Gothic Revival structure still housed many of its original fixtures, from arched entryways and high ceilings to pews and a rectory where club-goers delighted in snorting cocaine off the pulpit. But the cages hanging from the ceiling, host to a plethora of gyrating dancers, along with semi-naked gay boys bouncing off each other and Club Kids posing in outlandish get-ups, signaled a sea change from the church's early days of a far different type of worship.

On weekends—and on Wednesday disco nights—there was always a line of hopefuls outside the Limelight. With Austin and his friends dressed in leather vests and tight cut-offs, we never had a problem getting in. Half the time the doorman was gay, and they never carded too closely, anyway. One flash of our fake IDs, purchased from a shady vendor on St. Mark's Place, and Austin and I were in.

This particular Saturday, we reached the Limelight a little after midnight as was the plan—I'd learned since arriving in the city that DJs tended to play better music in the wee hours of the morning. Not that I was especially picky. In high school, I'd learned to like anything with a beat. My track teammates, mostly black girls and guys, had introduced me to Tupac and Notorious B.I.G. and perennial favs Salt-N-Pepa. In the off-season when I got home from school, I would turn on MTV Dance Party and practice the moves I'd seen my teammates make on the bus home from distant meets. I'd never imagined that I would someday be a regular club-goer in New York, but as it turned out, my after-school activities now gave me the confidence to join Austin and his friends on the dance floor.

Alcohol, of course, helped. By one that night, I was in the happy buzzed state two beers in under an hour tended to put me in. Not to mention, I loved dancing. Austin and I moved well together, all of his friends agreed. We didn't tell them we'd been dancing partners practically since the day he moved in next door. Selma and Claire had conspired early on in their friendship to send us into the city for dancing lessons. Selma always told me that she'd cut quite a rug back in the day herself, and I had no trouble believing her.

I was dancing with Austin, Tommy, Marcus, and several of their friends when the DJ slipped in Mary J. Blige. I whooped and slapped hands with Austin, who pulled me closer to grind briefly against his muscular frame. Then I pushed him away, laughing and spinning under the colorful flashing lights. Life was good. This was good, this moment, right here. I was glad he'd come back for me, glad I'd come back with him. If I'd had to lose Selma, at least I had my best friend beside me again.

Tommy leaned over and put a hand on my shoulder.

"Who would've thought a white girl could dance?" he shouted over the music, smiling down at me. Over six feet tall, with blond baby dread locks and an incredible body he maintained with a rigid workout schedule, Tommy was one of the beautiful people. And didn't he know it sometimes.

I stuck my tongue out at him and kept dancing.

A little while later Austin and I wandered off the dance floor. Back at the table where we'd left our drinks, we people-watched and played the Fag/SNAG/Foreign Guy game. The goal of the game was to correctly identify passing men as gay, Sensitive New Aged Guy (straight), or foreign. Each of these types tended to wear their hair long, dress in slightly effeminate clothing, and were easily distinguished from straight guys in baseball caps and T-shirts with beer logos, or Club Kids with elaborate hair pieces and carefully drawn-on eyebrows.

We were in the midst of checking out the guys crossing our line of vision when a group of three, all with longish hair, paused alongside the bar. One ordered drinks while the other two surveyed the crowd. I tried to figure out where I'd seen them before.

"Fags," Austin said, nodding toward them. Then he looked more carefully. "Wait. Never mind. Okay, the guy buying is bi, and the other two are SNAGs. Or maybe they're all SNAGs. Damn. My gadar must be out of whack. What's your call?"

The one at the bar turned around then, beers in hand, and

joined his buddies. Like, duh, Ash. It was Drew and his Frisbee friends, cleaned up and fully clothed for their night out.

"SNAGs." I took a swig from my Rolling Rock.

"You're probably right," Austin agreed. "The one with the drinks is cute. Too bad."

"Too bad," I agreed.

Drew kept looking around as his friends moved through the crowd. Was he looking for me? Had he really come here because I'd sort of, kind of invited him? Back in Tennessee, a guy like Drew wouldn't have looked twice at a skinny runner chick like me. Somehow, it didn't seem like a thousand miles should make such a difference.

Before I could decide whether or not to say hello, a blonde woman in Daisy Dukes and a halter top that showed most of her back and a good portion of her impressive cleavage made a beeline for Drew. I watched as they grinned at each other, hugged, and kissed. As the blonde backed off slightly, Drew looked over her shoulder right at me.

I pretended I hadn't seen him. Why had he even talked to me today if he was already hanging out with someone like her? I was neither blonde nor petite, and running was hardly conducive to the production of breasts like hers. Oh, well. As Selma would have said, no skin off my teeth. Or was it nose? I never could get her sayings right.

"Dance?" I asked Austin.

"Always."

I drained the rest of my beer and left the empty bottle on the table while Austin wrapped an arm around my neck and pulled me out onto the floor. His friends smiled and welcomed us back into their tight dancing circle. Tommy and I grinded thigh to thigh, and I couldn't help hoping that Drew was watching.

Dancing with the boys, I lost myself in the music. When someone tapped me on the shoulder, I barely noticed at first. The second tap got me to turn and look. Drew, his eyes dark under the psychedelic disco lights.

He leaned close. "How's it goin', Ashley?"

I spoke directly into his ear. "Not bad. You made it out tonight."

He nodded and gave me a thumbs-up. Austin's friends made room and Drew joined our circle. For a straight white boy he could dance, I soon discovered. Not hip-hop style but his own moves, fluid and athletic at once. No wonder Austin had thought he might be gay. Drew wasn't at all macho or self-conscious like most of the college boys strutting around the club.

Across the circle, Austin grinned at me. I wiggled my eyebrows back. One point to the SNAGs.

We stayed at the Limelight until three in the morning. Then Drew suggested we hit Around the Clock, a restaurant in the East Village that stayed open twenty-four/seven. Austin, Tommy, Drew and I took a cab down Fifth Avenue to Tenth Street and headed crosstown on foot.

Drew and I took the lead, Tommy and Austin strolling just behind us. I was amazed, as ever, by the number of people out this late at night. Not that it seemed that late. Looking up at the narrow patch of light-polluted sky visible between the buildings around us, I realized I hadn't seen a single celestial body since I'd arrived in New York, not even Venus pointing north in the early evening sky.

The club hadn't exactly encouraged conversation, so Drew and I exchanged data as we walked: last names, ages, where we were from, how we'd ended up in New York. Drew was from Western New York, I learned, near Buffalo, and had just started his junior year at NYU. We talked about the Limelight and our favorite music, discussed high schools and hometowns, and disclosed the color and make of our dream cars. Drew's was a red convertible BMW. Mine was a red Ford Ranger.

"Do you have any brothers or sisters?" Drew asked as we approached scaffolding that took up half the block between Fifth Avenue and Broadway.

I moved ahead of him down the narrow sidewalk corridor, ducking under an orange tarp that dangled from the construction walkway overhead. None of Austin's friends had asked about my family. I was pretty sure he'd warned them not to.

"I'm an only child," I told Drew over my shoulder. "My parents were killed in an accident when I was little, so I don't really remember them. My aunt raised me."

Accident was just vague enough. Most people's brains, I'd found, automatically supplied the word *automobile*.

"Whoa," Drew said as we reached the corner of Broadway and Tenth. Yellow cabs were flying south along Broadway, as usual.

"I'm so sorry."

"Thanks. But Selma, my aunt, was a great parent. What about you? Any brothers or sisters?"

"I'm the middle kid, and the only boy to boot. My older sister, Beth, just graduated from Vassar and moved to San Francisco." He seemed to consider me in the dim street light. "Did you notice that girl I was talking to right before you and I started dancing tonight? Blonde, kind of short, in cut-offs?"

I pretended to think. "Maybe."

"Cammie is Beth's ex-girlfriend. They dated at Vassar."

"That's cool," I said. So the Daisy Dukes girl was a lesbian. Interesting.

Speaking of gay... I checked behind us—a few paces back, Tommy had his hand on Austin's arm and was speaking urgently. While I watched, Austin pulled his arm away, clearly pissed. Wait, were they together? Sure seemed like it, but wouldn't Austin have told me?

"You're okay with the whole gay thing, then?" I asked Drew.

"What do I care who sleeps with who? I mean, whom. I just don't see what the big deal is."

"Good. Because Austin, my roommate, is gay."

Drew nudged my shoulder with his. "No, really?"

I shoved him back, pleased when he had to put a foot in the gutter to keep his balance.

"How do you know Austin?" he asked.

"We grew up together. He's actually the one who convinced me to come to the city."

"He's from Tennessee, too?"

Drew had refused to believe at first that I was really from Tennessee, given my lack of a discernible Southern accent. Typical Yankee.

"Yep," I said. "In fact, he's a fourth generation Chattanoogan."

"Was he out in high school?"

"No way. But I think I always knew on some level that he was gay. Or different, anyway. Was it like that with your sister?"

Laughing a little, Drew shook his head. "Not exactly. I heard rumors when I was in junior high and she was in high school. This guy Collin, whose sister was Beth's year, started telling everyone at lunch one day that my sister was a dyke. I beat him up, and then I went home and read my sister's diary."

We stopped at the light at Third and Ninth, waiting for Tommy and Austin to catch up.

"You read her diary?" I asked.

"I still feel bad about it. But I was only twelve. I promise, I haven't done anything like that since."

"Hmm. I'm not sure you can be trusted after something like that."

"No, you're right. I don't blame you."

Laughing, I poked him in the shoulder. "Kidding."

He looked over at me, smiling. "I know."

"Hey, there," Austin said as he and Tommy reached the corner. His grin was a little forced, and Tommy's face still betrayed little emotion.

"Yo," I said, smiling at Austin quizzically. Asking with my eyes, *You okay?*

He nodded almost imperceptibly. "Come on. I'm starving."

We crossed the street. The restaurant was next door to St. Mark's Bookshop, which had quickly become one of my favorite bookstores in the city. They had everything, from classics that were favorites of Selma's, to modern fiction by new and established writers alike. I loved to wander the cool, quiet aisles, looking through novels and magazines and hiding out from the hot, loud city outside.

Around the Clock was patronized by mainly young, hip people on drugs. Half the people in there on any given night were stoned and stuffing their faces in the midst of an attack of the munchies. Sometimes when we ate here, Austin and I would listen in on our neighbors' earnest discussion of the particular shade of yellow an egg turns when it has been fried sunny-side-up. We never sounded that stupid when we were high, Austin and I would assure each other.

We were seated upon arrival. The restaurant was crowded but not quite packed. In another couple of hours, after the bars closed, there would be a line out the door. New York is a city of lines, with queues to get into movies, museums, clubs, restaurants. Not surprising, I suppose, given the breathtaking number of human beings who call the city's boroughs home.

Our waiter, Jeremy, was a bald young man with an intricate dragon tattooed across his skull.

"That must've hurt," Austin said, eyeing the dragon as Jeremy handed out menus and described the special.

"Only a little," Jeremy said, gazing at Austin with sudden interest.

I looked at Tommy over the top of my menu. He was ignoring Austin.

We ordered pancakes, French toast, a veggie omelet, scrambled eggs, and bacon, all to be shared among the group. After ordering, we launched into a discussion of tattoos and pierced body parts. Drew admitted that he had a tattoo of the Schoolhouse Rock Bill—from Capitol Hill—on his ankle. This admission prompted a close examination of said body art, and we all agreed that it really did resemble the Bill of our childhood memories.

The food soon arrived and we dug in, conversation momentarily forgotten. Once we had somewhat satisfied our appetites, we resumed comparing our favorite childhood cartoons. We'd all loved *Speedracer* and *Superfriends*.

"Okay, so did anyone else notice that whenever the Wonder Twins activated, form of something," Drew said, "the guy always turned into ice or a bucket of water?"

"Totally," I said. "And the girl always took the form of an animal."

Austin nodded. "I used to wonder about that. Like, if they're really so magical, why are their powers so limited?"

No one was quite sure what a Power Ranger looked like, however, other than that they came in various colors.

"I sent one to one of my nieces for Christmas last year," Tommy told us, "and it turned out that I had bought," he paused for effect and ended in a deep voice, "The Wrong Color."

As we all laughed and made sympathetic sounds, I caught Austin watching Tommy with a bemused expression on his face. Then Jeremy reappeared with a fresh pot of coffee, and Austin smiled his flirty smile again. He was impossible.

Even three cups of coffee couldn't prevent me from yawning once my stomach was full and the hour hand on my watch had reached five.

"You ready to head out, roomie?" Austin asked.

"I think so. You guys don't have to come, though," I added, meaning him and Tommy. "I can catch a cab."

"That's okay," Tommy said. "I have to get going. I have to be in shape for a meeting at eight o'clock on Monday morning. If I get to bed soon, I can probably just be okay for work."

"That's what you get for always being Mr. Responsible," Austin said, outwardly cheerful. But I caught an edge to his voice, an undercurrent of tension pulled taut between him and Tommy.

"Want to catch a cab with us?" I asked Drew.

"Sure," he said, folding his napkin neatly beside his plate.

We split everything four ways and left with a last hail to Jeremy, who watched with regret as Austin turned away. Clearly Austin had worked his magic yet again. I almost rolled my eyes at Tommy, but then I caught the wistful look that crept over his features before the unfeeling mask descended once more.

God. Didn't they get sick of drama?

Tommy, who lived only a few blocks away on Fifth Street, kissed me and Austin both on the cheek, shook hands with Drew, and headed south on Third Avenue. I almost asked Austin what the deal was as Drew hailed a cab and directed the driver to his building just south of Washington Square, but the fifth degree could wait. No doubt he would have his own line of questioning to pursue.

At the corner of Thompson and Bleecker, Drew slipped out of the cab. He handed me a couple of bucks for the ride and a napkin from the restaurant with his phone number scrawled in black ink that had bled slightly through the filmy surface.

"Sorry, I don't have anything to write with," I said.

"That's okay. Just tell me and I'll remember."

I recited our number, wondering if this was his way of blowing me off. But as he closed the cab door and stepped onto the curb, he smiled at me so sweetly that I forgot my insecurities. Then it was just Austin and me again, slumped in the back of a cab traveling west through the Village at breakneck speed, our driver tapping the steering wheel in time to the Pakistani rap song playing on the radio.

"So," Austin said, his voice expectant.

"So."

"Drew seems cool."

"For a SNAG."

Austin shoved me sideways. "Why didn't you tell me you met someone today?"

I smiled, looking down at the crumpled Around the Clock napkin. "I didn't want to say anything, just in case."

Shaking his head, Austin caught my hand in his. "For a girl, Ash, you are way too repressed. No, wait, for a *human being*." He squeezed my fingers and let my hand go.

"Speaking of repression," I said, "what's up with you and Tommy?"

"I don't know. I don't get it. We have a good time together, but every once in a while, like tonight, he goes on these tirades and starts bossing me around like I'm his little brother."

"What happened tonight?"

"Nothing." Austin glanced away and brushed at his nose. A streetlight shone into the cab, and I could see blood on his fingers.

"You're bleeding," I said. "Your nose is bleeding."

"Shit." Austin stripped off his tight black T-shirt and held it to his face.

Faster than you could whistle, the cab came to an abrupt halt on the corner of Bleecker and West Tenth Street.

"Out," the cab driver said, shooing us from the back seat. "No blood in my car. Go!"

"But we're not—" I started to say as Austin and I obediently slid out onto the curb.

"Go!" the driver repeated, muttering something else under his breath.

Austin fumbled in his pocket. "What about the fare?"

The cabbie didn't even respond, just checked over his shoulder and pulled away, leaving us a couple of blocks from home. Austin never liked to be let off in front of our building, anyway, so it was a win-win, right?

"What luck," I said, slipping my arm through Austin's elbow. "Your bloody nose got us a free ride home."

"Real lucky," Austin said, and checked his nose. The tiny trickle had already stopped.

I tried to think of something to say as we walked home arm in arm, each of us keeping an eye on the shadows around us. José had been jumped the week before as he walked home alone after a movie at Bleecker Street Theatre, not all that far from here.

"At least we're not going home alone," I offered as Austin unlocked the front door.

"True." He smiled tiredly at me as we headed up the stairs. "By the way, have I told you lately I'm glad you're here?"

"No. But so am I."

We entered the apartment and locked the door behind us, twisting the three bolts shut and linking the chain across the edge of the door. You could never be too careful. Apparently the cabbie subscribed to this same philosophy.

I hugged Austin good night/morning, and then went into my room and checked to make sure none of his blood had gotten on me. Because even though the cab driver had muttered in his own language, there were two words I'd recognized: *faggot* and *AIDS*. And even though I hated myself for it, I couldn't help but worry about that bloody nose, too.

CHAPTER EIGHT

Drew remembered my number.

On Sunday afternoon, he called and invited me to dinner at a restaurant just off Washington Square.

"Um, okay," I said, mentally calculating the time remaining in the football game I was watching with Austin, José, and Ben, plus the time I would need to shower and walk to the restaurant. I'd only been out of bed for a few hours. "But let's make it six, okay?"

As soon as I switched off the cordless phone, Austin muted the game and said, "That was the cute SNAG from last night, wasn't it?"

José perked up. "The one you were dancing with? He was fine."

"Lucky girl," Ben put in.

"Whatever. It's not like we're going on a date or anything," I said, dropping back into the comfortable arm chair near the TV. Or maybe we were. I just wasn't sure I wanted to go out with a guy who, it appeared, had picked me up at Washington Square.

"It's a lot like a date," José said. "In fact, it is one."

"Aw, is our little girl growing up?" Austin's tone was faux syrupy.

"Piss off," I said, and threw a potato chip at him.

I'd been hanging out with Austin's friends all summer, but it still felt strange to hear them discussing my social life the way my track teammates would have. My female teammates, that is—the guys wouldn't have been caught dead dishing about dating or relationships, worried as they were that someone might think they were gay.

"Stereotypes often exist for a reason," I had heard Tommy, the sociology major, say more than once.

Bummer, that.

Drew was already at the bar, beer in hand, when I arrived.

"Hey, there," I said, sliding onto the stool next to him.

"Hi, Ashley." He smiled at me, and I noticed the dark smudges beneath his eyes. Like me, he appeared fresh from the shower. His hair was still damp and flowed over his shoulders. It was longer than mine. Prettier, too.

"Who's winning?" I asked, nodding at the television over the bar.

"The Yankees. The Indians suck this year. Do you want a beer?"

I shuddered at the thought of more alcohol. "No, but I'll take a coke."

Drew signaled the waiter. As we waited for my soda to arrive, I said, "Yankees or Mets?"

"Yankees."

"Giants or Jets?"

"Um, the Bills, of course."

"That's right, you're from there, aren't you? Giuliani or Cuomo?"

"Cuomo, of course!" He seemed almost offended. "My turn. Starks or Ewing?"

"Ewing. Starks is a punk."

"Good answer. The Doors or Nirvana?"

"Neither. Melissa Etheridge." Austin had introduced me to Melissa back in high school. I still loved her *Brave and Crazy* album better than anything else she'd done. "I've got one: Rock City or Ruby Falls?"

"What?" He looked at me blankly.

"You've never been to Tennessee, have you?"

Rock City and Ruby Falls are tourist attractions in the Chattanooga area. Along the main roads in Tennessee and surrounding states, there are legions of billboards and barn roofs emblazoned with the directives, "See Rock City" and "See Ruby Falls," left over from a decades-long advertising campaign.

"Nope. But I bet you've never been to Buffalo, either."

"You're right. I've only watched the Bills lose the last three

Super Bowls in a row."

Drew jumped off his bar stool. "I'm not even going to touch that one." But he was smiling. "Come on. Let's get a table."

We sat by the window where we could watch shadows from nearby buildings lengthen as we ate sandwiches and French fries and drank iced water. In between bites, we talked about our hometowns and the houses we'd grown up in.

"It's probably a good thing I lived in the middle of nowhere," I told Drew. "My aunt said she never thought I'd make it through middle school, let alone high school."

"Why not?"

"I used to do stupid stuff. Like when I was ten, I broke my arm jumping out of a tree. See?" I showed him my right forearm, where a jagged scar ran the length of the pale underside.

"So being a bike messenger isn't anything new?"

"Not really."

He took a sip of water. "What does your aunt think about you taking the year off? Was she for or against the idea?"

I looked down at my plate. "She never knew."

"What do you mean?"

"She died in February." I could say it easily now, aloud, in the middle of the day. "Cancer."

"God, I'm sorry," Drew said, reaching across the table to give my hand a quick squeeze. "You've been through a lot, haven't you?"

It was so easy for him to reach out like that, to imagine what someone else might feel. Me, I wasn't even sure what I felt myself, let alone anyone else.

"I have?" I frowned and moved my hand out of his reach.

"It seems like it. From the outside."

I shrugged and lifted my sandwich to my mouth, chewing by rote.

"Anyway, what's your event?" he asked, shifting his attention back to his food. "In track, I mean."

"Middle distance. What about you? What'd you do in high school?"

"Soccer and basketball," he said. "I wasn't bad, but I wasn't really good at anything, either."

"Except writing?" He'd said the night before that his goal in life was to win a Pulitzer. That's why he'd come to New York.

Supposedly it was the place to be if you wanted to be a writer.

"That, and throwing a Frisbee."

"My head begs to differ," I said, rubbing the spot where the Frisbee had made contact.

His smile was guilty. "About that…"

"What?"

"To be honest, I kind of aimed for you," he said. "I'd seen you running the past couple of weeks and decided I didn't want to always wonder 'what if' about you."

I stared at him across the table. *How sweet,* one part of my brain intoned. *Shut up, dork,* the other returned. "You hit me on purpose?"

He nodded. "But I didn't mean to hit you in the head. That wasn't part of the plan."

"First your sister's diary, and now this? I don't know, Drew. You seem sort of diabolical."

He laughed. "You're right, I'm clearly not to be trusted."

And yet, he all but exuded decency. Drew, I could already tell, was one of those comfortable, easy-going people to whom others confessed their innermost thoughts and feelings. He could almost even get me to open up.

We were almost finished eating when an unshaven man in torn clothes and a filthy, unraveling ski hat paused on the sidewalk outside the restaurant and looked in at us. Drew and I both stopped in mid-laugh and gazed out at the man. There we were in clothes and shoes that probably cost as much as a night's stay in a Midtown hotel, eating a dinner someone else had made for us while this man—and thousands of others like him—walked the streets of the city trying to line up his next meal.

"It's disturbing the way people end up, isn't it?" Drew said, picking at his sandwich. "I read recently there are more than twenty thousand homeless people in the city, and almost half are kids."

"Are you serious?" I'd had no idea the numbers were so high.

"Completely." He pushed his plate away. "It makes me feel guilty for having so much."

I knew what he meant. Since moving to New York, I'd grown accustomed to many things: to strange men making sexual remarks to me on the street; to the mingled smell of urine and rotting garbage strong in the air after a summer rain shower; to the reckless turn of yellow cabs through a crowded pedestrian crosswalk; to the flow of unrecognizable languages all around me as I crossed Midtown streets. But it still jarred me to see ragged men sleeping in cardboard boxes, hollow-eyed women towing their lives about in shopping carts.

A few weeks before, a bearded man had knelt on a pillow on Broadway, holding a sign that read, "Homeless vet. Please help." I'd dropped some spare change into his plate and looked down just as he lifted his gaze. Our eyes met and locked, though I don't think either of us intended it, and for a moment I could feel the man's humiliation, his despair, his utter emptiness as he knelt in the middle of the busy sidewalk with mostly uncaring people streaming past him. Shaken, I walked on, crossing the street against the light on my way to meet Austin at Tower Records.

I would never be homeless. At least, not in the technical sense, not with the trust fund and Selma's house waiting for me. But at the same time, I wasn't sure I'd ever have a real home with a family of my own, either. When I thought about my future, I saw myself as I was right then—alone, a bit lost, certainly not wife or mother material. Even before Selma got sick, I'd always imagined myself living on my own with a few close friends and a career that kept me busy. I couldn't see myself as part of a family, probably because I'd never known what it was like to have a mother and a father. Selma hadn't dated, so the only model I had for a successful adult relationship was Austin's parents. And look how that was turning out—a family therapist struggling to hold her family together, a school administrator unable to accept his own child.

When we were done eating, Drew paid the bill over my protests and asked the waitress to box up our leftovers. Then he took the Styrofoam container outside and offered it to the man in the unraveling ski hat, who was now leaning against the corner of a neighboring building.

"Thank you, son," the man said, looking down at the ground.

"You're welcome," Drew said. "Have a good night."

We walked to Washington Square and claimed a bench under a tree, discussing poverty and economic philosophy as the summer sun set beyond the NYU buildings that lined the park. Unlike many of the kids we grew up with, Drew and I both claimed to long for more meaning in our lives than the pursuit of gobs of money via a soulless white collar career. Even as I agreed to this last bit, I remembered with a start that I was already well-off, white collar career or no.

"It seems like people morphed into materialistic social climbers during the eighties, doesn't it?" Drew commented.

"My aunt blamed Reagan."

"*Reagan.*" Drew spit the name almost like a curse. "His trickle-down theory was utter crap."

"Total crap. But he's just the latest in a long line of people who blame the poor. Have you heard of Polanyi? He has this idea that industrial capitalism is responsible for destroying the basic social order that existed throughout history."

"Wait, was your high school uber-wealthy or something?" Drew asked. "I didn't learn about Polanyi until my sophomore year here." He waved at the NYU library just behind us.

"Not really," I said, "though the suburb where Austin and I grew up was definitely on the extreme end of comfortable. My aunt was the director of the local public library, and in the summers, she used to make me read one book for every four hours I spent playing outside. Economics wasn't exactly my favorite topic, but Selma knew how to make even the most boring book come alive."

I smiled, remembering how she would turn everything into a game. For Marxism, she enlisted a version of Rock, Paper, Scissors that involved paper clips as monetary units and a labor system that rewarded those who multiplied their clip collection and demoted those who lost theirs. For learning physics, she turned to crokinole, a nineteenth century board game that teaches classical mechanics (the motion of bodies under the action of a system of forces) as well as dexterity. She may not have been a model for successful adult relationships, but she'd loved learning, and she'd loved me. A kid could do worse, as Austin's friends demonstrated.

Ben, who hailed from Ohio, and José, who was from Long Island, hadn't come out to their families yet because they were afraid their parents would stop paying their tuition bills. Marcus, meanwhile, hadn't spoken to his parents in Rhode Island since he'd told them about his boyfriend two years earlier. The boyfriend had pushed and pushed for Marcus to tell his parents, and once he had, broke up with him because he couldn't deal with the fall-out.

Only Tommy's parents had offered their gay son unconditional support. An art history professor in Philadelphia, his father had responded with equanimity to Tommy's announcement at eighteen that he was gay. His mother, an artist, had blamed herself briefly, but had moved quickly beyond acrimony to embrace "the whole man," as she put it. His folks were regular visitors to his studio in the East Village.

As Drew and I sat on our bench people-watching, a man in suspenders and a bow tie walked past, playing a flute. A pair of teenaged boys with unkempt hair and tie-dyed shirts sauntered by in the opposite direction, debating the street value of certain drugs. They were followed by two youngish women taking a black Labrador retriever to the dog run at the west end of the park.

Soon a couple walked by, swinging a small, giggling child between them.

Drew glanced at me. "Can I ask you something?"

I closed my eyes, just for a second. I knew what was coming.

"Sure," I said, and sat on my hands so that I wouldn't feel the need to open and close them compulsively.

"You said your parents died in a car wreck, so I was just wondering how it happened."

Glancing over at him, I considered the question, which was really more of a statement, after all. He held my gaze, his face calm and relaxed, eyes enquiring.

"I don't really like to talk about it," I said.

"I can understand that." He paused. "Was it hard growing up never knowing your parents?"

I shrugged, gripping the wood slats of the bench. "As far as I'm concerned, Selma was my mother. I mean, I know she was my mother's sister, but she's the only parent I can remember."

"Was it harder losing her, then?"

Tears came out of nowhere, startling me. Just when I thought it was safe to go back into the water… I blinked and took a deep, steadying breath. "Well, yeah. It was freaking awful, actually. Still kind of is."

"I'm sorry," Drew said. "That was a stupid question. I was just trying to let you know that I'm here if you need to talk. I mean, I know I just met you, but I think you're a really cool person. That's all."

Now I felt like the ass. How could someone like him—all four of his grandparents were alive and well, he'd reported, and his parents were still so affectionate that he and his sisters sometimes complained about the PDA—know how to talk to a train wreck like me?

"It wasn't a stupid question. I'm just not particularly used to talking about it." I hesitated. "My parents weren't in a car wreck. It was a plane crash. The hydraulics went out during landing."

"A plane crash?" He frowned. "Was that in Chicago, where you were born?"

I nodded. "Selma came up and got me. I barely remember Chicago."

"So that's why you've never flown before."

At dinner, I'd said I didn't *like* to fly, not that I'd never flown before. The Orlando-Chicago flight had been my second and last experience on a plane. But there was no reason to tell Drew I had been on the flight as well. At least, not until I knew him better. Austin was the only person in New York who knew the truth, and I planned to keep it that way.

I actually had a fairly good reason to maintain secrecy: Every year or two a reporter had contacted Selma about interviewing me, but she always said no. When I was eighteen, she'd told me, I could make my own decisions about the media.

Now I was eighteen, and in only a few weeks, it would be the fifteenth anniversary of the crash. That was one of the reasons I had left my lawyer's contact information as my forwarding address for everyone except Austin's family. Leaving Tennessee had offered the added benefit of preserving my privacy in this, a significant anniversary year of the crash.

"Is it okay if we don't talk about it anymore tonight?" I asked.

"Of course. But if you ever need someone to listen, I'm here, all right?" And he covered my hand with his.

I couldn't imagine reaching for his hand like that. What if he pulled away? Or worse, what if he didn't?

"Thanks," I said. "Not that I'm not having a great time, but I should probably get going. I have to be at work early. The packages wait for no woman."

"I should probably get some sleep myself," Drew agreed, giving my hand a squeeze before letting go.

As we rose from the bench and headed out along Fourth Street, he told me that his summer internship as a fact-checker for Condé Nast had overlapped with NYU's fall semester by a month. Not great timing, but he couldn't turn down the money or the networking opportunity. Unfortunately, several of the magazines were approaching publication deadlines, which meant he and the other fact-checkers would be working long hours.

"How long?" I asked as we walked westward along Fourth Street.

"Sixty hours a week, on top of classes. It's just for the next couple of weeks. Once the internship ends, I'll have all the time in the world to hang out. Of course, then you'll be the one always at work."

Which meant he thought we would still be hanging out in two weeks. *Cool*, I told myself, irritated by the slight glow the realization had engendered.

We stopped at the edge of the park, and I smiled at him nervously.

"How about I call you in a few days when I know what my schedule will be?" he asked.

"Sounds good."

We both hesitated. Then he leaned forward and kissed me on the cheek.

"I had a good time tonight," he said as he pulled away.

"Me, too." I started to walk away. "Good luck at work."

"I think you probably need luck more than I do."

I didn't look back as I headed west across the Village, the evening darkening around me. Street lights flickered on, neon signs burning against the deepening dusk. A jet flew overhead, closer than I thought was truly safe. I shuddered a little. Why hadn't I told him the truth about the crash? My hesitation was rooted in more than just a need for privacy, I knew. It was almost as if I were trying to keep him at a distance—like if he never knew the truth, then he could never really know me. I would be safe with my secret in my black and white world of the trusted and the not.

Which was how I wanted it, I told myself as the sky grew dark and the city bright. Everyone was alone, after all. You were born alone and you died alone. You were better off if you could remember that and keep a part of yourself tucked safely inside, away from everyone else.

A homeless woman approached me on the corner of Seventh Avenue, but I avoided her gaze and brushed past. Hands balled into fists in the pockets of my khaki shorts, I crossed against the light and walked on, leaving her to beg for someone else's spare change.

CHAPTER NINE

September had brought cooler air that banished the humidity and improved moods across the city, but October brought warm air one day, freezing temperatures the next, and falling leaves that made the roadways and sidewalks slick wherever trees had been allowed to congregate. Every day that I took to the street on my bike, I became part of the frenetic flow. From the fortieth and fiftieth floors of Midtown buildings, I looked down from wide windows onto the snake of tiny cars and pedestrians swarming along the wide avenues. After each delivery, I couldn't wait to get out of the conditioned air and back into the jam of constant activity.

On the second Tuesday of the month, the fifteenth anniversary of the plane crash arrived. I checked the *New York Times* and *Daily News* before work and discovered an article in each that focused on the victims, their families, and the lone survivor, who had "recently graduated from high school but couldn't be reached for comment," according to the *Daily News*. I don't know what I'd expected, but after all the years Selma had spent warning me not to trust reporters, I was surprised at this seeming respect of my privacy.

At Mercury's, no one looked at me any differently than they had the day before. I spent the day on my bike as usual, glad for the distraction that messing offered. On the streets I could lose myself weaving in between skyscrapers built up and up, across bridges that had been funneling people across the East River for a century or more. From the outside—New Jersey, Brooklyn, the Bronx—

Manhattan rose up out of the water like some modern perversion of a monster with countless heads and tails. But when you were skipping along the monster's paved back, it seemed like the most normal place in the world.

Most days I averaged twenty-five or thirty runs a day in Manhattan and, more rarely, Brooklyn. At five each evening, sometimes earlier depending on my work load, I checked out at Mercury's and rode home to gorge myself on whatever food we had in the apartment. Some of the guys from the company had invited me out a few times to a messenger bar in Alphabet City, and I'd talked Marcus into going once before he went back to school. But he'd been right—all the guys did was drink and talk about messing, and then pull tricks in the alley outside the bar. I got plenty of time on the bike during the work week. I didn't need it after hours, too. Riding around the city was hard work, even if I was in good shape.

During the week, my schedule and Austin's overlapped mainly on Mondays, his night off. Occasionally I would run into him on the street on his way to work. On those evenings, I would accost him, trying to rub sweat on the collared shirt and slacks he wore to wait in. He would push me away, squealing like when we were kids and I would try to dunk him in Rainbow Lake. Ritual complete, I would turn for home and he would continue on to the restaurant for the dinner shift, where he was guaranteed to land copious tips and numerous phone numbers.

Once Drew finished his internship at Condé Nast, we hung out more, riding the subway up to 190th Street to wander Fort Tryon Park and the Cloisters, a miniature castle that housed the Medieval Collection of the Metropolitan Museum of Art; checking out a new Mexican dive in the East Village; sampling restaurants along Indian Row, East Sixth Street between First and Second; or catching a movie at one of the many nearby theaters. The "dates" ticked off, but our relationship remained mostly platonic, except for some hand-holding and a kiss or two. Anything more and I usually pulled away. Drew, a self-proclaimed feminist, tolerated my distance seemingly amiably.

He finally got frustrated with me, as I'd suspected he would, on the Friday before Halloween. We were lying on his futon facing each other, listening to a 10,000 Maniacs CD and talking about messing and school and our roommates and nothing at all, when he

97

reached across the space and tucked a loose strand of hair behind my ear.

"You know, Ashley, you're a really special person," he said, voice and eyes soft in the candle-lit room.

I just looked at him. Then a small laugh burst from my throat. I tried to rein it in, but too late.

Drew pulled away, staring at me. "What the hell? How is that funny?"

I bit my lip, swallowing the irrational laughter. "No, I know, I just hate the word 'special.' I'm sorry."

He rolled onto his back and stared up at the ceiling, arms folded across the front of his gray NYU sweatshirt. "I don't get you," he said. "I've been trying to figure you out these last few weeks, and I still don't get you."

I wanted to say I didn't get myself either. Instead, I rolled onto my back beside him. The bars on his window cast shadows across the ceiling. His room bordered the building's main fire escape, so his roommate's father had insisted that the building manager install iron gates with bars before Drew and Chris moved in. On a warm day the previous week, Drew and I had taken dinner out onto the fire escape to watch life in the Village below while we ate.

"So what's your deal?" Drew said finally, looking over at me.

I closed my eyes as Natalie Merchant sang about being blessed and lucky and knowing how something is meant to be. "I don't know. I'm sorry."

He sighed and rolled over on his stomach. I could feel him closer now, his body warm against my side.

"Ash," he said, and his voice was soft again. "Look at me."

Reluctantly I opened my eyes. His face was only a few inches from mine. I wanted to hold him, wanted him to hold me. Didn't I?

"What are you so afraid of?" he asked.

At that, I sat up and leaned against the wall. "I'm not afraid of anything," I said, and hugged my knees to my chest.

"Then why don't you let yourself feel anything?" he asked, leaning forward on his elbows. "It's like, I try to kiss you and you pull away. But I would swear you want to kiss me, too. So what's the deal? Do I repel you, or what?" He half-smiled at me.

I shook my head, chin on my knees. "No, of course not."

"Do you want to kiss me too?" he pressed.

"Yeah."

"Then what's the problem?"

"Look. Remember how I told you I don't have all that much experience? I mean, like, with sex and everything?"

"I remember." He gazed at me, waiting.

"Well, I haven't exactly had a boyfriend. Like, ever, if you know what I mean." I couldn't look at him.

Understanding apparently dawned. "You mean, you've never even kissed anyone?"

I shrugged, fiddling with the unraveling cuff of my Levi's. "No. Not really. Except Austin. We practiced on each other in middle school, and look how he turned out."

"Oh." He sat up next to me. "Okay. Well, are you attracted to me or not?"

"Of course," I said, frowning a little. At least, I thought he was attractive. That was the same thing as being attracted to him, wasn't it? "Are you attracted to me?"

"Uh, yeah, you could say that." He paused. "How did you manage to get this far without ever kissing anyone?"

"Part of it was that there wasn't much to choose from where I lived, and everyone thought Austin and I were together. But besides that, I used to fight a lot, you know, beat kids up?"

"You? I don't believe it," Drew deadpanned.

"Anyway, even after we were in high school, the boys remembered I'd kicked their butt when we were seven."

Once again I was sharing only half-truths, but I didn't want to admit to Drew, whose estimation of me seemed unreasonably high, that no one had wanted to kiss me because they couldn't forget my past. Even in high school, kids had whispered about the plane crash behind my back, calling me *witch* or, worse, *jinx*.

"So where do we go from here?" he asked.

"I don't know. You tell me."

He was so close now, his arm touching mine. Leaning over slightly, I let my chin rest on his shoulder.

"How about I kiss you and you see if you like it?" he suggested, slipping his arm around my shoulder.

I nodded, lifting my face to his. And he kissed me, his lips soft and warm against mine. I was liking it all right, when suddenly his tongue darted against my lips.

I pulled back, frowning a little. "What are you doing?"

"Kissing you," he replied, eyebrows lifting quizzically. "You know, like when both people open their mouths and, like, really kiss?"

"Oh. I knew that."

We looked at each other, and then Drew bit his lip. I could tell he was trying not to smile.

"I'm totally pathetic, aren't I?" I slid down the bed and covered my face with my hands. "This is so embarrassing."

"No, it's not," Drew said, sliding down next to me. He pulled my hands from my face. "It's sweet, Ash. I said you were special. I just didn't realize how special."

"Shut up!" I meant to hit him, but ended up sliding my arms around his neck instead. "I thought we were going to try the whole kissing thing?"

"I'm game if you are."

I pulled him toward me, closing my eyes as his arms folded around me and his lips settled against mine. His body felt warm and solid against mine. And all at once, I didn't want him to let go of me.

Which was the feeling I'd been trying to avoid all along, I thought later as Drew slept on the futon beside me. We'd fooled around for a while, taking it slowly in the face of all that I had yet to learn, until finally Drew announced that it was too late for me to go home. I'd borrowed his toothbrush and was wearing his T-shirt and a pair of his boxers. But I couldn't sleep. I lay awake watching him as the shadows shifted against the walls, across Picasso posters and a couple of framed line drawings Drew had done himself. Shadows shifted, cars passed below, and voices echoed off concrete. And I wondered what I was doing here, after all. Not just here in Drew's room, but in the broadest sense possible. Why hadn't I died in the plane crash? What had God, or whatever spiritual entity was out there, intended when he or she or it had spared me and only me? Why was everyone dead but me?

Tears slid down my cheeks, dripping from my chin onto the borrowed T-shirt. Eventually I slept, to awake in the morning with Drew's arm around me, the emptiness of the previous night forgotten. For a moment, half-awake in Drew's sunlit room, I thought I understood the meaning of it all. Then a truck drove beneath the window, brakes squealing the high-pitched squeal of all New York City trash trucks, and my inkling of understanding vanished.

"Don't go yet," Drew whispered as I stirred against him.

"I won't," I murmured back, content to lie in his arms on a chilly morning as the city came to life beyond the walls of his apartment.

CHAPTER TEN

The thing about riding your bike as fast as you can through Manhattan traffic is that the longer you do it without an accident, the bolder you become. The bolder you become, the more risks you take. Eventually even the most skilled—or lucky—rider makes a mistake, misses their line. Or someone else, intentionally or not, makes you miss it.

By the end of October, I'd been on the job for two months. I'd been doored a couple of weeks before, but I'd seen it coming and had managed to partially brake and brace myself, so the fall only left me with scrapes and bruises instead of breaks or sprains. My bike and I took a couple of days to recover, and then we were back at work, riding more slowly than before the incident, smart and steady like Marcus had taught me. Being richer than God, as Austin liked to call it, I could afford to dial back my pace. I'd become a messenger because I loved riding a bike and couldn't imagine what other sort of work I might do, other than library page. Libraries were indoors, though, and even on rainy days I would rather have been out on the streets than wandering the cool, quiet stacks.

Then again, it wasn't winter yet.

Even after getting my inaugural dooring incident out of the way—"It's like popping your messenger cherry," Marcus said when I told him a few days later—I still felt lucky to get on my bike every day and get paid good money to ride forty or fifty miles around the city while other people in possession of only a high school degree and limited work experience were flipping burgers and still living with their parents. Don't get me wrong—I would have taken a job at McDonald's over orphandom if I could. But in this life, I was glad to wear bike shorts and a sports bra instead of a polyester uniform and matching cap.

The day before Halloween, the temperature dropped from the mid-sixties to the mid-thirties, and I thought it might even snow as I shivered my way through the miserable afternoon. The next morning, it was seventy by noon, and I had to strip off my outer layers one after the other. *Crazy Northern weather*, I thought, shaking my head at a stoplight on Fifth Avenue as a runner in a skimpy Batwoman costume jogged past.

"Hey!" A voice sounded from my right elbow. "I know you. Fire Girl, right?"

I turned and squinted against the sun, lower now in the sky than it had been even a week before.

"Jeremiah," the speaker clarified, holding an effortless track stand. "You know, from Union Square?"

"Oh, right," I said, my brow clearing. Jeremiah, who, judging from the bag stretched across his shoulders, was a bike messenger.

He whistled. "You on the job, Fire Girl?"

I nodded just as the light turned. He set off, and I kept up with him. Not easily, and I could tell he was taking a bit off his usual pace, but we went down Fifth toward Broadway, me turning the pedals rapidly as I tried to keep up with his long, easy stride.

"Sweet," Jeremiah said. "Who you riding for?"

"Mercury's."

"The Boneta brothers? I didn't know they hired girls."

Women, I thought automatically. Although technically it was singular—Bridget, the ornery coffee drinker and bard fan, had gone over to another firm a few weeks before. "I'm the only one right now."

"They treating you okay?"

I hesitated, unsure of the etiquette. After all, he worked for a rival firm. "It's okay. Not great."

In fact, Fido had been sniffing around ever since Marcus went back to school, and I still didn't trust him as far as I could throw him.

"Sorry to hear that," my riding companion said, darting around a double-parked taxi. "If you can ride, you should get the respect."

I followed his line as best I could, admiring the speed of his decision-making as he slowed for a turning car and then sprinted across the intersection. I had to brake for a bus, but a long sprint got me close enough to almost catch him a few lights later.

"Nice riding," Jeremiah said, and held something out.

I took it—his business card. "Jeremiah Worthington," it said. And, "On The Job Messengers."

"You work for OTJ?" I asked, impressed. Even a rookie like me knew about the company run by a husband and wife team, both former messengers who occasionally took breaks from the office for a turn on the streets. OTJ was renowned for fair treatment of its riders and a team-like atmosphere that was the bane—and envy—of the other small firms in the city.

He nodded. "If you ever decide to jump ship, give me a call, okay?"

"Seriously?"

"Seriously."

"I totally will. Thanks, Jeremiah."

"My friends call me Spidey," he said, and laughed at my startled expression. "Be seeing you, Fire Girl."

He was off, maneuvering with ease through the congestion of Midtown on the way to the congestion of the Financial District. Try as I might, I couldn't catch him. But then, a rookie shouldn't be able to catch a legend like Spidey. He was known across the city as one of the best—experienced, smart, fast, quick to give back to the messing community. He had dominated the alley races for years before passing the torch. And he had given me his card.

At my next stop, I tucked the card away in the small zippered travel wallet I wore on a string around my neck. Jeremiah's offer warranted some serious thought, but not at this juncture. Right now I had a contract to deliver to a financial services firm on the ninety-fifth floor of the World Trade Center. On such a clear day, I knew from experience, I would be able to see past Ellis Island and the Statue of Liberty to the Verrazano Bridge, which was so long that the curvature of the earth had to be factored into its design. While I still wasn't a fan of heights or skyscrapers in general, I didn't mind the WTC as much as I had at first. The height might be dizzying, but the views were amazing.

Truly, I had the best job, I thought as I waited for the elevator to whisk me a quarter mile high in the sky.

*   *   *

A week later, I lay on the ground watching a car tire roll past my head so close my eyes almost crossed. In the time it takes to slide across rain-slicked pavement toward a car you think won't possibly be able to stop in time, I hated my job. *Never again*, I thought—assuming I survived.

This moment had been coming for two days. Or two months, depending how you looked at it. On Monday afternoon, as I cruised down Broadway thinking about my next bathroom break, a movement out of the corner of my eye caught my attention: Fido, riding hard, about to cut me off. The competitor in me rose, along with my feminist hackles, and I actually muttered aloud, "Oh no you didn't, bitch." Kicking it, I put on a burst of speed and held my line, forcing Fido to either brake or ram into me. He braked, and then swore loudly.

"Fuck you too," I said over my shoulder, as I nipped around a jay-walker. Fido turned off a block later without another word.

I told Steph about the encounter that evening as we left the office, me walking my bike next to her on the sidewalk not far from Mercury's.

"Are you kidding?" she demanded. "You're not, are you?"

"No."

"Damn it, Ash, you should have just let him go."

"But I had the right of way!"

"So what? Now he has an excuse to go after you. Don't you understand? He could really hurt you."

I shook my head. "I thought you, at least, would be on my side."

"I am," she said, her hand on my arm. "Believe me when I say that next time, you're better off letting him have whatever line he wants. It's not worth getting injured over. Or worse."

"Right," I said, only just eking the word out through my gritted teeth. "See you tomorrow."

"Ashley," she said, "wait."

But I just shoved my helmet on and set off across the city in the fading light of early evening.

Steph had been right, of course. Cutting Fido off had only made him foam at the mouth even more at the thought of taking me out. A couple of days later he had his chance.

This time I was in the Village, flying south on Seventh Avenue in a light drizzle. The weather was bad, but not terrible. Still, the rain muffled sound and distorted my sight, so that I didn't see him until too late. He gave one wolfish sidelong glance as he maneuvered into position beside me, and then he committed the bike rider's most indirect attack—he leaned on me.

If I had seen it coming, I might have been able to react. Or if it hadn't been raining, I might not have lost control. But Fido outweighed me by thirty pounds, easy, and the rain meant that my narrow tires had even less purchase on the road than usual. Two seconds and I went down, sliding across the nearest intersection into oncoming traffic while I heard Fido laugh in the distance. From my vantage point on the ground, I could see the cab driver's horrified expression as he hit his brakes and wrenched his wheel. He took evasive action, and that, in the end, made all the difference. We both finally stopped, his wheels scant inches from my head, my left leg and arm a scraped mess that would have been far worse had the pavement been dry. I lay on the ground, stunned, as the driver barreled out of his car.

"What the fuck do you think you're doing, bucko?" he shouted, his thinning gray hair standing up all over as if in surprise. He stopped as he got a better look at me. "Oh, shit, you're… I mean, are you all right? Can I call anyone?"

"No, I'm fine." I picked myself up, shaking a bit from reaction, and checked my bike and bag. "I'm really sorry. Another rider leaned on me."

"He what?"

"It was just a joke."

"Some joke," the cabbie said, his face dark. "I almost—"

"I know," I said. "But you didn't. It's fine."

Other cars were honking now, and in unison, the driver and I shot them the bird. Then he patted me awkwardly on the shoulder and said, "You be careful, okay? I have a daughter, and not a chance I would let her ride her bike in Manhattan. Too many crazies like your friend."

"Ain't that the truth," I said, and walked my bike to the curb as he got back in his car and drove away.

The frame was bent but rideable. I could finish up the job I was on, anyway, and call it a day.

At first the security guard at the downtown high-rise didn't want to let me go up, soaked and bleeding as I was. But I toned down my anger and batted my eyelashes, even though it was a betrayal of my principles to do so, and earned a ride to the architectural firm on the twenty-fifth floor.

"Where have you been?" the receptionist started. But then she saw my arm, grazed and bloody, and changed direction. "You poor thing. Do you need some ibuprofen? There's probably a first aid kit somewhere around here."

"No, really, I'm fine. Do you think I could get cleaned up in the bathroom, though? Normally I wouldn't ask, but..." I gestured at my body ruefully.

"Of course, sweetheart," said the woman, who was old enough to be my mother. "You take all the time you need. Are those the plans?"

Delivery complete, I retreated to the soothing, high-ceilinged restroom, lit by elegant sconces and offering a variety of carved soaps on a dish between two gleaming faucets. I turned on the hot water and dangled my hands under the steaming spray, examining my face in the mirror. Had I really almost been crushed by a taxi? Didn't that make what Fido had done attempted murder?

My stomach dropped and I closed my eyes, splashing my face again and again with hot water, until my skin was shiny and hot to the touch.

"Pain is weakness leaving the body," I murmured, and then again: "Pain is weakness leaving the body."

I called in from a pay phone in the lobby.

"I delivered the package," I told Steph.

"A little late, aren't you?" she chided.

"I kind of had an accident."

"Jesus, Ash. You okay?"

"Fine. But I had some help going to the ground."

Her voice dropped almost comically. "Fido?"

"How did you guess?"

"I'm telling you, that dog needs to be put down."

I laughed, and the rapid exhalation of breath revealed pain and tenderness in my rib cage. "You're preaching to the choir."

"You okay to ride, or are you calling it a day?"

"I think I'm done for the day. In fact, I think my bike is done for a few days."

"Too bad—I have a pick-up three blocks from you. I'll let the guys know you won't be back before the weekend. Take care of yourself, girl. I gotta jet."

We hung up and I thanked the security guard again, and then started home on my banged-up bike, my similarly banged-up body already stiff after a quarter of an hour out of the saddle. Tomorrow was going to suck.

Sure enough, I was even more sore the next morning. After dropping my bike off for repairs at Marcus's favorite bike shop in the East Village, I scrubbed out our clawfoot tub and soaked in a long, hot bath with lavender-scented bubbles, a vanilla candle flickering on the counter.

As I lay back in the tub, I remembered running into Jeremiah the week before. *If you ever decide to jump ship…* Was that what I should do? Fido's assault so soon after Jeremiah's offer certainly seemed like a sign, but could I really leave Mercury's and work for OTJ? Like most other messenger companies, Mercury's hired riders as independent contractors, which meant we were all self-employed. Riders moved from firm to firm easily, fluidly, going to whomever offered the best payment rate, busiest work load, most messenger-friendly terms. Being self-employed meant no health insurance and extra taxes, but it also freed you from the constraints of an employment contract. In theory, yes, I could leave Mercury's for OTJ. But would OTJ have me?

The morning rain cleared midway through the day. After watching soaps all afternoon with Austin, I headed out to meet Drew. I hadn't told him yet about the accident, and wasn't sure I wanted to. For one thing, it was embarrassing to wreck, especially as one of the few female messengers in the city. For another, I didn't want to have to explain about Fido the Dick's misogynistic streak.

But when I rang the bell and he jogged downstairs to meet me, I couldn't help the slight *oof* that escaped as he hugged me, his arms tight against my bruised ribcage.

Drew leaned away, frowning. "Did I hurt you?"

"Not you so much as the ground."

It only took him a second. "You had another accident?"

My backbone stiffened almost audibly. "Um, that would imply that I'd had an earlier accident, and being doored doesn't count. Besides, it isn't my fault some Neanderthal who doesn't think women should messenger decided to lean on me in the rain."

Drew's eyebrows lowered like said Neanderthal. "The asshole who's been hassling you?"

"One and the same."

"This morning?"

"Well, no," I admitted. "Yesterday."

"Yesterday?" He blew out a breath and shook his head.

"What?"

"Nothing. Only you have to quit messengering, Ash, before you really get hurt."

"It's okay, I have insurance," I joked.

He stared at me, disapproval evident in the set of his shoulders, mouth, eyes.

"This is why I didn't want to tell you," I said, backing away from him along the sidewalk. "I knew you'd react like this."

He followed me, still frowning. "Like what?"

"Like I can't fight my own battles."

"That's not it. I just don't think messengering is the best thing you could be doing, especially not if you want to run. Don't act like I'm the only one who thinks that. Austin doesn't like it, either."

"Maybe not, but he knows I'll do what it takes to stay on the job, and he respects that. He respects me."

When I'd come crawling home the night before, Austin had been about to leave for work. One look and he'd called in sick. While I took a long shower, Austin had wiped down my bike, ordered Indian for delivery, and picked up a movie at the tiny video rental shop around the corner. And not once had he said anything negative about my job, only about Fido and the things Austin and his friends would do if they ever caught him.

Not all gay guys were afraid to fight, he'd reminded me for the umpteenth time. Some of them were even pretty good at it because they had to be.

"Come on," Drew said. "I respect you."

"Right. You know what? I think I've had enough of straight guys for a while." And I turned and headed back down the sidewalk toward Washington Square.

"You know I respect you," he repeated, following me.

I reached the corner and looked around for a cab. Home was only ten blocks away, but I was tired and my body hurt. Besides, it wasn't like I couldn't afford it.

"Seriously, Ash," Drew said, his hand on my shoulder.

I shrugged away from his touch. "I *am* serious. Go home, Drew."

After a minute he blew out a noisy breath. Then he flicked his loose, beautiful hair out of his eyes and shrugged. "Whatever. Call me when you figure out I'm not the one you want to fight." And he turned and stalked home.

I watched him go, slightly stunned, and then looked around again for a cab. I couldn't believe he'd given up so easily. I mean, I had told him to get lost. I just hadn't expected him to capitulate so quickly.

Soon a taxi rushed toward me with its "Occupied" light off, and I flagged it down. The rain started up again as I rode home in twilight, and I slumped in the back seat watching water droplets slide down the cab windows. For once, I was glad not to have my bike.

Maybe Drew was right, and I needed to quit messing before I got seriously hurt. It was nice that he cared, right? And yet, something felt off about his reaction. I didn't need him to fight my battles for me or make pronouncements about what I should and shouldn't be doing with my life. He seemed to think he had the right to weigh in on my life, but we hadn't even slept together yet. What was he going to be like if and when we did?

As Friday and Saturday came and went and I didn't hear from Drew, I was relieved we hadn't gotten more serious. I didn't really miss him, not like I thought I should. Despite the fact he'd told me to call him when I was ready, I couldn't imagine being the one to call, not when he'd gone all caveman on me.

I know, slight exaggeration. But Selma had been an ardent though soft-spoken feminist, and had raised me to be wary of male claims of authority over female bodies particularly in the South, where such claims often come under the guise of chivalry. Drew had two sisters and a feminist mother, and belonged to a men's group on campus that had formed in protest against an epidemic of date rape cases at NYU. He was hardly macho or sexist, which made his attitude all that more difficult to analyze—where did his genuine caring end and innate chauvinism begin?

Apparently he realized this, though, because on Sunday afternoon when Austin and I came home from brunch with the boys, we found Drew sitting on our front stoop, a bouquet of wilting flowers on his lap.

"Good luck, bro," Austin said, patting his shoulder as he passed. He let himself into the apartment, leaving Drew and me alone outside in the cool, late autumn day, dying leaves swirling along the sidewalk in a brief gust of wind.

"Hi," he said, coming down the steps toward me.

"Hi." I folded my arms across my chest.

"So I've been thinking, and you might have been right. It's possible I shouldn't have said what I did."

I lifted an eyebrow. *That* was his idea of an apology?

"I'm sorry?" he added. And, holding out the flowers: "I got you these."

No one had ever brought me flowers before, and he'd obviously been waiting on the steps for a while. Besides, he was looking up at with me with such hope in his eyes that I couldn't stay mad.

"Come on, Tarzan," I said. "The game's almost on."

"Me can't wait." He grinned, hair falling into his eyes before the wind blew it back again.

"I'm serious," I said, returning to an old conversation, "you should wear a ponytail when it's windy. Otherwise you miss half of what's going on around you."

"Yeah, yeah," he said, and caught my hand as we headed into the apartment. "I missed you, too."

But that was the problem, I thought as we settled into the living room, television tuned to the Sunday afternoon NFL broadcast. I hadn't missed him much. In fact, I'd barely thought about him today until I saw him waiting outside the apartment, looking forlorn and tough at once.

Then he slid closer on the couch and took my hand again, and I had to admit that maybe, just possibly, I had missed the way he looked at me, the way he touched me, as if no one else in the world mattered nearly as much.

Was this really all there was to love? And if so, what was the big deal?

CHAPTER ELEVEN

On Monday morning, the phone rang at seven-fifteen. Blinking groggily, I grabbed the handset next to my bed.

"Hello?" I said, my voice low. Austin usually slept until at least ten even when he hadn't worked at the restaurant the night before.

"Fire Girl? It's Spidey. How's it hangin'?"

"Good," I said, biting my lip. I'd called him on Saturday, and when I hadn't heard back, I'd wondered if he'd been sincere. So what was it to be now? Good news or bad?

"I'm here with Mark and Leslie, the owners, and they're wondering if you might be interested in stopping by to meet them this morning."

My mouth dropped open. OTJ's owners wanted to meet me?

"Um, I would love to. But can we make it a little later? I'm supposed to pick up my bike from the shop at ten."

Jeremiah relayed the message, and then said to me, "Would ten-thirty work?"

"Yes," I said quickly.

"Great," Jeremiah said, "they'll see you then. And I hope to see you soon."

"Me, too," I said. Before I could thank him, the line went dead.

I turned off the phone, a dumb smile plastered across my face. I had an interview at OTJ! And all because I'd chickened out on my first-ever ride in the city. If I had persevered on that summer day long since past, I wouldn't now be lying in bed looking out over the neighbor's garden wondering if the coolest messenger company in the city would think I was good enough to be one of them.

Selma used to say, "Careful what you wish for, my sweet," whenever I announced that I was going after something I absolutely had to have—a seat on the class council, a win in an event I hadn't previously run, an after-school job that would help me save for a car of my own. And she'd almost always been right. Student council had been an exercise in frustration given the favoritism shown to a handful of members by the faculty advisor, a teacher barely out of college. Winning an event that wasn't mine only pissed off my teammates, and working at the country club reminded me that I was an object of pity mingled with fascination among some members of the greater Signal Mountain community.

But what was the worst that could happen if I joined OTJ? Maybe my luck was turning.

Selma also used to say, "You make your own luck." I hoped this was one of those times.

"You run the 3000? That was my event in high school," Leslie Jacob said, smiling at me as we sat together in the loft over the garage that housed OTJ.

"No way," I said. "Where did you go to high school?"

"Just outside Columbus, Ohio. What about you?"

"Chattanooga, Tennessee."

"Believe it or not, I've actually seen Rock City and Ruby Falls," Leslie informed me.

"That's awesome," I said, smiling back at her.

So far, our conversation had felt more like a meeting between two potential friends than an official job interview. We'd talked about how long we'd lived in the city—at thirteen years, she had me beat significantly—along with our favorite restaurants in the Village, the type of bikes we rode and the best places to run in the city. Hands down, we agreed, the reservoir at Central Park.

"Because it smells like water, not piss," Leslie had said, and I'd nodded, knowing exactly what she meant. Finding a place in the city to run—or walk, for that matter—where you weren't constantly assailed by the stench of urine was a serious challenge, and not one I would have expected before moving here.

By the time we got around to messengering, I was completely relaxed. The scent of coffee was strong, and the loft was clean and spacious, with granite counters and black appliances. The dark furniture balanced out the light from the high windows, while the well-worn wood floors looked inviting somehow, their flaws contributing a homey, lived-in feel to the loft's high ceilings and plentiful open space.

"Can you tell me a little about why you're thinking of leaving Mercury's?" she asked.

I hesitated. I didn't want to badmouth the Boneta brothers, not when they'd given me a chance.

"Jeremiah mentioned that perhaps you weren't welcome because of your gender?" Leslie prompted.

"Not being welcome is one way of putting it."

"In many ways, messing is a man's world. And men don't always respond well when we invade what they perceive to be 'their' territory."

"Tell me about it," I said, my voice more bitter than I intended.

I found myself giving her the blow-by-blow of Fido's assault the week before. Leslie listened, nodding and commenting sympathetically in all the right places much as Selma used to do. When I'd finished my story, I stared down at the table, remembering how Selma had always come to the rescue when I needed her—a Band-Aid with puppies on it if I skinned my knee, a piece of apple pie and cup of lemon ginger tea if I was upset. Since she'd gotten sick I'd been on my own, and now I wasn't so sure I'd done a very good job looking after myself.

"A similar thing happened to me when I was just starting out," Leslie told me, turning her coffee mug around on the table. "Only it was a guy from a different company, so the guys on my team went looking for the prick and, well, informed him that it wasn't okay to pick on female riders."

"Awesome," I said.

"I thought so. Have you been back on the bike since the accident?"

"I rode here from the shop on East Third."

"How did it go?"

I hesitated again. What would she want to hear? The truth, probably. "Honestly, at first, I found myself looking over my shoulder for him. It took about ten blocks, but I finally settled in."

"Good," she said. "That's really good. Some people aren't able to get back in the saddle after a fall. That's not a judgment—we're all who we are because of our experiences. But it would be a liability for a messenger. Tell me, what do you like best about the job?"

I glanced out the window above our heads, watching a pair of pigeons fluttering toward and about each other. "It's hard to narrow down. I like the freedom, knowing I'm on the move while so many other people are landlocked, anchored all day to one spot. I like the energy of the city, sleepy in the morning, revved up all day, impatient in the afternoon when everyone just wants to get the job done and go home. And I like getting glimpses of different companies and industries. This one time, I delivered a bottle of wine to a guy who gets paid by restaurants and caterers to pick their wine list. I mean, who even knew that career was an option?"

Leslie was nodding. "That is a great part of the job, isn't it? Okay, last question: Where do you see yourself five years from now?"

"In school," I said, "running."

Doh. I almost slapped my forehead. The answer had come out automatically, and probably had just ruined any chance I'd ever had of landing a spot at OTJ.

But Leslie was nodding again. "I appreciate your honesty. Messengering is a high-turnover job, and a dangerous one, as you know. But I like your attitude, and Jeremiah says you're a natural. His opinion carries a lot of weight as you probably know. So here's the story: I'd like to offer you a spot on our team. Does that interest you, Ash?"

"Of course." I grinned. "Totally!"

She laughed. "Normally I would say sleep on it and get back to me tomorrow, but it sounds like you've already made up your mind."

"I could get back to you tomorrow," I said a little uncertainly.

"No, I love the enthusiasm." She went through the terms— their riders were employees, not contractors, and earned a dollar more per delivery at each level than we did at Mercury's. "You'll be eligible for benefits after ninety days, but in the meantime, you can buy health insurance through the company for a reduced fee."

"That's okay," I said. "I have my own."

A stipulation of Selma's will had been that her estate should be used to pay health insurance premiums until I was twenty-five. She knew me well. I would never have spent the money if I'd had a choice. Insurance seemed like a colossal waste of money.

Leslie's eyebrows twitched upward at this news, but she continued: "You may already know this, but it's fairly typical to finish out the week for your current company when switching to a new one. Should we plan on seeing you next Monday morning at seven-fifteen sharp?"

"Yes, ma'am."

"Call me Leslie," she said, holding out her hand as she stood up. The interview was at an end.

Later, as I rode to Chelsea through light rain and stronger wind, I wondered how to quit Mercury's. Did I blame Fido? Mention Jeremiah and OTJ? Or did I just stop showing up like a couple of other riders had done since I'd started working there?

In the end, I didn't have to tell anyone about Fido. Steph had already blown the whistle on the bastard, and all the dispatchers who were on shift when I got there at noon waved at me more sympathetically than they usually did.

"Victor wants to talk to you," Steph said, her hand cupped over the mouthpiece of her receiver.

I nodded, suddenly nervous. I had left word that my bike would be ready sometime today. Was I in trouble for missing Thursday and Friday?

"Ashley! Have a seat," Victor said, jumping up from his desk when he saw me. "Can I get you something? Coffee, tea, water?"

"No, I'm fine." I sat down in one of the worn chairs facing his desk.

"Okay, my gir—I mean, you." He smiled nervously and perched on the corner of his desk, piled with papers and receipts and candy bar wrappers much as it had been when he'd offered me the job months earlier. "I understand there was some unpleasantness last week. Something to do with Aaron?"

I blinked. I'd sort of forgotten that Fido had a real name. "Yes. Actually, I wanted to tell you that I'm, well, I'm thinking of moving on to another company."

He nodded. "I'm not surprised. A girl's gotta do what she's gotta do. Where are you headed?"

"On the Job."

"Huh. They don't usually hire rookies. Good for you, Lake. No hard feelings?"

I shook the hand he offered. "I thought I'd finish out the week."

"Of course," he said, and waved a hand. "Go ahead and get back out there. And please, let me know if there's anything I can do to make your remaining time here go smoothly."

Bemused, I returned to the main room where Steph was just finishing a call.

"Lunch?" I asked, pausing beside her desk.

"Hell, yeah," she said, and picked up one of her many designer knock-off purses. "You can tell me what happened on the way."

We walked a block and a half to a Mexican joint. By the time we got there, I'd filled her in on all the relevant details.

"OTJ? Holy crap. You are the shit," Steph said, staring at me as we waited in line.

"I'm not, but my friend Jeremiah is. Or should I say Spidey."

"Wait, you're friends with Spidey?"

"Sort of. Not really. I met him my first week in the city, but I barely know him. I'm not really sure why he got me the job."

"Sheesh. Didn't know I was only two degrees away from bonafide messenger royalty."

The movie *Six Degrees of Separation* had come out earlier in the year, and everyone I knew in New York had become obsessed with how many degrees separated them from assorted celebrities.

"You start next week?" Steph asked.

"Yep."

"Lucky duck. I'll miss you, girl. Come see me sometime, okay?" she asked, slipping her arm around my shoulders.

"I will," I said, leaning into her half-embrace. I liked Steph, and had grown used to our daily interactions in person and on the phone. I would miss her, and no one else from Mercury's. Not a single other person.

Apparently it really was time to move on.

A few nights later, I was waiting on the sidewalk outside Drew's apartment building when a Trans-Am with neon pink windshield wipers—probably from Jersey, I thought automatically—slowed beside me. A teenaged boy with slicked-back hair and a gold chain dangling from his throat leaned out the passenger window. "Hey, baby. Wanna party?"

How original. I was about to retort with a certain gesture accompanied by a handful of the more wicked curses I'd picked up from my esteemed colleagues when Drew ducked out of the building.

"Too late," he said to the boy, sliding his arm around my shoulders. "She already has plans."

"Sorry, man," the boy said, and the car took off with a screech of tires.

I pushed away from Drew. "I could've handled that."

I'd gotten used to dealing with jerks, riding my bike around with my hair tucked up under my helmet. I was mistaken for a boy all the time, especially by cabbies who didn't think a woman could or would do my job. Recently I'd realized I was starting to think that a day that passed without at least one verbal wrangle was strangely disappointing.

"I was just joking," Drew said. "Are you mad, seriously?"

I shook my head and started walking west. "Nah. Come on. Race you to the train." And I took off.

"No fair! Cheater," Drew complained, running after me.

Tonight we were going to the cheap movies on Eighth Avenue to catch Disney's *Homeward Bound: The Incredible Journey*, in which two dogs and a cat try to make their way home to San Francisco through the rugged Sierra Nevada mountain range. I was convinced that we would be the only childless adults in the theater, but let Drew talk me into going. He'd already seen the movie twice, and pronounced it "devastatingly heartwarming." An oxymoron, I pointed out.

We took the A train to Columbus Circle, where we ascended into the noise of city street life. The sun was setting, not that it ever got dark in Manhattan. We walked a block south to the theater, bought our tickets from the machine, picked up popcorn and Twizzlers, and went to look for seats. Children under the age of ten occupied most of the seats in the theater, with an occasional adult trying to maintain order. We settled in, munching popcorn and listening to the competing strains of voices singing assorted tunes, most of which I was pretty sure I recognized from *Sesame Street*. All except a small boy in front of us who was mumbling the words to what sounded like "Here Comes Peter Cottontail."

I gestured toward him. "I bet he's seen this movie twice, too.'"

Drew threw a piece of popcorn at me.

"So," he said casually, "do you want kids?"

Whoa. A warning bell sounded in my head. Talking about children with Drew was not like talking about children with Austin.

Drew and I were arguably capable of reproducing together.

"I guess so," I said.

"Me, too. With the right person, of course."

"Of course."

I took a Twizzler from the package and began to nibble on it, bending it in half in order to bite equal amounts from either end, then bending it again and again until there was nothing left.

Drew watched me. "You know, you always eat Twizzlers like that."

"You better have some, or they'll be gone before the previews end."

"Like last week?" He reached for the bag and held it away from me. "How about I hold these?"

"Okay." I took the popcorn from his lap and started in on it. I'd only had time to grab a burrito on the way to Drew's after work—my next to last day at Mercury's, woo hoo—hardly enough to tide me over until dinner. "Fine with me."

He watched me chowing on the popcorn. "Damn, Ash, I swear I never knew a girl who could eat like you."

"It's because of the bike," I said. "I burn like a million calories a day. Hand me the Coke, will you?"

The Twizzlers were gone by the time the cat went over the waterfall. I had to admit, the movie was good. I even came close to crying when the dogs and cat—spoiler alert—were reunited in the wild. And when they—another spoiler alert—finally found their family, after surviving porcupines, mountain lions, and a thousand-mile wilderness trek? Devastatingly heartwarming, indeed.

Later, when we were back in the Village walking home after a satisfyingly large dinner, Drew reached for my hand.

"What are you doing for Thanksgiving?" he asked as we angled down a side street away from Sixth Avenue.

"I don't know." I watched our feet as we walked. He was wearing ankle-high Doc Marten's while I was wearing dark green Converse sneakers. Our feet moved in unison, jeans-clad legs swinging in time with our linked hands. "Probably have it with Austin."

"That's what I thought." He paused. "I was wondering, though. What if you came home with me for a few days instead?"

"You mean, to Buffalo?"

"Yes, to Buffalo."

"Um..." I chewed on my lip as we continued down the block, street lamps casting shadows in competing directions.

We were almost to the corner when he turned me to face him, his fingers gentle on my shoulders. "No pressure, Ash. I just think you'd like my family, that's all. And I know they'd love you."

I could see that he wanted to kiss me, and I wanted it, too, I was pretty sure. Wanted to feel his cheek against mine, his arms holding me. But I backed up a pace and stepped around him.

"Okay," I said. "I'll think about it. Um, thanks."

"Um, you're welcome."

We walked back to his apartment in silence. When we reached the downstairs door, I held back. He glanced at me, frowning.

"I thought you were coming up?"

"I think I might head home. I'm really tired, and tomorrow's my last day at Mercury's, so..."

Drew pushed his hair back from his face and shrugged. "Okay. Well, good luck tomorrow."

"Thanks." I leaned forward and pecked him on the cheek, but he caught me before I could turn away and tugged me closer, kissing me for real. I let him, trying to lose myself in sensation, but all I could think about was his invitation to celebrate Thanksgiving in Buffalo. With his family.

Finally he pulled away. "Why do I feel like I'm the only one in this kiss?"

"I'm sorry," I said, and backed away. "I'll call you, okay?"

"Right."

I waved once and then jogged away, picking up speed as I approached Washington Square. I wasn't running as much anymore, mainly on the weekends, which was okay temporarily but not long-term. At some point, I was going to have to figure out what I wanted. In more ways than one.

CHAPTER TWELVE

I hadn't realized how tense Fido and his goons had made me until I walked into OTJ Monday morning and was greeted *Cheers-*style.

"Yo, Fire Girl," Jeremiah said, giving me a bro hug.

Unlike at Mercury's, the other riders actually came over to greet me and introduce themselves. There was Dash, a skinny, twenty-something Irish punk with a Mohawk and eye make-up; Simone, a German woman who had been in New York for almost a decade; Clark, AKA Superman, a Jersey kid who looked about my age; Morrison, a messenger from San Francisco who had stopped in New York on his way home from the inaugural Messenger World Championships in Berlin, and stayed; Bennie, a thirty-something New Yorker with massive quads and a Jamaican accent; and Treat, a beanpole of a woman from D.C. whose nickname apparently derived from her fondness for Halloween. Leslie and Mark were there, too, as the official dispatchers.

Jobs were also handled differently from at Mercury's, I soon learned. The first assignments of the day, booked in advance, were doled out based on seniority. From there on out, Mark and Leslie tried to divide the work as evenly as possible among riders in different areas of the city.

"We find that morale stays higher if our riders are all pulling as close to the same amount of weight as we can reasonably manage," Leslie explained, outfitting me with a company pager and clipboard as Mark assigned jobs.

By seven-thirty, everyone was on their way out into the city streets, including me. What a difference a few days could make, I thought as I headed toward the nearby financial district. Without the stress of the morning melee at Mercury's, where riders jostled each other and vied for the dispatchers' attention, and without Fido and his buddies staring me down, I felt positively light as I zipped along the morning streets, dodging the occasional pedestrian and double-parked car.

Funny how sometimes you don't realize how anxious you are until the source of your angst is removed. Today was business as usual, really, since I had only switched companies, not careers. And yet, it felt like a new job whose rules and expectations I already understood.

I was going to like OTJ, I thought, slowing for a red light before weaving through the morning rush.

No doubt about it.

A few nights later, Drew and I picked up takeout and a video to watch at my place. Austin had the night off, but he and Tommy had dinner and dancing plans, so Drew and I had the apartment to ourselves. We ate pizza and drank beer during the first half of the movie, a classic romantic comedy starring Katherine Hepburn and Cary Grant. After we'd eaten, we cuddled on the couch. We missed the last part of the movie—Drew wanted to try again to seduce me. Between my work and his school schedule, his roommates and mine, we didn't get much alone time together.

The movie had already ended when we heard a key turn in the front door. We sprang apart guiltily, grabbing a blanket from the back of the couch. Austin shoved the door open, slammed it shut, and strode toward his bedroom without even looking at us.

"I thought he was with Tommy," Drew whispered, pulling his T-shirt down over his stomach.

"He was," I said, stuffing my bra between a couple of cushions. Then I handed Drew the remote and padded down the hallway to Austin's room. "A, it's me. Can I come in?"

"No. Go away."

"Nice try. I'm coming in."

He didn't answer, so I slipped inside and closed the door again, drowning out SportsCenter. I couldn't see him, but his breathing, harsh in the otherwise quiet room, carried down from the loft.

"I'm coming up," I said, and started up the ladder.

"Go away," he repeated, sniffing.

"I don't think so."

At the top, I climbed onto the queen-sized mattress and sat cross-legged in the middle. Austin was curled up against the wall, his back to me.

"What's up, dude?"

"Nothing." He sniffed again. "I'm fine."

"I can totally see that."

He rolled over and looked at the ceiling, only a few feet above the mattress. Abruptly he sighed, long and dramatic. "Okay, I'm not fine."

"What happened?"

"Tommy doesn't want to see me ever again." Austin shut his eyes, brow furrowed.

"What do you mean? I thought you guys were good?"

"We were." He rubbed his forehead, and I wondered if he realized that his mother did the same thing when she was upset. "At least, I thought we were. Tonight we went to dinner and back to his place, and we were on the couch eating ice cream, and I decided now or never. So I kissed him."

At first picturing Austin kissing another man had made me uncomfortable. You never see men kissing in American culture. Women kissing other women, yes, but the closest you come in our culture to seeing men physically together is when they roll around on the football field and slap each other's asses. After hanging around Austin's group of friends the last few months, though, I no longer even noticed if two people kissing were the same sex or not.

"How did he react?" I asked.

"At first he kissed me back. But then he backed off." Austin stared at the ceiling. "He said we could never be more than friends. I asked how he could say that when we both know there's more between us than friendship, and he—he just said it again. He said it didn't matter what was between us. So then I told him I didn't want another friend, and he said fine, we wouldn't be friends. Then he told me I should leave."

"And you did?"

Austin nodded. "He's probably already finished the fucking ice cream by now."

"I'm sorry," I said, sliding closer on the bed. "Give him a few days. Maybe he'll change his mind."

"I don't think so. He was pretty definite." Austin exhaled a short breath and pressed his clenched fists to his forehead. "God, I was so stupid. I can't believe I was so wrong."

"I don't think you were. I've seen how he looks at you, and it's not the way he looks at Ben or José or anyone else. Drew's noticed it, too."

Austin glanced at me. "Shit, I'm sorry. Drew's here, isn't he? I didn't even think."

"Don't worry, we were just watching a movie."

"Yeah, right. You finally getting some action?"

I shrugged, suddenly very interested in his ceiling. "Maybe a little."

"About time, girl. I thought you were going to be the big V forever."

"I still am. Nothing wrong with abstinence."

"Oh. My bad." Austin sighed again. "I guess we won't all be hanging out anymore."

I brushed Austin's hair back from his forehead. He shot me a look, eyebrows raised. Usually I didn't initiate physical contact, except to flick or punch him.

"Tommy will come around," I said. "I have faith. Don't give up, okay?"

He closed his eyes and expelled a long breath, and then he nodded. "Okay." He sat up and scooted closer to me. "Thanks, Ash," he said, and hugged me. "I mean it. Thanks for listening. I totally feel better."

I hugged him back. His body felt different from Drew's, bulkier and harder. But it still felt good to hold him. "You're welcome, A." Then, because all this hugging was still new to me, I pulled away. "We were just watching TV. Why don't you come hang out?"

"You sure I'm not interrupting?"

"Of course not, dork."

Drew had settled on a sit-com and was giggling like a little girl when we returned.

I sat down on the couch, elbowing him. "Good show?"

"The writing's actually decent. Hey, Austin."

"Hey." Austin sat down on the other side of him. Canned laughter echoed in the room. Austin frowned as he pulled a scrap of cloth from under a cushion, and then his brow cleared. "I believe this is yours, Ash?"

My bra. I grabbed it from him. Austin and Drew both snickered as I stalked to my room and threw the bra inside.

"You guys are so juvenile," I said, and sat back down on the couch. "It's not like I have cooties."

"She used to," Austin told Drew, "back in elementary school. Seriously wicked cooties."

"I'll bet," Drew said.

I pretended to ignore them. We sat on the couch in the dark living room, light from the television screen glowing on the walls and on our faces. It was nice to be home with Austin and Drew. Now all we were missing was Tommy.

On Sunday morning, Drew and I met for breakfast at Michael and Zoe's, a tiny bakery on Second Avenue that had the best hazelnut coffee I'd ever tasted. We ordered half a dozen muffins and two large cups of coffee, but by the time we'd paid there weren't any seats left inside.

"My place or yours?" I asked.

"Yours. Chris is hosting a study session."

Autumn wind whipped the streets. We were feeling lazy so, muffins and Sunday paper in hand, we caught a cab across the Village. We split the fare and strolled up the steps to my building, unlocked the door, and walked into the apartment in time to see Tommy, clad only in a towel, disappearing down the hall into Austin's room.

Drew and I looked at each other.

"Did you see that?" he whispered loudly.

"Um, yeah. Looks like things worked out after all."

"At least somebody's getting some," Drew murmured.

I punched him. "I thought you valued what we have."

"I do," he said, laughing. "No need to be so sensitive."

In the kitchen, we poured orange juice and set the still-warm muffins on a plate. Then we each took a section of the *Times* to the dining alcove. Perfect Sunday morning, I thought, smiling at Drew across the table. Selma would have agreed.

I glanced out the back window, where the trees were swaying in the wind. There were so many things I wished I could share with Selma—the view from the World Trade Center, the occasionally brilliant live music at Washington Square, the feeling of flying on the back of a bike down Ninth Avenue, where you could go forty blocks in a row with greens all the way. Shakespeare in the Park, the Met, MoMA, the American Museum of Natural History—and, of course, the New York Public Library. Selma wasn't a city person, but she would have loved visiting Austin and me here in our city.

I turned my attention back to the newspaper, full of tangible reminders of what a terrible place the world could be. Good for Selma, that she didn't have to read about the rise of Neo-Nazism in Europe; the hundreds of people being shot by snipers in Sarajevo each month; the debate over the ethics of cloning; the continued progression of the AIDS epidemic. Truly, there was at least as much misery in the world as happiness, I thought, turning the newspaper pages one after the other. Maybe more.

Only two muffins remained when Austin came into the living room, freshly showered.

"Hey," he said, not quite meeting my eyes.

"Hey. You okay?"

"Fine."

"Want a muffin?" Drew offered.

"Nah, I'm not hungry."

Tommy walked in just then. "Good morning," he said, nodding at us. He touched Austin on the shoulder. "I'm going."

They walked away, voices low. We heard the door open and close a few minutes later, and then Austin wandered back in and sat down at the table.

I touched his arm. "Did you and Tommy work things out?"

"Yeah," he said, his voice oddly flat. "Can I have a muffin?"

"Of course." I watched him closely. "Are you sure you're okay?"

"Just drop it, Ash." He devoured the muffin in a few bites, then stood up. "I'm going for a run."

Drew lifted his eyebrows at me as Austin all but stomped from the room, but waited until the apartment door closed behind my roommate before declaring, "That was bizarre."

I pushed my chair back. "What's up with that?"

"At least they're hanging out again."

"I'm not so sure that's a good thing."

"Me either." Drew stood up. "Hey, do you want to go for a walk? I was thinking of checking out Tower."

And the perfect Sunday continued. Sort of—as we cleaned up the kitchen, I couldn't stop thinking about Austin and Tommy. It wasn't like Austin not to tell me everything. Then again, with our opposite work schedules and our separate extra-curriculars, we hadn't seen each other as much lately. He was usually with his other friends, and I was either with Drew or sleeping.

"They'll be fine," Drew said, his hand on my shoulder as I paused by the dining room window, looking out.

"I know." I started gathering the newspaper for recycling. "Want to ride bikes to Tower? You could take Austin's."

"I would rather eat week-old leftovers out of a Midtown trash can. Anyway, I just had a better idea," he said, leaning in to kiss me. "We could stay here, all alone, and read the paper in bed. Or something…"

As his lips traced a feather-light path along the edge of my chin to the sensitive skin just behind my right ear, I shivered. Then I pushed him away.

"You can't just dangle a trip to Tower and then take it back. Come on. Last one there is a rotten—oh, wait, that's right, you're going on foot, aren't you?"

"Ha, ha," Drew said. "Seriously, Ash, are we ever going to talk about it?"

"About what?" I putzed about, pretending to look for my bike key lock.

"About why you don't seem to want to sleep with me."

Apparently this was the weekend for relationship show-downs. His bluntness left little room for equivocation on my part. Sighing, I took Drew's hand and led him to the couch.

"I'm sorry," I said. "You've been so patient, more than I have a right to expect, I know."

He made a frustrated sound. "It's not like that. Yes, of course I would prefer to be doing more than just sleeping in a bed with you. But I knew your situation when we started, and I'm the one who said we should take it slowly."

"Just not this slowly?" I asked, tracing his palm with my fingers. His hands were strong but soft, whereas mine were calloused from my grips.

"If you felt about me the way I feel about you, I don't think we'd be where we are now." He looked me in the eye, practically daring me to be honest.

And I should have been. I should have told him that while I liked kissing and cuddling and even sleeping in a bed with him, I didn't feel any urge to do more. What we did together was enjoyable, but I was just as happy with the occasional round of self-service. Happier, even, because then I didn't have to worry about his feelings.

"I'm just tired all the time because of work," I said instead, turning his hand over and fitting it into mine. "That's all. And it's different for girls. I want my first time to be right, you know?"

He sighed and leaned his head on my shoulder, uncharacteristically melancholy. "Yeah, I know."

Hating that I was the cause of his sadness, I proceeded to dig myself in even deeper: "Does the invitation to Buffalo still stand? Because I think I'd like to come with you, if you'll still have me."

Drew perked up. "Are you serious?"

"Of course I'm serious. Is that a yes?"

"It is definitely a yes."

"Good," I said, and leaned over to kiss him. "I can't wait."

But later that day, after Tower and lunch on Sixth Street and a walk around Washington Square, I told Drew I had to go home to corner Austin. While I cleaned every inch of the apartment and waited for my roommate to appear, I retraced my relationship history, such as it was. Why *didn't* I want to throw myself at Drew? Why, in fact, had I never wanted to throw myself at anyone? I'd had crushes in high school, usually on completely unattainable guys who didn't know I existed. Selma had encouraged open and honest communication about dating and sex, but she'd also admitted to being relieved when I chose to date Eric James, the soccer player everyone in town knew wanted to wait.

Eric and I had fooled around, but neither of us had any clue what to do. After a few mildly unpleasant groping sessions in his car, we'd agreed that we didn't have to be like everyone else at school. We could be together without the pressure of sex hanging over us, we agreed, congratulating ourselves on our ability to rise above the cultural norms of the American teenager. I'd been relieved to dodge a bullet—that's how I'd thought of it then, as if having sex with Eric, who I genuinely liked and who I knew cared about me, was something akin to a gunshot wound.

What was wrong with me? Was I naturally frigid? Inescapably narcissistic? Or was I so afraid of being a jinx that I couldn't stand to let anyone close, really close?

At ten-thirty, I gave up on Austin and went to bed, but only after checking the dead bolts and the window locks at least twice. New York was a scary place, as I well knew. Especially if you were all alone in the middle of the night.

Why had I wanted to be alone, again? Just then, shivering in my cold loft, my ears straining to hear any sound that didn't belong, I couldn't, for the life of me, remember.

CHAPTER THIRTEEN

By late November all the leaves on the trees in Washington Square had died and fallen into the gutters. I was wearing the same outfit almost every day to work now—thermal underwear, a fleece turtleneck, scarf, sheepskin-lined gloves, and a fleece cap under my bike helmet, rounded out with a GoreTex rain suit on wet days. Despite my seasonally appropriate apparel, my ears, toes, and fingertips always seemed cold. Sometimes in the middle of the night I would wake up to find my feet freezing, even in wool socks tucked beneath a down comforter.

OTJ continued to be as friendly and welcoming as Mercury's had been cliquish and dysfunctional. Often at the end of the work day I would head with the other riders to a bar just off Canal Street, where we would order mountains of food and gallons of drink and share stories of clients we'd dealt with, traffic situations we'd managed to survive, the latest bike-related gossip. At other times, we would talk for hours without even mentioning our bikes, instead dissecting our childhoods, families, hometowns. After only a month, my OTJ colleagues knew about the plane crash, Selma, even my waffling over Drew. No wonder everyone wanted to work there. The people were awesome, especially Leslie and Mark, who managed not only to be good bosses but also friends with their employees.

Leslie's college roommate, Camilla, a restaurant owner, regularly came out with us for drinks. When she found out I was a runner, she told me about her younger cousin who ran the 400 and 800 meters at Southern Arizona University in Tucson. SAU wasn't top twenty-five material, but it did boast one of the stronger Division I programs in the West.

"You'll have to meet Nicki," Camilla said. "I'm sure she'd love to run with you when she comes home for Christmas. Her parents live in Brooklyn, but she usually comes into the city to run at Central Park."

"Sounds great," I said, though I seriously doubted that an SAU runner would give a random friend of a friend of her cousin's a second thought.

Leslie and Mark were happy to give me time off at Thanksgiving. Messenger work tended to slow down during the holidays, Thanksgiving in particular. Frankly, Leslie told me, they would have been happy to close the offices for the week, but some of the riders couldn't afford to miss that much work.

Austin had taken my announcement that I would be celebrating turkey day in Buffalo in stride. He and Tommy were planning to spend the holiday with Tommy's parents, he admitted when I broached the topic a few days after the "most awkward weekend ever," as Drew and I referred to it.

"Wow, meeting the parents," I said, fishing. "You must be getting pretty serious."

"I could say the same about you and Drew."

Touché.

Austin had been shockingly closed-mouth about his relationship with Tommy. Drew said I was just annoyed because while I could dish out silence, I couldn't take it. He may or may not have had a point. Either way, I'd stopped prying, mainly because Austin had told me to "stop your damn prying."

Whatever. It was his life. Anyway, not like we saw each other all that much. When Austin did spend the night at our place, Tommy was usually with him. The group dynamic hardly contributed to long, deep discussions of inner-most feelings. They may have been gay, but they were still guys. As, apparently, was I when it came to emotional sharing, according to Drew.

The day before Thanksgiving, I caught a cab to Drew's, athletic bag slung over my shoulder. I hadn't known what to pack so I'd over-packed, naturally. I just hoped Drew and I weren't taking the same clothes, since we both tended to dress in jeans, khakis, and flannel shirts. It would be embarrassing to spend the long weekend at his family home in coordinated outfits.

Drew buzzed me in and I traipsed up three flights of stairs to find him in his bedroom throwing underwear and socks into an athletic bag. He hadn't showered or shaved yet.

"Um," I said, pausing in the doorway, "didn't that girl want to meet at the park at nine?"

A few weeks earlier Drew had posted a message on the NYU ride board, offering to pay for gas in exchange for a ride to Buffalo. A freshman from a town near his had responded.

"I'm ready." He pulled his NYU sweatshirt over his head, zipped the bag up, and leaned toward me, pressing his lips quickly to mine. "Morning."

"Morning," I said, and backed into the hallway. "I see you haven't brushed your teeth yet, either."

"I was just going to do that," he said, and detoured toward the bathroom.

Boys. Sheesh.

We made it to Washington Square at two minutes to nine. A blonde girl was waiting at the curb in a black Saab, hazard lights blinking.

"Nice car," I said to Drew, and then belatedly remembered that I could probably have talked Selma's attorney into letting me buy one just like it. After all, German engineering was freakishly reliable.

The girl lowered her window partway. "Are you Drew?"

He nodded. "This is Ashley."

"I'm Sarah." She smiled, looking freshly showered and decidedly Republican, I decided, in a white collared shirt and red blazer, her hair restrained by a thin gold barrette.

We set our bags in the trunk beside a set of matching luggage, then climbed into the car. Drew sat in front so that he wouldn't get car sick. As we headed crosstown to FDR, I wondered what someone like Sarah was doing at NYU, known for its progressiveness. Columbia seemed more her style.

Up FDR to the Third Avenue Bridge and I-87, the New York Thruway. Cars heading into the city were bumper to bumper. On our side, traffic flowed easily.

"Do you like Peter Gabriel?" Sarah asked, glancing over her shoulder at me after we'd reached the expressway.

"Totally."

Drew smiled back at me as if to say, *See? She's not all bad.*

Soon we were speeding north along the Hudson, "Red Rain" rendering conversation between the front and back seats next to impossible. I leaned my head back and looked out the window, watching the landscape change as we left the city behind.

Exhausted as ever from work, I fell asleep a few minutes later and only woke up when we stopped at lunchtime. This vacation I was going to get caught up on my sleep, if nothing else.

After our pit stop, I hummed along to the music—Van Morrison this time—and stared out the window again. This was my first time traveling north of the city since moving here with Austin. I'd been born at around this latitude, but the only place I knew even passingly well was Oshkosh, and I hadn't been there in years. The only other memory of the North I could conjure at will was Lake Michigan stretching out across the horizon, like the ocean.

In the South, I knew what to expect on a road trip: Cracker Barrel and Shoney's restaurants; signs for local businesses such as Bubba's Boots, Honest Abe Log Homes, and PoFolks Restaurant; rolling fields of corn, tobacco, and soybeans; signs for local caves and Civil War battlefields; fireworks stores built just off the interstate with huge multi-colored signs proclaiming their wares in letters that were often taller than the store itself; and ancient El Dorados with tinted windows speeding past pick-up trucks with Confederate flags in the back window, country music blaring.

Upstate New York held none of these things. There were pick-up trucks, but mostly they were fully loaded family vehicles with shiny bodies and hubcaps. Restaurant billboards advertised chains like McDonald's and Wendy's. And I only saw a couple of stores that featured lawn ornaments, with statues of deer and little Dutch people. Frankly, their selections weren't that impressive.

Up front, Drew and Sarah got to talking, and it turned out that she was studying government and public policy. She planned to go to law school and become a legal advocate for the disadvantaged. One weekend a month, she volunteered at an AIDS resource group that delivered meals and groceries to homebound AIDS patients. My initial impression of her had been about as far off as you could get. Another difference from the South—where I came from, money was almost always a marker of conservative "family" values. But in the North, the rich were just as likely to be progressive-minded as the middle classes, it seemed. More so, even.

Seven hours after we'd left the city, Drew announced that we were almost there. His hometown, Fairview, located on Lake Erie's south shore, was basically a suburb of Buffalo, only fifteen miles away. His father's pediatrics practice was in the city, as was the community college where his mother taught English literature. At a minor metropolis called Jamestown, we left the freeway and drove north, gradually climbing a long hill. A few miles later, from the crest of the hill, I could see a town just below us extending north toward Lake Erie.

"That's the Denny's where I used to hang out in high school," Drew said as we drove down Fairview's main street.

"You mean with all the cool kids who smoked and wore black?" I teased.

"Exactly. I used to sit in there with my friends trying to write song verses. I wanted to be a musician, but then I couldn't get a hang of the piano. Or the guitar. So that dream died."

"Now he sits around diners in New York," I told Sarah, "watching people and scribbling in his little notebooks."

"Turn left at the next light." Drew turned in his seat and grabbed my hand, smiling. "We're almost home."

I wondered if he could feel my pulse pounding in my fingers as we turned from the main road into a more residential area, leaving behind gas stations and fast food restaurants. Was he as nervous as I was? But then again, why should he be? I was the stranger, the one who would be meeting his family for the first time.

All at once I wanted to be back in New York with Austin and Tommy, getting ready to catch the train to Philadelphia. They would have let me come along if I'd asked, I knew. But I would be a third wheel, despite their assurances to the contrary. If Selma were still alive, I would have had a home of my own to visit. But then, if Selma had been alive, everything would have been different.

As we traversed streets that reminded me of home, I remembered the previous Thanksgiving. It had been a difficult time, with Selma weak from chemo and radiation. We were supposed to go next door for an early dinner, but in the end I had to call Claire and tell her Selma was too ill to make the short journey. As soon as we hung up, Bruce and Claire had packed up the food and brought it next door.

"If you can't come to Thanksgiving dinner," Claire had said, giving me a hug, "then Thanksgiving dinner will just have to come to you."

While they unloaded the meal, I'd gone up to the attic to look for the leaf to the dining room table, stopping short when I saw the box that held the scrapbook Selma had made me about the plane crash. Inside were clippings from the *Chicago Sun Times*, the *Tribune*, the *New York Times*, even *Life* magazine. She had pasted them into a photo album along with the pictures from Disney World rescued from my parents' camera. Somehow, just seeing that box broke my semblance of control. I'd sat down on the thin fragment of carpet covering part of the attic floor, and I'd sobbed and sobbed, venting the fear and sorrow that I couldn't let anyone see. And then I went back downstairs and blamed my red eyes on attic dust, pinning a smile on my face throughout the meal Selma was too sick to enjoy.

This year would have to be better than that, wouldn't it?

Drew's neighborhood was just what I'd expected—a quiet, residential street where old trees stood sentinel over well-maintained yards and large, Victorian-style homes. Multi-colored Christmas lights lined the evenly trimmed bushes at the front of the Ryan house, while white icicle lights dangled from the gutters. The house, two stories tall and significantly more spacious-looking than Selma's bungalow, looked well-loved and well-lived in.

Drew and I retrieved our bags from the trunk and bid Sarah farewell. She would be back to get us on Sunday. The Saab was pulling away when Drew's front door opened, and I took a step back without meaning to.

"Don't worry," Drew said. "They're going to love you."

"If you say so." I followed him up the front walk.

The entire Ryan clan was there to greet us, shivering in the cold air—Drew's parents Ed and Judy, his sisters Beth and Katie, even Toby the golden retriever.

"Come on in, kids." Judy's voice carried over the chorus of greetings. "Let's get out of the cold."

We were swept into the warm foyer, the scent of baking pies wafting from the kitchen. Ed closed the front door while Drew hugged his mother and older sister and gave his younger sister a high-five. I looked around, taking in wall-to-wall carpeting, floor-to-ceiling bookshelves in the living room packed with books and knick-knacks, various objects of framed art hanging on the walls. Then Judy Ryan stepped forward and took my hand in hers.

"You must be Ashley. We've heard so much about you." She had pale skin and dark hair that was just beginning to turn gray. She also had Drew's eyes.

"Yes, ma'am." The *ma'am* just slipped out, making me sound Southern as all get out.

"Call me Judy," she said, releasing my hand with a reassuring squeeze. "We're so glad you could spend Thanksgiving with us."

"Thank you for having me," I said, glancing over at Drew. He was kneeling on the floor, rubbing Toby's belly and talking to the dog in a low, rumbling voice. "I've been looking forward to it."

Drew's father, who looked like him only with thinning hair and wire-rim glasses, stepped forward to shake my hand. "I'm Ed. Nice to meet you, Ashley. Drew tells us you haven't been to Western New York before. What do you think of our part of the world?"

"It's beautiful."

"I'm Beth," Drew's older sister said, stepping forward. Her brown hair, the same shade as Drew's and their father's, was about an inch long all over except her bangs, which were longer and dyed blonde. Multiple ear rings dangled from her crowded lobes, the largest of which were women's symbols. "Do you want me to show you where you can put your bag and get cleaned up?"

"Sure," I said, trying not to sound too relieved. "That would be great."

"Good idea," Judy put in. "Then we can get caught up before dinner. You haven't eaten yet, have you?"

"No, Mom," Drew said, standing up and brushing dog hair from the front of his denim shirt. "It's not even five. You want me to come with you, Ash?"

"That's okay."

Beth took my bag, ignoring my protests, and led me up a carpeted staircase with a polished wooden railing. Upstairs we turned down a hallway and ended up in a room with a queen-sized bed, wooden dressers, and a window that overlooked the back yard.

"This is Drew's old room," Beth said as she set my bag on the floor near a dresser. "Mom changed it into the guest room once he moved to the city for good."

"Where's Drew staying?" I asked.

Beth blinked. "I just assumed he was staying in here."

"Of course," I said. "I didn't know if your parents were cool with it, is all."

"You don't have to worry about Mom and Dad. I've broken them in. But meeting the parents can be kind of rough, can't it?" she added, leaning against the dresser.

"It would be, if... I mean, Drew and I aren't actually serious. I just don't have any family in the area, so he thought it would be nice for me to have Thanksgiving here."

"He's a good guy," Beth said. "If there were more like him, I might even be tempted to date men."

Apparently she wanted it known up front that she was gay, maybe to see how the small town girl from Tennessee would react.

"I think the limited pool is why I've never had to meet anyone's parents before," I said.

We smiled at each other across the room. Beth would be a good ally to have the next few days, I decided. Not that meeting Drew's family was anything like battle.

Dinner, however, almost qualified. That night, we sat around the oval oak table in the dining room for close to two hours. The Ryans were a political family, avidly arguing about welfare reform and capital punishment, environmental regulations and public education. Even Katie, a junior in high school who still wore braces, knew what was going on in the world. I watched their interaction, speaking up every once in a while but mostly content to sit back and observe Drew's family. He and his father were more conservative than Beth and their mother. Katie was the least convicted among them, still reaching her own conclusions about various issues. And Beth, unsurprisingly, was the most liberal.

"Capital punishment is flat-out wrong," she declared halfway through a dessert of ice-cream and cookies. "Our society is so racist, sexist, and homophobic that people are still convicted of crimes they didn't commit based on their skin color or who they sleep with. The majority of inmates on death row are African American. It's not right to treat people with disrespect and cruelty and then to murder them when they turn around and take it out on someone else."

"Oh, come on," Drew said. "You can't tell me that someone like Ted Bundy deserves to live after raping and murdering, what, thirty-five women or more? And Jeffrey Dahmer, what about him? He deserves to be treated with respect of any kind? Tell that to the families of his victims."

"Two wrongs, Drew. You know?" Beth shook her head.

Judy leaned forward. "Not only is it two wrongs, it's giving those in our government power that I for one would rather they not have. Who's to decide which criminals deserve to die? Our judges? I would hope not. Not when there are still judges like that one in Idaho, was it? He reduced a man's sentence last year for killing his wife to time served because it was understandable that the defendant was driven to murder when he found out his wife was having an affair. Next they'll be sentencing women to die for killing their abusive husbands."

"Let's not cloud the issues," Ed said. "This is not a case of too much government power. That's not even what the issue of capital punishment is about. I agree with Drew—there are some people who are so inherently evil that they don't deserve to be part of society. I don't want my taxes to go to their upkeep in prison. Think of the good that money could do, in domestic programs for the poor, for instance."

"So you're saying we should stoop to their level, murder the murderers because you don't want to pay for their room and board?" Judy shook her head. "That is so simplistic."

Ed shrugged, brown eyes sparkling behind his glasses. "Nothing wrong with simplicity, I always say."

I couldn't believe they were squabbling like this in front of us. Selma had never had anyone to disagree with, as far as I knew, and Austin's parents had only ever argued behind closed doors.

"Anyway," Drew put in, glancing at me, "in case you couldn't tell, Ash, my parents are ex-hippies. Before my Dad went to med school, they both had long hair and went to sit-ins."

"We even saw Martin Luther King speak once," Judy said. "For a few years, though, we worried we'd pressured our kids too much to be like us. Especially Drew—when he was in junior high, he went through a conservative stage that had his father and I saying to each other, 'So this is how our parents felt when we came home from college and told them that everything they believed in was wrong.'"

"Come on, Mom," Drew protested. "I wasn't that bad."

"You certainly were," his father said.

"We were both convinced that Drew was going to be another Alex P. Keaton, you know, from *Family Ties*," Judy told me, ignoring Drew's dirty look. "He had the suits and the briefcase, and for a while, if you asked him what he wanted to be when he grew up, he'd say, 'I don't care as long as I'm rich.'"

"That's right," Beth said. "He wanted to be a lawyer, didn't he?"

"What do you expect?" Drew asked, changing tactics. "It was the eighties. Everyone my age wanted to be rich. Right, Ash?"

"I never wanted to," I said.

Ironic, then, that I had been excessively wealthy most of my life without ever knowing it. I hadn't told Drew about the money yet. Only Austin knew; and probably, by now, Tommy.

"Busted." Beth grinned at her younger brother.

Drew stood up. "Anyone else want more ice cream? Anyone but Ashley, that is."

I threw my napkin at him while his family looked on, smiling indulgently.

Later that night Drew and I bundled up and ducked out of the house for a stroll around the neighborhood. We wandered along the sidewalk, holding hands and talking idly. I watched stars appear overhead as the sky darkened, feeling myself relax when I hadn't even known I was tense. Sensory overload from the city, probably. Here was a way of life I recognized, a town whose pace was familiar. Street lights and tall buildings didn't block out the stars, and there wasn't even a hint of diesel fumes or police sirens in the air, just chimney smoke and dying leaves rustling in the breeze.

True, everyone in their comfortable houses looked and talked and dressed alike, but for me, that was okay because I was one of them. For Austin and Tommy, though, could it ever be like this?

"You're awfully quiet," Drew said as a car passed, momentarily illuminating us. "You okay?"

"Just thinking. Why does it have to be so hard to stay where you come from? There were kids back in Tennessee who did it, but I always knew that wasn't me. Even if Selma was alive, I wouldn't have stayed. And here you are, with this amazing family, and you're off doing your own thing."

"Everyone has to find their own way, Ash. My family's great and they love me, and I love them. But my parents are the ones who raised me not to settle for just anything. I bet your aunt was the same way."

Of course he was right. What if his parents got sick, though? How would he feel then? What if Beth wrecked her car and died in a hospital three thousand miles from home? American life was too fractured, with families splintering left and right. Didn't they realize how lucky they were to have each other?

"You really think my family is amazing?" Drew asked.

The cold night air felt good against my cheeks, and Drew's eyes looked almost black. I reached up and kissed his cheek, feeling the scratch of stubble against my chin.

"Yes," I said, and skipped away.

"Hey!" Drew laughed, crunching through dead leaves behind me. "Wait up!"

CHAPTER FOURTEEN

The following afternoon, I jogged downstairs ahead of Drew. Judy and Beth were already in the kitchen, aprons protecting their clothes from utensils and mixing bowls. Containers of food and dollops of cranberries and dressing cluttered the countertops. The smell of roasting turkey, strong throughout the house, made my stomach growl. Thanksgiving dinner was almost ready.

"Can I help?" I asked, pushing up my sweater sleeves.

"You could set the table." Judy gestured toward a tray stacked with silverware, plates, and cloth napkins.

"I'm on it."

It felt good to be doing something useful. That morning I'd slept later than I usually did, not rising until close to nine to go for a run. Leaving Drew snoring on his side of the bed, I'd slipped into spandex tights, a long-sleeved running shirt, my Sauconys, a fleece hat, and a windbreaker. Downstairs I said good morning to Judy and Ed sharing the newspaper over their morning coffee, and then headed out for a leisurely run around Drew's hometown. As I ran, I tried to imagine him as a child and teenager navigating these same streets. But I couldn't call up any images other than how he'd looked that morning, face unlined in sleep, hair tousled across the pillow.

By the time I'd gotten back and showered, Judy and Beth were already at work in the kitchen preparing for the big meal. Now, a little before one, we were almost ready to sit down. As I set the table, an image of Selma in the kitchen at home flashed into my mind's eye, and I paused in mid-fold of a napkin. This was my first real holiday without her.

It was strange. Because of what had happened to my parents and Selma, I could measure my life in a series of before and afters: Chicago was before the plane crash; Tennessee was after the plane crash and before Selma died; New York was after Selma died and before... what? What would come after New York? And would anyone die this time around, or would I manage to move on for once untouched by loss?

Drew came up behind me and slid his arm around my waist. "Hey, darlin'," he said, and kissed me on the cheek.

I flinched away, dropping a fork. It bounced silently against the thick carpeting.

"You okay?" he asked, frowning.

"Fine," I said, not meeting his eyes.

"Drew, get your butt in here and mash the potatoes," Beth said from the kitchen doorway. "We're not at Grandma's. You and Dad don't get to watch football while the women slave in the kitchen."

"We don't? What the hell?"

Beth glared at him mock threateningly.

"Okay," he said, laughing. "Mom, where do you keep the potato masher?"

"It's called a beater, Drew, and it lives with the toaster, right where it has lived since we moved into this house fifteen years ago."

Drew went to look for the beater, muttering under his breath about bra-burning feminazis.

"What was that?" Beth said, pausing in the frosting of a chocolate cake that was free of animal extracts of any kind.

Eyeing the chocolatey knife in her hand, Drew tried to look innocent. "Nothing. I think that was Ashley you heard."

"Whatever," I said. Then I walked over to where Drew was plugging the electric beater into the wall and murmured, "I'd be careful if I were you, Ryan. After all, I know about the diary."

He pretended to gasp. "You wouldn't!"

"Try me."

Thanksgiving dinner was much like the night before, with laughter and haranguing—mostly amiable—about society and politics and life on planet earth. This time I noticed that they rarely talked about their personal lives. I was used to Austin's family, who viewed life in terms of human development. But that was probably because Claire was a therapist and Bruce had been a guidance counselor for years before pursuing a career in high school administration. They were both almost too in touch with their emotional, spiritual selves.

I also noticed, as we passed dish after dish around the brightly lit table, the Ryan family's lack of religion. We didn't offer prayers before digging in, and no one mentioned God before, after, or during the meal. Even when they discussed issues with a moral side, like the death penalty or abortion, which everyone at the table agreed was a woman's right, they never mentioned religion. That, I knew, was because they were all to varying degrees practicing Unitarian Universalists. According to Drew, UUs believe in the practice of a good and moral life for the sake of that life alone, rather than for the sake of an imagined afterlife. The congregation he grew up in believed in secular humanism, not monotheism.

Selma would have liked Drew's family, I decided as I finished off seconds. She would have liked their house, their politics, the way they raised their children. Most of all, she would have liked how generously they opened their family to me. I knew that she, like Claire Taylor, had worried about me knocking around the house all alone after she was gone. And for a while, I had. But since moving to New York, I'd realized I didn't have to be alone anymore, not unless I wanted to. Being around the Ryans made me not want to.

After dessert, we sat back down at the table with the light a little lower, sipping from our respective drinks of wine, decaf coffee, and soda. We talked idly about the coming winter and the flavor of our drinks, and it was nice to be warm and full of good food in the Ryans' dining room, watching steam climb the windows as the day grew colder. I looked over at Drew, who was teasing Beth about something or other. I was glad he had invited me home with him.

"Everyone ready?" Judy asked as a lull fell over the table. They all nodded. "This is a Thanksgiving tradition," she said, looking at me. "We go around the table and say what we've gained since last year, what we appreciate about our lives. You don't have to say anything if you don't want to, Ashley, but we'd love to listen if you happen to feel like sharing. I'll start."

She cleared her throat and looked around the table, gazing upon the faces of her family one by one. "I know I always say this, but I am once again thankful for another year of health and success for each of my children. I am thankful that you are all here to fill this house with laughter and love. I am thankful for this family. Your turn, Katie."

Katie shrugged, trying to look bored but succeeding only in appearing awkward. "I guess I'm thankful that we're all here too. And I'm thankful that we didn't have to drive to Grandma's this year. Oh, yeah, and I'm thankful that I don't have to go to school till Monday." She grinned, braces shining in the overhead light.

Beth was thankful for being home for the week, since she wouldn't be able to make it for Christmas. She was also thankful for the new life she had begun to make in San Francisco, and her friends there.

Ed was thankful for his children and his marriage and for the home they had all made together. That was what he treasured most in life. I listened to his words and wondered if my father might have been at all like him. I hoped so.

Drew was thankful for the chance to follow his dream in New York, thankful that he still lived close enough to come home for the holidays, and thankful, he said, smiling over at me, that he hadn't come home alone this Thanksgiving.

It was my turn. I looked down at the wooden table, holding tightly to my cup of coffee as a blush warmed my face. "Well, mostly I'm thankful that you all let me be a part of this day. It's been really great. Thank you."

"You're very welcome," Judy said. "We're glad you could be here."

Ed pushed his empty coffee mug aside. "On to the next tradition. What does everyone say to a walk on the lake?"

"Aw, Dad," Katie groaned. "It's going to be freezing."

Judy's eyebrows rose. "I didn't think we raised any wimps." Then she glanced at me, apparently remembering my Southern roots. "I mean, if it's too cold, we don't all have to go, of course."

"Don't worry about Ashley," Drew said. "She's been riding a bike around New York all fall. By now she's toughened up to the cold. Right, Ash?"

"Right."

"Then let's get going before the sun sets," Ed said.

We took the minivan to the lake, Ed and Judy up front, National Public Radio out of Buffalo playing classical music. Drew and I sat in the very back, giggling at the story Beth told about her gay housemate who had recently come out to his parents.

"And they were like, 'Brett, we're so happy you've finally realized that you're gay! We joined P-FLAG two years ago.' And Brett was like, 'You did?' I told him they already knew, but he didn't believe me." She shook her head, Native American dream catcher earrings dancing with the movement.

"I know some people who would kill to have their parents react like that," Drew said.

"Me, too," I agreed.

Lake Erie was only a couple of miles from the Ryans' house. Lake Erie State Park, where they liked to walk, was another twenty minutes south. We parked in the nearly empty lot and piled out of the car, bundled in gloves, hats, and scarves. The temperature was in the thirties, but the wind off the lake would be strong, Ed and Judy kept warning me. I just nodded and smiled.

Erie looked more like an ocean than a lake. White-capped waves crested and pounded toward shore, washing over the deck of the long pier that marked the northern boundary of the park. Thick, gray clouds on the horizon obscured the light of the setting sun, darkening the sky prematurely. Gusts of wind whipped foamy spray up onto the sandy shore. This lake didn't resemble the calm, sunlit Lake Michigan of my childhood memories.

"The waves aren't usually this high," Drew told me. "Looks like a storm blowing in."

I shivered, watching the gloomy clouds creep closer. In the city, it was easy to forget the awesome power of nature. There the dangers were mostly of the human variety—crime, train wrecks, car accidents, terrorism. I'd almost forgotten the thrill of fear a storm could send quivering along my spine. I lifted my face skyward. I was out of the city, back in the real world at the edge of a thunderstorm.

"I think you're right, Drew," Judy said over her shoulder. "It does look like a storm out there."

She and Ed were walking arm in arm across the beach a few paces ahead of us while Beth and Katie had run ahead to the edge of the water, scattering seagulls in their path.

Drew took my arm in his, and I started humming a Toad the Wet Sprocket song about spotting the ocean at the head of a trail, in a place where everything was supposed to be better, to be safe.

Here and now, despite the storm closing in on us, I did feel better. Safe, even, with Drew beside me and his family around us, their warm, brightly lit house waiting for us, a beacon in the growing darkness.

The storm forced us to turn back sooner than planned. We were piling back into the minivan just as the first fat, cold drops of rain fell. Good timing, we all agreed, rubbing our hands together and stomping our feet against the minivan's carpeted floor.

"Your cheeks are red," Drew said, watching me.

"So are yours."

He lowered his voice. "I'm glad you're here, Ashley."

I stopped rubbing my nose. "Me, too."

Leaning against him, I looked out the window, keeping an eye on the storm.

Drew had a paper due the day he got back, so on Friday he locked himself in the den and got to work. Meanwhile, Katie went to a friend's house and Ed and Judy drove into Buffalo to check out the Thanksgiving weekend sales. They invited Beth and me, but we opted to amuse ourselves. We ended up in the finished basement where the Ryans kept a second TV and a Sega-Genesis game system. Beth had offered to teach me how to play Tetris.

"Drew says you're a distance runner," she commented, moving her head in the direction she wanted each floating geometrical shape to shift.

"I like to run." I stared at the screen, watching the shapes fall from top to bottom. Didn't look too hard. What was the big deal about Tetris, anyway?

"Do you want to run in college? Drew mentioned you were trying to decide where to apply."

Seemed Drew had talked a lot about me to his sister. I tried to ignore a twinge of guilt. "Ideally, I'd like to. But no one's exactly recruiting me."

I had a pile of applications waiting on my desk. Drew was pressing me to apply to NYU, but I wasn't sure I wanted to spend the next four years in New York.

"What were your grades like in high school?" Beth asked, her fingers flying over the controls. "If you don't mind my asking."

"Pretty good. Mostly As." Actually, all As until my senior year. Even then my teachers, knowing the situation at home, had taken pity on me. "Oh, and I got National Merit."

"You won a National Merit Scholarship?" Beth tore her eyes from the game long enough to look at me.

I shrugged. "I test well. Middle Tennessee State actually recruited me for academics. Their coach wanted me to run for them, too, even though my senior year was a bust. But I didn't want to stay in Tennessee."

"You should think about Vassar. Our sports are decent," Beth said, frowning as the Tetris shapes started falling almost too rapidly to control.

"Maybe."

Selma would have seconded the suggestion. She had asked me more than once to consider a private liberal arts college like Marian University, her alma mater, or Kenyon College, Claire's alma mater—a school where I could be a star on the track while earning an education superior to what a state university could offer. But I couldn't help it: I wanted Division I. I wanted to be an athlete at a big-time sports school. The way I saw it, my mind could and would be nourished throughout my lifetime. Selma had seen to that. But my body would be at its physical peak for only so long. At a school like Vassar or Kenyon, studies would always come before sports.

"Your turn," Beth said. Her score remained under Player One—15,432 points.

I could beat that, I thought, gripping the controls and staring at the screen.

"We're going to start you at Level Zero, just till you get the hang of it. Use the joystick to flip the shape, and the red button drops it instantly, okay? Got it?"

I nodded. I had it.

"Here goes." Beth hit the start button.

Turned out Tetris was a lot harder than it looked. I only got to 900 points that first game. Beth said that was really good for a beginner, then went on to score 17,000 in her next turn.

"You said before your senior year was a bust," she said. "Does that mean you didn't run?"

"Exactly."

I watched her hands on the game controls. They were smaller than Drew's, and paler. She wasn't as tanned as he was even though she was the one living in California. I liked the rings she wore, silver and chunky and tough.

"Why not?"

Up until now, no one in Drew's family had engaged me in conversation about my past. I had come to the conclusion that Drew had warned them not to.

"I wasn't getting along with my coach and I was burned out on running, so I quit in the fall. Took a break."

"Is that when your aunt got sick?"

She didn't look away from the glowing screen. Neither did I. I watched the colorful shapes fall, hypnotized almost by their twisting and shifting.

"Yeah. I didn't want to spend all that time running when I could be with her. And then she died and I got injured and I don't know, I guess I was depressed, because even after I could run, I couldn't. Not like before."

"And now?"

"And now I can again. When I can find the time, that is."

"I'm glad." She smiled at me. She had their mother's hazel eyes, too, green-gray with a lighter ring around the pupil.

The television beeped warningly, and we looked back at the screen.

"Aw, man, I'm dead." She laughed. "Your turn again."

"Ooh, only nine thousand. I can totally beat that."

We both cracked up.

I was really starting to like this vacation thing. Except the weather—typical November in upstate New York, Drew said, all blustery and gray. It was still dark outside Saturday morning when I slipped out of bed and pulled on my running clothes. Today was my long run.

Outside, I ran over to Lake Erie and headed south along the shore, breathing in time to the slap of my feet against the damp ground. The wind wasn't as strong today. It was raining, though, a damp mist that collected in miniature beads in my eyelashes, turning rays of light into rainbows. I lifted my face to the overcast sky as I ran. Running along Lake Erie while Drew slept soundly in his childhood home a few miles away, I was content.

Back at the house a little while later, I paused on the back porch to remove my dripping jacket, shoes, and socks. In bare feet, I padded inside. Drew and his mother were sitting on bar stools at the island in the middle of the kitchen. They both stared at me, and

I froze mid-step. I could almost feel the tension flitting from each of them to me and back again.

Then Judy smiled, not quite meeting my eyes. "Hello. How was your run?"

"Good, thanks." I tried to catch Drew's eye, but he wouldn't look at me, either. "Am I interrupting something?"

"No." His voice was low.

"Of course not," Judy said, but her voice sounded too hearty to me. "Would you like some breakfast, Ashley? Cereal, maybe? Or pancakes, I could fix pancakes."

"Cereal's fine. But do you mind if I throw my running clothes in the dryer? I didn't realize it was so wet out."

"Help yourself. Drew, didn't you say you needed to do some laundry, too?"

"Yeah." He jumped off the bar stool and left the room, still not looking at me.

"What's wrong?" I asked as soon as he was out of earshot. "What happened?"

His mother stared down at the countertop. "Nothing, really. We were just talking about a family matter."

In other words, none of my business.

"Oh," I said. "Well, I better hit the shower."

"Good plan." She rose and began clearing their breakfast dishes from the counter.

Upstairs I headed straight for the bathroom, stripping quickly and stepping into the warm shower. I closed my eyes, feeling my muscles loosen as the steamy spray washed the chill from my body. Something was clearly wrong in the Ryan household. Maybe it really was a family matter and had nothing to do with me, but I wasn't convinced. Had Drew told his mother about my hot and cold behavior? Had she told him he deserved better? I chewed my lip, worrying that Judy Ryan had seen through me with a parent's ability to recognize who was—and wasn't—good for her child.

By the time I headed downstairs again, the whole Ryan clan was up and around. Even Beth, who was tuned to West Coast time and had slept late all week, was in the kitchen, bleary-eyed over a cup of coffee.

"All warmed up?" Drew asked when he saw me.

I nodded.

He pulled up a stool next to mine and had a second cup of

coffee, chatting easily with me as I ate breakfast. Maybe his earlier reticence had really had nothing to do with me, I thought as I polished off my fourth pancake. Maybe.

"See, you guys? I told you Ashley could eat more than anyone you knew," Drew bragged.

Beth nudged me. "I think that's my baby brother's attempt at a compliment."

"Well, he is a guy," I pointed out. "You know how they can be about food."

"I can hear you," Drew said. "I'm sitting right here."

The weather kept us indoors most of the day. Drew, Beth, and I ventured out mid-morning to the video store. We rented *The Breakfast Club* and *St. Elmo's Fire* and sprawled out on the basement furniture eating microwave popcorn and reliving our Brat Pack days. Beth told me stories about Drew from high school. I told her stories about Drew from college. He pretended to ignore us but was secretly pleased, I thought, to be the center of attention.

That night, Ed and Judy took us all out to a fancy Italian restaurant in Buffalo. Beth, Drew, and I shared a bottle of red wine, and giggled in the back seat all the way home. Katie talked to their parents and looked scathingly at us. She was a peer leader in her school's "Just Say No" program. Give her a few years, I thought.

Back at the house we sat around the living room again, talking. This seemed to be the Ryan family's favorite pastime, debating current issues amongst themselves over hot beverages. I was going to miss these evenings. Selma and I used to talk over ice cream and pie, her favorite dessert. But our conversations had typically focused on what we had read or learned recently, rather than on current events. I couldn't believe she'd been gone more than half a year already. It didn't seem like that long, and yet, in a way, it felt like much longer. I watched Drew. I wasn't nearly as numb as I'd been when Austin came back to get me. Drew was definitely getting to me, breaking down my walls slowly. I just wasn't sure if I liked that or not.

Around eleven, Drew and I said goodnight to the family. Upstairs we got ready for bed, taking turns in the bathroom. I was already curled up under the sheets when Drew came into the room and stripped down to his boxers. His parents kept the house warm enough that neither of us had needed our flannel pajamas. He slipped into bed next to me and reached for the bedside lamp.

"Wait," I said, sitting up in bed. "Don't turn it off yet."

"I thought you were asleep already."

"No." I wrapped my arms around my legs. "What's up?"

He sat back, pulling the covers up over his abdomen. "What do you mean? Nothing's up."

I plucked at the comforter's stitching. "You seem different today, like maybe you feel differently."

"I don't feel any differently." He took my hand in his and wove our fingers together. "I guess I just got distracted thinking about tomorrow. We won't be together like this again for a while."

"I know." I rested my chin on his shoulder. "Your family's great."

"They like you too." He hesitated. "My mom said…" Then he stopped.

"What? What did your mom say?"

He stared down at our fingers laced together. "Nothing. She said she hoped you would come visit again sometime."

He wasn't telling me something. But just then, with the wind whistling audibly beyond the window, I didn't want to push him away by demanding to know what he and his mother had talked about that morning. Instead, I leaned over and kissed his cheek.

"I hope I visit again, too."

He smiled down into my eyes. "So do I."

A little while later I lay next to Drew in the dark room, staring at the unfamiliar ceiling and listening to him breathe. Tomorrow at this time we would both be back in our separate apartments in New York. With the end of the semester approaching, Drew would have to focus on school. As soon as we were back, I would get all caught up in messengering again, obsessing over food, sleep, the state of my body. These idyllic few days when I'd felt closer to him than anyone would be forgotten in the shuffle of our normal lives.

Was Austin lying awake tonight in Philadelphia, too? Or were he and Tommy sleeping peacefully in Tommy's childhood bedroom, secure in each other's arms? The latter, I hoped. Austin might not be telling me something—join the club—but we had been friends half our lives. The first time we rode bikes together, the day after they moved in, he'd asked me why I lived with my aunt. When I told him about the plane crash, he'd only frowned at the news and said, "That sucks." Then he asked if I had any cool scars, and that was that.

I used to wonder why he hadn't made a bigger deal over my past, but now I thought it made sense. He had been hiding a huge part of himself for so long. To him, it was only normal that I would have my own issues to work through.

Beside me, Drew snored softly. He didn't have any trouble sleeping, but then why would he? As far as I knew, there were no secret losses lurking in his past, only a lovely family that appeared perfect from the outside. Was that what set us apart from each other, or was it something else?

In the middle of the night, I woke to the sound of the house's bones creaking, and for a moment, I thought I was back in Tennessee, Selma asleep in the next room. Then I felt Drew in bed beside me, his back to mine. *I have to tell him the truth*, I thought, and then I fell back asleep as the wind whipped off Lake Erie, rattling the house and shaking the trees.

CHAPTER FIFTEEN

Over the next week, I almost told Drew about the plane crash half a dozen times. But each time, something stopped me. And then, I almost lost any and every chance.

Mid-morning on the first Tuesday of December, I was riding up Sixth Avenue, a cylinder of industrial blueprints strapped to my back. After I delivered the papers at Fifth and Thirty-Fourth Street, right around the corner from the Empire State Building, I was planning to stop for a snack at a nearby grocery store. By now I knew my way around the stores and vendor carts throughout lower Manhattan, since OTJ generally had me operating south of Union Square with the occasional trip to Midtown.

There I was, weaving around illegally parked cars, sprinting to make yellow lights, squeezing my brakes and checking traffic at reds. It had only been a week and a half, but Thanksgiving in Fairview felt like another lifetime, just like Tennessee. But that was one of the things I loved about messing—it didn't leave room to dwell on anything else. Messing was Zen in the form of the perfect line.

I was jolted from the flow in the time it took a Lexus to run the light at Thirty-First Street. Nowhere to go—a cab to my left pinned me in against the curb lined with newspaper vending machines and metal trash containers. I squeezed my brakes, but I was going too fast to stop. Brakes shrieking, my front tire crashed into the passenger door of the speeding Lexus.

At impact, the bike's velocity transferred into my body. I shot forward over the handlebars, over the Lexus, across the narrow side street. Flailing wildly, I slammed head-first into a pile of black trash bags on the opposite curb.

My body jolted to a stop. Immediately, a wave of nausea washed over me. As soon as the world steadied, I scrambled to sit up, pushing trash bags away from my face, my head, my body. I was buried in plastic that smelled of spoiled meat and things I didn't want to think about.

The Lexus driver had stopped his car and was hurrying toward me. Pedestrians and other drivers gathered around us. One man lifted my mangled bicycle out of the way of oncoming traffic while another called the police on a portable phone the size of his head.

I sat on my throne of trash, staring at the man who had nearly killed me. My heart was pounding. This wasn't supposed to happen. You weren't supposed to be riding your bike along, thinking about a nice mid-morning snack, and have some bastard try to run you down.

"Oh my God, I'm so sorry," the driver said, words spilling from his mouth. He didn't look much older than me, clad in jeans and a gray Columbia sweatshirt. "Are you okay? I didn't see you. Are you hurt?"

"Motherfucker!"

As if possessed, my body surged upward. Rage carried me into motion—my clenched fist caught him square in the mouth, and I watched as he crumpled to one knee before me, eyes wide in shock.

I shook my hand. My fingers hurt. So did my knees, I realized as my rage faded, only to be replaced by nausea again. My whole body was throbbing, I was going to puke, and I needed to sit down.

"You hit me," the driver said, a drop of blood reddening his front teeth.

"I know," I said.

And then an ocean rose in my head, obliterating everything else.

I wasn't out long. When I woke up, an EMT leaned over me, flashing a light in my eyes. Her jacket lapel bore a NYC Emergency Services patch.

"Welcome back, honey," she said. "What hurts?"

I had a horrible taste in my mouth. Looking down at my clothes, I recognized the foul odor that filled my nostrils. "Did I throw up? I'm sorry."

"I've seen worse. We got a live one," she called to her partner, who was unfolding a cot from the back of an ambulance.

"Glad to hear it," he answered.

"Where's my bike? And my bag?" I asked. "I have a delivery."

"Everything is right here. Now, what hurts?"

"I should be dead," I said, looking up into the woman's deep brown eyes.

"Not if I can help it."

After a cop showed up at the scene, the ambulance took me to the hospital. There, I refused to check in until one of the nurses called OTJ and told them what was going on. They let me talk to Leslie briefly, and she confirmed that the delivery had been made by one of New York's finest, probably the same cop who dropped off my messenger bag at the hospital.

"But that doesn't matter, Ash," she chided me. "Are you okay? Did you break anything?"

"Just my bike. I think I'm out this time, Leslie."

The pronouncement came out of some usually suppressed part of my brain, surprising me more than it did her, probably.

"Give it a few days," she said. "You might change your mind. In the meantime, call me when they release you, okay? Please? Everyone here will want to know."

I agreed, and then the nurse took the phone away and made me put on one of those horrible gowns with the ties that don't actually work. She pulled a blue curtain around my bed, but I decided it was mostly for show. Passersby could still see in, just like with my gown, the edges of which I tried in vain to keep together as the ER doctor examined me.

As the exam went on, the first doctor called in a second colleague, and then a third. They bent over my chart, speaking in low voices, glancing up at me every once in a while with expressions I couldn't read. The doctors and their minions scanned and X-rayed everything they could, poked and prodded my chest and belly. They bent my legs this way and that, listened to my heart and lungs, drew blood, and checked everything they could check.

Finally the original doctor sat down on the edge of my bed. He was an older man with gray hair and a chiseled face, and scribbled notes and codes on my chart as he spoke.

"You appear to be in remarkably good shape, considering. No

sign of a concussion, no breaks, no fractures, no abrasions even, and no apparent tissue damage. You'll be sore, though, for a good week to ten days. No riding a bike for a week, doctor's orders. By tonight, or maybe in the morning, you'll start feeling the worst of the muscular pain. Take ibuprofen but don't exceed 1500 milligrams in a twenty-four hour period. If the pain becomes unmanageable, come in so we can be sure there's no serious damage. Backs can be funny. You just have to wait and see." He looked up at me again, blue eyes serious. "I'd say you're one lucky young lady. Any questions?"

"If I don't have a concussion, why did I pass out?"

He glanced at his chart. "Apparently you lost consciousness from low blood pressure likely caused by a sudden onset of nausea, according to the paramedic's report. She further states that the trash bags you struck saved you from serious injury." He shook his head. "Let me amend my previous statement—you're one incredibly lucky young woman, Miss Lake."

As if I didn't already know that.

He squinted at the chart again, and then looked up at me. "For previous hospitalizations, you reported that you suffered a physical trauma at age three?"

I nodded, twisting the hospital band on my wrist around and around. "An accident," I said, hoping my voice didn't shake.

The last thing I needed was the press finding me now. The *New York Times* retrospective piece six weeks before had featured old photos of the crash scene, including one of me in my hospital bed. Imagine if the reporter learned that I was living in the Village, right under her nose.

The doctor nodded slowly, his eyes on mine. Then he reached into one of his coat pockets and drew out a business card. "Trauma can be a funny thing, too. You may experience some anxiety over your accident this morning, Ashley, or it may bring up old scars of a mental nature. If you experience any untoward distress, I hope you'll call me. I've been in this business a long time and could point you to someone who can help."

"I'll be fine," I said. After all, I'd been dealing with my demons for a decade and a half, and I hadn't freaked out yet.

Still, I took the card he offered.

After he left, I looked down at my my bony ankles and socked toes pointing out from under the hospital gown. Here was my luck again, popping up to save me from imminent death. Was it fate, destiny, karma, God? Who had placed those garbage bags in my path instead of a telephone pole or brick wall? A guardian angel, perhaps, whose job it was to see that I lived?

But why? Why me and not the others?

I shook my head, banishing the voice I'd lived with all these years, the question I never seemed able to answer. Why didn't matter. The fact was that I was still alive, and I owed it to everyone else from Flight 108 to do something extraordinary with my life.

What a fantastic job I had done so far.

The hospital released me after I signed some forms and provided proof of insurance. I hurried through the paperwork. Hospitals reminded me of Selma. In fact, the last time I'd been in one had been the day she died. I tried to shake the memories away, but this time, motion didn't help. I couldn't escape the image of Selma so small and still in her hospital bed, so gray and shrunken as her organs shut down, her heart rate slowed, her breathing became increasingly labored and then stopped, only to restart again—twice—as I watched, unable to stay but unable to leave, either.

Outside the sun still shone somewhere above the winter clouds, the city sidewalks overflowed as usual with lunchtime traffic, and pedestrians rushed past as self-involved as ever. Only I was different, rattled by the accident. But *accident* hardly seemed appropriate. The son-of-a-bitch in the Lexus had caused the wreck, not bad luck or providence or any other supernatural entity. I was glad I'd punched him. Served the bastard right.

I called Austin from a pay phone on the corner, hoping I would catch him at the apartment. He had switched shifts at the restaurant recently. Now he went in at one and left at eight—a much nicer schedule, Tommy and I agreed.

Austin picked up on the third ring.

"It's me," I said.

"Ash? What's up? I thought you were at work."

"I was. But I, um, kind of had an accident. I'm fine," I added quickly. "I just wanted to warn you that the police are going to drop my bike off at some point."

"The police? Are you serious? What happened?"

"A guy ran a light." I bit my lip, trying to blink back tears. "Look, I'm going to catch a cab home."

I had to get off the phone and stop thinking about what had

happened, or I was going to burst into tears there on the corner, surrounded by towering buildings and harried-looking people. *Stupid, stupid, stupid,* I chastised myself. I hadn't even been hurt.

"Wait, where are you? Do you want me to come pick you up?"

"No." I swiped at my eyes. "I'll be home soon."

I hung up the phone and limped over to Second Avenue. There, a taxi stopped and whisked me away, vomit-stained clothing and all. Slumped down in the back seat, my messenger bag on my lap, I watched the buildings and the people and the cars flash past beneath the gray November sky. I was freezing cold, desperately tired, and could barely stand the smell of myself. My whole body ached, including the knuckles on my right hand. The cops who interviewed me at the hospital had mentioned that the driver of the Lexus complained that I punched him, and he wanted to press charges for assault. But none of the witnesses at the scene could corroborate the driver's story. The witnesses clearly remembered that the guy had run the red light. However, they couldn't seem to recall whether or not I had punched him afterward.

"I wouldn't worry about it if I was you," the police officer had told me. He was middle-aged with thinning gray hair. "Just let me know if he bothers you."

He handed me a card with his name, rank, and number. Then he and his partner, a woman with red hair and a fixed scowl, had left the hospital, my ruined bike in the back of their patrol car.

This wasn't the treatment I'd expected from New York police officers. Among the messenger community, cops had a reputation for being hard-ass nitpickers who would sooner ticket a cyclist on the job than look at him. But maybe that was the key—*him.* Meanwhile I was a girl with a ponytail and puke all over my EMS ensemble, and maybe reminded the older cop, like the cab driver a few weeks before, of his daughter or one of her friends rather than the riff-raff he normally associated with messing.

Selma's face flashed in front of my eyes again, only this time I remembered the night my junior year of high school when I'd received my first speeding ticket on the way home from school.

"Next time," my aunt told me, "act helpless and cry a little."

I'd stared at her. "What?"

This from the woman who had raised me in a purposefully gender-neutral manner? The same woman who wrote letters to toy manufacturers and vacuum companies chiding them for the sexist overtones of their magazine and television advertisements?

She lifted an eyebrow. "If you're going to have to suffer under sexism, you might as well use it to your advantage every once in a while."

In the back of the cab, I blinked back more tears. Had she been watching out for me today? Maybe she was somewhere with my parents even now, and they were shaking their heads over the risks that I, their collective child, kept taking.

"That Ashley," I could hear them saying. "We knew she was going to be a handful the first time she climbed out of her crib."

I closed my eyes and rested my head on my raised arm, dozing a little as the cab sped across the Village.

The driver dropped me off in front of the apartment. I had barely finished paying when Austin appeared at my side. He put his arm around my shoulders and walked me into the building.

"I'm fine," I said. "I don't need help."

Tears filled my eyes again at the feel of his hands, gentle, on mine.

"I've got you," he said, and opened the apartment door for me. The bike was propped just inside, front tire twisted, frame bent and scuffed.

As he locked the door behind us, each bolt audibly snapping into place, I limped to my room. I needed to get out of these clothes as soon as was humanly possible.

He followed me. "The police came right after you called. I think they thought I was your boyfriend."

"Yeah?" I pulled a clean outfit from the dresser.

He watched as I stripped out of my shirt and silk undershirt. Under my sports bra, my ribs were already turning a nasty purple in places.

"It's not as bad as it looks," I said, turning away.

"Right."

He left the room while I pulled on fleece-lined sweatpants, a clean T-shirt, and a soft flannel shirt. I rolled my soiled clothes into a ball and left them in the corner, and then I checked myself over in the mirror. My face looked normal except for a small scratch on my chin. I *had* been lucky. As I stared at my reflection, time shifted and I found myself gazing upon my childhood face, examining the cuts, bruises, and scrapes from the plane crash. And the burns. I could remember Selma changing the dressings on the burns in the bungalow's guest bathroom. She kept all of my medical supplies on a shelf in the cupboard above the toilet. I vividly remembered standing on the toilet, reaching into the cupboard to find the gauze and the antibiotic cream. I wanted to help.

I blinked against the memory, willing it back into place. I didn't want to remember anything else, didn't want this latest near-miss to land me in a psychiatric hospital babbling nonsense, visions of broken bodies and burning airplane parts lodged in my mind's eye. There was a reason I couldn't remember, and now was not the time for my brain to release its stranglehold on my past. Frankly, I hoped it would never be time.

Austin was waiting in the living room. I looked at my watch as I eased myself down on the couch, propping my legs up on the coffee table. I was supposed to keep them elevated so that they wouldn't hurt as much.

"Don't you have to leave for work?" I asked.

"I called and told them I wasn't coming in. They understood." He sat down next to me on the couch, careful not to jostle the cushions.

"I'm okay," I said. "Go to work. I'm just a little banged up."

"A little?" he echoed.

"Okay, a lot. But you should see the other guy." And I giggled. I felt high. I was so tired.

"What do you mean?" Austin frowned. "I thought you hit a car."

I leaned my head against the back of the couch, sinking lower into the soft cushions. I wanted to go to sleep and disappear from the world. "I did. A freakin' Lexus from Westchester. I also hit the driver. With my fist."

"No wonder your hand looks like that. I thought you hurt it in the crash."

I flexed my swollen knuckles. "Nope. I punched him and then I passed out and puked all over myself."

Austin slid his arm around my shoulders. "I'm sorry. You must have been so scared."

I couldn't hold back the tears any longer. Leaning into Austin's side, I buried my face in his white Navy T-shirt.

He held me, his chin on top of my forehead. "Shh, it's okay. You're okay, Ash."

And somehow, all at once, I was crying for Selma and my

parents and everyone else who had been lost that October day so many years ago, all of the grief I daily tamped down rising and roaring to the fore. I cried out the sorrow and the fear until, finally, there was nothing bad left inside me. There on the couch, Austin's shoulder warm against my damp cheek, the smell of his deodorant a slight perfume through his shirt, I fell asleep.

I awoke disoriented a little later when he moved from my side. Blinking, I sat up.

"Sorry," he said, massaging his shoulder, "my arm is totally asleep. Why don't you take a nap in your room?"

"I'd rather stay here." I stretched out on the couch, resting my cheek on the pillow. I couldn't seem to keep my eyes open. "Go to work, Austin. I'll be fine."

"You shouldn't be alone," he said.

I burrowed deeper into the couch. "I'll sleep better without you here."

This wasn't entirely true, but he couldn't afford lost wages the way I could.

"You will?"

"I will."

"Okay. But only if you call Drew and have him come over when you wake up. I don't want you to be alone." He unfolded an afghan from the back of the couch as he spoke and tucked it around me.

"Yeah, sure." I yawned.

"Ash? You are going to call Drew, aren't you?"

Drew. There was something I was supposed to remember about Drew.

"Of course," I mumbled. "When I wake up."

"Promise?"

"I promise."

"All right, I'll go. What can I get you before I take off? Do you want some Sprite or juice or something?"

Wine sounded good, or perhaps something a bit harder.

"Sprite," I said, trying not to drool on the pillow as I spoke. "And Advil."

"Okay." He came back a few minutes later and set the cup on a coaster beside the bottle of Advil. "There you go. Anything else? The remote's right here."

"Thanks." I sat up just enough to pop a couple of pills, washing them down with soda. "Now go, okay? And don't tell Tommy about this whole thing. All I need is the two of you hovering over me like a couple of roosters."

He looked at me strangely. "You sound just like him."

"What?"

"Never mind. Go back to sleep." He leaned over and kissed my forehead, tousling my hair. "Sleep well, sweetie. Call me if you need anything. The phone is next to the remote."

I sighed, feeling the ache in my muscles already receding a bit. Ibuprofen, the wonder drug. "Thanks, Austin."

The door closed a few minutes later. I heard the bolts turn and Austin's footsteps fading in the hallway. Silence fairly echoed through the apartment. I sat up and looked around. Too quiet. I made my way to the stereo and picked a half dozen CDs, mellow music like Enya and Windham Hill. Then I stumbled back to the couch, pulled the afghan up to my neck, and buried my face in the throw pillow.

I dreamed as the afternoon darkened and shadows shifted across the walls. Dreams of screams and fire, red-tinged darkness and bright lights shining in my eyes. I couldn't get away from the fire. I couldn't move. I was trapped.

I awoke with a start when the doorbell echoed through the apartment, bouncing off the walls and ringing in my head. Automatically, I staggered to my feet. Pain shot up my thighs and down my calf muscles, and for a moment, all I could remember were the images from my dreams. They were dreams, weren't they? Or had I been in some sort of fire? Then it came back—the accident, the hospital, the doctor who'd recognized me.

I leaned against the wall and pressed the intercom button, trying to blink myself fully awake. "Yeah?" My voice squeaked out, strangled and hoarse.

"Ash? It's me," Drew said.

Dinner. We were supposed to have dinner.

"Are you ready?" he asked.

"Um, no." I looked at my watch. It was almost six. I'd slept the day away.

"Then buzz me in, will you? It's freezing."

I hit the buzzer, holding it until I heard the outer door open and close. Then I unlocked the apartment door and limped into my bedroom, turning on lights as I went. Enya was crooning in Gaelic on the stereo as I pulled a baseball cap over my messy hair and unwrapped a piece of gum. My mouth tasted like ass.

"Ready?" Drew called from the living room.

"Not exactly."

I glanced at myself in the mirror and tucked errant strands of hair under the edge of the cap. Time to face the music.

He was standing beside the couch looking at the bunched-up afghan and rumpled pillow.

"Were you asleep?" he asked. Apparently he hadn't noticed my bike in the dark hallway. "Wait. What's wrong?"

"Um." I started toward him, chomping my gum, trying to lose the cottonmouth. I needed more Advil. "I kind of got in an accident today. Just a little one. I was going to call you but I fell asleep."

"What happened? Were you hurt? Are you okay?"

"I'm fine." I waved a hand and sat down on the couch, wincing at the strain in my back. "A guy in a Lexus ran a red light and I biffed it. That's all."

"Oh, my God." He sat down next to me, looking me over. "Did he hit you? Did you hit your head?"

"I'm fine. I had my helmet on, and I didn't hit anything when I landed." I really was fine, other than a growing sense of righteous anger. "It was some jackass from Columbia. I was so mad, I punched him."

"You what?"

I laughed, then winced again as pain shot through my bruised ribs. "I know. Can you believe it? I gave him a fat lip. And I hurt my hand." I waved my swollen knuckles.

Drew caught my hand and examined it before looking up at me, his eyes troubled. "Why didn't you call me? My last class got out at two. I could have been here hours ago."

I glanced down at my sweats, playing with the draw string. "I was tired. I needed to sleep. It's not a big deal, Drew."

"It is a big deal. You could have died today."

"Technically I could die every day, and so could you. So could anyone."

He closed his eyes and took a deep breath, reminding me of Selma. She used to do the same thing whenever I got on her nerves.

"Did you at least go to the hospital?"

"Yeah, I did." No need to mention the ambulance ride just then.

"And they said you were okay?"

"Nothing ibuprofen can't fix. I'm okay, Drew. Really."

He leaned back next to me, his eyes on the opposite wall, and sighed. "You and your freaking luck. I just don't understand why you couldn't tell me."

"I'm sorry," I said, my hand on his. "I really didn't think it was that big of a deal."

"But you know it is. Why do you have to shut me out of everything?"

I frowned, pulling my hand away. "Like what?"

"You know."

I hesitated. It almost sounded like... "I don't have any idea what you're talking about," I tried.

"Yes, you do."

"No, I don't."

"The plane crash," he said all in a rush. "I know you were the only survivor. I know all about it. I've seen the pictures—you were in *Life* magazine, for Christ's sake."

I stood up and loomed over him, ignoring the stab of pain. "Who told you? Did Austin tell you? Did he?"

Drew pulled back. "No, it was my mom. I was asking her if she remembered a plane crash in Chicago when we were little, the one your parents were in, and she did. She said a girl about your age survived. She said she'd thought your name sounded familiar, and asked if it could've been you. I said no, you would have told me. But I wasn't sure, so I looked it up at the library over the weekend."

I shook my head. First the dreams, and now this? I couldn't be here. I couldn't do this. I stood abruptly and took a few steps, and then had to stop as a roaring sound rose in my head. I sat down on the floor, tucking my head between my knees. I never fainted. Maybe I was pregnant. Then I remembered that Drew and I had never actually had sex.

He knelt at my side, his arm around my shoulders. "It's okay, Ash, I'm here. I've got you."

Gradually, the world steadied and the nausea passed, leaving me more tired than before. I didn't want Drew to see me like this. As soon as I could, I pushed away from him.

"I think you'd better leave now." My voice sounded remote even to my own ears.

Drew rocked back on his heels, blinking. "Seriously? You want me to go, just like that?"

I nodded, holding my knees to my chest. My whole body ached. I couldn't get away from the pain.

"Tough shit, Ash." And he walked back to the couch and made himself comfortable.

I gaped. "Excuse me?"

"I'm not letting you run away from this."

He wasn't *letting* me? "Last time I checked, Drew, you didn't have any say in what I do or don't do."

"We're in a relationship, even if you'd rather pretend we're not. It's time for you to suck it up and deal."

"Actually, it's my life and this is my apartment. If I want you to leave, then you'd better leave."

Even as I spoke, I had a feeling that things were winding steadily out of my control. Why was I doing this? I didn't hate him. Why was I acting like I hated him?

"You are so fucked up," he said, and the depth of bitterness in his voice surprised me. "Even Austin thinks it isn't good the way you bottle everything up. I want to be there for you, but you won't let me. What are you so afraid of?"

"I'm not afraid of anything," I said. But we both knew I was lying.

And suddenly I did hate him. I hated him for laying me open with a look, a tone of voice, a few words; for stripping me down, my shortcomings revealed where neither of us could miss them. Tears crept from my eyes and slipped down my face.

Then Drew was beside me again. He pulled me close, sighing into my hair.

"Hey," he said, "don't cry. I'm sorry, Ash. Don't cry."

But I couldn't stop. The fire was still in me, still in and around me after all these years. I couldn't avoid it, couldn't outrun it. Just when I thought I had everything under control, back it came.

My eyes hurt from crying when I lifted my head from Drew's shoulder, my eyelids so swollen I could barely hold them open. All I wanted was to sleep.

"You okay?" Drew asked.

I bent my head, sniffling. "Fine."

But I wasn't, not really. This crying jag hadn't been about healing or release. It had been about buried pain exposed to light. I glanced up and caught Drew staring at me with a look I had never seen before in his eyes—pity. I swallowed, tasting bitterness, and pushed away from him to grab the bottle of Advil from the coffee table. "I'll be right back."

In the bathroom, I rinsed the tears from my face with cool water. I blew my nose, combed my hair, and put my hat back on, tugging the brim low on my forehead until it almost covered my red-rimmed eyes. Then I washed a couple of pills down with a glass of water. The liquid swished into my stomach, audible in the quiet room.

Back in the living room, I stopped in the doorway. "Are you hungry?"

Drew turned to face me, eyes serious, hands in his pockets. "Sure. I mean, if you are."

We stared at each other across the room, and it occurred to me that neither of us had expected what this day had given us.

I took a breath. "Look, Drew, I don't want to talk about this anymore tonight, okay? It's just too much for one day."

He nodded. "I know, Ash. I'm sorry. I wasn't thinking."

For once he had messed up. I relaxed a little. He wasn't perfect, either.

"You want to make dinner and watch basketball?" I asked. "The Knicks are on in a little while."

"Sure. Pasta?"

"Of course." I even smiled. "My specialty—rotini and red sauce."

"I'll get it. Just lay down and take it easy." He brushed past me, not quite meeting my eyes.

I stood where I was for a minute, listening to silence overtake the room as the CDs wound down. A breeze rattled against the window panes, the cold draft brushing against my skin. I crossed the room and pulled the shades, letting the Venetian blinds cover the windows. Inside the apartment, lamplight glowed on the peach walls. I curled up on the couch and turned on the TV, watching the news and waiting for Drew.

A little while later, Austin came home from work and sat down on the couch with us to watch the game. Soon after, Drew said he had to go work on a paper. He pecked me on the cheek and practically ran from the apartment. Couldn't blame him, really.

"I didn't think you'd call him," Austin said.

"I didn't. We were supposed to go to dinner."

"What's up with you guys? Seemed kind of tense in here."

I drew in a breath. "He knows about the plane crash. His mother remembered a girl my age had survived. Isn't that bizarre?"

"Not really," Austin said. "It was all over the news for a while. My mom always said it made a big impact on her, too, and we didn't meet you until later. She thought other parents could relate."

When the airplane cartwheeled across the runway, my parents had embraced each other, cradling me between them as the plane broke apart. That was the reason I survived. It hadn't been a matter of luck at all. My first mother's love had saved me, and my second mother's love had healed me.

Losing my parents had been difficult enough. How was I going to survive losing Selma, too?

"What'd Drew say?" Austin asked.

I shrugged, staring at the TV. I'd been watching the game since tip-off, but I wasn't sure who was winning or how much time was left. "He was pissed. Did you ever tell him you thought I keep everything 'bottled up'?"

"Well," he said, "that's taking it out of context. I mean, we were talking—"

"So you did."

"I didn't mean it in a bad way," he said, reaching for my hand.

"Right. And on that note, I'm going to bed." I stood up.

"Don't be mad, Ash."

"I'm not," I lied.

"Look, I'm sorry about everything you're going through right now," he said. "But it's not going to help if you push us all away. It's okay to need people."

Showed what he knew.

I retreated into my bedroom, undressed carefully, and crawled into bed. I didn't need them. I didn't need anyone. Curling into as tight a ball as my soreness would allow, I tried to sleep.

Deep in the night, when even the city streets were silent and still, I awoke with a start thinking, "I can't be here. I have to go."

But the memories that had come upon me while I relaxed in

sleep had me trapped. I couldn't stay but I couldn't escape either. I had to get away but there was no way out of my own mind. For minutes or possibly hours I lay rooted to the bed, unable to avoid the torrent of images and sensations flooding my brain. There was horror, disbelief, the red tint of pain, the terrible heat of fire. I kept thinking that if only I could leave my body, I would be okay. If only I could cease being me, the pain would stop. Wouldn't it have to?

At some point I slept again. When I awakened a few hours later to gray, autumnal light inching between the slats of the blinds, I couldn't recall what had tortured me so in the middle of the night. I remembered nausea, terror, the desire to leave my body. I remembered thinking that I couldn't possibly survive if I stayed where—who—I was. But when I tried to remember the details surrounding those desperate feelings, it was as if a wall had closed around them. Or if not a wall, then a kind of blurriness. A wall implies impermeability; the barrier in my mind was more tenuous in form and content.

I lay in bed for a while pondering the blockage. I sensed that if I really wanted to, I could eliminate it. Like a word that's on the tip of the tongue, my memories would prove attainable if I let my guard down fully. I wasn't a small child anymore, and it was possible that while my child's brain had been overwhelmed to the point of wishing for death when faced with the trauma of the crash—assuming, of course, these were the memories from which my mind so jealously guarded me—my nearly adult mind might be better able to contend with the pain and horror of what I had experienced.

And yet, what if it couldn't?

At least one type of pain was easily remedied. Wincing, I climbed down from the loft and went to find the Advil. For now, it would have to suffice. Only time would determine if the memories would come back again.

By God, I hoped they didn't.

CHAPTER SIXTEEN

A couple of nights later, I was lying on the couch watching a rented movie when the doorbell rang—Drew. I buzzed him in. He entered the apartment smelling of cold air and male sweat, his cheeks red and hair tousled by the wind.

"Hey," he said, and pecked me on the cheek.

"Hey." I resisted an urge to recoil from his kiss and locked the door behind him.

"What're you watching?" he asked.

"*Fried Green Tomatoes.*"

I sat down at one end of the couch, stretching my legs across the cushions so that he wouldn't sit next to me. He didn't seem to notice my reticence. Or maybe he was just used to it.

"Beth loves this movie," he said, dropping down onto the opposite end. "She loves pointing out the homoerotic stuff."

Homoerotic—you could tell he was the sensitive brother of a women's studies major. Normally I liked hearing him talk like a feminist. Tonight, though, it annoyed me, as if he were trying too hard to be something he wasn't.

"Uh-huh." I unpaused the movie.

Idgie and Ruth were having a picnic under a tree in an Alabaman field. As we watched, Idgie crossed the field to a dead tree where honey bees had built a hive, waved at Ruth, and then reached into the hive, searching for the honey. Bees clung to her skin, her clothing, and the piece of honey comb that she pulled from the tree's opening.

"You've gotta admit, that's pretty sexual," Drew said, smirking over at me.

"I guess," I said, and turned the volume up.

On screen, Idgie crossed the field again and held out the jar of honey to Ruth, who smiled and called her a bee charmer.

The week before in Fairview, Beth had said that in the Fannie Flagg novel *Fried Green Tomatoes at the Whistle Stop Café*, which the screenplay was based on, it was obvious that Ruth and Idgie were together. If you looked for it in the movie, she'd insisted, you'd find it too. Watching now, I was inclined to agree.

"I'm going to get a beer," Drew said. "Want one?"

"No, thanks."

I listened to him move about the kitchen, opening a bottle of beer and tossing the metal cap into the sink. I didn't want him here, I realized. I didn't even want to be around him. Before this week, I'd enjoyed being with him, and I might even have slept with him sometime soon. But Tuesday had changed everything. I would never look at him the way Austin looked at Tommy. Probably I would never even look at him the way Idgie looked at Ruth, and they were actors playing a part.

We watched the rest of the movie in silence. Drew drank his beer and I ignored him, willing myself to relax. I didn't need more tension at this point. My body was just getting back to normal after the accident.

I cried a little when—spoiler alert—Ruth died and Idgie sat sobbing at her bedside while Sipsy, the older woman who had cared for Ruth, covered a photo, and stopped the hands of the grandfather clock in the corner of the room. I knew how Idgie felt, in a way, as Sipsy held her and told her to let Ruth go.

Selma and I had always had this tradition of going to the movies together, especially over Christmas break when school and the library were both closed. Sometimes if we were feeling particularly decadent, we would go to a double-header. We'd seen *Fried Green Tomatoes* together at a multiplex in Chattanooga, and I remembered Selma tearing up at this same part. It hadn't occurred to me at the time that we would enact our own version of the scene a little over a year later in a hospital not far from that movie theater, while the clocks continued to tick and the birds kept singing as if nothing very momentous were happening.

When the movie ended, I turned the volume down. *Wheel of*

Fortune was on, Vanna White in her standard, sleeveless prom gown flipping letters on stage as the bell dinged.

"You know, Idgie sort of reminds me of you," Drew said.

"Yeah?" I tried not to let his perception affect me. What did it matter that Drew seemed to understand me the way no one else did, at times?

"Stubborn and volatile and all that."

Normally I would have laughed. Today I rolled my eyes and said, "Whatever," in a bored voice and watched Pat Sajak patronize his Middle America contestants.

"Chill, Ash," Drew said, teasing tone gone. "Don't take your bad mood out on me."

But he was part of the problem.

"Are you in love with me?" I asked.

"What?"

"Are you in love with me?"

Drew set his beer on the table. "Why are you asking that?"

"I just wanted to know, I guess." I knew I was being harsh, but I couldn't seem to stop myself.

"Well, are you in love with me?" he countered.

"I asked you first."

"That's mature. What's the matter, Ash? Afraid you might actually feel something if you let yourself? It's not that bad. You should try it some time."

The bitterness in his voice surprised me. "You don't even like me, do you?"

"That's not fair," he said, leaning forward on the edge of the couch. "You know I like you. I like the real you, the part you never show anyone except Austin, and me every once in a while. It just gets so frustrating, battling your walls all the time. Why won't you let me in? I'm not going to hurt you."

But he already had.

"It was my right not to tell you about the plane crash," I said. "Just because we hang out and do stuff doesn't mean you get automatic access to my whole life."

"But I let you into mine. You came home with me and you met my family, and we both saw how it could be away from the city."

"So I liked your family." I shrugged. "That doesn't mean I want to move in with you or anything."

"Oh, come on," Drew said. "Spare me. I haven't asked you for anything like that. I'm just asking you to let yourself feel, to be a normal human being. This is basic stuff, Ash."

His words stung nearly as much as his scathing tone. I folded my arms across my chest. "We can't all be normal, Drew."

"God!" He rocked back on the couch and stared at me. "You just don't get it, do you? I'm asking you to give me a chance, and you're doing everything you can to hold me at a distance."

I looked back at the TV. "Maybe you should take the hint."

He laughed a little, and the bitterness was back. He stood up. "Maybe I will. Give me a call when you're ready to discuss this in a mature way, okay?" He pulled on his jacket.

I watched Vanna flip over every *e* in the puzzle. "Whatever."

Even after the door slammed behind him, I kept watching the game show. The contestants turned the wheel and tried to guess the letters long after I had figured out that the place in question was "Between a rock and a hard place." Finally, impatient with their combined idiocy, I picked up the remote and began to channel surf.

The next morning, I woke up late, restless before I even opened my eyes. After three days of inactivity, I was tired of lying around the apartment like an invalid, tired of talk shows and soaps and syndicated repeats of *Family Ties* and *Cosby Show*. My mind craved activity. Unfortunately, my sore body won out.

Tommy and Austin went dancing that night. I lied and told them Drew might be coming over, just so they wouldn't feel guilty leaving. I hadn't told Austin yet about my fight with Drew. I didn't want to hear him echoing Drew's assertions that I was emotionally stunted.

As I lay on the couch that night drinking beer and watching yet another Knicks game, I thought about what Drew had said. Maybe he was right, and I shouldn't be holding him at a distance. He was sweet and open and funny, not to mention the most patient college student in the country, probably. What was I doing pushing him away?

I took a swig of beer. The Knicks were up ten points over the Pacers. Reggie Miller was out with a sprained ankle and Patrick Ewing was dominating the lane. Drew and his roommate were probably watching the game, too.

Picking up the phone, I dialed their number and waited, unsure what I would say. The phone rang four times, and then the machine picked up. I set the phone down. I didn't want to leave a message, not when he might be out with someone else. There were plenty of girls from school trailing after him, only too happy to open their lives to him, not to mention their bodies.

It was probably just as well if he dated someone else, I decided, slouching down amidst the soft sofa cushions and swallowing the rest of my beer. Because I was pretty sure I wasn't ever going to fall in love with him, and I had known for a while that that was what he was waiting for. I used to think it might happen, too. But apparently I wasn't meant to be in a relationship. I was just one of those people who was happier by herself.

I would call him in the morning, I promised myself, and got up to get another beer.

Morning came sooner than I expected. The telephone rang at two a.m., crashing into my dreams. Automatically I reached for the cordless phone in my loft.

"Hello," I said, voice hoarse with sleep.

"Ashley? It's Austin. Sorry to wake you up, but I'm at the hospital," he said all in a rush. "Beth Israel on First and Fourteenth, I think. Can you bring the car?"

I sat up, rubbing my eyes. "What's wrong? What happened?"

"It's Tommy. We got jumped. They hit him with a bottle and he's still unconscious. They don't know if he's going to wake up." His voice broke.

"Are you all right?"

"I'm fine. God, I can't believe this is happening. This is all my fault."

"I'm sure it isn't," I said, pushing the comforter down on my bed. "I'll be right there, okay? First and Fourteenth, you said?"

"Yeah. I'm in the Emergency waiting room. They won't let me back with him. The car's where it usually is, okay?"

"I'm on my way."

I climbed down from the loft and pulled on clothes quickly, still trying to digest what Austin had said. Had he and Tommy been gay-bashed? I shivered, hoping it had been an act of random violence. Somehow that wouldn't be as hard to accept.

I sped cross-town in Selma's station wagon, screeching the tires carelessly around empty corners. At Beth Israel, I parked in the visitor lot and hurried inside. Austin was in the ER waiting room, as he'd said, slumped down in a chair with one hand covering his face. His Fire Island T-shirt was torn and bloody, his pale blue jeans dirt-stained, his hair uncharacteristically messy.

I sat down in an empty chair and touched his leg. "Austin."

He sat up, and I tried not to react when I saw his left eye—the skin surrounding it was already black and blue, and the white of his eye had turned red.

"Thanks for coming so quickly. I know," he added, grimacing. "Lovely, isn't it?"

"Very pretty," I agreed, trying to keep my voice light. "I guess this is the week for hospitals. How's Tommy?"

"No change." He shook his head. "I wish they'd hit me, not him. Tommy's never been in a fight in his life. I keep thinking, what if we hadn't taken that street, what if we would've stayed longer at the club, what if I had kept my mouth shut... Then Tommy wouldn't be back there right now. I just can't believe this is happening."

I rubbed his back. "He'll be all right. He's tough. Tell me what happened."

He took a deep breath. "Um, we ran into Cruz at The Bar. He said Jodi was having a party and we should stop by. So we took off a little while later and headed over. Only we never got there—these guys jumped us on Avenue A and I guess someone called the cops because they showed up and called the ambulance."

"Was it a gay thing?" I asked, not sure how to put it.

"Yeah." His eyes were dark as he looked over at me. "They were Navy brats. Can you fucking believe it? On shore leave. Two of them took me on and two of them started in on Tommy. They kept calling us both fags and me a n----- lover. Jesus! What more do they want? We come here to get away from assholes like them. They have our hometowns and our families and we build our lives here where it's supposed to be safe, and then those fuckwits come into our city and attack us. It's not fair!"

I hugged him awkwardly, the metallic arms of our chairs between us. "I know," I said. "I'm so sorry, Austin. It's not fair at all."

"And the doctors." He pulled away. "You should have seen them when they realized it was a hate crime. They double-gloved just to look at my bruises."

At first I didn't understand what he was talking about. Then I clued in. "Oh. Well, there is a lot of HIV in New York."

"No shit," he said, looking over at me. "You think I don't know that? Tommy was bleeding, so I had to..." He stopped, looking down at his hands.

And there it was: the reason Marcus was so protective of Tommy; why Tommy had resisted getting involved with Austin for so long; why Austin had pushed me away after he and Tommy got together.

"Tommy's positive, isn't he?" I asked.

After a second, Austin nodded. "I wanted to tell you so many times, but he made me promise. It's been three years and he's been fine. He might be one of those people who never get AIDS. But what if he isn't? What if this screws up his immune system and he gets sick?"

"Take it easy," I said, squeezing his shoulder. "He's going to be okay. It'll be okay, Austin."

He leaned back in his chair, rubbing his forehead. I took his free hand and squeezed it, and we sat in silence. I wasn't surprised, exactly, that Tommy was HIV-positive. On some level, I'd suspected. But it wasn't something you could very well ask. Like any other secret, it was something that had to be shared by choice. Otherwise everything would get all out of balance.

A few minutes later a doctor approached us. "Mr—" he checked his clipboard "—Taylor? Your friend has regained consciousness. Would you like to see him?"

"Yes!" Austin leapt up. "Is he okay?"

"Looks like it." The doctor kept talking as he led us back into the main emergency room ward. "We'd prefer to keep him until morning, though, for observation. Your friend was very lucky. He has a concussion but his skull wasn't fractured, and he only needed a handful of stitches. Here we are."

Tommy's bed was in a smaller room off the main ward. He peered up at us through narrowed, bleary eyes. A small bandage covered the right side of his head behind his ear. The thought rose unbidden to my mind that at some point we might have to get used to seeing him like this.

"Hey," he said weakly, trying to smile. His voice came out scratchy and hoarse, far from its usual smooth baritone.

"Hey." Austin sat down in the chair next to the bed and took

Tommy's hand in both of his. "You had us worried there, bud," he said, failing miserably at sounding cheerful.

"Are you okay?" Tommy asked.

"I'm fine. I'm not the one who had a bottle broken over my head."

"That's what it was." Tommy closed his eyes, wincing.

"You okay, sweetie?" Austin asked, scooting his chair closer to the bed.

"Yes." But he didn't open his eyes. "Hurts to talk."

"You don't have to talk. Just rest. Rest and let your body heal."

Austin glanced back at me with worried eyes. I squeezed his shoulder. Tommy would be fine. He had to be.

I left the hospital an hour later after Austin insisted that he would stay and drive Tommy home in the morning. Reluctantly I let him twist my arm. One of us would need to be conscious tomorrow.

As the cab passed beneath yellow lights blinking against the brown-black sky, I realized with middle-of-the-night clarity that this week had changed life for all of us: Austin, Tommy, Drew, me. I wondered where we would be in six weeks, six months, six years. Would we all still be here? And how would Austin keep from catching the virus? No wonder Tommy had tried so hard not to fall in love with him. A positive with a negative—and here I'd thought I was cursed.

Back at the apartment, I crawled into bed and didn't open my eyes again until mid-morning. Then I opened the blinds and looked out at the back courtyard. Snow fell from light gray clouds, big, flat flakes drifting slowly to the ground. I watched the snow, thinking about everything that had happened recently. It was almost the end of the year, and I still didn't know what I'd be doing in either the near or distant future.

I glanced down at the desk where the applications were stacked, silently waiting. It was time to apply to school and get on with life. I couldn't stay in the city. New York was too harsh. I needed open skies and land that dominated people instead of the other way around.

I stretched, lifting my arms toward the ceiling. For the first time since the accident, my body felt almost normal. The applications could wait a little while longer. Right now, I was going for a walk in the snow. And when I got back, I would call Tommy's apartment because this time, it was my turn to help Austin. Or, at least, to try. I reached for my clothes.

CHAPTER SEVENTEEN

On Monday morning, I dropped by OTJ just before the work day started. Leslie and Mark and the riders gathered around me, patting me on the shoulder and telling me how glad they were to see me up and about. Leslie had come by the apartment the day after the accident when I was at my stiffest, so she in particular seemed glad to see me moving normally again.

I knew they were getting ready for the day to begin, so I didn't stay long. When I handed Leslie my pager and clipboard, she squinted at me.

"Is this because of your bike?" she asked. "Because if that's the case, I'm sure we can work something out."

I shook my head. "Thanks, but that's not it. I just can't afford the risks anymore, not if I want to run in college. I'm sorry."

"No need to apologize." Leslie reached out and hugged me. "You're welcome here anytime, Ash. In case you change your mind."

"Thank you," I repeated, "for everything."

The other riders gave me hugs and told me to stay in touch, and I knew they meant it. Once a messenger, always a messenger. Marcus was right—messing was more than just a job.

Jeremiah was last. "Take care of yourself, Fire Girl," he said, giving me a bro hug. "Be well, and don't be a stranger, hear?"

"I won't," I said, smiling at him. "I'll see you around."

"Counting on it."

Just before I left, Leslie pulled me aside. "Speaking of running,

Camilla was asking about you the other day. Do you remember she mentioned her cousin, the one who runs for Southern Arizona?"

Of course I remembered. The application for SAU was at the top of the pile on my desk. "I remember."

"Nicki's coming home for Christmas in a few weeks, and apparently she's interested in running with you. Think you're up for it?"

"Totally!" This was my chance to make a contact on the SAU team. Or at least, I reminded myself, to see if my goal of running Division I was plausible. "Tell her to give me a call anytime."

After a final round of hugs and fist bumps, I walked out into the December cold, just as glad to be headed home instead of out on the job. Christmas wasn't far off now, and while I may have been born in the North, I was a true Southerner when it came to snow.

Although if a certain SAU runner decided to invite me along on a winter run through Central Park, she wouldn't hear me complaining. Not one iota.

For the next two weeks, I went into virtual hibernation. I filled out applications, revised the previous year's essay, asked former teachers to write recommendations, and arranged for test scores to be sent to the schools on my list. As I wrote checks to cover the application fees, I realized just how expensive applying to college could be. With rent due and Christmas coming, I was working my way through Selma's money at a somewhat alarming rate. I was going to have to get another job soon.

I briefly considered holiday temporary work, but discarded the notion. There had to be some advantages to being ridiculously wealthy, such as not working retail in New York at Christmas. Besides, I had plans for the holidays. Austin's parents had invited us to spend Christmas in Signal Mountain, but Austin didn't want to leave Tommy on their first Christmas together. He told his parents they should come up to New York instead, not expecting them to agree, he reported later. But Claire and Bruce talked it over and called him back the next night to tell him they would be thrilled to spend the holidays in the city with him. And me. And Tommy.

One week before Christmas and the day before my nineteenth birthday, I completed my college applications. I had narrowed the pool to SAU and four other schools, all on the West Coast—University of Southern California, San Jose State University, University of Portland, and University of Washington. I suspected I would be accepted academically at all five schools. Whether or not I could make any of the running programs as a walk-on, however, I had no idea. USC and Portland were undoubtedly long shots, but midway through a long winter in New York, Southern California and the temperate West Coast sounded especially attractive.

As I dropped the last red, white, and blue Priority Mail envelope into the mailbox on our street corner, I said a silent prayer. Then I practically skipped home in fluffy snow flurries that drifted sideways through the leaden sky. Applying to college—albeit for the second time—was a sign I was back on the road I had veered off the year before. I still missed Selma, but I woke up each morning now with a renewed sense of anticipation. Not to mention, impatience. I wanted to know already where I would be the following autumn, the color of the sweats I would be assigned, whose stadium I would call home. Assuming I made someone's team somewhere, of course.

The very next day, on my first birthday without Selma, I turned nineteen. Austin, Tommy, and Marcus treated me to tapas and sangria at our favorite Spanish restaurant in Chelsea. Afterward we rented a movie and went back to the apartment, where I opened presents while the boys demolished a birthday cake Austin had made from scratch. Marcus had gotten me a cycling jersey from his favorite bike shop, while Tommy had picked out a white Don't Panic T-shirt that read "FAG HAG" on the front. I couldn't imagine ever wearing it, but in theory, it's the thought that counts.

Austin, meanwhile, presented me with a gift certificate to Urban Outfitters.

"I almost got you this totally rad sweater," he said, "but I figured you'd rather pick out what you wanted yourself."

I assured him he'd made the right decision. Austin was into the retro '70s look that had recently made a comeback in the fashion world, while I preferred the grunge look, also influenced by '70s wear. Thank God the '80s were over.

Tommy lit a joint for the four of us to share while Austin started the latest *Die Hard*. I had just taken my first hit of pot when the phone rang. I grabbed it off the coffee table, wondering who would be calling this late.

"Ashley? What's up!" His words were slurred almost unrecognizably.

I sighed. "You're drunk, Drew."

"Now why'd you have to go and say that? I haven't seen you in forever and now you go and tell me you're drunk. I mean, I'm drunk." He giggled. In the background I could hear music and raised voices.

I rolled my eyes at Austin, who paused the movie as I retreated to my room.

"What do you want, Drew?" I asked, straddling the wooden desk chair.

"I just wanted to call and say happy birthday. Is that so wrong?"

"No, it's fine."

"Someone had to do it." He wasn't laughing now. "You said you'd call."

"No, you said I should call if I wanted to talk."

"But I thought you'd want to."

Another burst of voices and laughter in the background.

"Are you at McSorley's?" I asked.

McSorley's was a bar in the East Village where you could get ten beers for ten bucks, as long as you bought all ten beers at once. Drew and his buddies liked to hang out there.

"How'd you know?"

"Go back to your friends," I said. "You must have exams pretty soon, right?"

"Monday. I go home on Wednesday."

I paused. This was not the time to talk. He was at a bar, and anyway, it was my birthday. "How about I call you this weekend?"

"You promise? You promise you'll call, Ash?"

"I promise."

"Okay. Well, I hope you have a shitty night. I am."

"I'm hanging up now."

"Don't bother!" And he slammed the phone down.

Outside the window, the falling snow was beautiful. Our neighbor's porch light caught each flake in a shimmering beam of light. Drew would forget about me, I thought as I returned to the living room. Soon, I hoped.

Austin glanced up from where he and Tommy were cuddling on the couch. "You okay?"

"Fine." I set the phone on the coffee table and grabbed the remote, curling up in the arm chair.

"Man troubles getting you down?" Tommy asked.

He was back to normal now, the blow to his head completely healed. Austin had told him that I knew he was positive, but we had yet to talk about it just the two of us.

"You know what bastards y'all can be," I returned.

"Ain't that the truth," they said in unison, and exchanged a look that was so sweet I almost felt like I shouldn't be in the room.

I glanced at Marcus, and he shrugged at me as if to say, *Lucky bastards.*

I took another hit from the joint as we settled back into the movie, but I couldn't concentrate on the flickering screen. Selma had always taken pains to make birthdays special, coming as mine did between the anniversary of the plane crash and Christmas. The previous year, as she'd done just about every year I could remember, Selma had made me my favorite meal, chicken casserole with mushrooms and wild rice. Then we'd driven to Signal Point and each read a letter out loud to my parents about the most recent year of my life. Selma wasn't religious—not that she ever admitted publicly to agnosticism in Tennessee—but she believed the soul didn't die with the body. My parents were still out there somewhere, she believed, watching over me.

That idea used to freak me out—was I really never alone? Not even in the bathtub or on the toilet? I confessed these fears to Selma when I was five, and she had the grace not to laugh at my childish literalism. Instead she sat me down at the kitchen table and explained that my parents would always be with me, but only when I wanted them to be. If I thought about them very hard and wished for them to be there, they would be. I wouldn't necessarily see them, but they would come.

The very next birthday we started the letter-reading tradition. In rain or shine, snow or sleet, we climbed up on the rock at Signal Point and broadcast our letters to the sky.

I hadn't written a letter this year. Without Selma, there hadn't seemed to be much point. Plus, now I would have to write two letters, wouldn't I?

Tommy fell asleep before the movie was half over.

"I think we're calling it a night," Austin whispered.

"Lightweights," Marcus said, but he was yawning, too.

I stopped the movie and rose, stretching. The pot had left my body beautifully mellow, if not my mind.

"Are you staying over?" I asked Marcus.

"If it's okay."

"Duh," I said, and went to get blankets and pillows out of the linen closet.

Austin followed me, purportedly to help. "You going to be all right?" he asked as I handed him the spare comforter.

"Yeah." I kissed him on the cheek. "Thanks for my birthday."

He hugged me. "You're welcome. I love you, you know."

No one had said that to me in so long. "I love you, too."

Back in the living room, Marcus made up his own bed while Austin half-dragged Tommy down the hall. I got ready for bed, trying not to think about the past. Wouldn't help. I was stuck in the here and now, and if I was smart, I would focus on what I had, not on what I'd lost.

Right.

An hour later, unable to sleep, I gave up trying and climbed down from the loft. Moving quietly in the dark apartment, I dressed warmly and let myself out into the cold night. It was late and not entirely safe to be out by myself. But new snow had whitened the streets and sidewalks and muffled the usual noise of the city. Huddled into a down jacket, my hair hidden under a wool cap, I walked the few blocks to the Hudson and stared out across the icy river to the bronze lights of New Jersey.

I cleared my throat and spoke tentatively. "Um, hello? Mom, Dad, Selma? I don't know if you're there. I don't even know if I think you still exist, any of you. I don't feel you here with me. I've tried. But I don't know if it's because I'm someplace I never went with any of you, or just that I'm forgetting you. Either way, I wish you were here."

Closing my eyes, I summoned a memory of Selma from years past placing the angel on top of our fake Christmas tree. Ever since I could remember, we'd had the same Charlie Brown-looking, plastic tree the top of which even Selma, five foot one if she was an inch, could easily reach. She'd always said she couldn't stand to watch a recently living tree wilt and die, needles falling onto the floor of our house like tears.

"Anyway," I said, focusing on New Jersey again, "it's been a strange year. Or half year. Austin has been amazing. I'm really

183

proud of him, and Tommy too. They're both such good people. I know you would love them.

"I mailed my college applications this week—not sure if you keep track of things like that. I should know in a few months where I'm going to spend the next four years. Not here, that's for sure. I like New York, but I feel lost. More lost than usual, I guess I should say."

Without a letter or any sort of living audience, I felt like I was rambling. Also, I was freezing.

"So I hope you're well, wherever you are. I hope you're together. I love you all and I miss you all and I always will. Goodbye."

As I turned back toward the city streets, I had the feeling that this might be the last time I spoke with my family. It just wasn't the same without Selma beside me to listen, to smile encouragingly with eyes that shone with love and sorrow and unmistakable pride. She'd believed in me always, believed that I was stronger and smarter and faster than the other kids, and because she saw me as whole, as a survivor instead of a victim, I could see myself that way, too. That would be one of the main challenges, I understood now—believing in myself when no one else had any reason to.

It was so cold that the tears froze on my eyelashes as I walked home, icy droplets that blurred my vision and painted rainbows around streetlights.

I kept my promise, albeit reluctantly. On Saturday I called Drew for coffee and we arranged to meet at a diner off Sixth Avenue, neutral territory halfway between our two homes. The prearranged time came and went, and Drew didn't show. I was about to leave when he finally walked in fifteen minutes late, cheeks red from the outdoors. He strolled over, hands in his jacket pockets.

"Hi, Ash." He seemed cool and aloof and together as he slid into the booth facing me.

"Hi, Drew." I didn't feel a thing, I told myself. Not even a twinge.

His hair was loose, falling around his face in brown waves. His summer tan was all but faded. Soon, I knew, he would have his winter tan. He'd shown me pictures of his group of friends snowboarding in upstate New York over break the year before.

"I'm sorry I called drunk on your birthday," he said. "That was really lame."

"It's okay." I shrugged, pretending his drunk dial hadn't bothered me.

The waitress came by and poured Drew a cup of coffee. I was already drinking tea. We sat looking every which way but at each other, steam from our drinks rising into the air between us. The Ryan family favorite pastime, except that we weren't saying anything.

Finally I broke the silence. "What did you want to talk about?"

"I was hoping you might want to, actually," he said, swirling his coffee.

I considered his words. "I don't think so."

"Look, I'm sorry about the night of your accident. I just didn't know how to react. I mean, it was like I'd found out you were a totally different person. Only it all clicked, too, in a bizarre way. Everything suddenly made sense."

"I wasn't something you had to figure out," I said. "I was your friend."

"Was?"

I shrugged and looked away.

"Well," he said, his voice thickening, "friends aren't supposed to lie to each other."

"I didn't lie. I just didn't tell you everything."

"But why not? Was it the diary thing? My sister's, I mean."

"No…" I realized he was joking and smiled reluctantly.

"Seriously, what was it about me that you didn't trust?"

"It wasn't you. I just don't tell people. It changed the way you see me. Admit it."

He frowned. "More than anything, it just makes me appreciate every minute I have with you."

"But I don't want you to look at me like that," I said, fiddling with my spoon. "I don't know how to explain it. I just want to be treated like I'm normal, not like I'm some freak to be pitied."

"But you are a freak," Drew teased.

I didn't smile. "No, Drew, I'm not. And I don't know how to be around you anymore without feeling like some sort of victim."

"But I don't see you as a victim at all. I see you as this totally strong person who I really admire. I don't know what I'd be like if I'd had happen to me what you've had happen to you."

I looked at him across the table. His eyes were reassuring, his voice earnest, his whole being devoid of the pity I'd glimpsed in him the night of my bike wreck. It was my feelings that had changed, not his. Or maybe they hadn't. Maybe I was just admitting, finally, that I didn't care about him the way he cared about me.

"This is it, isn't it?" he asked. "You don't want to be with me anymore, do you?"

I felt the same urge as ever to say what I knew he wanted to hear, but I'd owed him the truth for a while now: "No, Drew, I don't."

He expelled a short breath. "I wish I was as fucked up as you are, Ash. Maybe then I could turn my emotions on and off at will, too." He tossed a dollar bill on the table.

"That's not what I'm doing," I said. "I just don't trust you anymore. You're the one who screwed that up, not me."

"It's not about whose fault it is," he started. Then he stopped and shook his head. "Forget it. You wouldn't understand anyway."

"Fuck you," I said, throwing my own dollar on the table. "You don't know what it's like to be me, just like I don't know what it's like being you with your perfect little family and your perfect little life. But at least I never tried to tell you what was wrong with you." I stopped, breathing hard. Then I turned and walked out of the diner.

He followed me. "Ashley, wait. Come on."

I ran across the street just as the "Don't Walk" sign stopped flashing, leaving him stranded on the opposite side of Sixth Avenue. I kept running along the West Village streets, ignoring the looks of other pedestrians. I ran, breathing hard, feeling my stride lengthen and my feet pound the snowy sidewalk, and I didn't stop until I'd turned onto my street. Then I slowed and glanced over my shoulder. No sign of Drew.

Alone, my lungs smarting from the cold December air, I walked up the steps of my building. My first real break-up was official. So why didn't I feel more?

CHAPTER EIGHTEEN

The next morning, the phone woke me up. I rolled over in bed and nearly knocked it from the loft. "Shit." I looked at my digital clock—8:15. "I mean, hello?" My voice came out sounding like a frog's croak.

"Um, hi, is this Ashley?" a woman asked.

I cleared my throat. "Yes."

"Hey, this is Nicki Salvo. Camilla's cousin?"

"Oh." I sat straight up in bed, almost slamming my head into the ceiling. "Hi."

"I know it's last minute, but I'm thinking of going for a run and wondered if you wanted to come along. I'd love the company."

I tried to sound casual. "That'd be cool. How far are you planning to go?"

"Six miles through Central Park. Not too fast, just a re-introduction to the city."

"Sounds good." I paused. "Camilla might not know this, but I was in a bike wreck a few weeks ago, so I'd need to take it sort of easy."

"She told me. I just came off finals, so a nice, easy run sounds perfect."

"The finals of what?" I asked, picturing a meet in the Southwest or maybe California, where it never got too cold to race.

"No, I mean final exams."

"Oh." *Whoops.* "So where do you want to meet?"

"Where do you live?"

"The West Village."

"Sweet," she said, and even though we'd never met, I could tell she was smiling.

We arranged to meet at Columbus Circle in an hour. She would be the one in red tights, she told me.

After we hung up, I climbed down from the loft and hurried around the apartment, humming to myself as I got ready. This was really going to happen. I was really going running with someone from SAU. Unbelievable.

I got off the train at Fiftieth and jogged up to Columbus Circle, where I stretched out at the southwest entrance to Central Park as I waited. It had snowed the night before, and a fine layer of white powder clung to most exposed surfaces except the dirty piles of slush at the edge of Central Park South.

"Ashley?"

Stretching against the base of a statue, I looked up to see a girl my age, dark curls pulled away from her face in a ponytail, ears covered by a red headband that matched her tights. She was beautiful.

"You are Ashley, right?" she asked.

"It's Ash. You're Nicki?"

"Nic. Only my family calls me that."

I held out my hand. "Nice to meet you."

We shook, our gloves rasping. Except for brown eyes and dark hair, she looked nothing like Camilla, who was tall and curvaceous and dramatic. Nic, meanwhile, was built more compactly, though she still had more curves than me. Then again, so did most people.

"I know, I don't look like Camilla." She had a dimple in her right cheek and a slightly crooked front tooth that only made her look cuter.

"You don't sound like her, either."

"Give me a few days and I'll sound about as Brooklyn as it gets. Speaking of accents, I thought you were from the South."

"I am, but my family's from the North. When I'm down there, I sound native."

We looked at each other for a minute. Then she waved toward the park entrance.

"I'm warmed up. How about you?"

"Good to go."

"I thought 'good to go' was a West Coast thing," she said as we headed into the park.

"My roommate and his friends always say that."

"You live with a guy?"

"We're just friends," I said. "He's gay."

"Oh." Her forehead cleared. "I was thinking you were a little young to be shacked up with someone. You're younger than me, right?"

"I just turned nineteen."

"Really? Me, too, in September."

We reached the road and stopped, looking at each other. This was it.

"What exactly is an easy pace for you?" I asked.

Nic shrugged, tugging her headband lower over her ears. "Like, seven-minute miles?"

That *was* easy. "Okay."

She grinned. "Told you it would be slow."

We started our watches and headed off counter-clockwise through Central Park. Occasionally the wind gusted, dusting us with snow from trees overhead. The road been plowed recently, leaving the asphalt dark and damp beneath our feet, and the morning sky was clear, sunlight reflecting off the snow in white waves.

Our strides matched, long and loose, and our breath echoed rhythmically, steamy in the cold air. This would be the furthest I had run in several weeks. I tried to relax, blotting picturesque images of Arizona from my mind. I was just going for a leisurely run around Central Park. No pressure.

"Did you run track in high school?" Nic asked.

"Yeah. It was a small program, but our coach, Butch, ran middle distance at UCLA in the '60s. He actually missed qualifying for the '68 Olympic squad by a second and a half, so he knew what he was doing."

"Did you guys make States?"

"Sophomore and junior year. I did okay sophomore year, but I pulled a hamstring in the prelims junior year and had to withdraw."

I could vividly remember hanging out on the sidelines at TSU with Butch, knowing that if I had followed his advice and hadn't overdone it the week before, I probably would have been able to run my events. A solid performance at States that year would have cemented my standing among the scouts in the stands.

"What about you?" I asked. "What was your school like?"

"Pretty crazy. New York is not the easiest place in the world to run."

"So I've noticed."

"I spent a lot of time looking for open spaces, which kept me out of trouble for the most part. Your coach sounds like ours, except Diego came to the States from the Dominican to run in college. He wanted to try out for the Olympic team but the nationality thing messed him up. Instead he moved to New York and started teaching and coaching."

Her voice, I noticed, was respectful, bordering on reverent. "Did you guys go to States?"

"Every year. We even won it, twice."

"Nice."

As we ran together up the east side of the Park, alongside the snow-covered Sheep Meadow and past the glass-walled galleries of the Met, I felt a sense that this was what I was supposed to be doing in life—running and talking sports with someone who had the same addiction to endorphins and competition that I did.

At my prodding, Nic told me more about her high school team and about SAU. We kept up a solid pace, knocking the first three miles off in just over twenty minutes while Nic painted an appealing picture of her college program: a well-endowed athletic department with strong alumni support; an attractive campus in a naturally beautiful part of the country, all mountains and blue sky and sunshine; and a female coach who knew running and how to manage her athletes.

I'd heard of Marcie Andozzi, of course. Most people in the US who followed sports probably remembered that Marcie was a member of the Olympic track team in 1980, the year we boycotted. She had been ranked among the top women in the world in the 5000 meters at the time, widely considered a contender for gold. When the next Olympics rolled around, she missed qualifying because of injury, and that was it for her Olympic career. She'd won world titles on more than one occasion during a career that spanned twelve years before retiring and turning to coaching.

As we rounded the northernmost point of the loop up near 110th Street in Harlem, Nic guided the conversation back to me.

"Why aren't you in school now?" she asked. "I mean, your form is really good. You obviously know what you're doing. Was it grades?"

I watched the pavement moving rapidly beneath our feet, flecks of asphalt blurring together into a solid mass of dark gray. What story to tell? Drew's face flashed before me, and right then in the cold December morning, my breath showing white in the air as I ran beneath snow-laden trees, I wanted to tell Nic the truth.

"My aunt raised me," I said. "Last fall, she was diagnosed with cancer. It was pretty bad. I just couldn't do track when she was so sick. It didn't feel right, not when I had so little time left with her."

"She didn't make it, then?"

"She died in April. I decided to take a year to try to get my head together, you know?"

"That totally makes sense. I'm sorry," Nic offered. "Must have been awful."

"Thanks. It was. Sometimes it still is."

We finished the second three miles in twenty-three minutes. I was breathing harder than Nic, but other than the cold, my lungs felt good. No cramps, either, no muscular problems, and no joint pain. Awesome.

When we reached Central Park South, Nic said, "You up for a cool-down walk?"

"Sure," I said, trying not to sound too eager. Austin and Tommy and the boys were good friends, but sometimes it got old being one of the only women in a roomful of men.

Pausing every so often to stretch, we walked toward the Grand Army Plaza and Fifth Avenue. With less than a week until Christmas, the sidewalks were filled with shoppers and tourists come to see the Midtown Christmas lights and displays.

"Do you want to get breakfast?" Nic asked. "I know this place on Fifty-Eighth."

"Absolutely. I'm starving."

We walked to the diner Nic knew and sat in a window booth where we could watch cars zip past on Fifty-Eighth Street. The waitress poured our coffee and we sipped the hot liquid as we looked at plastic-coated menus. When we ordered, Nic finally sounded like she was from Brooklyn.

"See?" she said as the waitress walked away. "I told you I would sound like a local."

"You're still not as bad as Camilla."

"Bad? What, you trying to say we talk funny in New York?" she asked, exaggerating the accent.

I laughed. "You kind of just made my point."

We chatted about Christmas until the food arrived. Then silence reigned as we stuffed our faces with pancakes and hash browns and guzzled down orange juice and water. The only thing I was thinking about was getting some carbs into my depleted body.

Eventually our frenetic eating slowed and we leaned back in our seats.

"The food is really good here," I commented.

"I'm never sure if I love their food because it's actually good or because I'm so hungry when I get here."

I glanced out the window, remembering the previous day when I had sat in another diner in a different part of the city, fighting with Drew. I pushed away a pang of sadness. What did it matter? I'd be leaving New York soon anyway.

"You are applying to SAU, right?" Nic asked.

"I already mailed the application." I regarded her evenly. "Can I ask you something?"

"Of course." She stared back at me, her gaze warm and open.

"I know we weren't exactly pushing it today, but do you think I'd have a chance at walking on to the team?"

"I'd have to see you run more, but from what you said about your PRs, I think you have a chance. You could always come visit this spring, check out the school, maybe drop by a practice. I could introduce you to Marcie, if you wanted."

"You'd do that?"

"Why not? I only got a look myself because Diego knew Marcie's old coach. Like anything else, it's who you know. Where else are you applying?"

I told her and we talked about college and high school and the place of women's sports in each. This was a good time to be a female athlete, we agreed, better than any other time in history. But there was still a long way to go, too.

After a while, the waitress took our empty plates and topped off our coffee. We lingered in the diner, chatting as the sun climbed higher in the winter sky.

When the check came, we pooled our money and gulped down the dregs of our assorted drinks. Then we bundled up in headbands and gloves, and walked to the subway station.

"This was great," Nic said as we stood just inside the turnstiles, preparing to catch different trains.

"I'm really glad you called." I hesitated, not quite ready to say goodbye. What if I never saw her again?

"What are you up to today?" she asked.

"No plans. What about you?"

"I should get home," Nic said, sounding underwhelmed by the prospect. "Practically my entire family lives within a twenty block radius, and I'm one of the few who's left. Whenever I come home my aunts and my grandmother always make a big deal."

"You're welcome to hang out in the city with me," I offered. "I'm not planning to look for a job until after New Year's."

"Do you like movies?"

"I love movies."

"Awesome. Maybe I'll call you later tonight?" She made it a question.

"Cool." I heard the sound of a train entering the station. "Talk to you later."

"Later, tater." She smiled at me one last time and jogged off.

Following signs for the crosstown train, I headed through the station. The underground platforms smelled, as usual, of urine, but I hummed to myself as I rode escalators between floors beneath the city streets, actually skipping as I crossed the passageway between the 4 train and the N. The run had been wonderful, and so had the company. The pleasant exhaustion in my body made me feel like I was back in Signal Mountain, coming home to Selma's house after a long, satisfying practice.

This was what it was like to have a past, I thought a few minutes later, riding the N train under Midtown. Sitting in my seat on the half-empty subway car, I was conscious of my life before that time and that place stretching out behind me like a road, intersecting with the lanes of other people's lives. My family and I had traveled the same road for only a short time. Who would be my new family?

I watched my reflection flicker in the subway car window, wondering.

The phone rang that evening just as I was trying to decide what kind of pizza to order from Ray's.

"Hola," Nic said.

"How's it going?" I leaned back on the couch, balancing the

phone book on my lap.

"Good. I almost didn't recognize your voice, though," she said. "You didn't curse when you answered this time."

"Nice," I said, laughing. "How's the family thing going?"

"Lots of people pinching my cheek and telling me I'm not eating enough at that school of mine. The usual. They can't believe anyone would ever want to leave the city."

"Why aren't you like that?"

"I don't know. You must not be like your family, either, if you came all the way up here from Tennessee."

"I don't have much family. They're all pretty much gone, except for my grandparents and some cousins who live out west now. In Arizona, actually."

"Oh. Well, I guess I'm lucky, then," Nic said.

"You sound so sincere."

"No, I love my family," she protested. "Seriously. It's just sometimes they can be a little intense. You'll have to come over sometime so you can see what I mean."

"Okay," I said, trying to imagine what life in a big Italian family in Brooklyn would be like. Probably the opposite of growing up with a single, librarian aunt in a Tennessee suburb.

"You know how you said I sounded so sincere?" Nic added. "It reminded me of a scene from this TV movie in the eighties, *V*. Did you ever see it?"

"I love that show," I said, inordinately pleased she had caught the reference.

In high school, Austin and I had stayed up late every night watching the science fiction mini-series downstairs in his parents' basement, which was basically off-limits to the adults of the family. We spent much of our teenaged years down there listening to music and smoking the occasional joint. Austin's parents would have grounded him for life if they'd ever found out, while Selma, I suspected, might have grown some weed herself, though I'd never found any proof.

"I have a friend at school who taped *V*," Nic said. "Every once in a while we all get together and watch, kind of like going to *Rocky Horror*."

"I went to *Rocky Horror* a few months ago with my roommate and a bunch of his drag queen friends. Suffice it to say they all looked more feminine than I did."

"I know," Nic said. "One of my gay friends at school looks better in heels than I do. Walks better, too."

"I never could walk in heels."

"Honestly, I'm not sure why anyone would want to."

We both got quiet. The conversation seemed to have run its course, and I wondered if she wanted to get off the phone but was too polite to say so. Then I remembered—she had called me.

"What are you doing right now?" she asked.

"My roommate's at his boyfriend's, so I was about to order a pizza and watch some football." I paused again. "Any chance you might want to venture back into the city?"

"That'd be great," Nic said.

"Cool. Do you like ham and pineapple?"

"Love it."

"Sweet."

We hung up a moment later, and I stood holding the phone to my chest and smiling stupidly. I couldn't believe I was making a female friend, especially not one who just happened to run for Marcie Andozzi. It felt good, but slightly foreign, too.

Girls had always been this mystery to me. Because I'd been a tomboy my whole life, I'd never quite fit in with the female population of Signal Mountain. It wasn't that I didn't get along with them. I just didn't have much in common with girls like Jodie Kincaid, whose father owned the grocery store on Main Street. Jodie wore tight skirts and permed her blonde hair and chewed gum and smiled a lot. We were friends in that casual high school way, but the only summer we ever spent any amount of time together was when we both worked in the store as baggers. Jodie had worn her apron a bit tighter than I had, but no one ever gave me a hard time for refusing to wear makeup or for hanging out with guys. At least, not to my face.

Turned out Nic had been a tomboy growing up, too. We got to know each other better over pizza and beer that night, warm inside the apartment while the sky got as dark as it ever did in the city that supposedly never sleeps. Nic had grown up as I had, running and playing sports and befriending boys, mainly. But in her Brooklyn high school there had been other, tougher girls.

"Freshman year," she said, "I started hanging out with these girls who liked to party. Like, a lot. Fortunately Diego, my coach, got me straightened out. Without him, I'd probably still be stuck here."

I tucked my feet under me. "You don't like New York, do you?"

She shook her head, dark hair curling around her face. "It makes me completely claustrophobic, even for a little while. There isn't any uncluttered land left, just people and buildings everywhere. It's, like, soulless." She stopped and looked down at her plate. "But that's just my opinion. Millions of other people love it here, of course."

"I don't entirely get the attraction, myself. What's it like at SAU?"

"It's chill," she said. "This is what we do on Sundays—exercise in the morning, either run or hike up into the mountains, and then we all hang out at night eating pizza and drinking beer and talking about the meaning of life. You know, exploring our combined existential angst at having passed our impressionable years in the Reagan era. You'd like it there."

I smiled at her, feeling shy again. "If everyone's as cool as you are, I bet you're right."

"They're not. I'm going to grab another beer. Want one?" She'd brought along a six-pack of Dos Equis for our drinking pleasure.

"Sure."

I watched her leave the room, cute in her faded Levi's and an indigo Champion hoodie. As Camilla's cousin from Brooklyn, I'd expected her to be loud and slightly crass and a fan of acid wash. Instead she was thoughtful and sweet and funny. I closed my eyes, smiling.

Nic dropped back onto the couch. "Your beer has arrived, milady."

"Thanks. What are you going to do while you're here? At home, I mean."

She shrugged. "I'm not really tight with anyone here these days, and I only have a couple of weeks—gotta get back for indoor track."

"Oh. Yeah." I nodded and lifted my beer from the table.

"What about you? Plans for the holidays?"

"Austin's parents are coming to visit. His sister, too. She's a year behind me."

"Your parents aren't around, then?"

"No, they died a long time ago."

"What happened?"

"They were killed." I hesitated, thinking of Drew again. "It was a plane crash, actually."

"Wow, that totally sucks. I'm really sorry."

"Thanks." I glanced at her, but her eyes were sympathetic; no sign of pity there.

"One of my friend's fathers was killed in a plane crash," she said, "when we were in middle school. I used to hear planes flying over—we're in the landing pattern for JFK—and I would get scared. I even actually considered not going to SAU because I knew I'd have to fly back and forth. Crazy, right?"

I shook my head. "Not at all. It's like, you take for granted that this technology will just work, that it won't ever fail. But then it does, and walking everywhere, maybe riding horses, sounds pretty good."

"I thought about the horse thing," she said, "but it would take me like a month to get home, so..."

"Your coaches probably wouldn't like that."

"Exactly."

We exchanged a smile, and I noticed her dimples again. She was lovely, no doubt about it. What, then, was she doing hanging out with me?

I barely noticed time passing as we ate more pizza and talked the night away. Finally Nic looked at her watch and said she should be going. It was almost midnight.

I tried to talk her into staying in Austin's room. "The subways aren't safe at night," I said, sounding like a paranoid country bumpkin even to myself.

"Haven't you seen those signs on the trains—subway crime is down forty percent? Anyway, I've been doing this my whole life. Don't worry, okay?"

"Okay," I said reluctantly.

To be honest, I didn't like to sleep alone in the apartment. Austin was spending more and more time at Tommy's place these days. They tried to include me, but I knew they needed time together on their own, and honestly, sometimes being around them only reminded me of what I was missing.

I walked Nic out. The sky was bright with city lights reflecting on snow clouds. Shivering on the doorstep, I watched as she pulled on mittens and bright red ear muffs.

"It's too cold for muggers, anyway," she announced, and jogged down the stairs. "Thanks for dinner."

"Thanks for the beer."

"See you soon?"

"Definitely."

She waved and I did, too, watching as she headed toward Seventh Avenue. The streetlight on the corner flicked off just as she walked under it. I went inside, locking all the locks.

The apartment was quiet. I moved from room to room, pulling shades and turning off lights, insulating myself from the outside world. In the living room, I could smell faint traces of Nic's perfume, and I could almost hear her laughter still echoing in the air.

"Nic," I said out loud, testing the shape of her name on my tongue.

Sweet.

CHAPTER NINETEEN

For the rest of the week, Nic and I hung out daily. By Thursday we had run Central Park twice more; rented the original miniseries *V* and watched it in one sitting; gone ice skating at Rockefeller Center; and gone Christmas shopping together in Midtown. She even stayed over at the apartment one night, crashing on the couch after we watched *V*. In a matter of days, Camilla's cousin had become the person I spent more time with than anyone else.

Then Christmas Eve dawned, and we were both occupied with family, friends, and The Holidays.

The Taylors flew in Friday afternoon. Though Austin and Tommy had both been nervous about the visit, Bruce Taylor had clearly done some serious thinking over the past six months. He wasn't exactly warm, but he was undeniably respectful when Austin introduced him to Tommy at the airport. As he took Tommy's hand in both of his and smiled, I felt my shoulders relax, and sensed the same relief emanating from Austin and his mother. Maybe this visit had been a good idea, after all.

Back at the apartment, the Taylors were suitably impressed with the artwork, kitchen appliances, entertainment system, and quiet in the midst of the city. This was their first time in New York, and they admitted they hadn't been sure what to expect. Certainly not this level of comfort, Claire said as she stacked presents under the artificial tree Austin and Tommy had picked up at Gristedes the week before. Like Selma, Tommy couldn't stand the thought of killing a tree. He claimed it felt like animal sacrifice to kill a beautiful, healthy tree every year and dress it up with ornaments.

Apparently it was my destiny to be surrounded by pagans at Christmas.

We stowed the Taylors' bags and chatted over a snack of cookies and milk. Then Bruce and Claire announced that they wanted to go sightseeing, so we caught a train to Midtown and walked a few blocks to the Empire State Building. There were tourists everywhere, celebrating the holidays in the city. Our group of six fit right in. I watched the families around us, trying to figure out who was visiting and who, if anyone, lived in New York. Usually it was easy to tell—out-of-towners wore bright colors and brand new Yankees caps and Knicks T-shirts under their down jackets while locals wore almost exclusively black. Even I had succumbed to urban influence, and was wearing a black beanie with a matching North Face jacket, wool gloves, and fleece scarf.

At the top of the Empire State Building, I caught a security guard watching us: Tommy, Austin, his sister and parents, and me. We were a funny group, but not all that unlikely.

"What do you think?" Austin asked as we looked out over the Village, Chinatown and the Financial District in the distance.

"About your dad?"

"Yeah." Austin glanced over his shoulder as his father laughed at something Tommy had said. Tommy was smiling, finally, too.

"I think it's going great," I said.

"He's being cool, isn't he?"

"Totally."

"I'm a lucky man."

"Boy."

"Man."

I tickled him and he giggled, making my point, I felt.

There was a message on the answering machine from Nic when we got home. After Austin and Tommy called our favorite Chinese restaurant to order in, I took the phone into my bedroom. One of Nic's many female relatives answered my call. There were at least half a dozen aunts in the mix—typical Catholic family, in that respect. Nic's great-grandparents had landed on Ellis Island right after they were married. Camilla was named after their great-grandmother, who'd worked in a Chelsea garment factory until she fell over dead from a heart attack on a Manhattan sidewalk at age sixty.

"This is Ashley, Nic's friend," I announced into the receiver.

"Hello, Ashley. It's Aunt Maggie. We haven't heard from you today, have we?" A self-made business woman, Aunt Magdalena spoke in cultured tones that belied her Brooklyn upbringing.

"Not yet. How's Christmas Eve out your way?"

"The preparations are going well. We've almost got tomorrow's dinner ready. Except for the turkey, of course."

Each year on Christmas Eve, the Salvo family prepared an enormous amalgamation of Italian and American classic foods before heading out to Midnight Mass. They usually made so much, Nic had told me, that they feasted on leftover turkey, stuffing, lasagna, and pasta salad the whole week between Christmas and New Year's.

"I suppose I'd better hand the phone over to Nicki," she added. "You called just in time to excuse her from potato peeling, which is just as well because I was getting nervous watching her wield that knife."

Nic's voice came over the line. "What's up, Ash? How's the family thing going?"

I sat down on the floor, my back against the dresser. "Everyone seems to like everyone else. Even Bruce, Austin's dad, is being cool. What about you guys?"

"The usual drama. My cousin Ronnie, the one I was telling you about who quit school and started dealing—"

"The one whose father dropped him down the stairs when he was little?"

"Yep. He called up the house this morning and asked Aunt Maggie for money."

Aunt Maggie had begun her career at age fifteen working at the make-up counter at Macy's, and ended up vice president of marketing for L'Oreal. She was loaded, not to mention her skin was still smooth and youthful.

"What did she say?" I asked.

"She told him to get a respectable job that didn't involve preying on other people's weaknesses. Then she hung up on him."

"Go, Aunt Maggie."

The stories Nic told about her family sounded as if they belonged in one of those romance novels that spans six generations, the kind with the raven-haired beauty on the cover, standing straight and tall with her luscious breasts nearly falling out of her dress while a war rages around her. Or painted against an epic backdrop of green mountains and blue rivers, her breasts, again, generously highlighted in a lacy gown of some fashion. Selma had secretly loved those romances, the Barbara Cartlands and the Rosemary Carters and even the Danielle Steeles. She would have denied that to anyone but Claire or me, though. For some reason she was convinced that her reputation would be ruined if anyone found out that she read romances.

"Anyway," Nic said, "I just called earlier to say Merry Christmas, in case we don't get a chance to talk tomorrow."

"Merry Christmas." Beyond my door I could hear Tommy and the Taylors talking and laughing. "It's going to be crazy at your house tomorrow, isn't it?"

"Complete chaos. I'll probably be hanging at the kiddie table again, looking after all the little ones."

"Sounds like fun."

"It will be." She paused. "How long are Austin's parents here?"

"'Til Tuesday, I think."

"Isn't that a band?"

"You are such an eighties babe."

"You're just jealous you weren't as cool as I was in high school," Nic said. "You are going to come visit me before I take off, right?"

"Of course," I said, trying to ignore the twinge at the thought of her leaving. I chewed my lip for a second, then pushed ahead. "By the way, what are you doing for New Year's?"

"Hanging out at home and watching the ball drop with the family. Unless you have a better offer?"

"I was going to invite you to a party. But that probably can't compare to watching Dick Clark with your family."

"Gee, let me think. Where's the party?"

"At a bar in the Village. You could stay over afterward. This time I'd insist, dude."

"Okay, dude," Nic said. "This time I'd stay."

We hung up a little while later with promises to talk soon. I remained where I was, watching out the window as snow fell in the light from our neighbor's garden. So far this holiday hadn't been as hard as I'd expected without Selma. It just would have been so much better *with* her. I sat at the desk in my bedroom listening to the sounds of the Taylors in the next room, and tried to imagine what it would be like to walk into the living room and find Selma sitting next to Claire on the couch, festive in one of her traditional Christmas sweaters.

I closed my eyes and held the image in my mind, glad I could still picture her face and voice so easily. Then, sighing, I left the bedroom and joined Austin's family in the living room.

The next morning, Christmas Day, I awoke earlier than usual and lay in bed, staring at the ceiling. Julie Taylor slept on beside me, her breathing loud in the quiet room.

The night before, Austin had offered his parents the front room, but Claire was convinced that either she or Bruce or perhaps both of them would roll over the edge of the loft in the middle of the night and fall nine feet to their possible death on the hardwood floor. Instead, they decided to sleep on the fold-out couch in the living room, leaving the front room for Tommy and Austin. Tommy had wanted to go home to his own place, but Austin had called him chicken and Tommy had, predictably, risen to the challenge.

There we were, six of us in three rooms in every gender combination possible. I smiled at the thought: two men together in the front room, a man and a woman together in the middle room, and two women together in the back room. Not that Julie was my type, I thought as I looked over at her. Her hair was mashed unattractively about her head, and her mouth hung open, her jaw slack as her breath left her throat rather noisily. Definitely not my type.

I stared back up at the ceiling, reminded of a night I had spent with Drew shortly before Thanksgiving. We were in his room, cuddling and kissing and generally messing around. Both of our shirts were off, and I was feeling embarrassed about the minimal size of my breasts. They were only slightly larger than his.

"I think they're perfect," he'd said, slipping down on the bed so that he could kiss them.

As he did, his hair had spilled across my torso, and I'd looked down and found myself thinking, *He could be a woman, with all that hair.* At the time, I couldn't understand why the thought was not entirely unwelcome. Now I thought of Nic, imagining her hair splayed out across my chest.

Hmm. Definitely not unwelcome.

Quickly I blinked the thought away. Nic and I were just friends. If she knew what I was thinking, she probably wouldn't even be that.

The Venetian blinds were open enough that I could see more snow falling, the flakes slowly covering the previous night's drifts. Christmas morning. Hard to imagine that a year before, Austin had been on a ship in the Indian Ocean, Selma and I had still been together in Signal Mountain, and Bruce at least hadn't yet realized his son was queer. What a difference a year could make.

If I were honest, though, Selma wasn't the only one I missed. I tried to imagine what Drew might be doing—probably sleeping in his house in Fairview, warm and cozy under the new Laura Ashley comforter in his childhood room. I could picture the living room downstairs at his house, the den with its grandfather clock much like the clock in Selma's bungalow, the pictures on the walls of Drew and his family through the years. Was it the holiday making me miss his family, when I hadn't dwelled much on his absence before now?

A quiet knock sounded at the door, and Claire poked her head into the room. Her hair was loose around her face, her red plaid robe cinched about her waist. She'd had that robe for as long as I could remember.

"Merry Christmas," she whispered.

"Merry Christmas." I sat up, yawning and stretching my arms above my head, and gracefully cracked my elbow against the wall. "Ow."

Claire smiled. "Still a bony little thing, aren't you, my girl?"

My girl. Selma used to call me that, too. "Sometimes I forget."

"Would you like to join me for a cup of coffee? We haven't had any time yet, just the two of us."

"I'll be right there."

Everyone else was still asleep, including Bruce on the fold-out couch in the living room. So that was where Julie got her snoring from, I thought, Bruce's huffing drowning out our steps as we crept through the living room.

We took our steaming mugs to the dining alcove that looked out on the back courtyard, and sat facing each other.

"It's much quieter here than I expected," she said.

"That's what I thought at first, too." I cradled my cup between my hands. Had I really been here six months already? "We got an awesome deal with this place, though. It isn't typical of the rest of the city."

"Well, then I'm glad for the two of you. How are you doing here, Ashley? You seem like you've adjusted. Then again, I've never known you not to adjust."

"It's fine. I just can't wait to hear from schools, you know? I'm having a hard time being patient." As she sat back a little in her chair, I smiled. "Shocking, isn't it?"

"Terribly," she agreed, and took a sip of nearly white coffee. Selma used to keep extra half and half in the fridge just in case Claire dropped by. "You look so grown-up, both of you. I guess I have this city to thank for that."

I paused, knowing what she said was true. "Is it hard to have Austin so far away?"

"It is. I know he can't live in Signal Mountain, but I wish he felt he could live closer, or at least in a less dangerous city. New York is just so big. I'm afraid he's going to get lost." She waved her hand, encompassing the apartment, the neighborhood, the crooked Village streets.

"That's kind of the whole point," I said. "He blends in here, Claire. No place is one hundred percent safe. But in New York, everyone has their own quirks, and no one cares who or what you are. He's safer here than he would ever be in Tennessee."

Except when it came to Navy brats. Austin hadn't told his parents about the attack, and I wasn't about to mention it, either.

"But no one in Tennessee has AIDS," Claire said. "Or at least, not that many."

Austin hadn't told his parents that Tommy was positive, either, but was it possible that Claire had guessed? Or was her fear of AIDS entirely typical for a mother of a gay son our age?

"Anyway, enough about the Taylors," Claire said. "How are you handling the holidays?"

"It's okay," I said, thinking of Nic. "The runner I met, the one who goes to SAU—"

"Nicki, is it?"

I nodded. "She's really great. Being around her has helped me forget a little, I think."

"Distraction is good. I'm a big fan, myself." Claire sipped her coffee. "It's strange not to have the two of you next door anymore."

"I know. I was thinking this morning how even a year ago, I wouldn't have believed any of this."

"In some ways, I'm glad we're up here for the holidays. After last year, I wasn't looking forward to Christmas in Signal Mountain."

The year before, the Taylors had invited Selma and me over for Christmas dinner. Unlike at Thanksgiving, we'd at least managed to make it across the driveway this time. But Selma had been so sick from chemo and radiation again that she could barely eat anything. She spent New Year's Eve vomiting and having diarrhea; I spent New Year's Day cleaning and crying. Fun times.

"I know exactly what you mean," I said. "How's the family that moved into the house? The Alexanders, right?"

"They're a nice couple, in their thirties, I think I told you, with a nine-year-old girl. They only needed a place to rent while their house is being built closer to town, so I don't think they'll be there much past spring. You know, it's funny, but the little girl reminds me of you."

"What—a mouthy brat who hates Barbies?"

"Let's just say I've noticed she has a particular fondness for the word 'no.'"

"I'm glad someone's living there. I would hate for the house to be empty."

"Do you think you'll ever come back to Signal Mountain?"

I glanced out at the snow-covered garden. "I don't know. Without Selma, it just doesn't feel like home anymore. I'm not ready to sell yet, but maybe when the Alexanders move into their own house. Maybe then."

"Selma would understand, Ashley."

"You think so?"

"Yes, honey. She wouldn't want you shutting yourself up there on the mountain the way she did."

"Why did she move there, anyway?" I asked. "It couldn't just have been for the job, could it?"

Claire traced the rim of her coffee cup with one finger. "I don't have details, but I do know that it had to do with a broken love affair. That's all she would ever tell me."

"Selma? An affair? I can't imagine."

"Why not? She was young once, you know. Anyway, love doesn't just stop at thirty."

"I never said it did. But you can't honestly tell me you like thinking about your parents' love life."

Claire's parents lived in a retirement community in Florida, where they terrorized the local population every time they took their car out on the road.

"Point taken. Selma would have been thrilled to hear what you just said—as if she really were your mother. She used to say she felt like you were her child even though her sister gave birth to you."

"Really? I always felt like I invaded her life. It wasn't like she had a choice. She was stuck with me."

"You couldn't be more wrong," Claire said. "She used to tell me that she didn't know life could be so full before you came along. You were the greatest love of her life."

Tears pricked my eyes, and I blinked them away. *Ah, Selma.* Why had she gone and died on me? There was so much we hadn't said to each other, so much we never would be able to say now.

Claire covered one of my hands with hers. "I was worried about you last spring, honey, and even into summer, but now I see you're getting on fine. Soon, you'll see, a whole new world will open up to you. College is the path to the rest of your life. It's the start of everything."

"It is, isn't it? I think I needed to get away from home to figure that out."

"Selma would be so proud. Bruce and I are proud of you, too," she added, giving my hand a squeeze. "You've grown into a wonderful young woman. I'm so glad you're here with Austin to take care of each other."

"Me, too," I said, looking down at our clasped hands. Mine was bigger than hers now, and looked like the hand of an adult. When had that happened? Before Selma died? After I moved to New York?

Just then Austin's bedroom door opened and he wandered out, closing the door quietly behind him.

"Morning," he said as he noticed us sitting by the window.

"Merry Christmas," Claire and I chimed in unison, our hands falling apart.

"Merry Christmas," Austin said, and smiled.

CHAPTER TWENTY

Christmas with the Taylors was a definite success. Bruce and Austin managed to put their differences aside so much that they were on almost friendly terms by the time the Taylors caught their flight home on Tuesday. Even Julie, who had told Austin before the trip that she would rather celebrate the holidays in Tennessee with her boyfriend and his family, seemed disappointed to leave—Tommy had made it his mission to befriend her over the holidays, and few people could resist his charm.

On Wednesday, Nic and I met for an early run at Central Park. Afterward, we headed over to the diner on Fifty-Eighth, wolfing down breakfast while planning the next few days. Her flight to Tucson was set for Monday morning. Unless she got snowed in, Nic would be back in Arizona by this time next week.

"We're still going out on Friday, right?" she asked, glancing up at me across the Formica table.

"Totally." I hesitated. "By the way, I forgot to mention, the party is at a gay bar. Are you cool with that?"

"Why wouldn't I be?" she asked. "I can't wait to get away from my house. I'm starting to reach my limit with a couple of the aunts. You'll see what I mean if you come over for dinner on Saturday. You still up for that?"

"Of course."

"You don't have to, you know." She looked down at her syrup-streaked plate. "My family can be a bit much."

"I'd love to be there. If you want me to, I mean."

"I want you to."

She smiled up at me, cheeks rosy from the run, hair curling in wisps about her face and neck. I smiled back. Something about being with her made me feel like everything was as it should be, even here in the heart of the crowded, cold city.

Later, as I rode the train home alone, I tried to remember what life had been like before I met Nic. Even when the Taylors had been in the city, I'd talked to her every day on the phone. I'd barely had time this holiday season to get depressed about Selma. Or to think about Drew.

The season wasn't over yet, though, I reminded myself as I walked home along sidewalks encrusted with ice. Still time for disaster to strike.

Nic and I hung out in the city on Thursday, and then again at the apartment on Friday, sharing take-out, watching movies, and reading at opposite ends of the couch, poking each other every so often and giggling. On Friday night, we walked with Austin and Tommy to a bar on the main Village drag, where we ate Mexican food and drank tequilas. Marcus and Cruz showed up a little while later, and I introduced Nic to them. Austin and Tommy flitted about the bar, never far from us or each other. Meanwhile, Nic and I switched from tequila to beer and sat at a table with Marcus and Cruz talking and eating appetizers all night. We shared illicit cigarettes and, as the countdown to the New Year progressed on the TV over the bar, genuine amazement at Dick Clark's agelessness.

When the ball finally dropped in Times Square, the bartender blasted "Auld Lang Syne." Nic and I smiled at each other and slapped hands. But instead of letting go, our fingers caught and interlaced. I looked across the narrow table at her.

"Happy New Year, Ash," she said over the din.

"Happy New Year, Nic."

All around us, people were kissing and hugging and laughing. Should I lean in and kiss her?

Before the idea could crystallize in my mind, Austin and Tommy swooped in and pulled us up to dance. The music continued to blare through the bar, and we ordered more food and alcohol. The party went on, and I almost forgot about the moment when I considered kissing Nic.

Just before three, we caught a cab home. The taxi driver let us out in front of our building and we piled into the apartment. Nic crashed on the couch before I could offer up my bed, and was asleep in seconds, it seemed. Exhausted, I climbed up the loft ladder and fell asleep almost as quickly while outside the first snow of the new year floated gently to earth.

That night, I dreamed that Selma was there in the room, looking over me. The dream was so real that when I awoke in the early hours of the morning, I was sure that I felt her presence lingering in the darkness.

The scene in the bar came back to me, when I had looked at Nic across the table in the midst of the celebrating crowd and thought about pressing my lips to hers. What did it mean? Only I was pretty sure I knew, and even more certain I didn't want to.

I almost canceled. I almost called Nic that afternoon and told her I was coming down with a cold. But in the end, I couldn't bring myself to miss the chance to see her before she left for Arizona. We had promised to stay in touch, but who knew if I would actually see her again?

Saturday afternoon, I caught a train to Brooklyn. As it crossed over the Brooklyn Bridge, I listened to cars speeding along overhead and watched the East River below, white caps rushing inexorably toward the ocean. The last time I had been on this bridge, I'd been on the job, pedaling frantically to make a double rush delivery to an art gallery on the east bank. Not even two months later, I hadn't been on my bike in weeks. Strangely, I didn't miss messing as much as I'd expected. Must not be in my blood like it was for some of the riders I knew. Like running was for me.

Nic met me at the subway station. I saw her leaning against the wall by the ticket booth in black sweats paired with a dark green down coat. When she saw me, she pushed away from the wall and folded a copy of the *Village Voice* under her arm.

"Hey, you," she said, smiling into my eyes.

I felt my stomach flip over. "Hey."

"You okay?" she added as we paused before the stairway, people rushing past us up into the cold winter afternoon.

I looked at her, hair spilling across her shoulders unchecked, dark eyes shining in the light. "I'm great."

"Good." She tugged on my arm and took off, sprinting up the

steps in her hiking boots. "Come on!"

I ran after her into the world above ground. We were running east up a slightly snowy main street, through traffic lights and around cars and past corner stores. It looked just like parts of Manhattan, with mainly brick buildings built seamlessly along the street. This was where Nic had grown up, this very neighborhood, with the New York skyline just out of reach. Crazy.

After a few blocks, our joint burst of energy faded and we slowed to a walk.

"That's where I went to elementary school," Nic said, pointing down a side street at a large, square brick building a few blocks off the main road. "I started running home from school when I was in fourth grade."

I could picture Nic as a child, bossy and cute in plastic barrettes and overalls. She was the kind of girl I'd always wished would like me, but never seemed to.

"Austin and I rode our bikes to school," I volunteered. "We had a shortcut through the woods to the school yard."

"Woods," she repeated, and shook her head. "I wish."

She led me past the shoe store where she had bought every pre-college running shoe—she was a Saucony girl, too; past her family's favorite Thai take-out; and, finally, past the ice cream shop where she had worked in the summers to pay for said shoes.

"My parents were having enough trouble keeping us all in regular shoes, let alone cleats and spikes," she said. She was the third of six kids; her older sister still lived within a few miles of their childhood home, and her three younger brothers were still in high school.

Just past a flower shop, we turned south. A few more blocks and we turned again onto a short cul-de-sac. The highway whizzed off in the distance and I could hear the low throb of jet traffic overhead in the JFK landing pattern Nic had mentioned. Most of the buildings on her street were individual houses, two stories with garages and driveways. I'd pictured row houses or a townhouse even, but it turned out that Nic had grown up in a house a good deal larger than Selma's.

There were several cars parked in front of the house, and a beat-up RV took up most of the driveway.

"My aunts," Nic explained as we walked up the freshly shoveled front walk. "Most of them live in the neighborhood, except Angie, who lives in New Mexico, and Maggie, of course."

My hands were sweating inside my gloves as Nic led me up the front steps. Would they like me? Parents never liked me. Except Drew's—but they probably weren't such fans of mine anymore.

Nic paused, her hand on the doorknob. "Ready for the Salvos?"

"Sure," I lied.

She pushed the door open.

Immediately a wave of warm air tugged me inside, where I stood on a worn oval rug inhaling the smell of spices and baking bread. The entryway opened onto three different rooms and a stairway. There were women, it seemed, in all three of these rooms who, when they heard the door close, pulled themselves to their feet with varying degrees of difficulty and swooped toward Nic and me as we shed our winter outerwear.

"This must be Ashley," someone said.

"Oh, she's a doll."

"Come in, already. Come in out of the cold."

And "What? What did you say? Who is that?"

Nic looked at me, laughing, as a handful of middle-aged women accompanied by a pair in their seventies enveloped us into their midst and swept us away to the living room on a rising tide of English and Italian chatter.

I was led across the thin wall-to-wall carpeting and pressed into a worn arm chair. Nic sat on the footstool next to me while her relatives crowded around to ask me about myself. Where did I come from? Why wasn't I in school? What did I think of the President? Angelina, one of the older aunts, told me about the time she and her husband Jack had visited Mammoth Cave, Ruby Falls, and Rock City on a road trip fifteen years before. The youngest aunt, Miranda, a fortyish stockbroker, asked me how I liked the city.

My knee touching Nic's, I sat on that chair in the warm house and answered the questions as best I could. In such a group, there was no time to think about what I wanted to tell them and what I didn't. I explained my family situation, briefly mentioning the plane crash and Selma's death, and there were murmurs of sympathy all around. The middle-aged aunts told stories of families from the neighborhood who had lost sons in the Vietnam War or, more recently, to gang violence. The great aunts told stories of families decimated by World War II. Tragedy was everywhere, they agreed, and then we moved on to a discussion of what I had had for Christmas dinner and wasn't it nice that my boyfriend's family had traveled to the city to spend the holidays with us. Nic elbowed me in the ribs, and my protest that Austin wasn't my boyfriend died before it could cross my lips.

I sat in that chair for close to an hour, hearing and relating intimate stories with a room full of women who spoke English and Italian equally amongst themselves. The aunts all looked alike to me at first, with long dark hair and olive skin. I wasn't even sure which one was Nic's mother. But then Nic said something teasingly to one of the women in her mid-forties, and I noticed that this particular woman was wearing turquoise earrings that clearly weren't from around here. Bingo.

When the sisters started to argue about who had first taken the subway alone into the city so many years before, Nic leaned over and spoke in my ear.

"Sorry if they're a little overbearing."

I shook my head. "They're great. I'm glad you invited me."

She smiled into my eyes, her face close to mine, and I felt an almost physical jolt. I looked away, my smile slipping. *Chill, Lake*, I thought, but the admonition did nothing to slow my heart rate.

Then it was time to make dinner, even though it was only five and the meal wouldn't be served for another hour at least. Even leftovers took time to put together, Nic's mother said. Nic and I helped, warming up the mashed potatoes and buttering the loaf of French bread. The conversation, or rather the inquisition, as I came to think of it, continued unabated.

The men started arriving around five-thirty in sweaters and khakis and the long wool overcoats they wore into the city on weekdays. They were all businessmen of one sort or another, except a couple of Nic's cousins who were mechanics at an auto shop a few blocks away. One day they would own that shop, their mother told me proudly.

The men shed their jackets and strode into the kitchen to kiss their respective wives before retreating into the living room to laugh and argue amiably amongst themselves. It was so traditional—the women in the kitchen fixing the meal while the men had a beer and chatted with their feet up on the coffee table. What a far cry from Drew's family with his feminist mother, leftist sister, and mild liberal father.

Wait. I frowned. Why did I keep thinking of Drew? Meeting Nic's family was nothing like meeting the Ryans.

"What's up?" Nic asked. "You look like you want to hack that loaf of bread into little pieces."

I forced my shoulders to relax. "Nothing. I'm fine."

"Only fine?"

I glanced up at her. "Better than fine."

"Good," she said, and swatted my butt.

Camilla arrived a little after six with her long-term boyfriend— her "partner," as she referred to him—and came into the kitchen. She hugged me and told me that Leslie and Mark had passed along a message: "Happy New Year, and don't be such a stranger."

"Tell them hi," I said, a little guilty. I hadn't stopped by in a couple of weeks, not since I'd started hanging out with Nic.

Another cousin came in just then, too, Anita, a girl a few years older than us who worked in the mail room at a Midtown publishing company. She and Camilla hugged, and then Anita proceeded to talk ad nauseum about the hotness levels of her co-workers, some of whom Camilla apparently knew.

When Anita left to set the dining room table, Nic rolled her eyes. "She is so boy crazy it's painful."

"To each her own," I said, smiling to make the words friendly.

Nic looked down at the green pepper she was chopping. "Right."

When dinner was ready, Nic's mother rang a silver cowbell, and I watched as children and adults sprang from various parts of the house. Several boys came pounding up the basement stairs.

"Nintendo," Nic said, and I nodded in understanding. Gone were the days of Pac-Man, Space Invaders, and Asteroids. Now kids shut themselves inside dark rooms to play games like Super Mario Brothers and Mortal Kombat.

Since I was company, we got to sit at the adult table in the living room, while Nic's three younger brothers got stuck eating in the kitchen with the even younger cousins. Her older sister was in New Hampshire with her fiancé's family, while her older brother had joined the Army after high school. Currently he was stuck in Germany for the holidays.

By the end of the meal, I couldn't believe I'd ever had trouble telling the women in the family apart. Aunt Angie should have been born a cowboy because she loved horses and the West. She and Jack, a retired car salesman, had moved to New Mexico fifteen years before and had driven their RV back east this Christmas for the first time in five years. She spoke with a slight drawl, her words, slower and more drawn out, reminding me of home.

Then there was Aunt Maggie, the newly transplanted Floridian. On the outside, she was the consummate lady, her speech deliberately free of the Brooklyn accent some of her sisters had cultivated, including Nic's mother, Belinda. But during dinner Maggie had a glass of wine and loosened up and started relating rather risqué stories of her days in the corporate world—amusing accounts of people getting caught in assorted stages of nakedness, usually by company bigwigs. She refused to say if she had ever been caught herself.

Miranda, the youngest, was the biggest feminist among the group. I even wondered briefly if she might be a lesbian, since she wasn't married and her hair was shaved up in the back. But it turned out she was just obsessed with her work for Merrill Lynch and didn't want to deal with much of anything that didn't have to do with money. Except recipes—she loved to cook, and lamented that she never had time anymore to whip up a decent batch of bread.

We finished the meal and cleaned up the kitchen, then returned to our seats and lingered at the dining table over coffee and dessert while the young kids went off to watch TV and play video games. The men sat together talking about who was going to win the Super Bowl, which NBA teams were shaping up well. The women talked about people they knew and places they'd been and future vacation plans.

"Nicki tells us you've applied to SAU," Angie, the New Mexican, said to me.

I swallowed the bite of cannoli melting in my mouth and nodded. "It's one of my top choices."

"It'd be so awesome if you ended up there," Nic chimed in.

I nodded again, my eyes lingering on her dimples. If I went to SAU, we could hang out every day until we got sick of each other. Not that I could remotely imagine that happening.

"Well, you'll have to come visit us at the ranch if you do," Angie said. "We have more than enough room—and horses—to go around. I've been after Nicki to stay with us in the summers. This year she actually says she's considering coming out for a little while."

"Aunt Angie, you know I have to stay at school for summer workouts. Otherwise I'd be at your place all the time. It's beautiful," Nic added, glancing over at me. "You'd love it there."

"We've been raising cattle horses for twelve years now," Angie said. "Nic here has quite a bit of the horsewoman in her. That is, for an Italian." She winked at Nic.

A few minutes later Aunt Teresa, whose sons were the neighborhood mechanics, leaned across the table. "So tell us Nicki," she said during a lull in the conversation. "Do you have a boyfriend at school?"

The table got quiet. Even the men watched Nic to see what her answer would be.

"No, Aunt Teresa, I don't."

"Well, don't you worry," Teresa said, nodding. "You're a beautiful girl. One of these days you'll meet the right young man."

I hadn't known Nic for long, but I knew what the tilt of her chin meant.

"Actually, I did meet the right guy," she said pleasantly. "But he's a Black Muslim and his family didn't approve of me being Catholic, unfortunately."

I stared at her. So did everyone else at the table.

Then Anita tossed her head and said, "She's just kidding. She hasn't dated anyone since Billy."

"Is that true, honey?" Nic's mother asked.

Nic shot Anita a look. "Yep. Just joking."

"That Billy—now, there was a catch," Aunt Teresa said, and sighed.

Nic's mother enquired if anyone else would like more coffee, and the conversation moved on to the recent announcement that the West Coast coffee chain Starbucks would soon be invading the Big Apple.

A little before ten, Nic and I called it a night and went upstairs. Her bedroom was practically filled by a four-poster double bed and a wide dresser with a narrow mirror. A couple of posters of Boy George and the Bengals still decorated the walls.

"I can't believe you didn't take those posters with you to college," I said. "Cool bed, though." Without waiting for an invitation, I launched myself onto it.

"Thanks," she said, and closed the door. She stood with her hand on the doorknob, watching me. "My grandpa made it. We'll both be sleeping in here tonight. Is that okay?"

"Totally," I said, and then worried I may have sounded too eager.

"Good." She propelled herself onto the bed next to me. "So, the question of the night: What do you think of my family?"

I leaned back against the wooden headboard, setting a pillow between us. "I like them. The men seemed to blend together in my mind, but your aunts have a lot of, um, character."

"That's a polite way of putting it," Nic said, rolling over on her side to face me. "They liked you."

"They did?" I tilted my head sideways. "How can you tell?"

"Well, Angie asked you out to the ranch, and she's usually pretty picky about guests. She hasn't invited half of her own sisters out there. Not that some of them would dream of leaving the city for a week for anyplace other than Vegas or the Caribbean. Or Disney World, maybe."

Disney World. A memory flashed into my mind of my father carrying me on his shoulders so that I could be face to face with Big Bird. Weird. I hadn't ever remembered that before. I could picture Big Bird, huge and yellow, and almost feel the papery feathers of his costume against my fingers, but I couldn't picture my father's face.

"Earth to Ashley," Nic said.

I blinked, banishing the memory. "Sorry, I just remembered something from when I was little. From Disney World."

"You went there, too? We went when I was eight. How old were you?"

"Almost four," I said. "Right before I lost my parents."

I almost told her then. I nearly did—but while I didn't want my past coming between us later, I also wasn't ready for her view of me to change.

"Oh." Nic was quiet for a minute. "They've been gone so long—do you still miss them?"

I shrugged, staring up at the canopy of her bed. The cream-colored cloth draped down in the middle from the four posters, the overhead light shining dimly through the gauzy material.

"Sometimes," I said. "Not right now, when I'm here with you and your family and I'm all warm and full of good food. But other times, like when I don't feel well or I can't sleep, then it's harder."

She nodded. "Whenever something goes wrong, I start thinking of all the other disasters in my life, and I feel abysmally sorry for myself. The snowball effect."

"The damn snow. Does winter never end here?"

"Nope. That's why you should come to Arizona. Up in the mountains, it's freezing in the winter. But in Tucson, it's sunny and warm pretty much year round."

"Sounds wonderful," I admitted. "I hope I end up there."

"So do I," Nic said. Her hand rested on the pillow I'd placed between us. "You're a cool person, Ash. It's been great getting to know you."

"Same here," I said, and then smiled. "I mean, you're a great person, too."

"I knew what you meant."

Her eyes were warm and dark, and I glanced down at her lips, wondering if they would feel as soft against mine as they looked.

"So who's Billy?" I asked.

Nic rolled over on her back and stared up at the canopy. "Just this guy I dated last year. He was a couple of years ahead of me in high school and ended up at U of A on a basketball scholarship."

"Wait a minute. Do you mean Billy DiCiello? The basketball player who was drafted by the Sacramento Kings last year and everyone said what a waste?"

Nic rolled her eyes. "He'll get traded once he's past his rookie year, and then he'll have a career."

"How did you end up with him?"

"He came to one of my meets freshman year, and like an idiot I was all impressed by his big man on campus shtick. Little did I know he was sleeping with every slightly attractive female within a ten-mile radius."

"I could've told you that. I mean, look at him, Nic. He's a beautiful boy."

"*Boy* being the key word," she said. "But it made my family happy that I was dating a good Catholic from the neighborhood, even if his mother wasn't Italian. I think it made his family happy, too. Or his father, anyway, who really wanted him to be a star with the Knicks, settle down with a nice Italian girl, and produce a dozen grandsons."

"Yuck," I said, making a face. "Thank God you escaped that

fate."

"No kidding. I mean, no way am I ever going to live in New York again. Besides, the thought of giving birth to a dozen kids, while not a foreign concept in my family, does not appeal."

"You think you'll ever have kids?" I asked.

She shrugged. "I'm not sure. How about you?"

"I'd like to, some day." I hesitated. "Promise you won't freak out if I tell you something?"

She looked over at me quickly. "Promise."

"I haven't ever, well, you know, had sex. With a guy, I mean."

"You haven't?" Then she laughed. "Sorry, I'm not laughing at you. It's just, I thought you were going to say something else."

"Like what?"

Nic shook her head. "Nothing. It's stupid."

"No, really, what?" I persisted.

"Well, I kind of thought you were going to tell me you were, like, gay or something." She watched me, smiling this indefinable smile.

I looked back at her, struck by the sudden thought, *Oh my God, what if I am?* My heart seemed to pause as I stared into her eyes, and then it restarted double time. Of course I wasn't gay. So I really liked her and wondered what it might be like to kiss her. That didn't mean I was *gay*.

"Anyway, you're not missing much," she said, looking away first.

"What do you mean?" My train of thought had left me thoroughly confused.

"Sex with guys. It's not that exciting. Maybe the guys I've been with just weren't that great in bed, but I don't know." She snickered. "You have to admit, they are kind of goofy-looking naked."

"I thought I was the only one who thought that."

"No way! You should hear my aunts talk about their husbands. They toned it down today in your honor. That, and because my grandmother was here."

I was quiet, thinking about what she'd said. "Does your family really expect you to marry a Catholic guy?"

"Totally," Nic said. "And he has to be Italian, too. It's like, if I told them I made the Olympic team, they'd say, 'Well, Nic, that's wonderful. Maybe you'll meet a nice Italian boy to settle down with during those games over there in that Barcelona.'"

"Nuh-uh," I said, laughing.

"Yuh-huh."

"Come on, don't they just want you to be with someone who makes you happy?"

That was what Selma had always said. Though come to think of it, she'd always been a bit vague when it came to the gender of my future life partner.

"God, no. That wouldn't be nearly good enough. We're talking serious Catholics here, Ash. Remember when the Pope got shot back in the '80s? Aunt Teresa cried for weeks."

"Seriously?"

"Seriously." She rolled toward me again, toying with the seam on the pillow case. "I actually do have a Black Muslim friend at school, Rashad. He's always offering to come home with me and pretend to be my boyfriend, just to shock my many relatives."

"But they're your family."

"I know. I'm not saying I don't love them. I just don't want them running my life."

Her home life looked idyllic to me, but then again, I'd been orphaned twice. Possibly the grass would always look greener when it came to other people's families.

"What about Austin?" she asked abruptly. "Were his parents really cool about Tommy, like you said?"

"I think they'd both be happier if he was dating a nice white girl, of course. But Claire and Bruce are pretty accepting. They still want to be part of his life, so they're adjusting."

"Coming out to his family was brave," Nic said.

"The Navy didn't exactly give him a choice."

We were both quiet. I wondered what she was thinking as she hummed to herself and continued to toy with the pillow seam. I put my hand on top of hers, noting the smoothness of her skin and the similarity in our skin tone. As she stopped humming and looked up at me, her eyes narrowing, I glanced down at her lips, remembering the moment the clock struck midnight the night before.

Suddenly I jumped off the bed. "I have to pee," I said, and practically ran out of the room.

In the bathroom at the end of the hall, I locked the door and stood looking at myself in the mirror. My cheeks were flushed as if

I'd just run a race, and my heart was pounding. Why had I touched her like that? And what had the look in her eyes meant?

She was leaving in a few days, I reminded myself. No matter what did or didn't happen.

When I returned to her bedroom, Nic had already changed into a T-shirt and flannel boxers.

"Hey," she said, her smile shy.

"Hey."

She came toward me, and my breath caught. But then she continued past me to the door. "I'm going to get ready for bed, okay?"

"Okay."

Alone in her room, I considered knocking my head against the wall. At least that way my exterior would match my interior.

Five minutes later, we crawled into bed next to each other and pulled the sheets up.

"I'm really glad you came over tonight," Nic said.

"Me, too. Thanks for inviting me."

"Anytime." She started to reach for the bedside lamp.

"Wait, Nic." I stopped. I wasn't even sure what I wanted to say.

Her eyes were soft and so was her voice. "What is it, Ash?"

"Nothing. Only, good luck at school. I'll be rooting for you guys," I managed, mortified by my own incredible lameness.

But she didn't seem to notice as she smiled at me in the dimly lit room. "Thanks. Maybe you'll be doing more than rooting for us next year."

"I hope so."

"Me, too."

She flicked the light off, plunging the room into darkness.

"Good night, Nic," I said.

I felt her shift beneath the sheets, close enough to touch. "Good night, Ash."

Good night, John Boy. Selma and I used to call out the salutation at night, going through the routine from *The Waltons* as if there were more than just the two of us in the creaky old house in Signal Mountain. And speaking of family, why hadn't she ever mentioned gender when she talked about my future love life? Had she suspected about me, just as she had with Austin? And if so, had she been right on both counts?

I waited in the dark for Nic's breathing to steady. Only then did

I close my own eyes and settle down into her bed, giving way at last to fatigue while she slept on beside me.

CHAPTER TWENTY-ONE

With Nic scheduled to fly back to Arizona on Monday, Sunday was our last chance to hang out. After a late breakfast with her family, we headed into the city together. It was a cold day, the kind that hurt to breathe, so we decided not to go running. Instead we joined in the tourist pilgrimage to Midtown to enjoy the final weekend of holiday displays at Bloomingdale's, Barney's, Bergdorf's, and Saks. At Rockefeller Center, we grabbed lunch, admired the tree one last time, and rented ice skates for the second time in as many weeks. Because of an early obsession with roller skates, I wasn't bad. Nic, on the other hand, was amazing.

At first I just skated at the edge of the rink watching her cruise around backwards, spin in circles, and even throw a couple of jumps. Then she skidded to a stop beside me.

"Come on," she said, smiling as she held out both hands. "I'll teach you how to skate backwards."

Her teaching method involved standing close behind me and placing both hands on my hips, and then tugging me back toward her. I didn't mind, not even when, inevitably, we ended up on the ice in a tangled heap, laughing.

The day seemed to be speeding past. I wanted to reach out and slow it down somehow, but I didn't possess superpowers. Before I knew it, the afternoon had waned and evening was coming on fast.

"I wish you didn't have to go back yet," I said as we walked to the subway, down-encased arms brushing with each stride.

"I wish you were coming with me," she replied, and slipped her arm through mine.

We walked arm in arm towards the train, and I felt my face flush as people walked past, eyeing us curiously. *She's with me*, I wanted to boast. This incredible girl had picked me. But for what, exactly?

"Let's rent *V: The Final Battle*," Nic suggested as the train sped south across Manhattan.

"It's like five hours long. Anyway, I thought you had to go home."

She bit her lip. "I should, shouldn't I?"

No, I wanted to say. *Stay with me*. Aloud, I said, "Your parents are having that dinner for you tonight, aren't they?"

"Yeah," she said glumly. She picked up my hand and started tracing my palm with her fingers. "But I'd rather stay with you."

The feel of her fingers stroking my skin had unexpected effects—I actually felt a tingle work its way down my spine. Until that moment, I hadn't known my hands could be so sensitive.

"Me, too," I said faintly. "Be with you, I mean."

"Duh, Ash," she said, gazing into my eyes.

Just then a couple of guys standing near the opposite door whistled at us, snickering to each other. Nic immediately shifted into tough Brooklyn girl mode: "What are you looking at, pencil dick?" she demanded of the shorter man.

"Damn, bro," his friend said, laughter diverted. "She called you out!"

The little one's face darkened, and I tugged on Nic's hand as the train careened into the Fourteenth Street station. Not our stop but no matter, I decided as the shorter guy followed us to the doors and shot us the bird as we took off across the platform.

"I could have handled him," Nic grumbled.

"I'm sure you could have," I agreed. "But if we walk to Fourth, we'll have more time together *and* you won't have to ride to Brooklyn alone with them."

"True," she said, brightening. She slipped her arm through mine again. "Have I told you recently how glad I am we met?"

"I wouldn't mind hearing it again."

She smiled up at me as we climbed the stairs up into the cold evening, lights reflecting off the snow giving the city a glow like moonlight. A few blocks to the east lay Union Square, where I'd first encountered Jeremiah all those months before. To think—if I hadn't changed my route that day, I might never have met Camilla and, through her, Nic.

Ten blocks, it turned out, wasn't that far. We had to walk briskly to stay warm, so all too soon we were headed underground at the Fourth Street station. Before we reached the turnstiles, Nic turned to face me.

"You will come visit, won't you?" she asked, her eyes dark and intense.

"If you still want me to," I hedged.

What if I didn't get in? What if she changed her mind? What if she met someone else? Of course, that implied that I was someone myself.

"I'll still want you." She paused, glancing around at the people pushing past us. "I wish..." She trailed off, glanced back at me, and reached out to hug me.

"Me, too," I murmured, my arms around her, cheek against her hair. She was wearing a red hat and scarf of the same soft wool, and I buried my nose in the warm material. It smelled of wool, but even more, it smelled of her. I almost kissed her hair. Then, startled by the strength of the urge, I pulled away.

"You should go," I said. "Your family is waiting."

"I know." She reached out and touched my cheek, cold from the January air. "Take care of yourself, okay?"

"You, too."

I didn't let myself picture her on an actual plane. I couldn't think about air travel without recalling the crash. Sometimes I wondered if I ever would.

"I'll call you," she said as she turned away. "And you better call me back, you hear?"

Her combined Brooklyn/Southern accent made me smile. "I hear you. Bye, Nic."

"Bye, Ash."

She gave me one last smile, a bit wryer than usual, and passed through the closest turnstile. I watched her, noting the sense of loss creeping over me, until, just before she disappeared around a corner, she turned back and blew me a kiss. And then she was gone.

The emptiness of loss stayed with me the rest of the day and into the night. On Monday morning, I awoke early and lay in bed listening to the sounds of traffic beyond the apartment, trying to discern the dull roar of jets passing overhead. Was that her plane? Or that one? Or was she already long gone?

Turning over in bed, I buried my face in my pillow, squeezing my eyes shut tight. But the tears still found their way out, as they always seemed to do.

By the time the phone rang at dinnertime, I had checked CNN half a dozen times to make sure there wasn't any breaking news about an airliner from New York experiencing difficulties on its transit of the Southwest.

I grabbed the phone, ignoring Austin's questioning look.

"Hey you," Nic said, her voice tired but warm.

Tommy and Marcus were over for pizza and Monday Night Football, so I ducked into my room. "You got there in one piece."

"Thought you might want to know."

"Sure," I said, trying to sound casual—as if she hadn't blown me a kiss goodbye just before disappearing from my life for what might turn out to be forever.

In the background at her end, I heard a girl call, "Come on, hon. I've been waiting all day."

Hon? Waiting all day? What did that mean? A surge of what could only be jealousy expressed itself as a physical pain in my gut, and I realized Nic had only ever said she didn't have a boyfriend. She hadn't said anything about another girl.

"I actually have to go," I said. "Marcus is here and we're all having dinner."

"Oh. Okay, well, I have to go, too. I just didn't want you to be worried. About the plane, I mean."

"I wasn't."

Immediately I wished I could take the lie back. But then I heard that other voice, impatient again: "Nic, baby, let's jet."

"Just a sec, Jewel," Nic said. Then, to me, "I guess I'll let you go?"

"Okay. Take care," I said.

"You, too."

I waited, but she was still on the line. Then I heard the other girl's laughter, closer now, and the line clicked. I stood in the middle of my room imagining Nic being embraced by some college chick—*Jewel*—who had her shit together and wasn't in the least bit damaged goods.

Chewing my lip, I joined my friends. How was it that I felt a thousand times worse than when Drew and I had broken up?

"Was that Nic?" Austin asked.

"Yeah. She just wanted to let me know she got home."

"You two seemed awfully tight the other night," Marcus commented.

I shrugged. "Now that she's back at school, I'm not even sure we'll stay friends."

"Really?" Austin was frowning. "I thought you were talking about visiting her."

"So? You've been talking about going to California since I met you," I countered.

"Is that true?" Tommy asked, eyeing Austin. "Why don't I know this?"

Austin shot me a look. "Thanks, Ash."

"Anytime," I said, and took a swig of my beer as the conversation shifted to the mythical appeal of a fresh start in California, particularly among the gay community. California and Arizona were neighbors. Arizona, where Nic was doing something mysterious with someone I was pretty sure I'd never heard her mention but who had been waiting for her all day.

It didn't matter, I told myself, finishing my beer and going for seconds. Marcie Andozzi would never give an unknown runner a shot, especially one she hadn't seen in action. The last couple of weeks had been one extended daydream.

Time to wake up, apparently.

In Manhattan, winter dragged on. No longer was the snow fresh and soft and clean. By that first week in January, it had been plowed and re-plowed into ten-foot drifts along the edges of main roads, mountains of dirty snow mixed with trash and an occasional unlucky vehicle caught in the plow's path. At every corner, pedestrians had to scale a miniature frozen mountain just to cross the street.

I was tempted to hibernate in the apartment until spring, but I needed cash after the holidays. The day after Nic left I picked a temp agency out of the *Village Voice* classifieds and set up an interview. Later that same day, I caught a train to the agency in Midtown and interviewed with a bald man named Larry who told me that with my typing speed and library clerical experience, I should be easy to place. I left the office armed with a slew of brochures and time cards.

Selma had been right to make me take typing in high school, I had to admit. Too bad I wouldn't get the chance to tell her that. Then again, I thought as I rode the elevator to the ground floor and set off toward the nearest train station, Selma would have been leery of my signing up with a temp agency. But it was only for a few months. Then I'd have a little time to get settled wherever it was I ended up, and then college—real life—would begin. I pushed the thought of SAU and Nic out of my mind for the umpteenth time that day. There were other fish in the sea. Obviously.

The next day, Larry called and offered me a position for the rest of the week at a children's aid clinic in Chelsea, transcribing hand-written reports onto the computer. It paid twelve bucks an hour. I didn't even have to think about whether or not I wanted it. I had my first temp assignment.

The clinic was on a quiet street in Chelsea, housed in a square, gray-bricked building. For the next two and a half days I sat in a corner office, my back to a window that looked down two stories onto a cobblestone alleyway. I created records on the computer and filled them with stories of crack-addicted mothers and fatherless children. The lives of abused and neglected children passed from paper through my fingertips into the computer's memory. Alone in my cubicle, I read reports of mysterious scars and violent foster families, malnutrition and psychoses. And I'd thought I had it bad. In comparison to these kids, my life had been idyllic. Selma had loved me as if I were her own child, and so had Austin's family. I'd never had to worry about going hungry or sleeping on the streets or getting beaten up or raped repeatedly. How did these kids survive? Clearly some of them didn't.

On Friday afternoon, I finished the last report. Closing the file, I sat in my chair looking out the window, chomping spearmint gum in an attempt to get rid of the sour taste in my mouth. But the acid went deeper than the gum could reach, almost as if I knew too much now.

"Are you all done, sugar?" The voice startled me.

I turned away from the window. The social worker who had given me the files was leaning against the edge of the cubicle. I hadn't even heard her come in.

"How do you do this?" I asked.

She stood a little straighter. "Someone has to take care of these children, since their own families can't."

We looked at each other in the small cubicle: her, a large black woman in bright colors, me, a skinny white kid in gray and khaki. The distance between us wasn't only on account of race. It was also about money and privilege in a city that had long since run out of resources for its people. This was the darker side of urban life, a side of America people like me rarely glimpsed.

An hour later, I stood in line at the temp agency to pick up my check, and then stood in line again at a seedy check-cashing establishment one street over. I walked to Grand Central that night with a hundred and fifty dollars in cash buttoned into my back pocket. What a world, I thought, pushing my way onto a crowded Village-bound subway train. I didn't like this New York.

Back at the apartment, I checked the mail. Most of it was junk, but at the bottom of the pile I discovered a fat, brown envelope addressed to me. My heart pounded faster as I read the return address: *N. Salvo, Southern Arizona University.* Nic had written to me. Inside the apartment I paused, weighing the envelope in my hand. I wanted to tear it open, but instead I set it on the living room table. I wanted to feel clean when I read her letter.

I stood under a hot shower for a long time, trying to wash the city from my body. Needles of water pounded my pores. Eyes closed, I exhaled a long breath, willing negativity from my lungs.

Once I'd dried off and was warm in fleece-lined sweats, I sat down on the living room couch and opened Nic's letter. Inside the envelope she had included SAU's winter/spring training and competition schedules, as well as a couple of photos of the campus and surrounding area. There was also one of the team just after they'd won conference finals the year before. I sat back on the couch and read the accompanying letter, imagining the sound of Nic's voice as I read her words.

She had written the first three pages on the plane—about indoor track and the grueling schedule they would have until classes started again in a few weeks, about the displacement she always felt traveling between the two separate worlds of her life. It would be good to be back in sixty-five degree weather, but like always she felt withdrawal pangs from leaving home and her family behind, compounded by the fact that this time, she would miss me, too. She'd gotten used to seeing me, or at least talking to me, every day. She wasn't sure how that had happened in only two weeks.

Then she wrote, "Tonight there's a captain's meeting. It's a tradition—the night before the first indoor practice, we all get together and have a big dinner, and then we do a late night run up this paved trail at a place called Sabino Canyon, armed with headlights and flashlights and hydration packs. At the top we stop and sit in a circle and talk about our goals for the rest of the year while the moon rises over the city. It's awesome, and the only way it could be any better would be if you were there, too. Maybe next year you will be."

I blinked, the pieces falling into place. Jewel was probably a teammate excited about the evening's plans, not a girlfriend who had been waiting with bated breath for Nic's return. Crap. I was an idiot. Not that I didn't already know that.

Nic had appended a short message before she mailed the letter, much cooler than the intimate tone of the previous pages: "I talked to Marcie today before morning practice and told her about you. She said she'd be willing to meet with you if you set up a visit. So let me know if you're still interested. There's a home meet at the beginning of March that would be perfect. Call me—I think I told you the phone in my dorm room doesn't make outbound long distance calls, but I can receive them. Nic."

I set the letter on the coffee table next to SAU's schedule and looked toward the living room windows. Outside it was sleeting, a nasty combination of snow and rain that I was only too familiar with from growing up on Walden's Ridge.

I knew I should be thrilled after reading Nic's letter—apparently she really didn't have either a boyfriend or a girlfriend, and more to the point (in theory), Marcie Andozzi was willing to meet me. But one phrase kept echoing through my mind: "if you set up a visit…" There it was in Nic's neat handwriting on the white notebook page before me, the reality I had been steadfastly ignoring. In order to take advantage of the opportunity she was offering me, I was going to have to go to Tucson. No scouts would be flying in to watch my circuit of Central Park or Washington Square. I was going to have to book myself onto an airplane and fly, thirty thousand feet above the earth, halfway across the country.

I looked down at the letter lying half-closed on the coffee table and tried to imagine telling Nic I wouldn't be visiting SAU, even though she had given me an in on the team. But did I really want to pass up the chance at a college athletic career just because I was scared shitless of flying? Not only would I lose the chance to run, I would miss out on having Nic as a friend or—or whatever it was we were doing. We might write letters for a while or talk on the phone a few times, but our contact would eventually fizzle out because, after all, we were still mostly strangers, even though I woke up thinking about her every morning and fell asleep thinking about her each night.

Forgetting about SAU would mean forgetting about Nic *and* a shot at what I had always wanted.

So which loss would hurt more?

I didn't call Nic that night, only folded up her letter and tucked it away in my top dresser drawer. I didn't call her the next morning, either. Instead I went for a cold, slushy run around Washington Square Park, hoping I wouldn't run into Drew, and caught up later with Simone and Treat, the other female riders from OTJ. Sunday was the usual—brunch and the NFL with assorted gay boys, half of whom admired the on-screen athletic feats and the other half of whom were more interested in the players' tight pants.

By Sunday night, I had decided that Nic's letter required a bit more thought. I was going to call her. Really. I just wasn't sure when.

The following morning, Larry called to offer me a position at Maxwell's, a publishing company in SoHo.

"It'll probably last a few months," he said. "You'd be helping out in the photo department on the final stage of a series of children's text books. They need several people to help with the paperwork. What do you think?"

"Where and when?"

"SoHo, right now. Are you in?"

"I'm in." Not only did I need the money, I also needed something to distract me from Nic's letter.

The building was on the corner of Broadway and Spring, not far from On the Job. If the weather had been decent, I could have biked there in a quarter hour. As it was, I wrapped a scarf around my face and caught a train to Broadway and Prince Street. The building was only a block from the station.

On the third floor, the elevator doors opened onto a wide

hallway with a vaulted ceiling, red brick walls, and worn wooden floorboards. I wandered the length of the hallway until someone pointed me in the direction of the photo department.

There were five other temps already in the back corner of the main office, which was divided into cubicles. For the rest of the day we worked together sorting various photos and documents into half a dozen enormous filing cabinets. A little after four the head of the photo department, Andrea, a harried-looking woman in her early thirties, reviewed our work and interviewed each of us. She needed someone to temporarily fill the place of her assistant, Marian, who would be out for a month for her honeymoon.

Andrea offered me the position because, she said, I seemed like a hard worker and, more importantly, wasn't an artist likely to be struck by a creative urge that would lead me to call in sick. The other temps fell into that category, struggling actors, artists, and models who needed a day job to pay the bills. I assured Andrea that my only creative urges had to do with figuring out how to exercise in sub-zero temperatures.

"I can help you there," she said, and reached into her desk, covered in photo specs and galleys of the textbooks for whose production she was responsible. She pulled out a plastic card and slid it across the desk. "They just built a gym in the basement of this building. There's a work-out room in my condo, and this way I know you'll show up every day."

The next morning, the weather wasn't quite as frigid, so I walked to work through swirling snowflakes. I worked with the soon-to-be-married Marian all day, learning to track photo credits in the galleys. Each credit had to be checked and double-checked against various specs, or written photo proposals, then entered in a database. The work was actually interesting, and kept me from thinking too much about Nic and airplanes.

At the end of the day, I rode the elevator down to the basement. The building had been a factory in its former life and was in the midst of being remodeled, Andrea had told me. The gym was part of the remodeling project. One of the attendants checked my pass and gave me a tour of the facilities. There were a dozen exercise bicycles, Stairmaster machines, and treadmills, as well as a sauna and whirlpool in the women's locker room. After I changed into workout clothes, the resident personal trainer helped me design a program that would strengthen my leg and back muscles. I worked out hard, running on the treadmill for thirty minutes before following the circuit the trainer had prescribed, chanting my old mantra: "Pain is weakness leaving the body." Lord knew I had plenty of weakness to expel these days.

I was going to like working at Maxwell's, I decided that evening as I sat back in the whirlpool, steam rising around me. Now if only I knew what to say to Nic.

On Saturday, I rose early and dressed in running clothes, bundling up in layers to beat the cold. The gray sky was just beginning to lighten when I left the apartment. I caught a nearly empty train to Fiftieth and jogged the rest of the way to Columbus Circle. A little less than a month before, I had met Nic here at this very corner for the first time. And exactly one year earlier to the day, after two and a half miserable months, Selma had officially given up her fight against cancer.

"I'm sorry, Ashley," she'd said as we sat across the kitchen table, talking after dinner. "But I can't do this anymore. I can't pretend I have a chance when we both know I don't. So I'm going to stop treatment and work instead at enjoying the time I—we— have left."

I didn't say anything. I just stared down at the table pushing around crumbs from the Mexican casserole I'd thrown together for dinner. As the silence lengthened, she reached over and took my hand in her chilly one. Even before the cancer, Selma's hands and feet were always cold. Sometimes I wondered how she'd survived for so long in the North.

"I need you to know that I'm not doing this because I don't love you enough," she said. "I'm doing it because I love you too much to do this to either of us any longer."

At the southern edge of Central Park, I stretched and set my watch. Then I started my run. A few cars passed me on the way into the park, but mostly I was alone with the snow, my thoughts, and the very occasional human being. I eased into my pace, taking it slowly on the road that looped through the park. I wasn't running for time this morning.

Even though I'd known it was coming, Selma's death had still shocked me. I could remember practically every moment of the day I'd seen her for the last time. A warm spell had settled over the city that week, and that day, Claire and I had both worn shorts to the hospital.

One of the nurses, Shanice, stopped us outside Selma's room.

"Nancy says Miss Bishop had a bad night. She's been asking for you, Ashley."

Claire put her hand on my shoulder, but I couldn't tell if she was offering support or seeking it. "How bad?"

"I don't think there'll be another one for her," Shanice said gently.

It took me a minute to work out what she meant. Then I gasped, my hand rising to my mouth.

Shanice frowned a little. "Honey, you know where this train is headed."

"That doesn't make it any easier to hear," Claire said, her grip tight on my shoulder.

"Of course, you're right. I'm sorry," the nurse said, and slid her arm around my other shoulder. "We'll make sure she isn't in pain, sweetheart. I promise."

These two strong women were holding onto me offering me their care, but I couldn't seem to feel anything. Today was the day I'd been pretending wasn't coming. Sometime between now and nightfall, Selma would leave me. And then where would I be?

It took a while. But the morphine pump was on, feeding her the pain-killing opiate, so she never regained consciousness. There were no epiphanies, no heartfelt goodbyes, only a long, drawn-out end to months of suffering. After the heart monitor stopped for the final time, Claire touched my shoulder and left the room. I sat beside Selma's body, still wholly numb, until Claire returned with Shanice and a doctor who checked her vital signs.

"I'm sorry, honey," Shanice said to me. "It was just her time."

I shook off their comforting hands and ran from the hospital. Tears blurring my vision, I drove home. At the house, I changed into running gear and left again immediately. I ran through town and then, instead of following my usual loop home, I turned onto the two-lane highway that crossed the mountain and continued north. This road didn't see as much traffic anymore, not since the expressway had been built along the edge of Chattanooga back in the '70s.

I ran hard, away from Signal Mountain and the hospital in Chattanooga, away from the nurse's words echoing in my head: Selma had been asking for me, and I hadn't been there. Past kudzu vines and farms, under trees burgeoning with new growth, along pale gray asphalt I ran. I hardly noticed the miles passing beneath my feet. I didn't ever want to stop. If I stopped, then I would have to face the fact that she wasn't coming back. I couldn't stop, even as daylight faded and the sky turned indigo and stars opened their eyes above me.

Hours later and miles from home, my legs finally stopped working properly and I collapsed on the gravel shoulder of the old highway. I rolled over onto my back and lay on the empty road staring up at the deepening night sky. The air was cooler now. Insects called to each other and stars glimmered overhead. I didn't recognize the hills around me, shrouded in darkness. I was alone. Desperately, undeniably alone.

Lying at the edge of the road, I pictured Selma in her hospital bed, heard the nurse's words again. It couldn't be. She couldn't be dead. Tears coursed down my face as sobs tore from my throat, overwhelming the noise of crickets and cicadas and the wind. I'd never cried this hard before, not when I broke my arm jumping out of the tree house, not even when I crashed Selma's car on the W road and walked away with a tiny new scar to add to my collection. Both times Selma had been there to pick me up and nurse my wounds. But she was gone now, and this aloneness, this loneliness, was too much. I didn't think I could stand it.

I cried until my throat ached and my eyes swelled almost shut. I cried until it hurt to draw breath, and even after the sobs eased, I lay in the gravel sniffling and staring up at the stars shifting slowly above the earth. I was an easy target there on the side of the road, for rednecks or cougars or any other predator that might come along. But I didn't care what happened to me. For some reason, God or whatever was out there seemed to want me to stay alive, even as the people I loved most passed on. Selma had always said I had nine lives. Somehow, she seemed to think that was a good thing.

Despite the warmth of the day, the night was chilly. I was shivering by the time headlights flashed in the distance and a car wound its way along the road. I sat up, feeling the strain in my lower back, my right groin, my left hamstring, all my old racing injuries come back to haunt me. It was a good thing I'd already quit the track team; otherwise Butch would have killed me.

Claire pulled her minivan over and opened the passenger door.

"Thank God," she said, her face damp like mine. "I've been looking everywhere for you. What were you thinking, child?"

I climbed in and she wrapped me up in a blanket and drove me back to her house. There, she undressed me and helped me into a warm shower that brought my extremities tingling painfully back to life. She helped me to bed in Austin's room and sat beside me, stroking my damp hair as I slept. The next day I awoke hungry and sore, my muscles strained and stretched in all the wrong places. I couldn't run for weeks after that.

Now, almost a year later, my body was more than back to normal. Messengering had strengthened muscles I hadn't even known about. My legs carried me easily along the paved road through Central Park as snow fell and stuck to my eyelashes and I thought about how different my life had become. I didn't feel like the kid who had run away from the hospital that day. New York had changed me from a suburban Tennessee girl to a far more with-it young woman. My relationships with Austin and Tommy and Drew and Nic had changed me, too. Dating Drew had taught me about my own emotional tendencies, while being with Nic had triggered feelings in me I'd never suspected could exist. I might even be ready sometime soon to start dealing with them.

I ran through Central Park, savoring the feel of snow falling against my cheeks and mingling with tears on my skin. I still missed Selma so much, yet I didn't mind crying over her now. Though the future loomed before me unknown, at least I could feel again, love and pain and other emotions, too. But was it again or for the first time?

I ran on, footsteps falling one after the other on the damp road.

CHAPTER TWENTY-TWO

A couple of nights later, I pulled Nic's letter from the dresser. Lying on my loft bed with a candle flickering on the bedside table and an Indigo Girls CD playing on the stereo, I smoothed the folded pages and studied her rounded letters. She didn't write the way I thought she would. I'd expected her words to be short, letters narrow, but instead her writing looked laidback and soft, somehow.

I leaned back against a pillow, warm and tired from my workout and a huge pasta dinner. My stomach was full and I felt comfortable in my body, muscles long and tingly from forty-five minutes on the Stairmaster. The feeling reminded me of the night I'd spent at Nic's, when she asked me if I still missed my parents and I told her not as much when things were good.

Leafing through the envelope, I pulled out the picture of SAU's track team the day they won conference finals. Nic was in front, sitting on the ground with her arms across the shoulders of a couple of teammates. They were all laughing, happy in victory, and all at once, I wanted to be there, too. I wanted to be sitting beside Nic on the short grass outside a university athletic building, clad in red and black sweats with the cheesy picture of a desert cat, SAU's mascot, emblazoned across my duffel bag.

Before I could talk myself out of it, I reached for the phone and dialed the number she'd written at the end of her letter. It was two hours earlier in Tucson. She probably wouldn't even be home.

"Hello?" Her voice sounded across the miles, just as I

remembered it.

I swallowed hard. It had been two weeks since she'd left New York. What if I'd exaggerated the extent of our short relationship in my mind because I wanted her to feel about me the way I'd come to feel about her?

"Um, hi. Is this Nic?"

"Ash?" she said. "Is that you?"

"Yeah, it's me. What's up? How are you?"

"Fine."

She didn't sound fine. She sounded pissed.

I stumbled on: "Well, hey, I just wanted to say thanks for your letter. It meant a lot."

"Right."

"No, it did."

"Obviously."

"I know, I should have called sooner," I said, lying back on my bed. "I'm sorry. I wanted to. I really did."

"It's okay," she said, her voice cool now, dismissive.

"No, it's not. I want to explain. Will you listen?"

A voice sounded in the background, and the phone seemed muffled. Then she was back, just as subdued as before. "Yeah, okay."

Suddenly I knew what Drew must have felt, trying to talk to me after I'd already tuned out of our relationship. Had I ruined things with Nic before they'd even started?

"Your letter was lovely," I said. "Really lovely. I've read it like a hundred times, and I almost called you every time."

"Then why didn't you?" she asked, less distant now. "We went from talking every day, from Rockefeller for Christ's sake, Ash, to complete silence. What the hell?"

I took a deep breath. "Fifteen years ago, a plane crashed on landing in Chicago. Everyone on board was killed except for an almost four-year-old girl. Ring any bells?"

"I think so. Wasn't there some big anniversary recently?"

"There was, in October."

Nic was silent for a minute. "Wait. Are you saying that was you? You were on the plane?"

"I was the sole survivor, Nic, and when I got your letter, all I could think was that I'd have to take a plane to Arizona. But I've been thinking about it, and you know what? I have to get over this fear sometime. More people are killed in cars in a week than on planes in an entire year. I'm going to fly out there, okay? I'm going to fly out to visit you. If you still want me to."

She was quiet again, for longer this time. Finally she said, softly, "I still want you."

"Really? Seriously?"

"Of course, you idiot. But why don't you just take Amtrak?"

The train. Duh.

"You know," I said, "I never even thought of that."

"Is that really why you didn't call?" Nic asked. "Because you were trying to decide if you wanted to come out here badly enough to get on an airplane?"

"I know, it's totally stupid."

"No," she said, "it isn't stupid at all."

We were both quiet, and I wished I could see her face.

"Anyway," I said, trying to re-direct the conversation, "you mentioned the meet I should see is in March, right?"

"Yeah. We're hosting Brigham Young. You'll like this meet. It's like, all the urban people of color pound the little blond Mormons into the ground."

I cracked up, almost giddy with relief: She didn't hate me. She still lov—liked me. She still liked me.

I'd almost forgotten how easy it was to talk to her. We chatted about when I should come and what we would do while I was there. Then I told her about my temp job and my new workout routine, and she told me about the team and her practice schedule, and it was just like the past couple of weeks hadn't happened. Except that this time I couldn't hop on a train and meet her at Columbus Circle.

Finally I looked at the clock.

"I should probably get going," I said, "or else I'm going to need a nap at my desk tomorrow."

"Oh." She sounded as disappointed as I felt. "I guess it's pretty late back east, isn't it?"

"Yeah, and I have to work to save for that train ticket."

"Only six weeks away."

It sounded like an eternity.

"I can't wait," I told her.

"Me, neither."

I paused. "Well, take it easy. I'll be thinking about you."

"I'll be thinking about you, too. I'm really glad you're going to visit, Ash. Once you see this place, you won't want to go anywhere else."

I already didn't.

"I'll talk to you soon, okay?" I said.

"Okay. Bye, Ash."

"Bye, Nic." I waited, but I didn't hear a click. "Hey."

"Hey yourself."

"I thought you were hanging up?"

"I thought you were."

"Right. Well, goodbye," I said.

"Bye."

I waited another second, and then hung up and lay in bed, staring up at the ceiling. Something inside of me was different now. Some part of me that had been hidden deep inside—my heart or possibly my soul—had begun to reemerge. I had actually been willing to take an airplane to Arizona.

Only was it for the shot at the team or was it for Nic that I'd been willing to fly?

In the weeks that followed, my life fell into a routine—work all day at Maxwell's, work out in the basement gym, and hang out with Austin, Tommy, and Marcus or OTJ friends, and then talk late into the night on the phone with Nic. Tommy had a key to our apartment now, and sometimes he and I would make dinner before Austin got home from the restaurant. On those nights, we'd kick back with our food and hang out listening to music or watching one of the college or NBA basketball games that were always on. We never talked about his positive status or anything else potentially emotionally disturbing. We kept our interaction at the surface, but at the same time I felt like we were getting close in our own "emotionally stunted" way, as Austin liked to call it. Privately Tommy and I agreed that Austin and his whole family were too expressive. It just wasn't normal.

A month crept past, and I could tell my body was changing, my muscles getting stronger and more defined as I practiced with free weights the way the trainer had showed me. I spent long hours on the Stairmaster, stationary bicycle, and treadmill. I loved the Stairmaster, loved working my legs and lungs until sweat dripped from my skin. The exercise let me sleep at night after talking to

Nic, instead of lying awake in the loft missing her and worrying about my future.

Valentine's Day fell on a rainy Thursday that February. Austin and Tommy went out to celebrate. I stayed home and talked to Nic for an hour and a half, wishing I were in Arizona with her. Then I got ready for bed and fell asleep almost before I'd even settled into the loft.

Just before midnight the phone woke me. I struggled up from a deep sleep, fumbling for the phone before my eyes adjusted to the dark. Who was calling this late? Had something happened to Austin? Or worse, Nic?

"Hi, Ashley. It's me."

Drew. The nascent worry faded away.

"Hey," I said, rolling over and blinking as my eyes focused on the line of light coming in under my bedroom door. I'd left the living room lights off. Austin and Tommy must have come home.

"How are you?" Drew asked.

"Fine. Why are you calling, Drew?"

"Did I wake you up? You sound so grumpy."

His tone reminded me of some moment we had shared in the fall, and I pictured the way his hair fell across his face, the way his eyes crinkled at the edges when he smiled, the way he'd looked at me sometimes like I was the only person in the world who mattered. But I had never loved Drew. I had only wanted what he could give me—a sense of belonging, someone who loved me. I had used him badly; I just hadn't realized what I was doing at the time. Did that make it any less unforgivable?

"It's almost midnight," I said, my voice softer. "I have to be up early."

"Are you still messing?"

"No, just temping in an office until I leave New York."

"Do you know where you're going yet?"

"Not yet, but probably out west somewhere."

He was quiet. Then he said, "You were right about a lot of things, Ash. I think I thought you needed rescuing, but I only ended up pushing you away. I'm really sorry. I'm sorry I messed everything up."

"It's okay, Drew." Should I tell him about Nic? But at this point, there wasn't anything to tell. "Look, it wasn't all you. We both messed up. I won't hold it against you if you won't hold it against me. Deal?"

"Deal."

His voice coming out of the darkness was so familiar. I pictured him lying in his bed all cozy in his green and blue flannel sheets, the light from the street below casting shadows across his room. He really was a good guy, and I missed him as a friend. Not that I could tell him that.

"I'm sorry I woke you up," he said. "I guess I just miss you. I thought we'd be together tonight."

"I know," I said, staring at the light under the door. "I did, too."

As we sat in silence, Nic's face flashed through my mind. She was the one I wanted to be with now, not Drew. Only two weeks to go and then—what? I had no idea.

"Anyway, go back to sleep," he said. "I just wanted to hear your voice. That's bad of me, isn't it?"

"Not bad, exactly." I paused. "Look, I'll let you know when I leave the city, okay? That way you won't have to worry about running into me."

"I don't worry about running into you," he said. "Sometimes I kind of hope I will."

I didn't say anything.

"I definitely shouldn't have said that," he said, and sighed. "Take it easy, Ash. Tell Austin and Tommy I said hey."

"I will."

"Okay."

"Okay." I waited, but still he didn't say it. Finally, I did: "Bye, Drew."

"Bye."

I held my breath and listened for the click at his end. It came finally and I put the phone down. Nic's face still lingered in my mind. I missed her in a way I had never missed Drew. With him, I could take breaks from seeing him and not notice the difference. But with her, if even one day passed without a phone call, I was miserable. Talking to her had become an addiction of sorts, just like running.

The light from the living room beckoned. I crawled down from the loft and opened the door. Austin was wrapped in a red plaid blanket in the rocking chair next to the stereo, headphones clamped over his ears. I touched his knee as I sat down on the hardwood floor beside the chair. He jumped at the contact, eyes flying open. Then he pulled the headphones off.

"Way to scare the shit out of me," he said.

"Sorry."

He looked at his watch. "What are you doing up? It's way past your bedtime."

"I couldn't sleep. What's up with you?"

"Nothing."

"Must be something."

"No, really. Just, you know, Tommy."

"Is he okay?"

"Fine. Nothing like that." Austin leaned his head back and stared up at the ceiling. I looked up, too. It was one of those serrated paint jobs that made the ceiling look like a series of miniature mountain ranges.

"What about him?" I asked.

He closed his eyes. I could hear music drifting out from the headphones around his neck, Olivia Newton John's voice floating thready and tinny into the otherwise silent living room. I used to call her "Olivia Neutron Bomb" when we were in middle school, just to annoy him. How could I not have known he was gay?

"It's not a big deal," he said finally, looking over at me. "We went out to dinner and then to that show in the East Village, *Stomp*."

"How was it?"

"Awesome. Then we got dessert at Michael and Zoe's, and it was like the best night ever. Things are going really well, you know? But then we came back here, and I was just lying there thinking, 'What if this is our only Valentine's Day?' He could get sick at any time, and there's nothing I can do about it."

I nodded. "Freaks you out, doesn't it?"

"Totally. But at the same time, I don't think I'd love him as much as I do if I didn't worry about him so much. There's this part of me that I've always held back before. I've never let myself go completely. But with Tommy, it isn't worth it to hold anything back. I just want to be with him as long as possible, you know?"

I nodded again.

"It sucks that he's positive," Austin said. "I wish he wasn't, so much sometimes that it feels like I'm going to die. But if he wasn't, I don't think we would be as close as we are."

"When Selma was sick," I said, "I used to sit with her, and all of the walls between us just didn't matter anymore. I know it's different, but when you realize that someone you love is going to die, the petty stuff seems so stupid and the real stuff that much more important."

"Your senior year was pretty miserable, wasn't it?"

"Completely miserable. My life would be so different right now if she were still around." I shrugged. "But maybe that's okay, too. I mean, because of everything that happened, I came to New York with you and met Nic's cousin totally coincidentally, and now I have an in on SAU's team which I wouldn't have had otherwise. It's almost like now I'm on a better road than before she got sick. Not that I wouldn't trade a shot at SAU for her to be alive," I added quickly. "I don't mean that at all."

"Maybe you just mean that everything happens for a reason, even if it seems like utter bullshit at the time."

"You're pretty smart, Taylor. For a blond."

"Don't start on the blond jokes."

"Do you feel better?"

He nodded. "I think so. Thanks for listening."

"Anytime." I hesitated. "Can I ask you something?"

"Of course."

"How did you know you were gay?"

Austin looked over at me. "How did I know? I guess it took being cooped up with a couple thousand guys on a ship out in the middle of the ocean for me to admit it to myself. Then once I did, everything else from my past sort of fell into place. I realized I'd had crushes on guys my whole life."

"Really? Like who?"

"Um, you know, the usual. Movie stars. That kind of thing."

"Come on. You must've had a crush on someone in Signal Mountain," I pressed.

"Nope. Never," he insisted. "But why do you ask, Ash? Nothing to do with Nic, is it?"

I sat back, staring at him. "What do you mean?"

Austin shrugged. "Nothing. I just kind of wondered if she might not be completely straight."

"You did? Why?"

"Just a feeling. But who knows nowadays? It's getting harder to tell who's gay and who isn't."

I stood up, stretching. "Tell me about it. Anyway, I better get back to sleep. I have to be at work in a few hours."

He stood up, too, the blanket falling down around our feet. "Sleep well, Ash," he said, and hugged me.

I hugged him back. "You, too, Austin."

A feeling of serenity washed over me, and I knew: Whatever happened, everything would be okay. I closed my eyes, wishing that Austin could feel it, too.

Winter in New York continued throughout February with record snowfalls. I was busy all the time, working late sometimes at Maxwell's as publishing deadlines neared. After four weeks, Andrea's assistant, Marian, came back from her honeymoon. At that point, Andrea trimmed back my administrative duties and gave me sole responsibility for tracking photo credits for each of the galleys that had been printed so far. It was a solid chunk of work, but she said she knew she could trust my attention to detail. Or my obsessive-compulsive tendencies, as Nic put it.

Outside of work, I was getting ready for my trip to SAU, planning my route via Amtrak and training hard so that I'd be in good shape when I met Marcie Andozzi. I was running six miles on the treadmill five times a week, plus cross-training on the bike and Stairmaster. Every Saturday morning I caught a train to Central Park and ran a timed 5000 meters along a route provided by a local running club. My times were steadily improving, and already I'd smashed the PR I'd set in high school without anyone to push me but myself.

As the trip approached, I talked to Nic on the phone more and more frequently. At first it was once a day, but by the end of February, I was talking to her twice a day or sometimes even more.

The day before I was due to leave, I called her for the third time just before midnight my time.

"I can't believe I'll be there in a few days," I said when she answered the phone. I lay back on my bed, one fleece-encased foot hanging over the edge of the mattress. It was snowing again, and I was suddenly deeply relieved that trains weren't subject to the same weather delays planes and cars were.

"I know. It's crazy."

"How was practice tonight? Can you run on Saturday?" Nic had injured her quad a couple of weeks earlier and was just getting over the strain.

"You know it," she said, the usual brash confidence in her voice. Then she added, "At least, I hope so. It's still a little sore, but I think it'll be okay."

"Don't push it. You don't want this bothering you at Nationals."

"Assuming I qualify."

"You will."

We talked about her season, my upcoming visit, her classes, my job. An hour passed without me even noticing.

Then I checked my watch. "Dude, I gotta go. I'll see you on Friday."

"Dude, awesome!" She was making fun of me, something she never seemed to tire of.

"Don't forget to meet me at the train station, okay?"

"Somehow, I don't think I'll forget."

I paused. "Thanks again, Nic. I won't let you down."

"I know you won't," she said. "And you don't have to thank me. You deserve a shot as much as anyone else. Have a safe trip, okay? And don't worry. It's going to be great."

I turned off the phone and looked at my bags sitting by the door, waiting for morning. I was going on a trip. And at the end of it, Nic would be waiting.

Lying back, I tried to get some sleep.

CHAPTER TWENTY-THREE

Austin dropped me at the train station half an hour before my train was scheduled to depart.

"Have a great trip," he said, depositing my bag on the sidewalk. "Kick some butt, girl."

"You got it." I kissed him on the cheek. "Tell Tommy I said goodbye."

"Okay." He stood looking at me while people rushed by us. "It almost feels like you're going away for good now."

"It does, doesn't it?"

In a few months, we'd be saying goodbye for real. Once I left New York, I would only see Austin for occasional visits and major lifetime events—weddings, holidays, funerals. But those, I hoped, were a long way off. Especially the last one.

He punched me in the arm. "I'll meet you here next week, okay?"

"You don't have to."

"I want to, dumbass." He climbed back into the car. "Good luck!"

As he pulled Selma's station wagon back onto Thirty-Third Street, the Empire State Building looming in the background, I headed into Penn Station. Fifteen minutes later I was on an Amtrak Superliner, settled into my window seat in the train's upper level. I had my Walkman on already, my backpack under the seat in front of me, my athletic bag stowed in the overhead rack, and my chair reclined as far as it would go. I wouldn't be moving for a while.

247

The route paralleled my original journey to New York in reverse, hugging the coastline as we headed straight down the coast to D.C., passing through one heavily populated area after another. Tommy had said that the East Coast was one giant megalopolis from Boston to D.C.; on the train that day, I finally understood what he was talking about. City after city after town after town cluttered the East Coast. Streets littered with parked cars and empty fast food containers sprawled in all directions away from the train tracks. After a few hours, I wandered down to the Café Car both to sample its wares and to escape the overwhelming humanity beyond the train windows.

Back in my seat a little while later, I put my headphones back on and fell asleep to George Winston's *Winter Into Spring*. When I awoke with a start, we were already in D.C. I had managed to miss most of Maryland. I settled back in my seat, looking out the window as the train unloaded and reloaded. The stops were disconcerting, but at least I wouldn't have to switch trains until New Orleans.

Dusk had fallen by the time we left D.C. I shifted restlessly, trying to get comfortable. At least the "Passenger Comfort Kit" I'd picked up in the Café Car had been worth the six bucks—with an inflatable pillow, earplugs, blanket, and eye shade, the kit promised to make the next twenty-four hours more tolerable.

Maybe flying would be better, after all…

Nah.

Two days later, I awoke as the first rays of sunlight edged into my sleeping car. I had splurged for the second leg of my trip, laying out for a private bedroom with bathroom. I had slept almost eleven hours, and was looking forward to a hot shower—my second since boarding the train the previous morning—followed by a veggie omelet and fresh-brewed coffee in the dining car. Flying, shmying. After almost twenty-four hours aboard, I was pretty sure the Sunset Limited surpassed any first-class flight experience. Not that I intended to comparison shop anytime soon.

The landscape had changed again while I slept. The sky was still dark blue and wide, cloudless as far as I could see, but gone were the green trees and freshly plowed fields of East Texas. Now hills undulated into the distance, hinting at the mountains to come. The land around the train tracks was an almost uniform tan, its monotony only interrupted by the pale green of sagebrush and the darker green of the occasional hardy bush lining the flat-topped hillsides. There were few settlements between the main cities, and the ones we passed through seemed to be barely holding on in the unforgiving climate. This was the furthest west I had ever traveled, I realized. Selma and I had talked about a post-graduation road trip to the West Coast—we'd even debated between the station wagon and Amtrak—but obviously, that hadn't panned out. Now I was taking our trip without her.

As I stood beneath the hot spray, I wondered if I should call my father's parents, Judy and Sherman. They lived only a couple of hours from Tucson, just outside Phoenix, where they'd moved when I was in high school. Before that, when they were still in Wisconsin, Selma and I had taken an annual pilgrimage north to my parents' hometown. Selma had felt it was important I stay connected to my family history, particularly on my father's side. To that end, each June she would map out a semi-educational route—Wisconsin by way (loosely) of the St. Louis Arch, or the Badlands, or the ferry across Lake Michigan—and off we would go.

In the early years, we stayed with the Bishop side of the family. But after my maternal grandfather died, we took to staying with my father's parents in their beautiful old Victorian just down the street from the local university and only a few doors away from the elementary school where my mom and dad had met as kindergarteners. I loved visiting Judy and Sherman's house with its prolific pictures of my dad and his siblings. My favorite was the chronological array that angled in reverse up the walls on both sides of the house's central staircase. But after a week or more with the parents of the father I could barely remember, I was usually relieved to go home, too, where somehow Selma made it possible for me to just be me, instead of my father's ghostly girl-twin.

Wisconsin was all about ghosts, it seemed to me. Whenever we were in Oshkosh, we visited the graves of my parents and their parents and their parents before them, the Lakes and the Bishops and others stretching back to "frontier" times, when the earliest white settlers—our ancestors—had stolen the land from the resident Indians, Selma told me matter-of-factly, just as white people had done for centuries to native populations across this and other continents. On my father's side, there was believed to be some Ojibwe heritage, but as in many Midwestern families, that part of our legacy was not valued. The who and when of our native ancestry has been lost, along with the details of various European great-great-great grandparents, so that now the Lakes are just your average modern American family whose knowledge of our own past stretches back only a few generations.

Selma barely knew even that much about her side, besides what was public knowledge—William Carter Bishop, her father's grandfather, had been one of the principal founders of Oshkosh Manufacturing. That was about it—a historical footnote with few contextual details. From our stays with my dad's parents, though, Selma and I knew far more about the Lakes. Just as well, Selma told me—as a teenager, my mother had spent more time with her future in-laws than with her own father, a workaholic, alcoholic insurance executive for a company in Appleton. Judy and Sherman, it seemed, had treated my mother like a daughter long before she became their daughter-in-law. Perhaps that was why their sorrow always seemed nearly overwhelming to me when I was growing up—they lost two children in the plane crash, and then me, figuratively, when Selma took me back to Tennessee.

My freshman year of high school, Judy and Sherman had decided to sell their Oshkosh home and retire to Arizona to be closer to their kids, my other aunts and an uncle, all of whom had left Wisconsin for college and settled on the West Coast. When Selma told me the news, I locked myself in my bedroom and cried. It felt like the end of an era, and I suppose it was. Without the Lakes to visit, our regular Midwestern pilgrimages had ceased. We always meant to get to Arizona, but Selma had the expanding library and by then, I had a year-round training schedule I didn't like to put on hold for long road trips. Judy and Sherman still visited us every spring, even after their move, but I had yet to return the favor.

The last time I'd seen my grandparents had been at Selma's funeral. They'd stayed at their usual B&B for a week and would have been happy to stay longer or, better yet, take me back to Arizona with them, they told me. But I was an adult, or at least I thought I should be, and it felt strange to have my dad's parents in Tennessee. For all that they were family, I didn't know them very well. I thanked them for their generous offer and drove them to the airport and hugged them goodbye, my grandmother with her soft skin and permed hair, my grandfather with his strong grip and fondness for Old Spice, both of them smiling at me less desperately these days but still with a sadness that reminded me of everything I would never have. They'd invited me to Arizona for Christmas, but December had seemed too distant to make a commitment, especially when I still hadn't nailed down my college plans. Besides, Arizona was far away—really far away—and I didn't fly.

I did, however, like the train, I decided as I toweled my hair dry in my tiny private bathroom, the train rocking and rolling along its metal roadway. There probably wouldn't be time to visit my grandparents this trip. But next time, for sure.

Assuming there was a next time.

The morning passed quickly enough, the landscape gradually shifting from small, brown hills to larger, reddish-brown foothills, with jagged mountains and cacti visible in the distance. The closer we drew to Tucson, somehow the slower time behaved. As the final hour dragged past, buildings began to sprout up around the tracks. Small towns spaced miles apart blended together and ranged out across the desert toward the mountains. My seventy-five hour journey was coming to a close. Soon, very soon, I would see Nic.

Just before we pulled into the Tucson station, I brushed my teeth and hair, glad my sleeping car had a mirror. With a little powder to camouflage my shiny forehead and a dab of mousse to give my otherwise flat hair a bit of body, I felt positively refreshed, not like someone who had just traveled three days to reach her destination. Miracle of miracles.

I was the first person at the door of our car, backpack on my back, strap to my athletic bag slung over my shoulder. When the train stopped, I waited impatiently while the conductor opened the door and unfolded the stairs from the doorway. Then I jumped down and strode toward the station.

Nic was waiting at my gate just inside the sliding doors. She picked me up, bags and all, and spun me around, crowing, "Dude! You're here!" Then she set me back on the floor.

I smiled at her, feeling slightly dazed. "What's up?"

"Nothing," she said. "Just you, that's all."

We stood grinning at each other just inside the train station while people milled about us, hugging and talking and laughing. Nic looked the same, cute in her black baseball cap on backwards, a tight T-shirt, and cut-offs. Was Austin right? Could she be gay? She was tanned and freshly showered and I felt hot already in the jeans I'd donned after my shower that morning. I'd been away from Southern swelter for a while. Clearly it would take some time to rebuild my immunity.

"How was the trip?" she asked.

"Long."

She took my athletic bag from me, slipping the strap over her shoulder. "Well, you look great."

"So do you," I said, and then blushed.

"Come on." Nic slipped her arm through mine. "Let's get you to campus."

I let her pull me through the station and out into the mid-day sun. By the time we reached her friend's car in the half-empty lot, I could feel myself sweating. Surreptitiously I checked my pits for sweat marks. So far, so good.

"Hop in," Nic said, unlocking the car with the clicker and lowering my bags into the trunk.

"Nice ride," I commented, sliding into the spanking new red Ford Explorer.

"Belongs to my friend Rodney."

I wanted to ask who he was, I really did. Instead I fastened my seat belt and waited for Nic to whisk me off to SAU.

"So here's the dirt," she said, maneuvering the Explorer through traffic. "You, my friend, are here on an unofficial visit."

"You already said that like a hundred times."

"I'm just reminding you. That means you have to pay your own way for everything, capiche?"

"Capiche."

She slanted me a sideways look, flashing the dimples I'd been daydreaming about.

"What?" I asked.

"Nothing. You're just cute when you try to talk all New York."

She thought I was cute?

I was only half-listening as she started laying out the NCAA recruiting rules that governed my visit. She could have been talking about Arizona's gross domestic product and I would have kept on smiling stupidly at her. It was as if my life had been operating in two dimensional black and white, and now, since I'd stepped off the train station platform into her arms, color and another dimension had returned.

She stopped. "What?"

"Nothing," I said. "You're just cute when you try to talk all jock."

Behind dark sunglasses, her eyes narrowed and dropped to my lips. I held my breath, but she looked back at the road, hands fixed on either side of the steering wheel.

As we drove on through the city, I made myself focus on things outside the car: the endless blue sky and arrow sharp sunlight; the mountains in the distance, brown and serrated and close in one direction, green and farther off in another, almost black and imposing in yet another; and closer in, streets with names like Broadway and Park Avenue incongruously lined with Spanish stucco homes, cacti, and tropical flowers. Talk about a change from New York—the day before I left, a storm had dumped three more inches of snow on the city, lifting the season's grand total to almost twice its average. Meanwhile, here in sun-drenched Tucson sprinklers painted tiny rainbows in every other yard. I hung my arm out the passenger window and inhaled the desert air. At last, I could breathe again. After months of frozen hell, I was finally warm.

I recognized the SAU campus right off from the view book the admissions office had sent: new-looking buildings with stucco walls and red tile roofs, tanned students in sandals and tank tops, and even more sprinklers running on lush greens.

Nic pulled into a half-full parking lot next to the athletic building.

"I live over there," she said, pointing toward a modern, ten-story building a little ways from the athletic complex. "But I thought you might want to see the track first."

Squinting in the bright sunlight, I looked around at the old and new buildings of the athletic complex. "This is it, huh?"

"It is." She slung my athletic bag over her shoulder and headed across the parking lot to the stadium.

The track, painted in the school colors of red and black, looked new. We dropped my bags at the entrance and walked down a concrete ramp. At the end, I stepped onto the track, feeling the springy surface absorb the impact of my footsteps. Stopping in the center lane, I looked down at the numbers painted in staggered intervals across the lanes, memories colliding in my mind—my first race in middle school, when I came in first by a full minute; States my sophomore year, when I realized I might actually have a shot at a big-time program; and then States again my junior year, when I watched those dreams fizzle for what I thought would only be another year but became, it had seemed, forever.

Selma had been with me at each of those key moments: hugging me after my first major victory; cheering me on in the stands at States; watching anxiously at the edge of the track after I pulled up short in an early heat the following year. She'd never missed a single competition. At the start of every race, I would search the crowd for her white hair, her smiling face, and I always found her. She would lift her right hand, thumb poking up in a most un-librarianish way, and I would nod at her. It was my pre-race ritual, and neither of us ever missed it.

I lifted my face to the sunshine. A breeze drifted through my hair, pulled away from my face in a barrette, and I sensed it—she was here with me, now. I hadn't felt her with me much in New York, but she was here on this track in Arizona. Maybe it was that this was the first track I'd set foot on since her death, or maybe it was that I could finally let myself feel her presence. Either way, this was where I should be, I could feel it. This place, this school, could be home. If only they wanted me.

All at once, I remembered Nic. She was standing off in the furthest lane watching me.

"You look happy," she said.

"I am."

And I was. This was all I needed—a wide sky filled with light, a spring breeze against my skin, and a million-dollar track beneath my feet. And, possibly, her beside me, finally close enough again to touch.

"Are you hungry?" she asked a little while later as we followed the sidewalk toward her dorm.

"No, I ate a big lunch on the train. I'm tired more than anything. I slept in a train seat night before last, and I still don't think I've recovered."

"I bet you could use a massage."

"That would be amazing. Do you guys get them from trainers, or actual massage therapists?"

"No, I meant I'd give you one," she said. "You're a prospect on an unofficial visit, remember? No perks allowed. Except, of course, from me."

As we neared the dorm, she pulled out her keys. Most athletes who lived on campus lived in her building, she'd told me—it was the closest dorm to the athletic complex.

Before Nic could unlock the front door, it swung open.

"Hey, Nichole," a guy our age said. "Who's your friend?"

"Don't call me that," Nic said, but she didn't sound all that annoyed. "Ash is visiting from New York. Jesus runs the 800."

"So you're the prospie," Jesus said. "We've all heard a lot about you. Seriously, a lot."

Nic whacked him.

"I mean, it's nice to meet you," he said, rubbing his arm. "Will we see you at practice later?"

"I think so. Only to observe, though," I added, remembering Nic's list of what a prospect on an unofficial visit could and couldn't do.

"Now I have something to look forward to," Jesus said, smiling suggestively.

Nic gave him the finger as we headed into the building. In reply, he blew her a kiss.

Inside, I looked around interestedly, aware that there was a (perhaps very slight) chance that I would be living here myself come fall. There were several rooms off the entryway, one of which had couches and a TV. A couple of pop machines stood just inside the front door beside a pair of pay phones. The tile floor looked like it had been scuffed by at least a hundred pairs of athletic shoes.

"Don't pay any attention to Jesus," Nic said. "He thinks he's irresistible. We can take the elevator," she added, leading me toward the back of the building. "Unless you want to take the stairs?"

"The elevator sounds good," I said, recalling that she lived on the seventh floor.

As we rode up, Nic explained that while I was allowed to stay on campus with her, I would have to pay the "regular institutional lodging rate," which added up to seventeen dollars per night.

"Geez, did you memorize the NCAA handbook or something?" I asked, teasing.

"No, I just want this to go well. Is that so bad?"

I propped my sunglasses on top of my head and looked down at her. While we were apart, I'd forgotten she was a couple of inches shorter than me. Her personality made her seem taller, somehow.

"It isn't bad at all," I said.

She gazed steadily back at me until the ding of the elevator doors distracted us both.

Her room was at the end of the hall, her door decorated with postcards and a plastic message board with the note "Go Desert Cats!" scrawled across it.

"Athletes get singles," she explained as she unlocked the door. "Back the other way, past the elevators, there's a kitchen and a bathroom."

She held the door open for me and I stepped past her. Her room wasn't anything like I'd expected. It was on the corner of the building, with wide windows that looked out in one direction over the lawn we had just crossed toward the stadium in the near distance, the other toward the mountains at one edge of the city. Instead of shots of Michael Jordan and Flo-Jo, the posters were muted abstracts and black and white images of city and countryside. The only athletic poster featured a woman and man running along a dirt road, lake and mountains in the background, the inscription "Welcome to the Real World" etched just below the image. A map of the world hung above a futon covered with a dark brown bedspread and a Mexican blanket of muted greens and grays.

I stood on the green and black rug in the middle of the room, looking around in admiration. "Nice room."

"Thanks." She hung her keys on a hook just inside the door. "I got totally lucky in room draw last year. Most of the sophomore rooms aren't this big. Have a seat," she added, waving toward the futon and the bean bag chair in the corner of the room. "You can leave your bags wherever."

Nudging my bags out of the way, I stepped out of my Converse tennies and tumbled down onto the futon. The night before, as the rocking of the train lulled me to sleep, I'd realized I never slept well in New York. The constant noise and light were not conducive to a good night's sleep, which meant I had months of poor sleep to catch up on.

The frame creaked as Nic sat down beside me. Not that sleeping was necessarily my first priority.

"Want a back rub?" she asked.

I thought of Austin's comment again. Was she or wasn't she? And was I or wasn't I?

"You don't have to," I said.

"I don't mind. That way you can relax and I can tell you about your schedule this weekend."

"My schedule," I repeated. Then I rolled over onto my stomach, my heart rate already amping up. "Go for it."

She straddled my hips, most of her weight on her knees pressing into the mattress, and went to work on my back. Her hands moved quickly over the bunched-up muscles along my spine.

"You have been lifting, haven't you?" she said after a minute.

I grunted as she kneaded a particularly tight knot. "Didn't believe me?"

"You're broader than I remember." She pushed and pulled on my back. "Relax, Ash. I'm not going to hurt you."

If only I could be sure... I closed my eyes and tried to loosen up.

"This is the plan so far," Nic went on. "I have a class in a little while I thought you might like to attend, History of Native Americans from 1500 to the Present. What do you think?"

"Um-hmm."

"Then we have practice four to six," she continued, "and dinner with the team, and then maybe if we're back early enough, we can hang out with a friend of mine, Rodney."

Rodney again? I craned my head around to look at her. "The guy with the Explorer?"

"The same. Turn your head back around."

I obeyed reluctantly. "So what's up with you and Rodney?" I asked, trying to sound nonchalant.

"Wait, do you mean...?" She snorted. "Um, he's gay, so nothing is 'up.' I would have told you, idiot. Besides, with a name like that, did you seriously think he would be straight?"

The pillow muffled my relieved laughter.

Nic continued down the list. "Saturday is the meet, and afterward we'll probably have a team party and everyone will get totally plastered since we have Sunday off, and then on Sunday we can do whatever we want. I was thinking maybe we'd go someplace so you could see the local sights..."

My eyes were shut and I was warm (it was Arizona after all) and the breeze floating in the partially open window above the bed was gentle, and Nic's weight felt solid and real against me, her hands soothing now along my sore back, her voice soft in the dorm room, and the hum of the miniature refrigerator next to the bed lulled me into a half-awake hazy world where everything was good and I was happy.

Until I felt a string of drool drop toward the pillow. Horrified, I opened my eyes, sucking in the saliva before it could fall.

Nic stopped mid-sentence. "Did you just drool on my pillow?" she asked, extricating her legs from mine and flopping stomach-down on the mattress beside me.

"I think I caught it in time."

"You better have."

"No, I totally did."

We were lying on her bed, warm colors and earthen tones of her room all around us. The world beyond the window was red clay and cacti this time, not the snow-entrenched, night-shadowed streets of Brooklyn. Being at her house a few miles from Austin and the Village had been good, but this was better. This was a future I could earn, and possibly even choose.

"Speaking of schedules," Nic said, looking away from me to frown at her watch, "I have to grab some food before class. Are you sure you don't want anything?"

"Nah, I'm fine. In fact, I could use a nap."

"Cool." She slid off the bed and pulled a backpack from under the futon frame. Grabbing a couple of books from the desk near the door, she tossed them in the pack and readjusted her baseball cap. "Are you really going to sleep, or should I leave you the keys?"

I was yawning as she finished the question. "Take the keys."

"There's Gatorade in the fridge if you get thirsty, and some fruit if you get hungry. When I get back we'll head out to class, okay?"

"Okay." I stretched lazily on the bed.

She slung the pack over her shoulder and opened the door. "Oh, and Ash."

"Yeah?"

"Try not to drool on my pillow, will you?"

"I didn't—" I started, but too late. She'd already closed the door.

As her footsteps receded, I climbed off the bed and opened my athletic bag. I was too hot in these clothes. I pulled out a pair of khaki shorts and a white T-shirt, inhaled deeply of their dryer sheet scent and pulled them on, tucking my jeans into the only empty pocket of my bag. Good thing I'd shaved my legs on the train.

Stretching out on the bed again, I looked out the window above my head. Blue sky as far as I could see. It was probably cold and gray in New York. Shutting my eyes, I snuggled into the bed. Would I even be able to sleep? I wasn't sure. But it didn't matter. I was in Nic's dorm room, and I wouldn't have to leave for three whole days.

In my dream, a hand touched my cheek and lingered.

I opened my eyes. Nic was standing across the room with her back to me. It was a quarter to two already, according to the clock on the mini-fridge next to the bed. I'd been asleep for almost an hour.

"I didn't hear you come in," I said, stretching.

"Yeah, but you wake up really quickly. I forgot that about you." Frowning, she pulled a desk drawer open and fumbled through a stack of papers. Then she stuffed a folder into her pack and finally looked up at me. "Ready?"

"Sure." I sat where I was on the bed, holding my knees loosely to my chest. "You okay?"

"I'm good. You?"

"I'm good, too. I know I haven't been here long, but it already feels like this is where I was meant to be, you know?"

Nic nodded. Then she looked away from me, searching through the open desk drawer again. "Of course, you haven't tasted the cafeteria food yet. That may change your mind."

"I doubt it," I said, sliding off the bed. I stepped into sandals and pulled on a baseball cap. Then I paused. "Wait, is it okay to wear hats in class?"

Nic smiled. "Yes, Ash. This isn't high school."

"I knew that."

"Sure you did." Her smile was definitely more of a smirk now.

Out in the hall, I waited until she'd closed the door before pulling her into a pretend head lock.

"I'd be careful if I were you," I said, holding her against me. "You never know what a crazy bike messenger might do."

"Former bike messenger," Nic pointed out, and tickled me until I let go.

"True," I admitted. "Though I prefer the term *retired*."

"Uh-uh. Come on, Miss Retired Bike Messenger. Your first college class awaits."

Her arm still around my waist, we headed toward the elevator, and I remembered the feeling I'd had in New York as we walked underground from one train station to the next—somehow, this amazing girl had picked me. I still didn't know for what, exactly, but I couldn't wait to find out.

CHAPTER TWENTY-FOUR

The room where Nic's class took place was nothing like my high school. Instead of linoleum tiles and beat-up desks with gum stuck to the underside, the second-story classroom was more like an auditorium, with wall-to-wall carpeting and stadium seats, each with its own retractable desk. I sat at the end of a row watching Nic take notes and listening to the professor's description of the Anasazi tribes that had once lived in the Arizona desert. The slides the professor shared were fascinating—I had never heard of cliff dwellings before, and hadn't realized the Southwest had been settled since before the beginning of written history.

"College is awesome," I said to Nic as we left the building.

"It is, isn't it?"

Just then, a guy in jean shorts and a tank top caught up to us from behind.

"Hey, girl," he said, and kissed Nic on the cheek.

"Hey, yourself. This is Ashley, from New York. Ash, this is Rodney."

He smiled at me, shaking his brown-blond hair out of his eyes. "Well hello, Ashley. I've heard all about you." He held out a hand, muscular shoulders rippling in the sunshine.

"Nice to meet you," I said, clasping his hand.

"You're visiting at a perfect time," he said. "Spring in Arizona is gorgeous."

"I know. It's going to be hard to go back to New York next week."

"Hopefully you'll be back before too long," Nic put in.

"Hopefully."

Rodney glanced at his watch. "I'm late for a meeting, but I'll see you later. It was nice to finally meet you, Ashley."

Finally? "You, too."

He jogged off, attracting interested looks from men and women alike.

"Austin would be totally hot for him," I said. "So would half his friends."

"He's beautiful, isn't he?" Nic agreed, squinting after him as we strolled on. "The thing is, he doesn't even know it. He's so into swimming, he doesn't have time for anything else. He actually just came out at the beginning of the year, and he still hasn't dated anyone. I think he's scared of AIDS. Not that I blame him."

"You know Tommy, Austin's boyfriend?"

Nic nodded.

"He's HIV-positive. That stays between us, though, okay?"

"No problem." She reached out and touched my arm. "God, he's so young. It must be hard on all of you."

"Tommy and I are alike in a lot of ways, one of them being that neither of us talks much about what we're feeling. We basically ignore the whole thing, which drives Austin crazy."

"Why don't you talk about how you feel?" Nic asked, nudging me with her shoulder to make me turn onto a different sidewalk.

I shrugged. "I don't know. Why, are you like totally in touch with your emotions?"

"I *am* Italian, Ash. Talking about our feelings, usually at volumes wholly uncomfortable for others—it's sort of in our genes."

For a moment, I envied her. Selma had always told me we descended from practical, uber-competent Midwesterners for whom the laconic comment, "Could be worse," was a cherished state of mind. My mother's more volatile temperament, which I'd inherited, had been considered a weakness, and so my mother had worked hard to suppress her feelings, to curb her "excessive" emotional life.

Selma didn't want me to do the same thing, she told me, and yet I could tell that my likes and dislikes, intense as they were, did not sit easily with her or with the majority of our oh-so-Southern neighbors. Denying my feelings had become a habit, even when

Selma tried to get me to open up. Besides, I couldn't help thinking that if I delved too deeply into the mysteries of my own mind, I risked undoing the protective shield around my memories of the accident. After my recent half-remembrance, this was not a risk I wanted to take.

And yet... I glanced sideways at Nic, who was gazing out over an almost too-green lawn where students in shorts and tank tops tossed Frisbees and juggled hacky sacks. Wouldn't there be something liberating about being able to talk openly with someone else? Someone you, say, loved, and who loved you?

"What's up?" she asked, her hand reaching out to touch my elbow.

"Nothing," I said, and moved to a safe distance that I maintained the rest of the walk across campus.

At the gym, a woman in SAU sweat shorts was waiting for us. She nodded as we approached. "Salvo. And you must be Ashley Lake."

"Ash, this is Trinity Jackson," Nic said, "one of Marcie's assistants."

Trinity held her hand toward me, and I shook it, careful not to squeeze too hard or too light. I had read somewhere that the handshake could make or break a recruiting trip. Fortunately, Marcie's assistant didn't seem to dwell unduly on the strength of my grip.

"Welcome to Arizona," she said briskly. "We're glad you could make it. I trust the trip from New York was a long one?"

"Very."

"Nic tells us you're from Tennessee originally."

"That's right. Chattanooga."

"I've been there," Trinity said. "I ran a couple of meets at UTC for Georgia Tech, back in the day."

"Georgia Tech?" I repeated, my hopes sinking. Yellow Jackets were not traditionally fans of those of us who hailed from the Volunteer State.

"That was a long time ago." She smiled slightly. "Well, maybe not that long. Anyway, come on, Ashley. I'll give you the guided tour."

As Nic fell into step beside us, Trinity stopped and raised her perfectly sculpted eyebrows. "Don't you have physical therapy, Salvo?"

"Aw, Trin, my leg feels a thousand times better."

"I'm sure it does. Now, beat it."

Grumbling, Nic squeezed my hand and mouthed "Good luck" where her coach wouldn't see.

I nodded and watched her leave, my stomach flip-flopping. She was the one person who seemed to want me here almost as much as I wanted to be. Without her, I would have to work to sell myself to these people, to convince them that they needed an unknown middle distance runner from suburban Tennessee in their program. Fan-freaking-tastic.

Trinity led me through the athletic complex, showing me the indoor track and tennis courts, the swimming pool, the basketball courts, and the weight room. The facilities were impressive. The buildings were new, the courts all in good condition, and the indoor track top-notch. In the training room, Nic sat on a table with a heating pad wrapped around the top of her leg. She waved, the look she gave me almost as anxious as I felt, and I understood: Official or not, this interview would determine my fate at SAU.

Trinity saved the administrative offices for last.

"Marcie should be in her office," she said as we crossed into the coaches' wing. "She wanted to meet you before practice."

As Trinity knocked on a partially open door and stuck her head in, I took a settling breath. I was about to meet Marcie Andozzi, running legend and the person with the power to decide my future. We'd spoken on the phone once before the trip, but this would be completely different.

"Come in," Marcie called, her voice low and clear. She stepped from behind her desk as Trinity waved me in. She was taller than I'd expected.

"Welcome to Southern Arizona University, Ms. Lake," she said, meeting me in the center of the room.

I shook the hand she extended while sunlight, filtered through half-open Venetian blinds, cast stripes across our hands. Her grip was firm. I hoped my palms weren't sweating. I hadn't felt this nervous since Selma's funeral. The thought calmed me—nothing could be as bad as standing up in a packed church to eulogize my mother-aunt, and I'd somehow managed to survive that experience.

"Thank you," I said, my voice steady. "It's good to be here."

As Marcie walked back around her desk, Trinity sat down and motioned me into another chair. Once seated, I crossed one leg across the other, barely controlling the urge to fidget.

Opening a drawer, Marcie pulled out a manila folder and opened it. "Look familiar?" she asked, sliding a sheet of paper across the desk.

It took me a second to recognize the athletics form I had torn out of the SAU guidebook and mailed to the athletics department back in December. I had filled in high school, age, weight, sport of interest, events and times, and athletic honors received. When I filled out the form, I hadn't met Nic yet, and definitely hadn't dared to dream of sitting in Marcie Andozzi's office discussing my desire to be part of her program.

I handed the form back. "Yes, ma'am."

Everyone was quiet for a minute, until I cleared my throat and started to wiggle one foot. Trinity looked down at it. I stopped.

Marcie tapped the desk with a pen. "Ms. Salvo says you're the real deal, Ms. Lake. What do you think?"

"I'm not sure what she meant," I said carefully, "but if you mean can I run, then the answer is yes. I can run."

I met her eyes. She didn't scare me. In my lifetime, I had leapt into bottomless pools of water, ridden my bike through rush-hour traffic in the city of all cities, and held my aunt's hand as she drew her final breath. Marcie Andozzi intimidated me, sure, but she didn't frighten me.

I held her gaze until she nodded and smiled. She actually smiled.

"Well," she said, turning over the form I'd filled out and consulting what looked like handwritten notes, "it appears that your high school coach agrees."

"He does?" I asked before my brain could stop my mouth.

Trinity shifted beside me, and I wondered if she was shocked by my lack of filter or merely disgusted.

"Yes, he does," Marcie confirmed. "Trin here pulled your form off the pile when she saw your times, and Mr. Halvorson and I spoke at some length in January, just before Ms. Salvo returned singing your praises. Do you know what he told me, Ms. Lake?"

That I was a mouthy, mutinous teen with a mountain-sized chip on my shoulder? I shook my head.

"He said you are the best natural runner he ever coached. He also said that you are loyal, mature beyond your years, and one of the toughest people he knows. He is of the belief that I would be lucky to have you in my program."

Butch had said that? About me? I was the only Ashley Lake at Red Bank High, as far as I knew, so it wasn't like he could have confused me with someone else.

I swallowed. "Oh, is that all?"

Silence again, and then both coaches laughed. Not hard, but enough that I relaxed slightly.

"Actually, that's not all," Marcie said. "He shared some of your story, too, but I'd like to hear from you why you didn't compete spring of your senior year."

I'd been expecting this question, had prepared for it, even. "My aunt raised me, and during cross country, she was diagnosed with stage four metastatic cancer. She was my only family. I knew I couldn't commit fully to my team or to my sport, not when things at home were so uncertain. I decided that while I could always run, I wouldn't always be able to spend time with her."

"And now? Do you regret that decision?" Marcie asked.

I shook my head. "Absolutely not. Do I regret that she got sick? Of course. I regret that instead of running spring season, I was waiting for her to die. I regret that she didn't see me graduate from high school or go on to college. But no, I don't regret my decision."

Marcie nodded. "You know, on paper you look great. On video, too. It was really the lack of senior year stats that made me hesitate to get in touch, but now that you've explained, I think I understand."

"Um. What video?" And then I remembered—a friend of Butch's had created recruiting videos for anyone who asked. I'd quit before it had been finished. Or so I thought.

"Your coach sent us a copy of your recruiting video," Trin said, her head slightly tilted.

"Oh, that," I said. "Awesome."

"You said your aunt raised you," Marcie continued. "Does that mean you'll be making this decision on your own? Or is there someone else who can claim you as a dependent?"

Given she would have been a teenager at the time, it was possible she remembered the plane crash. It was also possible Butch had spilled the beans when they spoke.

"My parents were killed in a plane crash when I was little. Did my coach happen to mention that, too?"

She inclined her head. "He did."

"And did he also mention that I survived the crash?"

"That fact did come up."

I hesitated. "And do you have any questions about that?"

"Should I?" She frowned. "Do you have injuries or other issues related to the accident that I would need to know about?"

"No," I said quickly. "Not at all. It's just, people always want to know what it was like."

"I see." She folded her hands on top of her desk. "I suppose you know I was on the Olympic team the year we boycotted?"

I nodded.

"The first thing most people ask me even now, a decade and a half later, is how it feels to have missed out on the Olympics. But I don't see myself as a failed Olympian. I see myself as a runner who was lucky enough to enjoy a long career in the sport she loves; a coach who works hard to help her student-athletes achieve their very best in the classroom and on the track; and, perhaps most importantly, a mother to an amazing little girl. You see, Ashley, I don't mind how other people view me. I know who I am."

Just then I wanted to be her. Or, at least, as well-adjusted as she appeared to be.

We talked a little longer about SAU and the program, about her coaching style and her philosophy of education. She inquired after my weekly mileage and whether or not I had access to a track for workouts, and then she asked me if I had any questions. I'd checked out a recruiting book from the library before the trip, and now I recycled a handful of the questions I'd studied on the train: How many seniors were graduating? Did she plan to remain as the coach of the team into the near future? And finally, where did I stand on her recruiting list?

"To be honest, you're in the middle of the pack. But if you can get yourself into some USATF-certified races this spring and send me your official times, I have a feeling you'll be moving up. There may not be any scholarship money at first, but we may just find you a spot on the team. Depending on how your spring goes, of course."

"I can do that," I said eagerly. "New York has tons of road races in the spring and summer, all over the boroughs. I already started making a list."

"Excellent," Marcie said. "Road isn't the same as track, of course, but it'll do for our purposes. And now I have a question for you: Are you planning visits to any other schools?"

"No." I knew from the book that it was important to be forthright with any coach who showed even slight interest.

"Have you applied to any other schools?"

"Yes, and I received invitations for unofficial visits to two others—University of Portland and University of Washington."

"The Pacific Northwest," she said, nodding. "Why aren't you visiting, then?"

"When it comes down to it, I just can't see myself there."

"And can you see yourself here?"

"I think so." I nodded. "Yes, I can."

"Okay, then," Marcie said, and stood up. "Thank you for coming in today. It's been a very enlightening conversation. Trinity will help you find a comfortable spot on the hill to watch practice, and then I hope you'll join us for our team dinner tonight and the meet tomorrow."

"Absolutely," I said, and shook the hand she offered again. "Thank you, Coach. I really appreciate the opportunity."

"You've earned it, Ms. Lake. What you do with it is up to you."

And with that, Trin escorted me from the office. She waited until we were out of the coaches' wing to clap me on the shoulder.

"Nice job, Lake. You handled yourself really well in there. You studied up, didn't you?"

"I may have had some time to kill on the train."

"Being prepared is never a bad idea, especially when you only get one shot." She reached into her sweatshirt pocket and pulled out a card. "When you get back to New York, give me a call and let me know what your racing schedule looks like for the next couple of months. Try to get in at least five races before May, if you can. We like to have our fall squad firmed up before the end of spring season. By the way, would you be available to attend captain's practices this summer?"

"You mean here in Tucson?"

Trinity smiled. "I don't mean in New York, that's for sure."

"Yes," I said quickly. "Totally."

"Good."

And that was that. We walked outside, me restraining myself from skipping, Trinity watching me try to act nonchalant with a knowing smile. I'd met Marcie Andozzi, and she'd dangled a carrot before me: If I performed well this spring, I could have a spot waiting for me here. Maybe.

I knew it still might not work out, but that *maybe* was a heck of a lot more than I'd had to look forward to a week, a day, even an hour earlier. Marcie's offer meant that I had something tangible to work toward. No more waiting and wondering. Once I was back in New York, I only had to stay healthy and run like I knew I could, and SAU and all it represented—an amazing coach, supportive teammates, a new home where I truly belonged—could be mine.

Outside in the bright sunshine again, Trinity got me situated on the hill at one end of the stadium in a slice of shade, and then I was on my own watching the team file out in pairs and small groups, clad in skimpy runner's shorts and tanks in the school colors. The guys were tall and muscular, the women fitter than any group of female runners I had ever seen. Nic came out toward the end, stepping gingerly on her injured leg. I knew what that was like— sometimes just the memory of an injury could play tricks on you.

She looked up, found me on the hill, and waved. I knew she wanted to know how the meeting had gone, so I gave her a shrug and a thumbs-up and then another shrug. She nodded, and then a girl with short hair and a tattoo of a barbed wire band encircling one bicep walked up behind Nic and appeared to whisper something in her ear. Nic turned away from me, laughing at whatever her teammate had said.

I didn't like that girl, I decided on the spot. I didn't care who she was. I did not like her.

Practice began, and I tried to focus on my potential athletic rivals instead of dwelling on who Nic may have spent time with since coming back to school in January. I would know if she had a girlfriend, wouldn't I? Or would I? It wasn't like I'd exactly opened up myself. I wasn't even sure which way she swung the bat, as Austin would have put it. All I knew was that she had dated Billy DiCiello and that she pinged Austin's gaydar. Oh, and that she had blown me a kiss in a train station once. There was that.

After practice, I was relieved when Nic made a beeline for my spot on the hill, the girl I'd decided not to like trailing her. *Please don't let her be Jewel*, I thought as they reached me. The idea of tattoo girl calling Nic "baby" made me ill.

"How did it go?" Nic asked, grasping my hand.

"I'm Cat," the other girl added before I could answer, waving at me from a slight distance.

Cat. I'd definitely heard Nic talk about her before. But what had she said? Nothing that set off any alarms. Of course, that was before I saw the way she followed Nic's every move.

"Ash," I said, nodding stiffly. "It went well," I added, looking back at Nic. I smiled down at her, holding onto her hand almost in defiance. "Marcie says I've got a shot. Just depends on my spring season."

"Are you running for a community college?" Cat asked.

"Ash doesn't need a transition school," Nic said dismissively. "Are you running the Chase Manhattan in a few weeks?"

"Already signed up. There are a bunch of races in April and May, too, though some are farther out."

"Good thing you have a car," Nic said, her smile intimate.

"Exactly."

After a second Cat cleared her throat, and Nic and I stepped apart.

"Anyway," Nic said, "Cat's our ride to Trinity's for dinner. You ready?"

"Sure," I said, eyeing the other woman warily again.

Nic and Cat stopped in the locker room to grab their gear. Another runner joined us on the way out to the parking lot—the infamous Jewel, a sprinter from Joplin, Mississippi.

"Trinity makes a decent pasta sauce, even if she doesn't have any of the motherland blood in her veins," Nic said as we walked, with a half-smile that only I saw.

"Are you trying to say black people can't cook pasta?" Jewel challenged.

"Not at all," Nic said insincerely.

"Mm-hmm," Jewel said. "Cause I'd like to see you try to fry a chicken, little girl."

"We don't fry chicken in my family," Nic said. "We sauté it in wine sauce."

"Like you ever sautéed anything in your life," Jewel said. "You forget, we've all seen you in the kitchen with your Campbell's soup and your Lipton noodles."

"Nothing wrong with convenience," Nic protested.

"Or laziness," Cat said to me.

I shrugged. "I'm not really much of a cook, either."

"I knew you'd have my back," Nic said, holding her hand up for a high five.

When I ignored her, she shoved me sideways. I caught her elbow and brought her back, tickling her until she gasped for mercy. By then we'd fallen behind Jewel and Cat. I heard Cat mutter something that sounded like "effing personal best," and Jewel chortled. Beside me Nic stopped abruptly.

I stopped, too. "Are you okay? Did I hurt you?"

"No, I'm fine," she said, and started again after her friends.

When we reached Cat's Mustang (of course she drove a muscle car), Nic called shotgun, which left Jewel and me sharing the narrow back seat.

"Nic says you run middle," Jewel said as we left the parking lot.

"Yeah. And you're a sprinter?"

We talked about running for a bit, and about our hometowns. Most of the other girls on the team were from California or Texas, Jewel told me. It would actually be nice to have another SEC girl on the team, she allowed.

Up front Cat cranked the radio, and we all sang along to a Madonna song. As we headed off the campus that was beginning to feel familiar to me, singing along while the flower-lined streets flashed past, I felt again that this was what my life was supposed to be like.

And, God and Marcie willing, it would be.

CHAPTER TWENTY-FIVE

Saturday morning dawned cooler than I expected. I rose early and changed into running clothes, watching Nic sleep. She didn't have to be up until after seven, and it was only just now six. To my East Coast body, though, it felt late. Double-knotting my laces, I lifted the keys from the hook by the door and left the room.

I jogged down the seven flights of stairs as a warm-up and sat outside on the front steps to stretch. No one else was up this early on a Saturday morning. Some of the dorm's residents had probably only gotten to sleep a few hours before. But not us. After spaghetti, French bread, and a group screening of *Chariots of Fire* at Trinity's house, we'd been back at the dorm ready for bed by 10:30. Nic liked to get at least eight hours of sleep the night before a meet.

Only instead of going straight to sleep, we'd stayed up talking until almost midnight. As I started off along the sidewalk, sidestepping stray sprinklers, I tried to remember what we had talked about. Her ex-boyfriend, my ex-boyfriend (strange to think of Drew that way), her childhood in Brooklyn hanging out with her brothers and their friends, my childhood on the mountain hanging out with the boys. We were a lot alike, Nic and I, despite the fact she had grown up in a Northern city of nine million people and I had grown up in a Southern suburb. Just different enough to make it interesting.

Matching my breathing to the tread of my feet, I settled into the rhythm of the run. I wound through campus, passing buildings Nic had pointed out to me the day before. Compared to the West

Village, getting around SAU's campus was easy. There were signs and campus maps everywhere.

Water droplets glistened on well-tended lawns as the sun rose over the mountains and cast its light across campus. Running in the morning here reminded me of springtime in Signal Mountain, warm and sunny, though much dryer than I was used to. Could I be happy in the desert? Nic said the summers were scorchers here, but I was used to that. Honestly, I was just looking forward to getting away from humidity of any kind. Besides, I'd be willing to risk hellfire and damnation to run for Marcie Andozzi.

Hellfire and damnation—funny my mind had gone there. According to the Bible bangers I'd grown up with, homosexuals were bound for hell, no doubt about it. If I ended up here, would something happen between Nic and me? But hadn't it already? The night before, she'd fallen asleep first, and I'd lain beside her in bed wondering what Cat was to her, wondering what I was to her. I'd almost woken her up and asked because I recognized the look in Cat's eyes whenever she smiled at Nic. Whether Nic knew it or not, Cat was smitten.

I ran my usual five-mile pace along the streets around campus, managing to go over only slightly before finding my way back to Nic's building. I ran into her in the bathroom on her floor, where she was toweling her hair dry, a white terry-cloth robe tied loosely around her waist. For a moment I could only stare at the damp patch of skin between the curves of her breasts, paler than the sun-kissed skin at her neck.

"Morning," I managed.

"Morning. Nice run?"

"Not bad. You shower before a meet?"

"I don't feel awake otherwise."

I slung the towel she had loaned me over the door of a cubby. "I'm going to get cleaned up, okay?"

"Best news I heard."

"Do I smell that bad?" I asked, alarmed.

"No, of course not." She watched me pull shampoo and soap from my travel bag. "That's just what my dad always says."

"Oh." Relieved, I rezipped the travel bag. "I left your room unlocked."

"Cool." She turned away. "See you in a bit."

I closed the door to the shower and stripped, setting my dirty clothes on the part of the bench closest to the shower curtain and my clean clothes on the other half. I missed the comfort of my bathroom back in New York. One thing about college that I actually might not be thrilled about, I thought as I stepped under the lukewarm spray. But there was always off-campus living. I pictured a cute adobe house with Nic and some of the other girls, Jewel maybe, or Gwen, a middle distancer from LA who had been especially friendly at Trinity's house. We could have meals together, and watch movies, and do homework, and give each other back rubs... My mind returned to Nic's skimpy robe, and I shut my eyes, dunking my face under the spray. Maybe I should take a cold shower.

Back in Nic's room fifteen minutes later, I watched her get ready for the meet. First, she laid out her uniform—tank top, shorts, sports bra, duofold socks, and track shoes. Then she packed everything in her red team bag along with toiletries for afterwards. Last, she pulled on the SAU sweat jacket over her collared shirt and khaki shorts. It was too warm for long pants.

"Are you nervous?" I asked from where I lounged on the bean bag in the corner.

"Always, even when I know we'll kill them. BYU isn't known for their track team, especially their women." Nic brushed her damp hair away from her face. She used a black rubber band to secure the ponytail and a small red scrunchy to hide the rubber band. Then she looked at me in the mirror. "Ready?"

"If you are."

I pushed myself up from the floor and stepped into my Tevas. In my navy Nike shorts and white tank top, my goal was to get a tan. My skin was beginning to turn brown already from the couple of hours I'd spent in the sun the day before. I intended to be dark by the time I returned to New York to wait out the rest of winter.

People always had a hard time in the summer figuring out my ethnic background. From my father's side of the family, I'd inherited long muscles and dark hair, eyes, and skin. From my mother's people, I had taken small features and delicate hands. In the pictures of my family Selma kept for me, my mother always looked like a skinny, red-haired kid next to my tall, dark father. They had died in 1978, so inevitably in the photos they were wearing bell bottoms and beads.

I used to wonder what they would have been like in the'80s.

Would my mother have jumped on the fitness bandwagon and become a buff redhead with a frizzy perm and a collection of spandex? Would she have gone back to work once I was in school and started wearing frilly fronted shirts with little red string ties at her throat? Would my father have begun to lose his thick, longish hair?

"What are you thinking about?" Nic asked, her eyes on mine in the mirror.

"Hair," I said. "Come on. You don't want to be late."

Nic looked at her watch. "Plenty of time."

But she followed me to the door, took one last look around the room, and grabbed her keys.

"What about hair?" she asked as we headed down the seven flights of stairs.

"Oh, you know. Nothing really," I said. "Last one down is a rotten banana!"

I started running down the steps, letting gravity do most of the work.

"It's *egg*, you cheater," Nic called after me, laughing.

I took the last six steps in one leap and burst from the stairwell into the outdoors—and nearly landed in a sprinkler. Catching my breath, I waited for Nic.

She came through the door a few seconds later, her pace far more sedate than mine.

"Sorry, but I can't risk another injury," she said as I fell into step beside her. "Marcie would kill us both."

The stadium hulked in the distance, obscuring our view of the gym. I matched my pace to hers. Ours legs were almost the same length, but hers were more muscular than mine, bulkier from the shorter, faster distances she ran.

"Probably a prospie faux pas to injure one of the star sophomores," I commented, resisting the urge to grab her hand.

"I'm not a star," Nic said, elbowing me. "But yeah, a major faux pas."

"You are too a star," I teased, skipping ahead.

"No, I'm not. Geez, you're hyper today, aren't you?"

"Si, senorita. Je suis tres hyper." I giggled and ran back toward her.

"Language problem?" she asked, eyes hidden behind dark sunglasses.

"I think I finally recovered from the trip out here." I breathed in deeply, tasting desert dryness and a hint of sage. "I feel, like, giddy or something."

"Well, it's cute on you."

"You're not so bad yourself," I said, but she only smiled and walked on in silence.

We were almost to the gym. As we rounded the edge of the stadium, a charter bus slowed on the road and pulled into the gym parking lot.

"There they are," Nic said. "The rich, blond Utahans. It'll be fun to demolish them."

"Uh-huh. Well, you whoop 'em good, y'hear? I wanna see them girls goin' down like roadkill on that track," I announced in my best redneck drawl.

Nic stared at me in horror. "Good God, you really are from Tennessee!"

"Damn straight, girlie."

We were in the gym now, heading down the tiled hallway toward the locker room, both of us blinking like a couple of cats in the sudden gloom of indoors.

I stopped beside the locker room door. "I'll be in the stands," I added in my normal voice. "Good luck today, Nic."

"Thanks. Stay out of trouble."

We hesitated, eyeing each other. Then I held up my hand and she slapped it before ducking into the locker room.

I'd wanted to hug her. I almost had, too, until I remembered that there were people all around us, as in coaches and teammates and parents. Not ours, but that didn't matter.

I wandered outside and sat in the front row of the home team side of the stadium as other fans began to filter in. Slipping my sunglasses back on, I turned my Yankees cap backwards and leaned back in my seat, face upturned to the sun. I could get used to all this Vitamin D.

A few minutes later, someone tapped me on the shoulder. "Hey, Ash."

It was Rodney. As he sat down beside me, I tried not to stare too obviously at the muscles peeking out from under his turquoise tank top. Damn. I wished I had definition like that.

"How's it going, Rodney?"

"Good. I went for a swim this morning, so the day started

well."

"I know what you mean," I said. "I went for a run. It's nice being up before everyone else."

We watched the teams warming up. The rhythm of the meet was just starting to roll—the placement about the track of starting blocks and hurdles, the progression of events and the order of runners. When it came, the first crack of the starting gun jolted me half out of my seat. This was a part of running I hadn't quite realized I'd missed—the waiting around, nervousness building, then setting out at last, pacing myself on endless loops of the track, saving one last bit of energy to smoke the girl trying to pass me on the last lap. I'd even missed those horrible moments when it became clear I hadn't kept my own pace and couldn't make that final burst.

"You want to be out there, don't you?"

I'd nearly forgotten Rodney. Blinking behind my shades, I leaned back again and lifted my face to the sun. "Yes. But it's cool to watch, too."

As Nic had promised, BYU's track program was not strong. Rodney and I caught as many events as we could, meandering through the stadium as the sun climbed higher in the sky and the meet progressed. Rodney told me about the team members he knew, filled me in on SAU sports gossip, and generally kept me company. I was glad he was there.

Nic was scheduled to run the 800, her main event. Sometimes she ran shorter or longer distances, I knew, if they needed runners to round out events. But today, since she was just getting over the quad injury, she would only run the 800. Rodney and I returned to our seats and watched the start of her race in silence. Nic, one of her teammates, and one of the BYU runners got out to an early lead over the rest of the field.

"You know, I've never seen Nic open up to anyone the way she does with you," Rodney commented.

"Really?" I watched Nic, her muscular legs pounding against the cushiony track. "Not even Cat? They seem pretty tight."

"Cat wishes," he said.

"What about Nic? Does she wish, too?"

He laughed a little. "I think you know what Nic wishes."

Did I? If only I could be sure. But maybe he was saying I could be.

Nic and the other two frontrunners finished the first lap at a pace that would automatically qualify them for Nationals. Not bad.

I changed the subject as they attacked the second lap: "Have you been friends with her a while?"

"Since freshman year. We were in a couple of the same classes first semester, and then we just started calling each other. Sometimes we would talk on the phone for hours, even though we only lived a couple of buildings away."

"Sounds like Nic," I said. "I don't even want to see my phone bill this month."

"Do you live by yourself in New York?"

"No." I kept my eyes on the race. Half a lap to go and the front pack was still pretty tight. They should be making their moves anytime now. "I have a roommate. We're subletting his friend's apartment until June."

"You live with a guy?"

"Yeah, but he's gay. He's planning to move in with his boyfriend when the sublet is up."

Austin had given me the news over dinner one night when Tommy had to work late. He'd been glowing when he told me, and I'd been so happy for them both I was pretty sure I'd glowed, too. Or maybe that was just all the wine we'd consumed.

"Oh." Rodney mulled the information over. Then he said, "What will you do then?"

"Good question. Hey, she's making her move. Check it out."

Nic was kicking it on the final turn, churning her legs faster and catching the other two napping. She finished a couple of strides ahead of her teammate and a full two seconds ahead of the BYU girl. Not a bad run, I thought, checking the board. Bummer—just over qualifying time. With some real competition, I figured she and the other SAU runner would both have qualified for Nationals.

Walking it off, Nic checked the unofficial time on the board and shook her head. Turning, she slapped hands with the other runners as they crossed the line, and then took a couple of cool-down laps with her teammate, a girl named Jackie. Afterward, they walked to the edge of the track for a brief conference with Marcie and Trinity. At one point, Trinity gestured to where I was sitting in the stands. Nic nodded, got ice from the trainer, and headed our way. Still on prospie babysitting duty, apparently. Not that I minded.

She made her way to our section, saying hello to various parents and students as she took a seat next to us and propped her leg up, ice pressed to her quad.

"That was great," I said. "You have an awesome kick."

"Thanks." She smiled, almost shyly. "I've been working on that with Trinity. It felt really good today."

"How's the leg?" Rodney asked.

She made a face. "Kind of sore. Not as much when I was running as now. The ice should take care of the worst of it."

"After the adrenaline wears off, right?" I said. "I hate that."

Nic nodded. "Did you guys see that girl try to cut me off on the second lap?"

"The blonde?" Rodney asked innocently. All three of the BYU runners had blond hair.

"Ha ha," Nic said. "The one who stuck with us. She totally tried to trip me."

"Missed it," I said. "We were too busy talking about you, I guess."

Nic looked at us. "What do you mean, talking about me?"

Rodney smiled. "Oh, I was just telling Ashley about your long line of one night stands with half the football team, that's all."

"Pretty interesting stuff," I added.

"Funny. I'm not the only one who hasn't had a date recently," Nic said. "Am I , Rodney?"

He blushed. "I'm going to get a drink. Either of you guys want anything?"

"A Gatorade would be great," I said, pulling a couple of bucks from the inside pocket of my shorts.

Rodney waved off the money. "Don't worry about it," he said, and jogged off.

"That shut him up," Nic commented.

"Right? I mentioned something about Austin and Tommy earlier and he got all quiet, too. Guess he's not cool yet with the whole gay thing."

"It's so lame. Not Rodney. I mean society. Sexuality shouldn't be such a big deal," Nic said, looking over at me. "It's only part of a person. It's not their entire identity."

"What's the team like? I mean, are people out?" I asked, thinking of Cat. You would have to be blind to think she was straight.

"It's a tolerant place. Beth, one of the other assistants, has a girlfriend, and Marcie has made it clear she doesn't care who we date as long as we're in healthy relationships."

I noticed she hadn't answered the second part of my question, but Rodney came back with the drinks just then, and Nic returned to the SAU bench shortly after.

The rest of the meet flew by. Soon the only events left were the men's and women's 400 relay. Neither race was even close, and the meet ended with a hiss instead of a bang. SAU took the day with 130 points to BYU's 58—a shellacking by anyone's standards.

The stadium emptied quickly. Rodney and I headed to the gym to wait for Nic. They always had a quick post-meet talk with the coaching staff, Nic had told me, and then showered and changed. After a dual meet like today, with only one round of mostly uncontested competition, the men's and women's teams usually got together to celebrate.

With my fake ID and New York's lax policing policies, I'd gone out a fair bit over the last year, but it had been a while since I'd gone anywhere with large numbers of straight people. Not exactly the scene I'd been hoping for, but it would be good, I supposed, to see what life as an SAU runner was really like.

Wouldn't it?

We hung out with Rodney the rest of the day and into the evening. After a long dinner and a short beer run, it was almost eight by the time we got back to the dorm. Rodney went his own way while Nic and I grabbed the elevator to her floor. We still had an hour before we had to meet downstairs to catch a ride to the off-campus party.

Back in Nic's room, I stepped out of my sandals and dropped onto the bean bag.

Nic hung her keys on the hook and sat down on the futon. It creaked under her weight.

"Nice tan lines, Lake." She pointed at my feet.

I wiggled my toes. The Tevas had left wide bands of pale flesh across the tops of my feet. "At least I wasn't wearing those dorky teams shorts today."

"I knew you were gonna talk shit about that," Nic said. "Just wait'll you get here. Then you'll be wearing those same shorts, little girl."

"Little? Who you calling little?" I jumped on top of her, holding her down with one hand and tickling her with the other.

"Okay, okay, I take it back," Nic said through her laughter, trying to fend me off. "Uncle! Uncle, Ash!"

"Okay." I relented, flopping back on the bed beside her and staring up at the ceiling. I wanted to do a lot more than tickle her, and the urge freaked me out a little. I'd never felt this way about anyone, not even Drew. Especially not Drew.

Nic rolled over on her side to face me. "Do you like the Grateful Dead?"

"Totally. Austin and I went to a Dead concert his senior year and got so baked we couldn't drive home until the next morning. Selma and his parents thought we were lying dead on a road somewhere."

"You guys must have been a scary pair in high school. Okay if I put the Dead in?"

"Yeah. 'S cool."

"Too bad it's season or we could smoke a little."

She didn't look at me as she got up and crossed the room to her CD player. Nic was on full scholarship at SAU, which meant the athletic department paid for everything. The money she made with her campus job during the year and in the summers was spending money. Her room, like the other jock rooms I'd seen, rocked—CD player, futon, fridge, and plenty of food and drink, of course, for the growing athlete.

"You smoke?" I asked, watching her rifle through her CD collection.

"I get high like once a year, but only in the off season. You know, don't really want to pollute the lungs all that much. Plus those random NCAA drug tests.... But it's fun to let go sometimes and just chill."

She put in a Best of the Dead compilation CD and we reclined against the pillows, legs touching, and looked through the photos she had taken the summer before at the Grand Canyon. I had a hard time focusing on the pictures, too aware of Nic's body next to mine on the futon. This was getting out of hand, I told myself, but I stayed where I was, close enough to smell her shampoo every time she brushed a hand through her hair. Meanwhile the sky outside grew darker and the air breezing through the partially open window got cooler.

Finally Nic got up and shut the window. "We should probably get going," she said, glancing at the clock. It was almost nine.

I didn't particularly want to go to the party anymore. I wanted to stay in Nic's room with her, talking and listening to music. The last official party I'd gone to had been at the apartment of some of Drew's NYU friends—before Thanksgiving, before Drew and I stopped hanging out, before I knew Nic existed.

"By the way," she said, crossing to her dresser and pulling open a drawer. "Just to warn you, these parties can be kind of meat markety. Everyone brings like a hundred friends from various dorms and people get totally trashed and hook up. Typical college party."

"That's a typical college party?" I asked skeptically.

None of the parties I'd been to with Drew had been remotely like the scene she'd just described. Drew's friends liked to get a little drunk and a little stoned and watch sports on TV, play card games, listen to grunge music, and go out to clubs later. This sounded more like a frat party.

Nic shrugged. "For a state school, it's pretty typical. Usually Jewel and Cat and I take over a side room and chill. You can brave the masses if you want, or you can hang with us."

"I think I'll stick with you guys," I said. "What're you wearing to this thing, anyway?"

We went downstairs dressed almost alike in shorts, sneakers and T-shirts. But Nic's cut-offs were short and tight, while my khakis were longer and looser. The rest of the team from the dorm was already waiting. We went outside and piled into an Isuzu Trooper. Everyone in Arizona seemed to have either four-by-fours or convertibles. I didn't think I would mind that.

I watched the streets pass as we headed to the party, the lights of the city bright against the mountains. Tucson reminded me of Chattanooga in a lot of ways, and with Nic as my personal guide, I already felt more at home here than I'd felt in New York, ever. What if Marcie decided she didn't want me on the team? Where would I be then?

Nic was sitting in the seat in front of me. As if she could read my mind, she turned around and flashed me a smile. I smiled back, feeling something inside me relax. If I was supposed to be at SAU for the next few years, I would be.

I just had to be patient and let it happen.

CHAPTER TWENTY-SIX

After breakfast the next morning, Nic and I filled half a dozen water bottles and borrowed Rodney's Explorer. Our intended destination: Sabino Canyon, a popular hiking area in the foothills of the Catalina Mountains just north of the city.

"It's not exactly green by East Coast standards," she cautioned as we left campus. "But there's this awesome trail, Seven Falls, that we can hike with lots of great places for a picnic."

I was looking forward to spending time with Nic, just the two of us out in the desert foothills on our own. At the dorm, there was always something going on or someone dropping by.

"Did you have fun at the party last night?" she added, her hands loose on the steering wheel.

"I did," I said. "I like Jewel. Teri too."

The night before, Nic, Cat, Jewel, her girlfriend Teri and I had taken over a smaller room at the party, just as Nic had predicted. We drank beer and played quarters, getting mellower as the evening progressed, while the rest of the off-campus house pulsed with loud music and echoed with the laughter of the more intensely party-minded.

"So, Ashley, Nic says you took a train out here?" Cat had asked during a lull in conversation, taking a puff on a cigarette. One cigarette between five people didn't really count as smoking, we'd all agreed. She passed the cigarette on to Nic, who was looking at me and didn't notice until Cat tapped her hand.

"Yeah. Amtrak," I said.

Nic took a puff, blew the smoke out in rings, and handed me the cigarette.

"A train? You're crazy," Jewel said. "But I hear you run a mean 5000, so that's all right. You think she's going to take Gwen's scholarship?" she added to Nic.

"Wait," I said, "I'm not here to take anyone's scholarship."

"Gwen is on shaky ground," Cat put in.

"Her grades are beyond bad," Jewel agreed. She focused on me again. "But what do you mean, you're not taking anyone's scholarship?"

"Marcie said there might not be any money, assuming I even make the team."

"No way," Cat said. "Coach wouldn't bring you out here just to tell you to get lost."

"I paid my own way," I said. "She didn't really bring me here."

"She called and invited you, didn't she?" Nic reminded me.

"I guess so."

Without Nic's intervention, though, would Marcie have called me? Maybe. Butch, after all, had given the hard sell, miracle of miracles. Probably it had been an alignment of the stars, as Selma would have called it, that led Marcie to extend the invitation.

"You mean your parents paid your way," Cat said.

"No, I mean I did." I gulped down some beer.

"What are you, emancipated or something?" Jewel asked.

"Not exactly. My parents died a long time ago."

"Shit," Cat said. "What happened?"

"Plane crash. I was in it, too, but I walked away."

It was easy to say here in this dark back room, the window open, cool air and the smell of tropical flowers drifting in on the breeze. My parents and a hundred other people had died and I had lived, and now, fifteen years later, I was sharing a cigarette with this group of women, one of whom I liked way too much for a potential future teammate.

"That is messed up," Jewel said. "I had you all wrong, Lake. I thought you were just some suburban brat who could run."

"Well, I'm still from the suburbs and I can still run, so..."

They laughed.

Then Teri, who was from Phoenix, said, "Check this out." She lifted her black SAU T-shirt, and even in the dim lighting I could see the puckered skin of a scar that marred her ribcage. "I got that in a drive-by when I was thirteen. I didn't even know the shooter."

"Wow," I said. "That must've pissed you off."

Teri nodded. "You know, it did."

We were all quiet for a few minutes, smoking down the cigarette and drinking down our beers. Eventually the conversation turned toward easier topics like classes and the team and general campus gossip, the five of us continuing to chill in the back room while the "real" party raged on just beyond the closed door.

"They liked you, too," Nic said now, slowing the Explorer and turning into the driveway of a small grocery store. "Ready to stock up?"

"I can always eat."

Inside, we picked up sandwiches, trail mix, Power Bars, and half a dozen other snacks. Then we headed north into the foothills. A half hour out of the city we turned into a nearly full parking lot, where we found one of the last open spaces.

"Crowded much?" I asked.

"Told you it was popular."

We paid the parking fee and caught a tram a couple of miles up the canyon to the Seven Falls trail head, applying sun screen to any and all exposed skin as we went. Mid-morning, the day wasn't too hot, but the sun was bright as ever. Baseball caps and sunglasses on, our backpacks filled with water and food, we set out on the trail lined with spindly bushes and the prong-armed cacti that Arizona is famous for.

"Did you know some of these saguaro cacti are a hundred and fifty years old?" Nic asked. "In late spring, they have these really beautiful flowers that only bloom at night."

"Cool," I said, and gulped down more water.

Like Nic, I was carrying one of my water bottles by hand and took a sip every few minutes. It was only seventy-five out, but the desert air could be devious, she'd said. Better to drink before you got thirsty.

The trail meandered through a gorge, following a creek between progressively steeper slopes. The trail itself remained fairly flat and dusty, except at spots where it crossed the creek. The water was cold—snow-fed from the mountains, Nic explained—and I was careful not to fall in as I leapt from rock to rock across the flowing creek.

"During the monsoon season, the water runs even higher," Nic said at one point as we forded the creek for the fifth or sixth time. By now we were high enough that a glance back down the canyon revealed sunlight reflecting in the distance from the cars and buildings of Tucson.

"Monsoon?" I repeated. "The desert has a monsoon season?"

"The desert doesn't, but the mountains do. In the fall, these trails can get pretty dicey with heavy rain and flash floods."

"I totally wouldn't have expected that here."

Nic stopped and waited for me to catch up. "Unexpected isn't all bad. Look at us—when Camilla mentioned Leslie and Mark had a messenger who moonlighted as a runner, it never occurred to me that Marcie would end up inviting you to campus."

"I know, right?" I said, and slapped her shoulder like a future teammate would do.

What I really wanted was to touch the jade necklace resting in the V-neck of her tank top, or smooth away the drop of unblended sunscreen on her forearm. I wanted to put my hands on her in a distinctly non-teammate way, and that was the problem. Or, rather, a symptom of the actual problem: how I felt about Nicki Salvo, sophomore sprinter for the SAU Desert Cats.

Slowly she reached out and cupped my shoulder, her fingers soft against my skin. "Ash," she said, her voice low, eyes hidden behind her sunglasses.

"Yeah?" I could barely breathe, and not because of the dryness of the air.

Just then a family of hikers we'd passed earlier came around a bend in the trail. Nic released me and stepped back, smiling politely at the man, woman, and their three children.

"Good morning," the man said, his eyes glued to Nic.

I couldn't blame him, really, though I did want to whack him upside the head. Nic nodded coolly, smiling more warmly at the mom and kids. The youngest, a boy with curly dark hair and a missing front tooth, grinned at us as he passed, and I remembered when Nic had asked me if I wanted kids. I did. I wanted a daughter or a son of my own, one who looked my mother or father, or possibly like Nic. I wanted a family that belonged to me, one that I could belong to. And I wouldn't die on them, either. If I could help it.

We hiked on through the canyon, following the walls of the gorge up and up. The Seven Falls outlook was two and a half miles up the mountain. We took it slowly, resting frequently. Nic's leg was a little sore from the previous day's competition, she admitted.

"Trinity would kill you if she knew you were here, wouldn't she?" I asked when we stopped for a break a little while later.

"Pretty much. Don't mention it, okay?"

"I don't know, Salvo. I think you're going to have to do some convincing to keep me from talking."

"Shut it," she said, laughing, and shoved me sideways.

We'd stopped on a rock ledge about five feet up from the creek bank. Now I let myself teeter over the edge, pretending that she'd pushed me harder than she had. It wasn't much of a fall. I rolled when I hit the ground and bounced back to my feet, laughing.

"Ashley!" Nic exclaimed, peering down at me. Her brow cleared as she caught my laughter. "Are you okay?"

"Totally." I grabbed a hold of the ledge and climbed back up. "That was fun."

Nic just looked at me, shaking her head wordlessly.

"What?" I asked.

"Your poor aunt."

I wiped my dusty hands against my shorts. "I know. If I could do it over, I would try to be better. The only thing I ever really did for her was get good grades."

"I doubt she thought that."

I shrugged, looking out across the saguaro cacti and the rocky canyon walls that narrowed the sky above us.

"Do you miss her?" Nic asked.

"Not as much as I used to. All my life, I'd been planning to leave her—for college, for a career, for my own family. It wasn't like either of us ever thought I'd stay in Tennessee. She didn't want me to stay because of her, and I didn't plan to."

"And yet...?"

"And yet, I was the one who was supposed to leave, not her. It was so fast. I mean, it wasn't. It seemed to take forever at times. She was in so much pain." I shook my head. "I didn't know anyone could hurt that much."

"Do you mean her, or you?"

I closed my eyes against the bright sunlight. "Both, probably."

Nic's hand was warm on mine. "Do you think she would be happy if you ended up here?"

I remembered the feeling I'd gotten the first time I stepped onto the SAU track—as if Selma were with me and at peace all at the same time. I glanced at Nic, smiling. "Yes, I think so."

"And would you? Be happy here?"

Her hand was still on mine, and her skin was flushed from the heat, her lips moist from the water she had just sipped.

"Yes," I repeated, wondering what she would do if I leaned forward and kissed her there at the edge of the creek with half the population of Tucson traipsing past on this lovely spring day.

"Good. Because I'm happy you're here."

"You are?"

"Of course. It felt like I was waiting forever. When you didn't write back or call at first, I started to think I'd been imagining things."

"What do you mean?"

Nic looked at me evenly. "Do you really not know?"

My heart pounded in my ears. I was aware of the warmth of her hand holding mine, the sound of birds singing in the bushes, the rush of water just below us. Of course I knew. How could I not?

Nic jumped up. "Forget it," she said, and leapt from the ledge to the trail, wincing a little before turning away from me.

"But…" I trailed off. Rising, I went after her. Why hadn't I said anything? I'd wanted to, only it was as if my vocal cords were frozen.

We were both quiet for a little while. Then, gradually, we started talking again, about school and movies and Marcie and the rest of the sports world at SAU. Soon we were back to normal, the break on the rock ledge forgotten for now. Mostly.

The trail led around twists and turns into gradually lusher land, ending abruptly at a series of waterfalls. Seven, to be exact, stretching away above us on what seemed like intentionally built red rock terraces. We spread a sheet out along a huge boulder that overlooked the clear, deep pool of water at the base of the first set of falls. It was just past noon, and we were the only people here. For now.

On the sheet, we took off our shoes and made ourselves comfortable. I tucked my socks into my shoes and wiggled my bare toes in the open air. It felt good to be half-naked in the Arizona sun.

Beside me, Nic arranged herself so that her tan would be even and closed her eyes. "Wake me up in fifteen minutes so that I can flip over, will you?"

"Yeah, yeah. Flip this."

She opened an eye. "Excuse me?"

"Nothing."

"Uh-huh. Because don't think I won't throw you over the edge like I did before."

I laughed. "In your dreams, Salvo."

I leaned back on my hands and watched the water falling. I tried to watch single drops make the plunge, but it was too hard to keep track, especially with Nic lying only inches away from me. The breeze occasionally gusted our way, covering us with tiny drops of spray from the waterfall. New York seemed a million miles away, my Tennessee childhood even farther.

A little while later, Nic rolled to her front and cradled her head on her arms. I was already on my stomach facing the waterfall, tossing small pieces of slate and clay into the pool and trying not to think about the expanse of skin her skimpy outfit afforded.

"Is that a scar?" she asked, her finger tracing a line along my shoulder.

I'd forgotten the small mark might show. "Yeah."

"What from?"

Turning onto my side, I faced her, hiding the mark. That particular scar, along with half a dozen others, was the faded remnants of a burn from the plane crash.

"Is it from your days of terrorizing the boys of Signal Mountain?" she added, teasing.

"Not exactly." I paused. Drew had never noticed the scars because we'd dated in the fall and I had enforced a strict lights-out policy whenever we messed around. But I didn't want to hide them from Nic. "It's actually from the plane crash."

We regarded one another there on the rock, drops of water brushing our skin as the breeze changed directions.

"Have I mentioned how glad I am you survived?" she asked.

"No."

"Well, I am." She reached across the red rock and covered my hand with hers again. "Really, really glad."

I turned my hand over in her grasp and laced our fingers together.

"Me, too." I looked into her eyes, searching, but I didn't see any pity. Just warmth, and something else.

"Why don't you lie down?" Nic said. "Come here." She pulled me close, cradling my head on her shoulder.

"This is nice," I said, feeling unbelievably safe in her arms.

"Isn't it?"

And just like that, I fell asleep.

When I woke up an indeterminate amount of time later, there were other people at the falls, including a trio of college boys who were determined to impress us with their derring-do, leaping from our boulder into the deep pool below even though the water was glacial. Literally.

Nic rolled her eyes at me and we moved further up the canyon to eat our lunch in peace as the boys wrestled and shivered behind us. We shared our sandwiches and water, a new sort of openness settling into place between us. I would start a sentence and she would finish it, both of us laughing.

At one point, I offered her a grape, and she held my wrist as she ate from my fingers, her tongue swirling over my skin briefly. I almost gasped, my face flushing with the heat that flooded my body. Nothing with Drew had ever felt like this, not even when we'd been in bed touching each other in far more intimate places. And Nic and I hadn't even kissed yet.

"Do you want to go back to my room?" she asked, her voice low.

"Totally," I said, and started shoving food and picnic supplies willy-nilly back into my pack.

The hike down to the tram stop only took an hour. We were hurrying, or at least I was. I couldn't wait to get back to her dorm and lock her door against the rest of the world. Our arms kept brushing as we hiked down the trail, and it was all I could do not to pull her behind a cactus. Assuming she wanted me to. Which I still wasn't sure of. Though I had my suspicions.

In the car, I thought she might kiss me. But then another car pulled up behind us and put their blinker on, and Nic had to back out to give them our spot. I reached over and took her hand as we drove toward campus. She looked at me quickly, and then faced forward again, her dimples showing.

Back on campus, we practically ran to her dorm. There were already a couple of people waiting for the elevator, or I probably would have kissed her as soon as the doors closed. As it was, we stood at the back of the elevator, hands clasped, bodies touching, smiling at each other out of the corners of our eyes. I counted the floors impatiently as we rose slowly, slowly, slowly. Finally the doors opened on seven and we fled down the hall, giggling.

At her room, as she fumbled for her keys, I suddenly realized my bladder was about to burst. Nic had gone at the visitor center at Sabino Canyon, but I hadn't.

"I have to pee," I said, backing away.

"Really?" She sounded disappointed. "I mean, okay. Of course."

"I'll be right back," I promised, and then turned and sprinted down the hall.

In the bathroom, I peed what felt like a gallon, and then raced back to Nic's room. I heard voices as I approached, and slowed. What the hell? I stopped in the doorway. Rodney and Cat were sitting on the bed, Nic not far off on the bean bag chair.

"Surprise," she said when she saw me at the door, a fake smile pinned to her lips. "Look who dropped by?"

"We're taking you out," Rodney announced.

"It's your last day in Tucson, and you haven't done anything touristy or even had any real Mexican food yet," Cat put in. "What kind of hosts would we be if we let you leave without seeing Old Tucson or trying a Mama Cassidy's burrito?"

Mama Cassidy's wasn't the burrito I was interested in, but I didn't need to tell Cat that, I realized as she smiled at me, her eyes hard.

I strolled across the room and dropped down beside Nic on the narrow bean bag, my weight sending her rolling into me. She had to put her hands on my chest to stop herself, but she didn't protest or pull away.

Glancing up at Cat, I tried not to smile too triumphantly. "Sounds good," I said, my arm around Nic's shoulder. "When do we go?"

Old Tucson, an Old West theme park complete with cowboys and dancing girls, was actually kind of great. Nic and I strolled behind Rodney and Cat, our hands brushing, our bodies turned toward each other as we explored the old-style frontier town. But it wasn't the historic scenery that had me all in a tizzy. In the Grand Palace Saloon, Nic tugged me into an alcove, pushed me against a wall, and kissed me. Maybe it was because I wasn't expecting it, or possibly because I'd been waiting for this moment for months, but her kiss seemed like no other kiss I'd ever experienced. I wrapped my arms around her neck and pulled her closer, tasting the sun and salt on her lips.

All too soon she pulled away.

"Later," she said, her voice breathy.

"Yes," I agreed before following her back out into the bar.

The restaurant they took us to after Old Tucson was kitschy and cute, with wide booths that allowed for a shocking amount of physical shenanigans to go on unseen by those on the other side of the table. I know this because Nic and I piled in on the same side and spent the next hour all but feeling each other up under the table.

It started innocently enough—I dropped my napkin, and when I leaned down to get it, my cheek brushed against Nic's bare leg. It was soft and smooth, and I may have lingered a little, inhaling the scent of her skin. Then I felt her shiver, and I grabbed the nearly forgotten napkin and sat up again, smiling a little smugly to myself.

Not even a minute passed before I felt it—the tips of her fingers sliding along my leg, then wandering over to my inner thigh. My shorts were too long for skin-on-skin contact, but that didn't stop me from literally jumping.

Rodney frowned. "What was that?"

"Nothing," I said quickly. "I thought I saw a bee."

"I think it was just a fly," Nic said, appearing to peruse the menu. Meanwhile, her fingers were still on my thigh, rubbing oh-so-gently.

I held up my own menu and grabbed her hand. "Stop it," I whispered from behind the raised menu.

She withdrew, but arched an eyebrow at me. "Don't start something you can't finish," she whispered back.

The rest of the meal went on like that, each of us goosing the other at irregular intervals, until finally, toward the end of dinner, she didn't flinch away when I slid my hand across her thigh. In fact, she shifted closer to me, an unspoken invitation for me to explore even further.

But I couldn't. Much as I wanted to be daring, much as I wanted to touch every inch of her body, I didn't want to do it here with Rodney smirking—he had finally caught on—and Cat glowering. I pulled my hand away and left it on my lap. Nic looked down at the table, her brow creasing momentarily. She didn't try to touch me again.

Cat didn't give up easily, that much was certain. After dinner she tried to convince us to rent a movie to watch in her room, two floors down from Nic's. When that didn't work, she attempted to lure us into hanging out with beer.

"We're in season, Cat," Nic said. "You know the rules."

The previous night they'd explained that everyone on the team agreed to abide by the same rules—no smoking at all, and no drinking the night before any team activity, be it practice or a meet. That left only Saturday nights to party, and even then, they weren't supposed to have more than three drinks.

"No, I know." Cat's shoulders slumped. "Okay, then, I guess I'll see you tomorrow."

"Tomorrow," Nic said, and gave her a fist bump.

"Bye." I nodded at Cat.

"Bye." Her voice was flat.

We took the stairs, Nic moving ahead of me determinedly. Ever since the moment in the restaurant when I'd backed off, she hadn't seemed to want to look at me. When we reached her room, she unlocked the door and hung her keys on the hook. Then she went over to her desk and started fiddling with her books.

This was not how the night was supposed to end. A few hours earlier I'd only wanted to be alone with her, and the feeling had seemed mutual. She was the one who'd kissed me in the Grand Palace Saloon.

"Nic?" I tried.

"Yeah?" She had a notebook open now, and stared down at it.

"Shouldn't we, I don't know, talk or something?"

She closed her eyes, and then she set the notebook back on her desk and turned to face me. She looked nervous, and knowing that I wasn't the only one, realizing that she felt that way because of me gave me the courage to walk over to her.

"Hey," I said, and lifted my hand to the curve of her cheek. "What happened?"

"You tell me," she said, her eyes fixed on my right shoulder. "I keep reaching out to you and you keep pulling away."

That was exactly what I'd done to Drew, and look how that had turned out. But this was different. She was different.

"I'm sorry," I said. "I've just never done this before."

She looked at me at last, her eyes quizzical.

"Drew is the only person I've ever been with, and even then we weren't really together."

Her eyes widened. "Wait. You said you'd never had sex with a guy."

"I know. I haven't."

"I thought that meant you'd been with girls."

"What? No way," I said, shaking my head.

"Then why would you qualify it like that?"

"I didn't realize I had." I hesitated. "Have you been with girls before?"

"Girl, singular," she said. "Jackie Moriarty in tenth grade, and only a few times. Seriously, you're really a virgin? Like, a total and complete virgin?"

I shoved my hands in my pockets and backed away. "Sorry to disappoint you."

"Ash," she said, and reached for me. "Come here. I'm sorry. I didn't mean it like that."

"Then how did you mean it?"

She didn't answer. Instead, she slipped her arms around my neck and pulled me against her. "Come here," she repeated, softer now. And then she kissed me again.

My arms went around her and I pulled her close, and I didn't care that I was in an SAU dorm room on an unofficial visit because nothing mattered except Nic's lips, and her hands sliding under the hem of my tank top, and we barely stopped kissing long enough for her to slip the tank off over my head. And then she was backing me toward the bed and pushing me down. She pulled off her own shirt, her hair loose and cascading over her shoulders as she leaned over me.

"Is this okay?" she asked, her eyes shining.

"God, yes," I said, and reached for her.

"Wait."

I watched as she moved purposely about the room. When she returned to bed, the room was lit only by a couple of candles on the nearby dresser and Sarah McLachlan's voice crooned from the stereo on her desk, a cassette I had sent her a few weeks earlier.

Candlelight an irregular halo in her dark hair, Nic lowered herself onto me slowly. I caught my breath as her hips settled into mine, her hair a curtain that blocked out everything else.

"Ash," she breathed, and then her lips closed on mine, soft and teasing at first until, a growl of frustration rising in my throat, I flipped her onto her back and pressed down against her. I needed her. I had never needed anyone as much. For a moment, the thought broke against the tide of my wanting, but then she slipped my sports bra off over my head, and I gratefully, ecstatically ceased thinking.

We slept, eventually, wrapped around each other in her bed. When the first light of day edged into the room, I opened my eyes and lay beside her trying to remember every second of the previous night. I knew that for a lot of people, their first time wasn't particularly memorable. That was not the case here. I'd reached a happy ending, so to speak, before, both with Drew and on my own, but I had never been brought to the point where I forgot myself. Somehow I doubted I'd quite returned the favor, but Nic had seemed happy, too. Several times.

I couldn't help comparing our night to what I'd had with Drew. And yet, there was no comparison. Drew had taught me to be more comfortable with my body and that there were certain things I liked and others I didn't, but messing around with him had always felt like, well, messing around. With Nic, I'd touched her because I wanted to, not out of some sense of sexual quid pro quo. We'd kissed for what felt like hours because I couldn't get enough of kissing her, and not once had my thoughts wandered the way they frequently had with Drew. With him, I would notice that we were kissing, or that we were lying in bed together, or that he was touching me. With Nic, the physical sensations had swept me along, my mind and body melded in a way I was used to only experiencing during a good run. Runner's high, I'd always called it. Looked like I would need to find a new term.

Beside me, Nic stirred lazily.

"Good morning," she murmured, slipping her arm around my waist.

"Good morning."

Now what?

"I am in so much trouble," she murmured, her head on my shoulder.

"You are?"

"Mm-hm. The SAU prospective host handbook clearly states

it's against the rules to seduce your prospie."

It took me a second to realize she was joking. "Nice."

She rolled on top of me and kissed me, and I soon forgot all about prospie rules, morning breath, and the fact that I was due to leave Tucson in a matter of hours.

Not for long, though. It was after eight by the time we resurfaced, and my train departed at one. That only left us a few more hours together. Fewer, really, because Nic had two classes this morning.

"Are you crazy? I'm not going to class," she said when I asked her what time the first one, Spanish Lit, started.

"You can't skip," I said. "Marcie would kill me."

She paused in pulling on the previous day's T-shirt. "You are so cute, but that's not how things work here. I've only had one professor who had an attendance policy, and as long as our grades are decent, Marcie doesn't care what we do."

"Oh. Well, good, then."

Nic finished dressing and sat down on the bed beside me. "Do you really have to go back to New York? Didn't you say your grandparents in Phoenix asked you to come live with them?"

I stared at her. "Yeah, but I told Austin I was coming back. And I have a job. I can't just not show up."

"No, I know. Forget it." She leaned over to kiss me again. "I just wish you didn't have to go."

"Me, either," I said, holding her tightly. "I thought being apart the last couple of months was bad. Now it's going to feel like torture."

"Tell me about it. Every night I'm going to have to lie here alone wishing you were here."

"You will? Be alone, I mean?"

She leaned back so she could see my eyes. "Of course. Won't you?"

"Um, yeah," I said. "I'm the virgin here, remember?"

"Not anymore."

We hadn't done a whole lot more together than Drew and I had, and yet, it counted as so much more.

"True," I said. "But I live with a gay guy, and you live in a dorm filled with people who would be more than happy to help you forget about me."

"You're the only one I'm interested in."

"Really? What about Cat?"

She bit her lip. "You noticed that."

"Kind of hard not to notice when someone is obsessed with your girl."

"She's not obsessed." Nic paused. "So I'm your girl now?"

Flustered, I sat up straighter against the pillows, holding the sheet up to my collarbone. "I didn't mean it like that."

"It's okay if you did," she said. "Honestly."

"Yeah?"

"Yeah. Now get dressed or we're never getting out of here."

Which would have been fine with me, I thought as I pulled on the previous day's outfit. More than fine, really.

The next few hours escaped when I wasn't looking, and then somehow it was time to borrow Rodney's Explorer for the short trip to the train station. As we got nearer, I felt my throat closing up, my eyes going all tight like I was going to cry. I blinked hard, reminding myself that Marcie had said I had a chance, that Trinity had asked me when I could be ready to move to Tucson. I would probably be back here in a few months, ready to start my new life. Probably.

But what if I wasn't? What then? SAU was a good school, smaller and more selective than the average state university, but with my grades and test scores, I didn't think I would be rejected. Still, would I come here if Marcie didn't offer me a spot on the team? Could I move to Arizona for Nic? I knew what Selma would have counseled: I would be better off going somewhere that offered the full student-athlete experience I craved, rather than sacrificing my dreams for someone I barely knew.

Maybe I wouldn't have to choose, though. All I had to do now was stay healthy and do well in a handful of tri-state area runs, and I might have everything I wanted. Including, possibly, Nic, who felt like someone I had known far longer than a couple of months. Over the past few days, she had become the most important person in the world, as far as I was concerned, and now we were saying goodbye for who knew how long.

Neither of us spoke as we walked from the car to the station, her with my athletic bag, me with my backpack and the gift she'd handed me just before we left the dorm.

"But I'm the one with a job," I'd protested when she handed me the SAU bookstore bag, warning me not to peek inside until after the train left Tucson.

"Whatever," she'd said. "I can buy my girl things if I want to."

"Your girl, huh?"

She'd lifted her chin and said, "Yeah. You got a problem with that?"

"Nope," I'd said, smiling down at her, and pulled her close for a final kiss before we left the safety and privacy of her room.

Inside the station, we sat close together in the waiting area, not looking at each other. A few feet away, a straight couple was practically having sex on one of the benches. I glanced away from them, resenting the freedom they probably didn't even know they had. I wanted desperately to kiss Nic goodbye, but I also didn't want to worry that some redneck asshole would follow her back to campus. At least we weren't guys. There was nothing that enraged a redneck quite like seeing two men in love.

"I wish you didn't have to leave so soon," Nic said. "It feels like you just got here."

"I know. But at the same time, I've gotten used to this place. New York is going to seem like this big, ugly, loud place."

"Don't forget dirty."

"Thanks," I said, and shoved her sideways. Or at least, I meant to, but somehow I only ended up tugging her closer.

She leaned her chin on my shoulder, just for a second. "I can't wait until you come back."

"Same here. I'm going to miss you so much."

"Me, too." She sighed, her breath warm against my neck.

It was killing me not to touch her. I was almost relieved when the PA system coughed out the boarding call for my train. We stood up and stared at each other, and then we hugged, holding onto each other tightly. After a minute, she kissed my cheek, quickly, and pulled away, not meeting my eyes.

"Have a safe trip." She handed me my bag. "Call me when you get there."

"I will." I hesitated, feeling my throat tighten again. "Write to me, okay?"

"Of course."

I started to turn away, but then I stopped. "You won't forget about me, will you?" It came out as a plea that I immediately regretted. It was just that I couldn't stop thinking about the fact that she would be here with Cat and a plethora of other students who would be happy to share her bed, while I would be off in New York waiting to find out if I could ever even come back to Tucson.

"Ash," she said, her eyes bright with the same tears ambushing me, "I haven't stopped thinking about you since the first time we ran Central Park. Do you think I could now that we've actually been together?"

Letting my bags drop, I wrapped my arms around her. And all at once, standing in the middle of the Tucson train station, I understood that I loved Nicki Salvo. I was in love for the first time in my life, and Selma would never get to meet her.

"I don't think I can leave," I said when she pulled away.

"I know," she said, and smiled. "But you'll be back, I know you will, and I'll still be here. I'm not going anywhere."

The boarding call for my train sounded again over the speakers, and Nic leaned forward and kissed me on the lips. With people brushing past, I kissed her back, but it wasn't at all like being in her dorm room, with the candle flickering and Sarah McLachlan singing and the breeze tousling the curtains. We were kissing in the middle of a public space in Tucson, Arizona, with strangers passing close enough to touch. I stepped back, my cheeks hot. The Southwest, like the Southeast, isn't known for being particularly liberal.

"Sorry. I wish…" I stopped, looking at her helplessly.

"So do I," she said. "Go. I'll talk to you soon, okay?"

I nodded. *I love you*, I thought, but I couldn't say it out loud. It was too soon, not to mention too clichéd. She was my first everything, but what if she didn't feel the same way?

Steeling myself, I turned and walked out onto the platform and down along the side of the tall Amtrak sleeper cars. I looked back once and Nic was still there, watching me leave. My breath seemed to freeze inside my chest, and I had to force myself to keep moving forward. Leaving was almost as bad as being left. I climbed aboard, waved at her one last time, and found my private room on the upper level. It was on the side opposite from the station, so I wouldn't be able to watch Nic as we pulled out of the station, assuming she was still there. I stowed my luggage, pulled a Gatorade from my pack, and settled onto the sofa bed as the train started moving, Nic's gift bag on my lap.

Inside, an SAU T-shirt and baseball cap were hidden under tissue paper. There was also a postcard from the Grand Canyon on the back of which Nic had scrawled, "I miss you already. Kick ass this spring so that we can be together this summer. Oh, and so that you can join the team and kick ass at SAU, too, of course." She had signed it, "All my love, N."

All my love. I looked out the window, barely noticing the receding cacti and the approaching mountains, the blue sky and the bright sunshine. She loved me? She loved me. It said so right there on the back of the picture of one of the world's Seven Wonders. All my love.

I would be back, I decided, channeling Nic's optimism. Even if there wasn't a spot on the team for me, I would have to come back. Given I could count the number of people I loved on one hand, walking away from her just didn't seem like an option, especially as it turned out that she, apparently, loved me back.

The train soon left Tucson behind and I settled into the ride, my thoughts jumbled. Being with Nic had changed everything. I wondered again if Selma had suspected I wasn't straight. I wondered if Claire and Bruce and Austin suspected I wasn't straight. I pulled my Walkman out and put in a Melissa Etheridge tape, listening more closely to the words than I usually did. I had three days to figure it all out. Three long days to relive every second of the weekend, starting with the last twenty-four hours.

I closed my eyes and listened to the music in my headphones as the train carried me back east.

CHAPTER TWENTY-SEVEN

Austin was waiting for me when I got back to New York. He hugged me inside Penn Station and led me outside to the station wagon double-parked half a block away, blinkers on. Nic was right—after SAU's pristine campus and surrounding environs, New York seemed downright filthy. The mountains of dirty snow still piled on the corners of every intersection didn't help, either.

I had barely buckled my seat belt when Austin said, glancing over his shoulder before pulling out, "Spill it, Ash. Who did you sleep with and how was it?"

I blinked, trying to process his question.

"My money is on our little Nic, of course," he added, "but you've had your dark horse moments, so..."

"How did you know?" I asked, finally recovering my voice. I had spent part of the trip home rehearsing how I would tell Austin. So much for those plans.

"It's all over your face. I do believe you've gone and fallen in love, my friend."

"Great, I've been gay for less than a week, and already I'm horrible at the closet."

"Nah. No one else would even be able to tell you got laid, let alone by a girl. Now give—was it Nic?"

"Duh," I said, and grinned so widely my face actually hurt.

We spent the short ride home discussing my enlightening weekend in Tucson. Tommy was waiting at the apartment with dinner ready and candlelight flickering, which of course reminded me of Nic.

Tommy hugged me and then exchanged a look with Austin. "Nic?"

Austin smiled smugly. "You owe me twenty bucks."

As Tommy reached for his wallet, I glanced from one to the other. "You bet on whether or not I would hook up with Nic?"

"Not if, but when," Austin clarified. "He figured you would fall into bed right off the bat, but I know you a little better than that. I mean, look at ole Drew, or BB, as I used to call him."

"BB?" I asked.

"Blue Balls. Poor guy. You never did put him out of his misery, did you?"

Tommy handed Austin a folded bill, and then smacked him on the arm. "Behave."

"She started it," Austin said.

"Did not."

"Children, let's not fight. Ashley, you've been away for a long time, and I've made a lovely dinner. Let's celebrate—to Ash and Nic."

"About effing time," Austin added.

We clinked wine glasses and partook of the delicious quiche that Tommy had prepared. Toward the end of the meal, Austin caught me checking my watch, trying to gauge what time it was in Tucson. Two hours earlier, which meant I may or may not catch Nic at home.

"Go," Tommy said finally. "We'll clean up."

"Thanks," I said, and practically fled to my room.

"Tell your girlfriend we say hi," Austin called as I closed the door on his knowing smile.

Nic picked up on the second ring, and I sat down at the desk, realizing how much I missed her. On the train, the constant sense of motion had allowed me to suspend reality temporarily. But now I was home in New York, and she was in Tucson, and the earliest we might possibly see each other was in three months.

"Hi," I said softly. "It's me."

"You made it home," Nic said, and I thought I detected relief and sadness both in her voice. Or maybe that was just what I wanted to hear.

"I wouldn't call New York home, necessarily," I said. "But it's good to see Austin and Tommy. They said to tell you hello."

"Really?"

"Get this—they had a bet going about when you and I would hook up. Can you believe it?"

"Absolutely," she said, laughing.

An hour passed far too quickly, and finally Nic admitted that she had skipped dinner to wait for my call.

"Dude, you have to eat! You're a scholarship athlete," I scolded her.

"I know, and I will. Don't worry, I made noodles while I was waiting."

She had waited beside her telephone for my call? Obviously she was still enamored with me enough to skip dinner. This, I decided, was a Very Good Sign.

It took us another few minutes to hang up, with the requisite "You hang up," and "No, you hang up" exchange eating up even more time.

"Go eat," I finally ordered her. "You need to build your strength back if you're going to qualify for nationals."

"Yes, ma'am."

We hung up at last, and I wandered back into the living room where Austin and Tommy were hanging out on the couch watching *Friends*. I sat down next to Austin and leaned my head on his shoulder. He slipped an arm around me and kissed my hair. He was a lousy stand-in for Nic, but anyone would be. At least I had my best friend and his boyfriend to get me through the next few months before I moved on and left them behind for yet another new life.

I was getting tired of starting over. Admittedly I'd only done it once so far that I could remember, but I knew intellectually that June would mark my third big reset. Why couldn't everyone I cared about live in the same place, anyway? At least my grandparents were in Arizona, along with a few of the cousins I vaguely remembered from our summer visits to Wisconsin. Every summer except the one when my other grandfather died, my aunts and uncles would arrange their own visits to the Midwest around the trip Selma planned for us. They'd wanted to maximize family time, Selma explained. So practical, those Wisconsinites.

Sitting on the couch with Austin and Tommy, I considered calling my grandparents. I'd talked to them a few times since Christmas, but it had been a while now, what with planning for my trip and all. What would I tell them, though—that I had just spent a long weekend in Tucson and hadn't even called? That I may or may not be attending SAU next year?

Better to wait, I decided, until some of the bigger questions had been answered. In the meantime, maybe I should get a wall calendar and cross off each day with a big red X. Speaking of cliché... But I didn't mind being a cliché if, in the end, I wound up in Arizona with Nic and the rest of the team.

Aargh. How was I going to make it through the next few weeks, let alone months?

I slouched lower on the couch next to Austin and stared at the television, trying to imprint the images and voices on my distracted brain.

At first, as expected, I couldn't stand being back in the loud, dirty city. But after a couple of days, my trip to Arizona was a blur of good memories. After a week back in New York, limited once again to communicating with Nic solely via the telephone, it was almost like I hadn't ever left, other than the whole falling-in-love-and-sleeping-with-a-girl thing.

My second weekend back was the NYPD Versus FDNY 5 Mile Run through Central Park. It wasn't USATF-certified, but the course was similar to the one I'd been running on Saturdays and would make a good warm-up to real competition. I'd pre-registered, but I still got to the registration site, an elementary school on the Upper East Side, excessively early, dragging Austin, Tommy, and Marcus along to cheer me on.

"You've got this," Austin said when I came back from my warm-up run and started stretching in place, waiting for the race to begin. "You're totally going to clean up."

The day before, the weather had warmed up, and overnight the temperatures had only dropped partially. At nine in the morning it was already in the mid-forties, which made me happy. I hated running in cold weather, especially when I knew Marcie would be reviewing my times.

The race attracted lots of beefy cops and firemen, so Austin's prediction was actually pretty accurate. I lined up close to the front and stood swaying and stretching, clad in black tights, a long-sleeved white tech shirt, and a black, fleece-lined earband. Thin running gloves finished off the outfit and kept my fingers from freezing. These I pounded together now as I sized up the competitors lining up near me. A handful of the guys pushing their way to the front looked like real runners, but only one other woman appraised me coolly as I returned the favor. About ten years my senior, I was guessing she would be my competition.

"Found your peeps?" Austin asked from behind the nearby barrier.

I nodded and held a hand up to my friends. They slapped it, one after the other.

"You go girl," Tommy said in a fake queen accent that made Marcus snort.

"I intend to."

I flashed them a quick smile, reached for my watch, and hit go on the stopwatch function as the crack of the starting gun echoed through Central Park.

It had been a while since I'd been in an actual race. What came to mind as we set off along East Park Drive was not all the races, cross country and stadium track, that I'd run in high school. Instead I pictured Midtown traffic and imagined myself on a bike weaving in and out among the buses and taxis, jockeying for position at each intersection, the sweet sensation of freedom when I would hit a long stretch of timed lights, like on Sixth Avenue between Midtown and SoHo, and I would be part of the flow of the city. That was what running was like—finding your place in the pack and then holding your pace, going with the flow until you became part of it.

The woman runner and I fell into step together, running side-by-side as if we had done so a hundred times before. I let myself be pushed a little, faster than I normally trained, but it felt good. I felt good and the morning was warmish, and I actually caught glimpses of yellow and white and blue crocuses poking up beneath still-bare trees at the edge of the road. Finally, spring was within reach.

I pictured Nic as I had a thousand times in the past week—leaning over me, her hair a curtain that blocked out the candlelight—and I picked up my pace a little more. I was running for her, and to her; for once, I had a destination in mind instead of merely escape. It felt good. It really did.

The woman and I ran together until the end. Then, with the finish line in sight, she kicked it. I reached inside and assessed my reserves. I still had energy to spare, so I emulated her kick. When I caught her, she expelled a breath somewhere between annoyance and acceptance, a sound I recognized as I passed her and, fifteen seconds later, crossed the finish line in the lead.

I slowed, and she caught me in return, clapping me on the shoulder as we jogged.

"Nice race," she said, smiling at me.

"You, too." I smiled back.

And then I did remember all of the races in high school when a runner I'd beaten congratulated me, or when I commended someone else who had managed to slip away from me. That was one of the things I loved about running—you battled and battled, and then at the end of the day you shook hands and wished each other well out of respect, in the name of sportsmanship.

Because it could always be you who lost. And if you raced enough, it would be.

By the end of March, my New York life had settled into a steady rhythm. I almost felt like I really was in-season as I continued to work out during the week and race almost every weekend. Butch's advice came back to me in chunks, and I implemented ideas I'd formerly resisted mostly because I thought Butch didn't like me—or maybe it was that I didn't like him. On Trinity's recommendation, I also checked out a handful of books on training from the library, and used the charts and schedules to plan when to taper my weekly running and cross-training activities to better avoid injury. A pulled groin or hamstring now could doom my college plans. Or at least, my plans to attend SAU.

The weather continued to improve, and with it the moods of many New Yorkers. Even the most diehard city resident couldn't resist the return of sunshine and birds to the streets and parks of Manhattan. At work, our deadline of June first was rapidly approaching, but we were in good shape, Andrea said, thanks in large part to my work. I was ready to be back in school, but it felt good to be part of the team at Maxwell's, too. Maybe my children would someday use the text in their studies, and I would be able to tell them about the crazy year I worked in New York City. Although perhaps they didn't need to know that I'd taken a year off before college, or that I'd worked as a bike messenger, or about the weekly excursions to gay clubs back before Austin and Tommy fell in love and settled down.

This train of thought made me wonder what secrets had died with my own parents. I'd never gotten to know them, not the way I knew Selma, and they'd never had the chance to know me, either. Had they realized this in the seconds before they died? Or had it happened too fast for thought, only reaction?

These were questions the answers to which I would never know, and that was okay. Soon I would have plenty of other answers, whether I liked them or not. In fact, they had already started. My college acceptance letters began to arrive at the end of March, with no surprises—I got in to each of the schools I'd applied to. Meanwhile, I'd been in regular touch with Trinity through a new form of correspondence, e-mail. Nic and I had been e-mailing, too, in addition to the usual long letters and nightly phone calls. The days were ticking by and the races were going well, from my perspective. Nic and Trinity thought so, too. By mid-April, I had bettered my PR in the mile and the 10K, both on certified courses. The only thing left to improve on was my 5K time. If I could do that, Trinity confided on the phone one evening, then we'd be talking.

In late April, I got my chance: the Sarah B. Cook Race against Cancer in Central Park, a USATF-certified 5K course. Early that Sunday, the last in April, I rose and caught the subway to Fiftieth Street. Tommy and Austin were in Philly for the weekend and Marcus had exams coming up, so for this one race, I was on my own. As the sun rose over the quiet city—Sunday mornings were by far my favorite time in New York—I jogged up to Columbus Circle, reliving the morning I met Nic. How far we'd come since that snowy day when she walked up to me for the first time and I could only stare at her, aware at some level that my life had, in a moment, changed. Again.

The night before, I'd wanted to talk late into the night, and perhaps to have some extra-curricular phone fun, but she'd insisted I needed my rest. Besides, she had a party to go—the women's team had qualified at a meet earlier in the day for Nationals for only the second time in school history, the first in Marcie's tenure. SAU was headed to San Diego in June.

I was thrilled for Nic, who would be running the 800 against the nation's best, but I couldn't help wishing I was there to help her celebrate. Even more reason I needed to run well, I told myself after I'd picked up my number and pinned it to my tank top—the day was dry and already warm, especially for the time of year, and expected to get hot. At the start line, I noticed the same couple of dozen runners I'd seen every weekend for a month now, chatting with each other as they elbowed the recreational runners out of the way. The woman I'd beat during my first race in New York back in March was there, and we nodded at each other, all friendly and serious at the same time.

"What splits are you going for?" she asked me, stretching her quad.

"Five thirties," I answered. "I really want to break seventeen. You?"

"Five-forties, if I'm lucky."

"Want to do five-thirty-fives for the first two?" I asked. "We could pace each other."

She tilted her head. "What are you, eighteen?"

"Nineteen."

"I'm thirty. That means no matter what, I win my age group."

"Assuming no one else beats us."

She glanced around. "I've been running in the city for five years, and I can say with confidence that none of this lot are going to give us any problems."

"Does that mean you want to run together?"

She held out her hand. "Why not? I'm Carrie, by the way."

"Ash."

We synched our watches and waited for the air horn that signaled the official start. Then we were off, matching our strides and our breathing as we wound through the park.

"You a student?" Carrie asked.

"No, but I hope to be soon."

"Where?"

I gave her the brief version of my current saga, and she made appreciative sounds in all the right places. I checked the odometer on my watch. We were a little under, so I speeded up slightly.

"What do you do?" I asked after a little while.

"Reporter," she said. "*Daily News.*"

A warning bell rang in my head, and it took me a second to remember that I was a celebrity of sorts, given my sole survivor status and the years Selma had hidden me away. It had been months since the fifteenth anniversary of the crash had rekindled the spotlight on the mysterious girl who survived, but I wasn't taking any chances. I kept the conversation firmly on Carrie, practically drilling her on her work.

Finally she gasped, "No more talking."

So we stopped talking and ran on under the laden boughs of magnolia and cherry trees, their spring blooms vivid against the cloudless blue sky. On days like this, it was hard to believe that only five months before, Nic and I had run the park drive edged with snow, our skin protected by fleece and wool. Now the grass in the fields was green, the spring flowering trees in full bloom, and even the deciduous trees we passed were hazy with the yellow-green fuzz of new leaves just embarking on the short single season of their lives.

At the two and a half mile mark, we were at 13:49. At this rate, I wasn't going to break seventeen.

"Go," Carrie said, pushing me forward. "Just go! You can do it!"

I reached inside, testing, feeling. I felt good. Could I do it? Maybe.

"Towanda!" I said, and kicked it.

The finish line was on a straightaway, which meant I could see the clock from a fair distance out: 16:41, 42, 43, 44... I put my head down and gritted my teeth and ran harder than I had since high school. I imagined Selma in the stadium back home, leaping out of her seat to cheer me on. I pictured Nic in Arizona, waiting for me. And I ran.

Just before the finish, I checked the clock again. 16:53, 54, 55... I crossed the finish line at 16:59. One second to spare—I'd done it. I'd broken seventeen and clocked a new PR on a certified outdoor course. That would have to move me up on Marcie's list, wouldn't it? *Please, God or whomever*, I thought, lifting my face to the sky as I slowed to a walk, *let it be enough.*

"Way to go!" Carrie said when she caught up to me.

We fell into step and jogged on down the road at an easy pace, cooling down after the big push.

"Thanks," I said, and smiled at her. "What about you? New PR?"

"Yeah," she said. "This is my first sub-16:45, so thanks, kid."

We slapped hands, jogged a little ways, and then turned to head back to the finish line. We grabbed water and a snack, then stretched out together and took a short walk across a nearby field to look at the spring flowers close up, chatting the entire time. She wasn't from New York either, it turned out. She'd come from Michigan to the city for graduate school—Columbia School of Journalism—and stayed.

"Do you miss Michigan?" I asked.

"A little. Are you familiar with the area?"

"I was born in Chicago and I used to have family in Wisconsin, so I've spent some time in the area. I love the Great Lakes."

"Me, too. I remember one of my grad school classmates from Texas arguing with me about Lake Michigan—he was convinced there couldn't possibly be a lake so big you couldn't see across it."

"Texas," I said scathingly.

"Exactly. Pretty soon, you'll be practically neighbors with Texas."

"Only if I'm lucky."

She shook her head. "It has nothing to do with luck."

"My aunt used to say we make our own luck."

"Smart lady, your aunt. Does she live in Wisconsin?"

"Not anymore."

Carrie and I both stuck around for the awards ceremony. I'd finished first among all women, and she'd finished first in her age group. After my name was called and I'd gone up to pick up my medal, I walked back to where Carrie was still standing, guarding our gear. As I approached, our eyes met.

"Your last name is Lake?" she asked. "And you were born in Chicago?"

I grabbed my bag and started to back away. "I have to go."

"Ashley, wait. Please."

I could have run. We both knew she couldn't catch me. But I had been running for so long.

"You're her, aren't you?" she asked.

I hesitated, and then I nodded.

"No one's ever interviewed you. Your family always protected you."

I nodded again.

"Any chance you feel like breaking the silence? With me, for example?"

"If I say no, will you write the story anyway?"

"Not without your permission. There's this pesky thing called ethics that we journalists try to live by."

"Really?" I asked, thinking of the paparazzi who shadowed movie stars and made their lives hell. Or as near to hell as those who were rich and beautiful and adored by millions ever got.

"Maybe not all of us," she admitted. "But I'm one of the good ones. You can trust me."

"In that case, I don't think I am ready."

She sighed. "All right. Guess it was too good to be true."

"Seriously? I'm really not going to wake up tomorrow and find my face and story plastered across your paper?"

She frowned. "Of course not. It's your life, and we were talking as fellow runners. I'll respect that."

"Wow. Thank you." I held out my hand, and she shook it. "I think you just redeemed my faith in humanity. Or, at least, in the press."

She smiled. "I'll take that as a compliment. And just so you know, if and when you are ever ready, I would be honored to tell your story. I think you could be an inspiration to others who've experienced great loss, as well as to the people who lost family members on that flight."

"Me? An inspiration?" I repeated.

"Yes, you. Look at what you've managed to accomplish. Most people don't have your prospects, even the ones who haven't had great tragedy shadowing them."

"But I don't even remember the plane crash," I told her.

"You don't?"

Dang it. Somehow I kept forgetting she was a reporter who may or may not keep her word about revealing my life history and current whereabouts.

"Don't worry," she added. "I won't use that. But I hope you'll think about it. Your story could help others, I genuinely believe that."

I stared at her earnest expression, her face still red from the run. Was she right? Could I help other people just by sharing my story? Could something good really come of something so terrible? All those people, including my parents, suddenly gone from the earth without a warning, in many cases without even remains to be buried. And here I was, an adult of sorts, whole and intact and on my way to possibly, maybe being happy with someone I loved. The plane crash had happened to me, and Selma's cancer, too. But I was going on, trying to be happy. Just like Tommy and Austin were doing with the specter of AIDS hanging over them, just like Jewel's girlfriend Teri had done after being randomly shot by a decidedly imperfect stranger.

"I'm not sure I agree," I finally told Carrie, "but I'll think about it. Seriously, it would be nice for something positive to come out of what happened."

"Something already has," she said, and touched my shoulder. "You survived, and I would bet my last dollar that there are those whose lives are better because of it. I mean, look at me," she added, her tone lightening. "I just ran a PR thanks to you."

I laughed. "Good point."

After the awards ceremony ended, we walked toward Columbus Circle together, her headed for the East Village, me to the West. Before we parted, she gave me a card with her work contact information, her home phone number scrawled on the back.

"Do you have e-mail at work?" she asked.

I nodded. "I'll have it at school next year, too."

"Good. That's the best way to reach me."

"You're really not going to write about anything I told you today?" I couldn't help asking.

"To be honest, I'll probably go home and write down some notes. But no, I won't do anything with them unless you tell me to. Deal?"

"Deal," I said, holding out my hand.

She slapped it. "You keep running, Ashley."

"You, too."

We smiled at each other, and then I was turning away and jogging across Central Park South. The weather was perfect, warm and sunny but not too hot yet. I dodged foot traffic, heavier now mid-morning than when I'd warmed up before the race, and contemplated going public with my story. What would SAU think? What would Nic think? What would Selma have thought?

She had worked so hard to protect me from the press, to shield me from any potentially negative effects from the plane crash. But it was part of me, just as she was, and pretending something hadn't happened was starting to seem to me like a massively flawed approach. If Carrie was right, maybe I had the uncommon opportunity to help others. What if, with her help, I actually managed to turn tragedy into hope?

When I reached Sixth Avenue, I headed south along the

sidewalk. I'd missed riding my bike through the city, though to be honest, I hadn't missed freezing my ass off or risking my athletic future. But now it was spring, and the warm air felt wonderful. Maybe I would run home. It was only three miles, which would bring my total on the day to 10,000 meters. Besides, it would be nice to explore the city while I still could. One way or another, I wouldn't be in New York much longer. Even if Marcie didn't want me, Nic did, and the feeling was mutual.

I couldn't wait to tell her about the race, and Carrie, and the idea that Carrie had planted in my mind. Unfortunately, the phone call would have to wait, something that I was growing either increasingly better or far worse at dealing with, depending on the day.

Today, I decided as I ran slowly down Sixth Avenue, the sun peeking around buildings and the shade perfectly cool, was one of the better days.

Midweek I was up to my eyeballs again in work, running forgotten as I vainly searched for a lost photo spec among the files strewn across my desk. When the phone rang, I considered letting it go into voicemail. At the last second, I slipped a pen into the file where I'd left off.

"This is Ashley."

"Hi, Ashley. This is Marcie Andozzi from SAU. Have you got a minute?"

I gulped and my hands twitched and I almost knocked over my water bottle. "Um, yeah, I do. What's up?"

"I just wanted to follow up on your times. Seems like you've had a busy spring. How are you feeling?"

My stomach felt like it had dropped into my kneecaps. "Good, thanks. Everything's great." I paused, pleasantly surprised by the steadiness of my voice. "So, Coach. Do you have news for me?"

"Yes, Ashley. I have a proposal to make. Are you ready to hear what I have to offer?"

No, my subconscious wailed. "Sure."

"All right, then. Ashley, I'd like you to run for me beginning this fall. I checked with Admissions, and you were among the first batch of applicants accepted. They tell me you're eligible for a National Merit scholarship."

That didn't surprise me. It was the first part of what she'd said that I was having trouble with. "But wait—you're saying you want me on your team? Like, seriously?"

She laughed. "Yes, like, seriously. The National Merit scholarship doesn't count toward the team's financial limits, but it will count toward your grant-in-aid limit. This means that, like most of my other athletes, you'll be on a partial athletic scholarship. Is finding money for college a concern for you?"

"No," I said, swallowing hard as realization sank in. She had called to offer me a place on the team, not to extend apologies or excuses for why it wouldn't work out. "Partial is fine. I mean, it's better than fine. Thank you so much."

"Does that mean you're committing to us?"

"Yes," I said. "Yes!"

"In that case, you're very welcome," Marcie said. Then she turned brisk again. "I'll have our staff send you the NCAA letter of intent and other paperwork. Once you've read through everything, you can call me with any questions or just sign the papers and send them back. We'll get the ball rolling from there. Do you think you can be in Tucson by July first? I'd like you to participate in some of the captain's workouts this summer."

"July's perfect." I was almost dizzy, thinking about moving to Tucson in a few months. Wait until Nic found out.

"All right, then," Marcie said, and I could hear the smile in her voice. "Welcome to SAU Track and Field, Ashley."

"Thanks, Coach," I said. "This is so amazing!"

"Between you and me, I think we can build you quite a career at SAU. All I ask of my athletes is that they trust me."

"I will." I was one of her athletes now. God, I liked how that sounded.

"Excellent. Well, look for the letter in the mail. And in the meantime, take good care of yourself, Ashley."

"I will," I said, smiling stupidly.

I hung up the phone and stared at it for a minute, then picked it up again and punched in Nic's number. I knew she was in class, but I left her a long, rambling message. Then I went and told my boss, Andrea, the good news. She gave me a hug and ordered me to take an early lunch. Outside, I wandered the cobbled streets of SoHo. It was warm for April in New York, and I found myself eyeing the messengers who passed. Leslie—I should thank Leslie. I owed her big time for my shot at the big-time.

The door to OTJ's garage was open to let in the spring air, and Leslie and Mark were both there along with Morrison, the transplanted Californian, pulling dispatch duty.

Leslie was on the phone but waved me over. Within a minute she had wrapped up the call and dispatched it to Simone, waiting on the other line. Then she dropped the receiver and turned to me. "I hear you might be headed to Arizona."

I nodded, smiling. "I actually just got offered a scholarship to run at Southern Arizona University." I used the full name intentionally, testing the sound and feel of it. Yep—pretty sweet.

"I'm happy for you, Fire Girl. So how does it feel to achieve your dreams?" she asked, smiling back at me.

"Pretty freaking amazing."

She held up her hand and I slapped it. "Hey you two," she called to Mark and Morrison. "Ashley landed herself a spot at Southern Arizona. She is officially a Desert Cat."

"Boo-yah," Morrison called, covering the phone with one hand and giving me a "hang loose" wave of thumb and forefinger with the other.

"Congratulations," Mark mouthed, giving me the more traditional thumbs-up. I nodded at them both.

"Anyway," I said, "I know you're busy, but I just wanted to stop by and give you the update."

"That's not the only update you have to share, is it?" Leslie asked pointedly.

"What do you mean?" I felt my cheeks warm.

"I thought I'd heard you had some personal news to pass along. Something about a certain sprinter whose cousin happens to be my best friend?" And she wiggled her eyebrows in a comical way.

"Oh, that," I said, my mind going a thousand miles an hour—how did Camilla know? Had Nic told someone in New York who had told Camilla? Or had she come out to her cousin?

"Yes, that," Leslie said. "Congratulations are definitely in order. I've met Nicki a few times, and she is quite the catch."

My cheeks were blazing red by now. "Yes, well…"

Leslie laughed. "I can see I've caught you out, so to speak. We can change the subject if you like."

"Yes, please."

We chatted a little while longer, and then the phones started ringing again, and Leslie gave me a hug and told me not to be a stranger for the next couple of months. She was already picking up the phone as I turned to leave: "On the Job. What can we do for you?"

CHAPTER TWENTY-EIGHT

The phone was ringing as I let myself into the apartment that night after working out at Maxwell's. Austin was at the restaurant, and Tommy wasn't here, so it was just me and Nic and our long-distance connection.

"I'm in!" I said as soon as I established that yes, this was my girlfriend calling the second practice let out.

"I know! I can't believe it!"

I paused in pacing the living room, phone glued to my ear. "You can't?"

"Not like that. I mean I'm dumbfounded, bamboozled, astonished."

"Yeah, those don't really sound any better."

She laughed. "How about this: I'm thrilled, and I can't wait to see you, teammate!"

I winced. "I'm pretty sure teammates shouldn't date, so…"

"What's going on, *chica*? You just got a Division I scholarship offer. You should be bouncing off the walls."

"I am. Or I was, earlier."

Her tone lost its teasing edge. "Is this not what you want?"

"No," I said. "Of course it is. It's exactly what I want." I took a breath. "But before I sign the letter, I have to tell you something."

I could almost feel the temperature drop over the phone line. "What kind of something?"

Clearly she thought I was going to say something like *I cheated on you*. This was not going well. I could be such an idiot.

"It's nothing bad," I said hastily. "Only, well, I love you."

At first she didn't say anything, and my heartbeat accelerated in panic. Oh, God. She didn't love me. I had just ruined everything.

"I love you, too," she said.

I let out a breath. "Really? You're not just saying that?"

"No, Ash," she said, and I could hear the smile in her voice. "I wouldn't say it if I didn't mean it. I was just shocked, that's all. I didn't expect you to say it first."

"Neither did I. But damn it, I love you," I repeated, and laughed. "I totally love you!"

"You're not going to break into Olivia Newton John, are you?"

"Um, no. But for the record, those lyrics are 'I *honestly* love you.'"

"You would know that."

"Duh, I live with a gay guy."

"Not for long," Nic said. Then she paused. "Actually, how much longer?"

"The sublet is up at the end of May, and so is my temp position."

"And then are you coming here? Please, please tell me you're moving here."

"Yes," I said, deciding on the spot. "Then I'm moving out there."

"Thank God."

"I know, right?"

We chatted a little longer about the impending future, and then I brought up my conversation with Leslie.

"So how exactly does your cousin know about us?"

"Oh, that," she said, a little sheepishly. "I meant to tell you: I sort of came out to my family."

My chin literally dropped. "You *what*? When? And more importantly, why?"

"I did it because I'm in love and I don't want to have to hide it. I don't want to hide you. You're amazing, Ash, and I want everyone else to know it."

I dropped onto the couch, stunned as ever by my luck. It was almost as if the plane crash and Selma's cancer had gotten all the bad luck out of the way, and now things could be good from here on out. Intellectually, I knew that happily ever after was a fairy tale. But just then, it almost seemed within reach.

"Wow," I said, resting my head against the back of the couch. "How did it go?"

"Predictably—my mother went all silent but deadly, my father said he loved me no matter what, and Camilla said Aunt Teresa had to be revived with smelling salts."

I laughed, easily able to picture the scene she'd described. "Seriously, are you okay?"

"I don't know." Her voice lost its brash edge. "My mom just seemed so withdrawn. I don't see how we're ever going to get past this."

We sat quietly listening to each other breathe over the phone line, thousands of miles apart as we had been for months. But not for much longer now.

"You know," I offered, "the same thing happened with Austin and his dad, and six months later they're doing much better."

"In six months it'll be Halloween, and you'll be more than halfway through your first semester."

"Can you believe it? Oh, that's right, you can't."

"I wish you were here already," she said for the hundredth time since March.

I pictured her lying on her bed in a tank top and the men's boxers she liked to sleep in. "So do I. You don't even know how much."

"Tell me again when you're coming to Tucson?"

"I'll leave New York at the beginning of June. There are some things I have to do in Signal Point—"

"I thought you weren't going to sell the house?"

"I'm not. But I have to see the property manager, and I should talk to Selma's lawyer about paying for college." I hadn't told Nic yet that she was dating a millionaire. It kind of felt like something I should do in person. "And then I'll get back on the road. It should only take, what, ten days or so?"

"Nationals will be over by then, so we should be back."

"And LSU will have another title to add to the, what, six others?"

"Seven, I think."

Louisiana State was the favorite again to win it all on the women's side of the upcoming championships. Only the best of the best were worthy of being named a Lady Tiger. Though personally, Nic and I had agreed, far better to be a Desert Cat than a "lady" mascot of any sort. After all, it was the twentieth century. One of Nic's rival high schools had been cursed with "Maroon Giants" as their mascot, and had actually inflicted "Lady Maroon Giants" on their girls' teams. Talk about cruel and hilarious at once.

We could have kept on talking forever, of course, but Nic had a paper due in history and I still had to replenish my carbs.

"Hey, Ash?" she said just before we hung up.

"Yeah?"

"Thanks for going first. I know it wasn't easy."

"You're worth it."

"I do love you," she said.

"I know." And I hung up while she was still half-laughing, half-sputtering at me.

I bounced around the apartment waiting for Austin to come home, but he didn't. A little after ten, I tried him at Tommy's.

"Guess what?" I said when Tommy handed him the phone.

"What?"

"I got offered a spot on the SAU team."

"Holy shit!" His voice grew muffled. "Ash just found out she made the team at SAU!"

I could hear Tommy in the background whooping it up.

Austin came back. "Nic must be psyched."

"I think the other thing I told her might have made her happier."

"Ashley Lake, you did not confess your undying love to your long-distance girlfriend." He sounded almost stern.

"I did."

"Did she say it first?"

"No, I did."

He covered the phone for a second, and I could hear them talking again. Then he said, "My work here is done."

"Ego much?"

"Whatever. Nic can try to take credit for taming you, but we all know who you see on a daily basis."

"You mean my boss, Andrea, right? Because I barely ever see you anymore, roomie."

"Good point. Hey, it's supposed to be nice tomorrow. Want to play hooky and go to the Sheep Meadow?"

I thought about the deadline looming at work, about the files scattered across my desk rife with post-its. Then I thought about the day in the not-so-distant future when I would pack up Selma's station wagon and drive away, leaving Tommy and Austin to life in New York without me.

"Damn right," I said. "Count me in."

After we hung up, I got ready for bed. I wasn't sleepy, so I took a book to bed and tried to focus on the words that formed sentences I couldn't seem to digest. Finally I gave up and lay in the dark listening to the sound of countless unseen strangers living their lives in the rooms and buildings around me. Soon, I would be gone from this place. I tested the thought, like pressing on a bruise. But the idea brought no pain because leaving New York meant I would get to live in the same city with Nic, who loved me so much she had told her family even before I told her I loved her, too.

What would happen now? Part of me worried about accidents, injury, an act of terrorism that would keep me from achieving the dreams that were almost within reach. After all, I was cursed, wasn't I? But another part remembered what the therapist I'd seen a few times my senior year at Selma's insistence had said when I offered up the cursed theory: "I hate to tell you this, but you're just not that important, Ashley. The world doesn't revolve around you."

I knew what she meant—I was just another person among billions on the planet. And yet sometimes I still felt that by surviving the plane crash, I had made some sort of deal with the devil that meant my life would be easy while those I loved would be beset by illness, bad luck, even, worst of all, death.

If the therapist was wrong, if I was carrying some sort of bad karma that only affected the people I cared about, it wasn't fair of me to be with Nic, let alone contemplate planning a future with her, was it?

I'd asked her this late one night a couple of weeks earlier, when our future together still seemed precarious. She hadn't laughed as I'd worried she might. Instead she'd listened carefully, hearing me out before saying, "I don't think the world works like that. At least, I've never seen any evidence. Have you?"

"Just me."

"But your life hasn't been easy. Sure, you're smart and a really talented runner, but the one time you remembered the crash, if that's what happened that night, you told me you were a wreck. Besides, just the fact that you worry about being a curse to others—that's not easy, Ash."

I hadn't thought of that. "Good point."

"Don't take this the wrong way," she said, her voice hesitant, "but do you think it could be an excuse you've created, like subconsciously, to protect yourself from getting hurt?"

Whoah, what?

"I mean," she added, "you lost your parents when you were little, and then Selma when you were older. Now Austin is with Tommy, and I know they're careful, but he could get sick too, you've said as much yourself."

"You're right," I said slowly. It was like I was outside myself all of a sudden, looking in on the inner workings of my mind. "The whole cursed thing is an excuse, isn't it?"

"Not necessarily. This is just a theory."

But the theory had clicked in my brain, and in the days and nights since our conversation, it had evolved into something like fact. Casting myself as a jinx gave me an out, a loophole in any relationship. I could retreat when faced with a challenge, assuring myself that I was in fact protecting the other person from a terrible fate. How generous of me. And how chickenshit.

Now as I lay in the loft, my mind spinning with all the things I would have to do in the next month to get ready to move to Tucson—at least I had a month this time to get ready, rather than mere hours—I knew that I probably wouldn't be able to relinquish entirely the idea that I was a human bad luck charm. But at least when those feelings cropped up in the future, I could remind myself that they were mostly a defense mechanism. Facing that fact might just keep me from running away from the best things in my life.

Carrie, the reporter, would love this angle, I thought as I lay in my loft bed in the West Village, waiting for sleep.

As predicted, the hot weather persisted throughout that night and into the next day. Austin came home late the following morning, and after packing a picnic lunch, we caught the train up to Central Park. There, we walked to the Sheep Meadow, spread out a sheet, and started munching on grapes and yogurt.

I took off my shoes and dug my toes into the grass. "It's always sunny in Arizona," I said, picturing the Seven Falls trail, Nic looking sexy and adorable in her hiking garb.

"Have you told your grandparents yet?"

"No, I thought I would call them this weekend."

"They're going to be happy to have you nearby."

"I hope so."

He hesitated. "Can I come visit you, maybe in the fall? Once you're settled, I mean."

"Of course." I looked over at him, my eyes shaded by sunglasses. "Actually, I was planning to ask you—what do you think about driving out there with me?"

"Seriously?"

"Yes, seriously."

He tilted his head sideways. "How long would it take?"

"Probably about ten days, including a stop in Signal Point. I'd pay for your plane ticket back, of course. Maybe Tommy could even fly out and meet us for a few days at the end."

"Let me talk to him, okay? But my first thought is hell yeah."

"Sweet."

The idea had occurred to me the previous night as I lay in bed thinking about everything I still had to do and everyone I would be leaving. Austin and I always had fun on road trips. Besides, who better to help me start this latest new life?

"You know," I added, "I was just telling Nic I wished you guys lived in Phoenix or something. Or even LA—it's only ten hours away."

"You never know. Turns out New York is one of the unhealthiest places to live if you're positive. Maybe the desert air is just what he needs."

I paused. "How's he doing?"

"Good," Austin leaned back on his hands, lifting his face to the mid-day sun. "Really good, actually."

"And you?"

"I still feel like I'm waiting for something bad to happen, but he's got a great attitude. I'm trying to stay upbeat because whatever is going to happen will happen, you know?"

I nodded. I did know. "You can call me anytime you need to talk, okay?"

Austin half-smiled. "Damn, Ash, you must be in love if you want to talk about actual emotions."

"Shut up," I said, and threw a handful of grass at him.

He just shook the strands out of his hair.

"Anyway," I said, tossing a grape into the air and catching it in my mouth, "can you believe it's been almost a year already since we moved here?"

"Long enough for you to have gotten pregnant and had the kid by now," Austin said, tossing his own grape into the air.

It hit him between the eyes and I tried not to laugh. He pretended to glare at me as he picked the grape off the sheet and popped it in his mouth.

"Technically that's not even possible," I said.

"That's right—you and ole BB never did the deed."

"We almost did a couple of times but I always backed off. Nic says I'm a gold-star lesbian since I've never had sex with a guy." I tossed another grape into the air and caught it.

"How do you do that?" Austin complained, throwing up another grape. This time he caught it. "Oh. That's not so hard."

"Unlike some of the things you've had in your mouth." I laughed at the look on his face. "Sorry, I've been hanging around gay boys too much."

"Apparently. That was pretty good, Ash."

A little while later Austin took his shirt off and I stripped down to my sports bra. We sunbathed in comfortable silence for a bit. Then Austin turned his head so he could see me. "Can I ask you something?"

"Depends."

"You called yourself a lesbian—does that mean you think you're gay?"

"As opposed to bi?"

He nodded.

"I'm pretty sure I'm gay all the way. What about you?"

"Definitely all about the boys."

"You always were a bit of a cream puff."

"I'll take that as a compliment coming from a gold-star dyke like you."

I rolled onto my stomach and rested my chin on my forearms. "Was it hard coming out after growing up in the South?"

"Kind of. Even after I joined the Navy, I kept trying to prove to myself that I was straight. But I finally had to deal with the fact that I didn't really like sex with women."

I lifted my eyebrows. "You're saying you've had sex with a woman."

"Those first few months in the Navy, a couple of times. Actually, once before that, too."

"Like in high school?"

"Um, yes."

"You had sex with someone in Signal Mountain?"

He wouldn't look at me. "It's no big deal."

"Who was it?" I demanded. "Out with it, Taylor."

He ducked his head. "Betsy Smithers."

"What? How have you never told me this before? Of course, I probably wouldn't have told you either if my first time was with the queen of the Signal Mountain white trash."

"When did you become such a snob, little miss millionaire?"

My face fell. "Thanks for reminding me I'm an orphan."

"Sorry," he said, "I was just joking—"

"Got you!"

"I can't believe I fell for that."

"Neither can I."

"You know," he said, "I've kind of gotten used to having you around, even if you do eat more than two teenage boys put together."

"Hello pot, please meet the kettle."

He shoved me sideways. "Seriously, jackass, I'm going to miss you."

"I know. I'm going to miss you too." I reached out and squeezed his hand, and we sat there for a few minutes hanging onto each other.

"Did I tell you I'm thinking about going back to school?" he asked. "Tommy thinks it's a good idea, and we all know how my parents will react to the news."

"That's awesome. Maybe you could try out west for school, if you're serious about getting out of New York."

"That's my plan, if I can talk Mr. East Coast into relocating, that is."

"He'll go if you do, won't he?"

"That remains to be seen. You and Nic are lucky—you've got at least a couple of years before you have to figure out what comes next."

"True."

"So do you think she's the one?"

I rested my chin on my forearms. To the north, the twin towers of San Remo protruded above trees that were finally turning green again after the long winter.

"I don't know if I believe there's only one person out there, but right now, I can totally see myself building a life with her."

"Just like a lesbian, already planning the wedding."

I almost pointed out that I wasn't the one moving in with my boyfriend after only six months, but their situation was different. They didn't know how much time they would have together.

"I don't know about a wedding," I hedged, "but I could definitely see raising a family with her."

"We're too young to have kids."

"To have kids, yes. To think about having kids, no."

He shook his head. "Lesbians."

I paused. "Do you ever wish you'd gone to college instead of the Navy?"

"No. It's different for you, Ash. You're an athlete, and you have to be in school to compete. But for me, it would've just been wasted time at this point."

"Because of Tommy?"

He squinted at a guy who walked by just then, selling cold drinks out of his cooler. "Because of Tommy. Unless they find a cure, he's going to die, no matter how much either of us pretends he won't. And then maybe I'll end up doing all those things I was supposed to—go to school, get a real job—just so I can fill up the time. Because that's all I'm going to want to do—keep busy so I won't notice how much I miss him."

I put my hand over his again.

"Sorry," he said, managing a slight smile. "Didn't mean to be a downer."

"You're not a downer," I assured him. "I'm glad you're talking about it, Austin. You need someone to talk to so that you can be there for Tommy. I almost wish I weren't leaving."

He looked down at our interlaced hands. "But it's good you're leaving. I'm happy for you, Ash. Everything's going to be so great for you out there. I'm just going to call you all the time."

"At least we already know what our phone bills will look like."

Our last couple of bills had been worrisome due to my habit of calling Nic whenever I felt like it.

Austin sat up. "Hey, want to play catch?" he asked, pulling a Nerf football from his pack.

"Of course," I said, standing up beside him. "Wait, is that the football Selma gave you for your birthday the year you moved to the mountain?"

"Yep. My mom found it and brought it along at Christmas. Y'all ready for this?"

"You know it."

"Then go out," he said, palming the football.

I turned and ran across the Meadow, trying to dodge park-goers while looking back over my shoulder for Austin's throw. When he launched the Nerf in a perfect spiral, I stretched my arms out and caught it.

We played football in the grass that afternoon, laughing and cavorting just like in elementary school when we used to throw the ball around in his backyard for hours at a time, perfecting our form. Sometimes Selma would walk over to Austin's house after work and we'd have dinner with the Taylors at their picnic table in back, football lying momentarily forgotten on the patio.

As a kid, I was sure I would be the first woman to break into the NFL, if only I wanted it badly enough. Encouraged by our families, Austin and I both believed then that we could do anything we wanted. Now, as we played with the old Nerf in the Sheep Meadow at Central Park, I thought that maybe we both remembered that feeling of endless possibilities, come back to visit for a spell on a warm spring day.

CHAPTER TWENTY-NINE

Six weeks later, Marcus and I helped Austin and Tommy move into their new place. The apartment was in the West Village, so Austin didn't have far to go. Unfortunately, Tommy was the one with all the furniture. And clothes.

"I've never seen this many clothes before in my whole life," I said as Marcus and I each carried an overflowing laundry basket into Tommy and Austin's new bedroom. There were already boxes of jeans, shorts, shirts, and sweaters stacked nearly to the ceiling, not to mention the sea of suits in drycleaner's plastic hanging in the closet. "Will they even fit in this apartment?"

"You've led a sheltered life, haven't you?" Marcus said, wiping the sweat from his forehead. It was only eleven, but the heat and humidity had already begun to settle over the city. Ah, summer in Manhattan.

"You should talk," I said. "At least I was allowed to watch MTV."

While he was training me for Mercury's, Marcus had admitted to unqualified nerdishness in high school, which he blamed on excessively strict parents.

"Liar," Austin said, walking in just then with Tommy. "You only watched MTV when Selma wasn't home."

Marcus lifted his eyebrows at me.

"Anyway, that's it," Austin added. "I do believe we're done."

"Sweet. Is my stuff in the other room?"

I would only be in New York for a few more days. My job at

Maxwell's had ended the week before. On Tuesday, Austin and I would drive to Arizona, where Tommy would meet us. Afterward, they would come back to New York without me.

"Yep. We just have to set up the futon," Austin said.

"We really have a guest room, don't we?" Tommy asked, smiling at him.

"Yes, sir, we do."

Marcus and I exchanged a look, and I could tell he was also tempted to point out that the guest room was actually more of an oversized closet. We both refrained, not wanting to disturb how happy Austin and Tommy were in their new place. Moving had taken its toll, of course, and they'd bickered over little things just like any other couple. But mostly they'd grinned continuously as they arranged the furniture and hooked up the TV and stereo in their new living room.

"Let's go to brunch," I said. "My treat."

"You're on," Marcus said. He was back at Mercury's for the summer, and back to eating everything in sight, too. This would be my last chance to buy him a meal for a while.

That night I lay on the futon in the guest room, staring at the ceiling. The closer I got to leaving New York, the harder it got to sleep. Too many questions running through my mind: Would I like Tucson? Would I succeed at SAU? Would Nic and I make it as a couple?

The window was open a little, barless since we were on the fourth floor and the fire escape was in Austin and Tommy's room. I could hear a car alarm going off in the distance. I knew that alarm. I hummed along as it blared across the night:

"Enhh enhh enhh enhh, oooyoo oooyoo oooyoo oooyoo," and on and on, until finally the car beeped twice and quieted down. A few minutes later another pedestrian drifted too close to a parked car. The alarm went off, and I sang along with that one, too.

In some ways I was going to miss New York, I realized as I lay on the bed singing along with car alarms on the otherwise quiet West Village street. I was going to miss Austin and Tommy and Marcus the most, but also Sunday morning runs around Central Park, with the sun rising over Museum Row on Fifth Avenue; the haphazard conduct of taxis driven by unshaven men with funky hats and very little knowledge of English; the cobbled streets of SoHo with thirty-somethings in BMWs and Armani suits on their way to the financial district. I was even going to miss the attitude that this city was the center of the universe, and that anyone who didn't realize that was a cretin. In point of fact, New York is epic, with lights that obliterate celestial patterns and buildings that shoot up ever higher above the earth's surface, swaying in the wind. Not to mention all the energy coursing through the streets. There's always something going on in New York.

But leaving meant going someplace new with someone new. Now whenever we talked on the phone, Nic and I made plans for the summer. She had a job on-campus that would let her remain in her dorm room, and for at least the first few weeks, I would crash with her. After that, we would see.

I lay in Austin and Tommy's spare bedroom that night pondering my future and the past and the present all rolled together into one. These were my last real days of freedom. No more wondering what might be, planning an unknown future. The choices I had already made would dictate the changes ahead.

Once, just before she got sick, Selma and I had sat at Signal Point gazing out upon the lush Tennessee Valley a couple of thousand feet below. She'd put her arm around my shoulders and we'd leaned together as the sun set, listening to the wind and watching clouds drift overhead. I'd known then, without consciously knowing, that my home was with Selma. I belonged with her.

Then she died, and I went away to a strange city to look for a new feeling of home. And while I looked, I stumbled across the very life I had nearly convinced myself I would never need.

Eventually, the song of the car alarm lulled me to sleep beneath the starless New York sky. In the morning I woke to sounds of Austin and Tommy moving about the apartment, laughing and shushing each other. I lay on the futon, remembering my dreams as the sun rose over the buildings on the block and the city woke from its shallow slumber. I had dreamed of red earth and blue sky and sunlight. Selma was there, and Nic, too, in the center of it all, I thought. But I couldn't be sure as wakefulness intruded, driving the fragile memory of dreams from my mind.

Tuesday morning dawned cool and cloudy, the smell of rain strong in the air. Austin, Tommy, and I carried my bags out to Selma's car. There wasn't much more than I'd arrived with other than some new clothes, shoes, and baseball caps. I wore a CK T-shirt, a pair of cut-offs, and my Yankees cap backward, leather Tevas strapped to my feet. My city girl clothes, as Austin liked to call them.

"Drive safely, you guys," Tommy said as Austin and I tossed our backpacks in the back seat and the tape collection up front.

"We will," I promised.

I stood with Tommy on the sidewalk, at a loss for words. How did you say goodbye to someone who might not be around much longer, or might live for another fifty years?

Our eyes met and held. Then he stepped forward and wrapped his arms around me. "I'm going to miss you, hon."

"I'm going to miss you, too," I said, swallowing past the lump in my throat. I squeezed him, feeling his body strong and vibrant beneath my hands. He was so healthy. It seemed impossible that a virus could be working its way through his body, attaching itself to cell after cell, weakening his immune system. I wished I could lay my hands on his skin and destroy the disease with the power of touch, but my powers didn't extend that far.

I pulled back. "Anyway, we'll see you next week, okay?"

"Looking forward to it," he said. "I've always wanted to see the Grand Canyon."

Before I die. He didn't say the words, but I was sure we all thought them.

Then Austin kissed Tommy and we piled into the station wagon that had brought us to New York almost a year before. We waved as we drove down the West Village street. I looked back at Tommy, his baby dreads poking up from his head in disarray. He waved once, and then I lost sight of him.

It was early still, before the morning rush hour. I asked Austin if he would drive up the West Side Highway to the George Washington Bridge so that I could get one last view of the city as we left. He obliged, and I stared at New Jersey across the Hudson and looked up at the bridge towering in the distance, trying to memorize everything I saw. It was harder than I'd expected, this leave-taking.

Then we were on the bridge skimming over the water and I was looking over my shoulder through the back window at the New York skyline up close for the last time for who knew how long. I looked and looked at the familiar sights while Natalie Merchant rocked out on the radio. And I wondered, remembering my months-old promise, if I should have called Drew to say goodbye.

I turned back around in my seat as we crossed into Jersey. "Thanks for coming with me," I said, looking over at Austin.

"Thanks for inviting me."

I watched mile markers pass, counting them. Only nine hundred more miles to Chattanooga. We drove south and west, the sun climbing higher in the sky behind us. I pulled out my shades and slipped an REM tape into the stereo. This was it. At the other end of the road, Nic and Marcie and the stadium where I'd felt Selma's presence were waiting.

I hung my arm out the car window and smiled over at Austin. "Here we go," I said.

Austin smiled back at me, turned up the music, and drove on.

Here we go.

ABOUT THE AUTHOR

Kate Christie lives with her family near Seattle. A graduate of Smith College and Western Washington University, she spends her days crafting marketing copy and her evenings trying to stay awake at the keyboard long enough to meet her goal of 1000 words a day, deemed by Ray Bradbury to be the minimum daily output for any writer. Sometimes, she even succeeds.

To find out more about Kate, or to read excerpts from her other titles from Second Growth Books and Bella Books*—*Gay Pride & Prejudice*, *Family Jewels*, *Beautiful Game**, *Leaving LA**, and *Solstice**— please visit www.katejchristie.com. Or visit her blog at katechristie.wordpress.com where she occasionally finds time to wax unpoetically about lesbian life, fiction, and motherhood.

www.ingramcontent.com/pod-product-compliance
Lightning Source LLC
Chambersburg PA
CBHW070643180626
46817CB00006B/2221